GILCHRIST

CHRISTIAN GALACAR

GILCHRIST

A NOVEL

Book design by Maureen Cutajar
www.gopublished.com

ISBN-13: 978-1975802028
ISBN-10: 1975802020

To the memory of my father.

Prologue

LAKEMAN'S LANE (1931)

1

"What the hell are you doing? Hold that goddamn thing steady!" Mullins shouted over the sound of the crane.

The entire crew of a dozen men had gathered to watch. It was the biggest tree they'd felled since starting the job. Side bets had been made as to whether or not their equipment could even move the thing.

"I got it," John Dennison said, carefully working the crane's controls. Though only in his twenties, he was a skilled operator. He had been doing it since he was a kid. His father had taught John everything he knew, but he didn't want to think about his father right now. The boom lowered slowly, and the massive log it was hoisting inched farther out. After a few feet, the crane started to bow forward and lift the treads off the ground. Dennison reacted, raising the boom again, and the crane squatted back down.

"Jesus Christ!" Mullins threw his hands in the air.

"It's too heavy," Dennison said. "It isn't meant for something this big. Why don't we just drop it and push it with the dozer? It's safer."

"It ain't too heavy. You just don't have a damn clue how to run that thing. Just take it slow, and it'll be fine. You don't worry about what's safe. That's my concern."

Dennison ignored Mullins. The guy didn't know what he was talking about. He started letting the load line out to bring the swinging log down. But before it touched the ground, Mullins was running over.

"Just what the hell do you think you're doing?" he said, out of breath. He was a fat man with a taste for afternoon gin. His face was the hypertensive shade of a ripe plum.

Dennison worked the controls, eyes focused ahead. "I told you it's too heavy, and yellin about it isn't gonna change a damn thing. So I plan to set this down, go have myself a smoke, then I'm gonna get in the bulldozer and push that log the way we should've done from the start. How's that sound, Will?"

"You little prick, if I tell you to do something, then you do it. That's how this works."

"That so?"

"You're goddamn right."

With the log settled in the dirt, Dennison jumped off the crane and looked at Mullins. He was dog-tired and didn't want to deal with his bullshit right now. Mullins was an okay foreman—not an okay guy, though an okay foreman—but he didn't know when to admit when he was wrong, and that was dangerous with this sort of work. To top it off, it had been a long day. Hell, it had been a long summer. The crew had been out there since June, building the road to Lake Argilla. Lakeman's Lane was the name Gilchrist's town officials had decided upon.

"Last I checked," Dennison said, "you ain't got no one else qualified to run equipment. So what choice do you have?"

Mullins's face showed a brief moment of embarrassed shock. Then, considering the crew watching, he pulled it into a hateful scowl. Without further warning, he cocked his arm back and took a swing.

Dennison ducked, then lunged forward and wrapped his arms around Mullins's stout body, driving him back. "You gone done it now, you fat shit."

"Get that sumbitch," one of the crew said.

"It's on now," another yelled.

Others had started to laugh and cheer.

Mullins and Dennison jostled in each other's arms for a few seconds, then fell over in an awkward embrace and started swinging in the dirt. Before long, a few of the crew ran over and pulled them apart. Mullins bled from a cut above his eye, and Dennison from his nose.

One of the men tried to put a hand on Dennison's shoulder to calm him down, but Dennison jerked away. "Don't touch me," he said, and stormed off into the woods.

"Where the hell do you think you're going?" Mullins yelled after him.

Without turning around, Dennison yelled back, "I told you, I'm gonna go have a smoke, and then I'm gonna get in that bulldozer and push that goddamn log. Then I'm going home."

There was a pause. Then Mullins, in a defeated voice, said, "Well, hurry up. It'll be dark soon."

Dennison continued into the woods to find a place to sit. He just wanted a few minutes away from that moron so he could calm down.

2

Dennison sat on a rock at the shore of Lake Argilla and blew a wad of bloody snot from his nose. The bridge of it throbbed with its own dull heartbeat. He fingered a Lucky Strike from his pack and lit it. The sun was setting over the trees across the water. He was thinking of his father, who had died a few weeks ago of a massive heart attack. Dennison had been the one to find him on the floor in the garage. They used to come out to the woods and go fishing a lot when John was a kid.

Those were good times, weren't they, Pop?

He took a drag, then held out his hand and looked at his knuckles. They were nicked and scuffed with dirt. His hand trembled from the adrenaline coursing through his bloodstream. Mullins was lucky they had been pulled apart. He might've killed the guy.

"Moron," he said to himself, and dropped his hand to his lap.

He couldn't wait to be done with this job. Recently, he had been thinking about heading west to see if he could find something else to do with his life. He was a good machine operator—despite what Mullins thought of him—and he knew it wouldn't be too hard to find work. He had never been away from Gilchrist before, and he thought it was probably time. There wasn't a whole lot left for him here.

"Johnny, is that you?" a familiar voice said from behind him.

Dennison wheeled around on the rock. He felt the blood drain out of his face as his skin chilled and broke out in gooseflesh.

"Dad?" he said, shock washing over him. His Lucky Strike fell in the mud and hissed as the ember went out.

3

Mullins was climbing over a pile of cut logs when his foot slipped down into a seam and his ankle got pinned. He tried to yank up on it, but a log above him shifted, threatening to roll down on him and crush his leg. He remained still, trying to assess the situation. He'd gotten himself into a fine pickle. The crew was about fifty feet off in the distance, drinking coffee and mulling over the evening's excitement. The last thing he wanted to do was call to them for help, especially after what had happened with Dennison. He'd looked like a fool enough for one day. If he kept at it, he would lose all respect. And without that, the job would never get finished. On the other hand, he didn't want to end up a cripple, either.

He bent down to inspect the situation better. Maybe if he could slip his foot out of his boot, then—

The sound of the bulldozer's diesel engine grinding to life startled him. He looked up and saw the exhaust pipe cough black smoke. The rain cap bobbed up and down on the muffler. Then he saw Dennison sitting behind the controls, staring at him. Great, he thought. Just the guy he wanted to find him like this.

Mullins hesitated. But after a moment or two, he waved his hands over his head to make sure Dennison could see him. He was thirty feet away, on the other side of the little clearing where they kept the equipment parked. "I'm stuck!" he shouted reluctantly, pointing to his leg.

Dennison continued to stare at him, his face a blank slate. Then he pushed a lever forward, and the dozer began to creep and squeak toward Mullins.

"What're you doing? Stop fooling around. Come give me a hand," he yelled.

But Dennison just adjusted a few more levers and maneuvered the dozer, pointing it directly at Mullins. Then he pushed the throttle all the way forward, and the engine wound up, jetting smoke from the exhaust. The treads started to *cleak-cleak-cleak* louder and faster.

Mullins began to feel the first traces that something was wrong. "Cool it, asshole!" he shouted. "Shut that thing off and come help me. You're gonna shake one of these logs loose. It's not funny."

The dozer was only ten feet away now, and Mullins could see Dennison's face clearly. But it wasn't his face that drummed up a sense of disquiet in Mullins… it was Dennison's eyes. He didn't recall Dennison having such bright green eyes. Almost unnaturally green.

The bulldozer's blade started to lift, adjust… and aim.

"Shut that thing off this second. I swear to God I'll fire you and find someone else."

Dennison didn't slow or change course, and Mullins knew he was in real trouble.

"Help! Somebody help!"

He heard people scrambling through the woods. Thumping footsteps. Or maybe it was his own heart trying to pound its way out of his chest. The dozer kept coming. He could see the rust and caked mud on the blade. Pieces of dried tree root. The bolts. The welds. The gouges in the steel from rocks.

His gaze met with Dennison's horrible eyes right as the bottom edge of the blade pressed against his lap and started to push him back against the logs. He heard two loud pops and felt the biggest pain of his life as his legs were crushed, and then severed. He looked down and saw gouts of blood pouring over tree bark.

Then Mullins lost consciousness.

AUGUST 1966

Chapter One

BAD NEWS

1

The silence settled like a cold slab between them, had happened that way since they lost Noah. Moments without forced conversation filled too quickly with unspoken accusations. Their life was supposed to be different, supposed to be perfect. Other people had these problems, not them.

Peter and Sylvia Martell sat in the waiting room. They couldn't look at each other without seeing the word FAILURE in giant blaring letters. Their lives were contaminated—infected—with the word, although neither would say so. They'd been evicted from their former life. The life where she smiled honestly and he didn't drink so much—hell, they both drank too much. The life where they hosted dinner parties and people could talk about their own children without that look surfacing in their eyes that seemed always to say: *These poor, unfortunate people. I can't imagine…*

Peter picked at the knee of his pants, working on the seam of his khakis, trying not to think about what might be coming.

Every so often, as to not seem beaten down by it all, he forced himself to look up and make eye contact with his wife. Sylvia nursed the paper cup of water the receptionist had given her, feigning polite smiles when the air grew too stale with tension. Her face wanted to be stoic, but the burden was too much. There was a time when she could hide things well, but those days were gone. Neither Peter nor Sylvia was a bad person, but both feared the other thought they were. And that might've been at the heart of the thing.

Peter picked up the copy of *LIFE Magazine* sitting on the table beside him. It was the August 12, 1966 issue. The cover showed a bullet hole in a window and a blurry silhouette of a tower in the background. The headline was in bold black letters: THE TEXAS SNIPER. Below that, in smaller white print: "Store window shattered by bullets fired from tower in background by Charles Whitman."

Peter cleared his throat. "Every time I see this, I think it can't be real. What would make a person do something like that? Kill a bunch of innocent people for no reason? I mean, what's the damn point?"

Sylvia glanced at the magazine cover but didn't say anything. Peter could tell she was nervous, preoccupied.

He dropped the magazine back on the table. He had already read the article on the shooting last week, when the issue first came out. "Is your sister still coming for dinner tonight?"

"I think so." Sylvia crossed her legs, then swept the edge of her hand over her wool skirt, ironing out the already flat fabric.

"That'll be good. You haven't seen her in a while," Peter said. "Is she still with that teacher?"

"Arthur?"

"Yeah, that's it."

"Yes, he's coming, too." Sylvia started picking at the side of her thumb with her nail—her anxious tic. The skin there was raw and cracked.

"We should stop and get some wine on the way home," Peter said. "Maybe a bottle of nice scotch or something."

Sylvia checked her nails. "That's a good idea."

The receptionist came and stood in front of them, holding a clipboard in both hands. She had it pressed against her bosom in an officious way. "Dr. Carlson will see you now. Just this way."

Peter looked at his wife and placed his hand over hers. "Everything will be okay. I'm sure of it. I love you, no matter what happens."

Sylvia smiled noncommittally. "Okay," she said, sliding her hand out from underneath his. "Let's get this over with." She stood and shouldered her purse, pressing her fingers against the side of her auburn hair. Peter stood and dropped a hand into the pocket of his tweed sport coat. Then the Martells followed the receptionist through a door marked PATIENTS ONLY and down a tiled hallway that smelled strongly of antiseptic.

At the end, the receptionist took a right and stopped outside a doorway. "You can have a seat in here. The doctor will be right with you." There was a brass plaque beside the door that read EDWARD CARLSON, MD.

Peter followed Sylvia in, and the receptionist closed the door behind them.

They were not in an examination room. They were beyond that phase. In fact, if either of them never had to set foot in another exam room again, it would still be too soon. They were in the doctor's personal office. The room, with its dark-wood paneling, was a place where long-awaited test results were discussed. A large oak desk sat in front of three tall bookcases filled with thick leather-bound medical reference books. Covering the walls were framed pictures of sailboats and nautical maps, and in one corner, which seemed to be designated for them, his diplomas—Boston College and Harvard—were hung. The one from Harvard was for their medical program. Graduating class of 1945.

In the opposite corner was an antique globe supported by an elegantly carved wooden stand. Deep-green wall-to-wall carpeting covered the floor. Two chairs sat in the middle of the room, facing the visitors' side of the desk. Sylvia sat in one and set her purse on her lap. Peter went over to the globe, spun it slowly, and stopped it with his finger. It came to rest on the coast of Africa. He sighed, spun the globe again without waiting to see where it would stop, and took the seat next to his wife. He swept away a few strands of his dark hair that had fallen across his forehead.

The cold slab settled between them again. And the Martells waited without speaking. A clock on the wall beside them ticked along in the silence, a lonely sound in the hollow heart of something dark on the horizon.

2

It was two thirty by the time Dr. Carlson came in. A tall, lean, handsome man in his late forties, with short black hair and smart features, he was a presence. "Peter, Sylvia, good to see you. Sorry to keep you waiting."

"Hello, Doctor," Sylvia said, her big blue eyes following Dr. Carlson as he went behind his desk and sat. He was wearing a lab coat with gray slacks, a white collared shirt, and a thin black tie. He pulled the stethoscope from around his neck and dropped it on his desk.

He started patting his pockets. "I just need to find my glasses. They were short on eyes the day they made me. I can't read a thing without them." He checked the top of his head, but they weren't there. He started picking up papers on his desk.

Peter stared at him, his gaze searching Carlson. After a moment, he closed his eyes, his index finger and thumb rubbing together in little circles like he was rolling a pill. He could hear the blood running in his ears, the low *thump* of his heartbeat. He focused. The world around him fell away, then returned. "Do you have a jacket?" he finally asked, opening his eyes.

"Yes." Dr. Carlson stood and crossed the room to a coat rack beside the door, where a gray suit coat hung.

"Check the inside pocket," Peter said. "The left."

"Ah. Found them. Thank you. That was pretty good, Mr. Martell."

"You bet. That's where I always keep mine," Peter said.

Sylvia glanced at him. Peter didn't wear glasses, not even to read.

Dr. Carlson returned to his desk, sat down, and put them on. "Okay, that's better." He opened a file in front of him and skimmed through it. The situation had the flat taste of chalk. The reading of the file seemed like a formality, as if he already knew exactly what he was going to say.

"Some office you have here, Doc." Peter gestured vaguely around the room.

Carlson smiled modestly. "Thank you."

Sylvia slid to the edge of her seat and set her purse on the floor. Her legs were crossed at the ankles, her posture stiff.

There was something noble about the pose. She looked like a person prepared to face a firing squad, at peace with whatever was coming her way.

"So…" Dr. Carlson closed the file and leaned forward on his elbows. He rubbed his hands together dourly, his face sobering. "Let's get right to it. I have both good news and bad. The good news is I can find absolutely nothing wrong with either of you. We'll get that out of the way. You're healthy."

Peter touched Sylvia's arm and smiled. She looked at him, but her face didn't match his spirits. "What's the bad news?" she asked Carlson.

He sighed. "Well, that's just it. The bad news is the same. I can't find anything wrong. By all medical standards—according to all the tests we've run—you and your husband should be perfectly capable of having another child."

Sylvia deflated with a huff and fell back in her chair. It was almost as if she'd *wanted* there to be something wrong because at least then she would have a definitive answer—a target at which to aim her frustration. "But we've been trying for over a year now. There *has* to be something wrong."

Peter looked at his wife. "You heard Dr. Carlson, the tests said we're fine. Maybe it's just going to take some more time."

Sylvia closed her eyes, clenched her jaw hard enough to ripple the soft sides of her face.

"Well, no, I didn't say that everything was fine," Carlson said, holding up a hand. "What I said was that I can't find anything wrong with either of you. An absence of evidence doesn't mean there isn't something we simply cannot find. Infertility is an area of medicine that is still quite new, and often the cause is idiopathic. The science and research simply isn't there yet."

"Infertile?" It seemed to be the only word she'd heard, the one for which she'd—they'd both—been waiting. Sylvia was at the edge of her seat again. "Is that what you just said? Infertile?" she repeated.

"How do you know that?" Peter said. "It doesn't make sense. We had a baby three years ago, and it was never a problem then." He looked over at the globe. He thought of the coast of Africa and how his finger had landed and stopped the world spinning.

Sylvia reached over and put her hand in Peter's, bringing his attention back.

Carlson crossed his arms on his desk. His eyes were emotionless and steady. He was a man doing a job. "Medically speaking, after a year of trying without success, we will generally diagnose the cause of failed conception—provided you *are* actively trying—as a fertility issue. It can be a problem in both men and women. And as in your case, where you both appear to be healthy, it can simply be an unexplained reason. Medicine isn't an exact science. I know this isn't easy. But you need to understand that I am not telling you that you'll never be able to have another child. Not at all. Fertility is an area of medicine where so much is still unknown. We get it wrong sometimes. It's just the nature of it. People absolutely still conceive children after attempting for much longer periods of time than a year, and the reasons for the difficulty are often never known. This time next year, you could very well be parents again."

Peter shook his head and opened his mouth to say something, but his wife beat him to it. "So what next? You're saying you think it's a fertility issue with one of us, or both of us, or... or—"

"Yes, or neither of you," Carlson said, finishing Sylvia's thought. "That's what I'm saying. I sincerely do wish I could offer the two of you something more concrete—vague answers, I'm sure, aren't what you were hoping for—but at this time, we have to work with what we know. In this case, you're both young, healthy adults, but you're having a difficult go of getting pregnant. Your position is hardly unique, although I understand that doesn't make it any less frustrating."

"What do you recommend we do?" Sylvia asked. "I don't want to give up."

"And you shouldn't." Carlson's up-shifting tone suggested he was about to make his closing point. "I would advise you to keep trying like you've been doing. The only way to guarantee you *won't* get pregnant is to stop attempting altogether. And there's a lot of research currently being done in the area of hormone treatment, which is something that might be an available option in the near future. I'm not able to say when—or even *if*—for sure. But it can be comforting to know that new advancements in medicine are made every day."

Sylvia nodded as if she'd decided something. "Okay." She blinked twice, both times hard enough to wrinkle her nose. It was another tic of hers—one Peter thought was cute. "Okay... okay." Her finger picked at the side of her thumb. It was starting to bleed.

Peter looked curiously at his wife. "Are you all right?"

Sylvia smiled a plastic smile. "I'm fine. Yes. We'll just have to keep trying. That's all. Dr. Carlson is right. We shouldn't lose hope." She faced her husband, met his eyes briefly, then looked down and picked up her purse. She set it in her lap and sat straight and proper, hands clasping the straps of her bag. She was done here, had heard all she needed. "We won't give up."

Peter nodded blankly, unable to find anything suitable to say.

Carlson filled the dead air. "And if you do decide to continue trying, I'd recommend making a follow-up appointment for three months from now, just to see how things are going. You can schedule it with Wendy at reception."

"Okay. We'll do that," Sylvia said. "Is there anything more?"

"Not unless you have any questions," Carlson said. "I'd be happy to answer any you or your husband have. And consider that a standing offer. If you should think of something tomorrow, or even next week, don't hesitate to call."

They had nothing more to ask.

3

Sylvia stared out the window as Peter drove home. He fiddled with the dial on the radio but couldn't find anything he wanted to listen to and eventually shut it off. They rode in silence, until they turned off Route 2 and onto the main strip of downtown Concord.

"I'm sorry," Sylvia said, cutting the stillness inside the car.

"For what?" Peter asked as he pulled onto a narrow street that fed into a small shopping plaza, and parked in a space in front of the liquor store. He put the car in park and looked up at the sign hanging from the brick building: CONCORD WINE AND SPIRITS. Below that, in cursive: "Est. 1944, Concord, Massachusetts."

"I don't know. I just felt like I should say that."

"Want to talk about it?"

Sylvia pressed the edge of a finger under her eye, catching a tear before it could track through her makeup. Then her lower lip trembled, and it was all coming up. "I miss Noah. I miss him so much. And I feel like we're being punished for what happened to him. Like we don't deserve a second chance."

"Oh, hey, that's not true at all. No one's punishing us. We did nothing wrong. It was an accident. A horrible accident, that's all."

"I'm such a bad person." Sylvia glanced at Peter with a shameful look in her eyes.

"No you're not. Why would you say such a thing?"

"Because."

"Because what?"

"Because it's not your fault. I know that. None of this is," she said. "But I find myself blaming you sometimes. Even though I know you're trying as best you can."

Her words felt like a slap, but Peter understood it and bit his tongue. Instead, he leaned over and put his arm around her. He didn't know whether he was legitimately trying to console her or if he just didn't want to have to hear her cry. He was sick of tears.

"It's not as bad as you think," he said. "And you've never blamed me. *I've* never felt that way, at least."

"Yes, I have. Maybe I've never said it, but I can feel the way I act toward you. And sometimes I do think it outright. Sometimes I think it was stupid that you insisted on writing with your door closed. Maybe if you'd kept it open, you might've heard something sooner. And I blame you for that." She broke down sobbing, her hands covering her face. "And I blame myself. It was such a waste."

A car pulled up beside them, and a man and a woman got out and went toward the store. Peter watched them for a moment. He watched them smiling at each other, happy and excited about whatever they were discussing. Maybe a great future was still waiting for them—one without tears, endless doctor's visits, and funerals with small caskets. They had to be about the same age as he and Sylvia. The man held the door for the woman, and he followed her. The faint jingle of the entrance bells filtered into the car.

"It's okay. I know this is hard. But you heard what the doctor said—we're perfectly healthy. That's a good thing. There's nothing wrong with me, and there's nothing wrong with you." He rubbed his wife's back rhythmically as he spoke, as if he were trying to hypnotize her. And perhaps he was.

"I don't want to do dinner tonight. I'm cancelling," Sylvia said. "I'll call Evelyn when we get home."

Peter was actually relieved to hear her say that, but he had to give at least one show of effort; he didn't want to seem too eager. "Are you sure? Maybe you'll feel better when we get home. I'll go in here, get some wine, and we'll have a few drinks and put today behind us. What do you say? Maybe that will change your mind."

Sylvia pushed herself up and wiped her eyes. "I just want to go to bed." She pulled a tissue from her purse and dabbed her red-rimmed eyes.

"Bed?" Peter checked his watch. "It's not even five o'clock. Don't you think maybe—"

"I know what time it is. I just don't want to think about anything anymore. I'm tired, Peter. I'm just tired."

"Okay. Say no more. I understand. Just let me run in real quick, and we'll go home. I actually wouldn't mind a quiet night. I have to be in Boston tomorrow morning to meet with the publisher about foreign rights stuff."

"All right," Sylvia said.

Peter regarded her. God knew he had seen her sad since their son died, but something had changed. She looked broken, and all he wanted to do was fix her. That was all he had ever wanted to do—to fix them, to get them back to normal. But the damage seemed such an impossible thing to mend.

Sylvia was looking straight ahead at the brick wall of the building, wringing the wadded piece of tissue in her hands. It was covered in little dots of blood from the raw flesh on her thumb. Her knuckles were white with strain, her eyes unblinking.

He opened the door and swung his legs out with a long sigh. "I'll be right back. You want anything?"

"No, thank you."

Peter got out and shut the door. He stood outside the car for a moment. The heat from the engine drifted up from the undercarriage, carrying with it the smell of rich exhaust and asphalt. It was a summer smell that only seemed to exist on hot days. And it was hot. He ran his finger around the inside of his collar and looked around the parking lot. It was a strange kind of desert. Desolation in the middle of a bustling town.

He removed his jacket, opened the back door, and tossed it on the seat. He watched Sylvia take a small pillbox from her purse and finger out one of her Equanil. The tranquilizers might've been the glue keeping their marriage together. Over the last few months, she had worked herself onto a steady schedule of the drug: one every morning with her coffee; one at night before dinner; two an hour before sex (or as she always referred to it: "trying to conceive"); and a few here and there when needed, just for good measure and to keep the anxiety from creeping in.

Sylvia popped the little pill in her mouth, jerked her head back, and swallowed. Then she went back to staring vacantly ahead.

Peter watched her a moment longer, a sinking feeling in his heart. He wanted to tell her he loved her and that everything would be all right. But at that exact point in time, he wasn't so sure he believed it. Sometimes things weren't fine. Sometimes the broken thing stayed broken until it was thrown away.

He shut the door and went inside.

4

Peter was having a dream. He was kneeling, bent down, and looking at an elderly reflection of himself in a river. When he focused on the constant burbling of moving water, the sound seemed to wax and wane, becoming a rhythm, as if the water itself were breathing. He broke away from his reflection and looked around the sad landscape. An ominous red sky cast a sick light over everything. In the distance, a dilapidated church stood in the middle of an empty field that looked scorched. He went to it. The doors were open, and he could see inside. The pews were covered in blood.

Something moved behind him. Many somethings. He turned around. They were pouring out of the ground like black ropes of oil. But the ropes had eyes. And the ropes slithered. And the ropes had teeth. They were all whispering, and it was one word hissed over and over again: *Gilllchrissst… Gilllchrissst… Gilllchrissst…*

One snaked across the back of Peter's calf, latched on to him, and bit. He looked down and the ground was covered with them. He tried to scream, but no sound would come.

He awoke.

Sylvia was snoring when Peter opened his eyes. He caught his breath and picked his watch up off the nightstand: 3:27 a.m. He sat up, drenched in sweat, and searched around the floor with his toes until he found his slippers. A twinge of fear needled his mind as he thought of his foot touching something slick and slithery below, but he wasn't sure what that something was exactly. The dream was already disintegrating and taking on a lost and distant feeling like a fading echo. It left behind only its disquiet, not its details.

He went to the bathroom. He needed water. His mouth tasted like a New York drain gutter. He hadn't intended to get drunk when they had returned home, but after Sylvia had popped a few extra Equanil and followed through on her promise to go to bed early, he had decided to have a drink or two while he did a little writing on his new book. But as was often the case, one or two drinks became the whole bottle. Then after the bottle was gone, it became whatever else was in the house.

He bent over the sink and drank directly from the faucet, lapping the cold water like a greedy dog, each sip feeling somehow purgative. He straightened and looked at himself in the mirror. To spare his eyes, he hadn't turned on the light, but he could still see his reflection. He looked worn out. A hint of something familiar touched him, but it was too faint, and he was too tired to grasp the connection to his dream.

Peter went back to the bedroom and stood at the foot of their bed. He watched Sylvia sleep. She snorted, cleared her throat, and rolled over on her back, kicking her leg out from under the covers. She threw her arm over her head, her hair somehow remaining perfectly neat. She really was a beautiful woman.

Five minutes passed. Maybe ten. The house was so silent, so still. Memories of their happier past seemed to have real volume when he replayed them in his mind at this hour, as if he could reach out and touch them. But behind it all, looming overhead like a storm cloud, was a very real thought. All he could think about was how easy it would be to pack a bag, leave, and never come back. Walk away from it all. That might be the only way either of them could ever have any sort of good life again. Death had hardened the soil of their hearts, and now no new love could grow.

The thought sickened him, and a surge of guilt rose up in him for even having it. He would never leave her. He loved her, and they would make it through this together. They would ride it out, no matter what.

That's right, he thought. *No matter what.*

Peter got back into bed, but he didn't sleep.

Chapter Two

DALE'S DELIGHT

1

Peter saw the highway sign when he was seven miles from home. He'd driven that stretch of Route 2 between Boston and Concord at least a hundred times and had never noticed it before. Perhaps because it wasn't the type of thing you did or did not notice, he thought, not when you've seen it so many times that it's become part of your landscape. Not when you already know the way. You don't read the signs when you already know the way, do you?

In bold white lettering over the bright-green background, the sign read CONCORD 7, LEOMINSTER 30, GILCHRIST 48.

Gilchrist, he thought. *Something had said* Gilchrist. *Something had…*

And there it clicked. All at once, the dream resurfaced like a thunderclap in his head, and he remembered it all: the old church, the red sky, his aged reflection staring up at him from the water, and the black snakes that had oozed like tubes of oil and slithered over his leg.

Gilllchrissst… Gilllchrissst… Gilllchrissst…

Peter shivered, and his skin broke out in fat bumps of goose-flesh despite the sweltering heat inside his car. He had always been a vivid dreamer, but he hadn't dreamed one that bizarre in a long time, and somehow, this one felt a little too close for comfort.

A car honked behind him, breaking his concentration. He glanced down at the speedometer. He had dropped to almost forty miles per hour. The speed limit along that stretch of road was a posted fifty-five.

"Pass me if you don't like my driving," he said, pressing his foot down on the accelerator. "There are two damn lanes. What're you honking for, jerk?"

The white Chevy Impala put on its blinker, changed lanes, and sped around him. Peter checked as the car went by. The driver, a bald man holding on to wispy patches of gray along the sides, scowled at him and shook his head.

"Yeah, yeah… sorry, pal." Peter waved a half-hearted apology as the man went by, offering a sarcastic, apologetic smile. Baldy didn't seem to care for it. He flipped Peter the middle finger, and soon after, Peter was looking at the Impala's rear bumper pulling away up the road. If this were another time, if he were ten years younger, he might've tried to mess with the guy, see if he could goad him into a race, but those days were behind him. Besides, the slant-six under the hood of his Dodge Dart wouldn't stand a chance against the monster V8 the Impala was probably packing.

He sighed and looked at his watch. It was twenty past noon. He settled back into his seat, dropping his hand out the window. Letting it rise and dip in the wind, he felt like a fighter pilot controlling the flaps of a plane every time the air caught his fingers and changed their direction. In the serenity of that moment, the thought returned to him: *Gilchrist. What the hell is in Gilchrist?*

And wasn't that a good question? Probably it was nothing more than a coincidence that he'd heard the name in his dream and then seen the sign the very next day. Those weren't exactly two obscure or unreasonable things to connect. The sign was a sign. That was all. He'd more than likely just seen it after repeated trips by it, and for some reason, the information had finally bubbled up to the surface and combined with whatever other nonsense was floating around in the mixing bowl where dreams were made.

Another sign passed overhead: MA-2 WEST – CONCORD. Then below that: WALDEN POND NEXT LEFT.

Nothing about him wanted to go home. He'd already exhausted his agenda for the day, and he was starting to get hungry, not to mention thirsty. The idea of a cold beer and some food didn't sound half bad at all. A little hair of the dog would take care of that last little edge of hangover that the aspirin hadn't killed. What did he have to lose?

Several minutes later, when the Concord exit approached, Peter did not turn off. Instead, he continued on. Forty-one miles to go.

2

Gilchrist seemed to emit a strange, almost nostalgic energy that Peter felt the moment he turned onto the downtown strip. Nothing looked familiar, but damned if he didn't feel like he had been there before.

He drove slowly up what he could only imagine was Main Street, eyes searching for a place that offered food and drink. It didn't take long for him to spot what he was looking for. A modest corner building at the first intersection he came to had a neon Pabst sign in the window. The establishment was called Dale's Tavern, according to the lettering above the door.

Peter went through the intersection and parked in front of a place called Tedford's. It looked like a hardware store. He got out and crossed the street to Dale's.

As Peter was approaching the bar, hand about to reach for the door, it burst open. A man sort of stumbled out, head down, as his finger dug around inside a pack of cigarettes. Peter stalled and stepped back. The man looked up, gracelessly pushing a comma of greasy brown hair off his forehead. His nose was reddish-purple and fat with broken blood vessels.

"Wuhcha fuggin want here, pal?" the man slurred, one eye half shut. He hitched up his pants slowly with one hand and took another step out the door, letting it slam behind him. "Ain't nothin here for ya. G'home b'fore this place swallas you up."

"All right, if you say so," Peter said dismissively, giving the man space to walk by. He had dealt with enough drunks in his time to know it was best not to engage someone in the throes of a blackout. Things could easily go from friendly to aggressive in a matter of seconds, the simplest things interpreted as a call to battle. He had been that way more times than he cared to remember.

"I sed wuhcha fuggin doin? You come here, gonna stay here." The man lunged at Peter, grabbed him by the shoulders, and licked the side of his face. He reeked of booze, body odor, and a lifetime of cigarette smoke.

"Get off me." Peter tore himself away.

The man broke away and started laughing, cramming a bent cigarette into his mouth. He stumbled past Peter, who was standing there, shocked, and started weaving up the sidewalk, searching his pockets, presumably for a lighter to fire up his crooked Pall Mall.

The door opened again, and another man came out, this one tall, middle-aged, and wearing an apron. "He give you trouble? I just gave him the boot."

Peter wiped his cheek on the sleeve of his shirt. "Huh? No. No, not really. Just…"

"He lick you?"

Peter smiled. "Is that what that was?"

The man laughed. "That's Benny. He does that from time to time. He's mostly harmless. Doesn't bite, is what I mean. Were you trying to come in?"

"I was thinking about it. Anyone else going to mistake my face for an ice cream cone?"

"I can't promise you that." The man smirked. "But I can promise you that our beer's cold and that Benny won't be back to bother you."

"You serve food?" Peter asked. "I wanted grab some lunch."

The man straightened and folded his arms, straddling the doorway. It was a look of pride. "Best burgers in town. The Dale's Delight, it'll blow your damn hair back. Guar-own-teed. Some might tell you Diane's up the road is better, but they'd be lying… or plain wrong. She uses that lean beef."

"Sounds good to me," Peter said.

"Come on in. I'll fry you up a couple. First beer's on the house to make up for Benny's bad first impression."

He followed the man inside.

Dale's was a classic dimly lit local bar, and it was just the kind of place Peter had been looking for. It was the type of joint where the burgers were greasy and the beer was cheap and cold. A couple of lone patrons were at the bar when he came in. They both turned around, regarded Peter for a second, then went back to gazing down into their beer glasses, perhaps searching for whatever it was they felt but could never describe had passed them by. The air smelled of long nights and pool chalk. A jukebox was pumping out Johnny Cash's "Folsom Prison Blues."

He grabbed a seat at the bar, exactly halfway between the two old beer-gazers sitting at opposite ends. The man in the apron walked around a large wooden column and went behind the bar. He pulled a beer from a tap into a tall glass and cut off the head with a butter knife. "Who should I make this out to?" he asked, setting it in front of Peter.

Peter took a long sip, then reached over the bar. "Peter."

They shook hands.

"Good to meet you. Name's George. Don't think I've seen you around here before. I'm usually pretty good with faces."

"As good as Benny?" Peter offered a smirk that said his comment was all in good fun.

George leaned back against the bar and laughed. "Good one. All right, not bad."

"I'm just passing through," Peter said. "I don't live too far from here."

"Where're you from?" George picked up a dish towel and started folding it.

"Concord." Peter took another sip, baring his teeth as the cold carbonation stung his mouth. "Thanks for the beer, by the way. Cold as promised."

"Oh sure, I've been to Concord before. It's nice," George said. "You want me to grab you a menu, or should I set you up with a couple of Delights?"

"Depends. What comes on a Delight besides full-fat beef?"

"The works, which includes my wife's homemade sweet pickles—best you'll ever have—plus bacon, cheese, and barbecue sauce. You won't leave hungry… or disappointed. I can assure you of that." He flicked a thumb over his shoulder, pointing to a small cardboard cutout on the wall that read SATISFACTION GUARANTEED, and once more, he said, "Guar-own-teed."

Peter thought for a moment, and decided he could indeed take down two burgers. "I'll take two… make sure no onion, though. It'll be repeating on me all night if I eat any onions."

"No onions, no problem. So two Delights, *sans cebollas*, coming right up. That's Spanish for *onion*, in case you flunked high school." George winked at Peter. "Want another beer while you wait? I fly solo until about four o'clock, so things can go a little slow this early."

"Yeah, I'll take another. Thanks."

George pulled another beer from the tap and set it in front of Peter. He disappeared through a swinging door behind the bar. For the brief moment it was open, Peter could see into the small kitchen, the engine room of the bar. When the door closed, he took down the rest of his first beer, slid the empty glass to the edge of the bar, and brought the fresh one in close to his chest. Then, with no one to talk to, he let his eyes drift down into his glass.

"I know you," a voice said from down the bar. It sounded accusatory in tone, but also mixed with gentle interest. "Yeah, yup, I sure do recognize you."

Peter glanced in the direction of the voice. The old man's eyes lit up when Peter looked at him. Peter smiled politely back.

The bar relic slid down two stools, eyes narrowing as if switching to some kind of investigatory focal strength. "Yeah, yeah, I thought I placed you when you come in. You were on the back of my wife's book. She read that damn thing every night for a week. Cried at the end and wouldn't shut up about a fella named Boone for the next month." He slapped his hand on the counter. "Author!" he said, with the deciding finality of a judge. "That's you. You're the author." He screeched with a wheezy laughter that broke up into a cough.

"I think you might mean Boothe," Peter said, trying not to come off as self-righteous.

"What's that?" the man asked, wiping his sleeve over his mouth.

"The character's name in the book... it's Boothe, not Boone. Was she reading *Jupiter Place*?" Peter suddenly felt arrogant for correcting the man, and even more so for saying the name of his book out loud like it should mean something.

"Yeah, that was it. Sorry. I'm no reader myself. But my wife is." The old man moved down another stool. "So did you write that?"

"I did," Peter said.

"I knew it. Oh man. We got someone famous sittin right here." He perked up and looked over Peter's head to the man sitting at the other end. "Hey, Alton, get this... this fella is a writer, and a famous one."

Alton didn't seem to care. "Is that right?" he said, drinking his beer and never looking in their direction.

"Not a fan, I guess," Peter said softly, but not without humor.

"Forget him. Hey, let me buy you a beer." The old man dropped a wrinkled five-dollar bill on the table.

"No, that's okay, really."

The door behind the bar swung open, and George came out, spinning a bag of hamburger buns closed with a twist tie. He dropped them on the table beside him. "What's all the commotion out here, Walt? What're you shouting about? It's too damn early for shouting."

The old man patted Peter on the shoulder as if staking a claim. "You know who this is, Georgie? This ain't no ordinary customer."

"Don't call me that, Walt. Nobody's called me Georgie since I was a kid. I didn't like it then, and I don't like it now," George said calmly, but with an underlying toughness in his voice that suggested a person might do well to heed his warning. Then he looked curiously at Peter. "I know his name's Peter. And he's hungry and likes cold beer. That's about the long and short of it."

"The man's an author. Peter…" Walt started snapping his fingers, searching for a last name.

"Martell," Peter said, when it became clear Walt was going to be snapping all night.

"A writer, huh?" George gave a slight frowning nod that looked something like approval. "We had another writer in town once. It was a few years back. The horror guy. Declan Wade was his name. He rented a place up at the lake. You ever heard of him?"

"Sure I have. He's good," Peter said. "I've only read one of his novels, *Gray Dawn*—I don't really read that kind of stuff anymore—but I know he sells roughly a gazillion books a year. He's a hell of a lot bigger than I am, that's for sure."

"He seemed like a nice enough fella. Pretty much kept to himself." George took the empty glass from in front of Peter, dipped it in a sink full of sudsy water, and placed it on a rack. "So if horror isn't your thing, what're your books about?"

Peter sniffed. It wasn't a derisive gesture; it was one of lived frustration. He hated that question, and yet it always seemed to be the first one people asked him when they discovered he was a writer. "I wish I knew," he said.

That was the answer—or some variation of it—he always gave. And that was because it was the truth. There were only so many ways to bend the truth when one wanted to keep the heart of it intact. That was why lies were easier. A person can go at them, shape and reshape them with a jackhammer, and they still come off the line pretty much as good as the next one and the next one after that.

"Tell me, how does a person write a book if they don't know what it's about?" George asked.

Walt followed up: "Yeah, that don't make no sense to me, neither." His face was cramped into a raisin of confusion.

Peter felt the beer starting to kick in. His nerves took their claws, one by one, out of the meat of his brain. His neck warmed. "Writing a book is a strange thing. It can mean so many different things to so many different people at so many different times. I guess after a while, I kind of lost track of what the stories were ever even about to begin with. But that's assuming I ever really knew in the first place…" Peter gulped his beer. "Which I didn't."

"So you do know, or you don't?" George asked.

"I do…" Peter paused for dramatic effect again. "And I don't."

"So which is it?" Walt inched even closer, and Peter could smell the body odor coming off the man. Not as bad as Benny's had been, but close.

"Both and neither," Peter said.

George laughed. "I think you're full of shit. That's what I think."

"I am…" Peter downed the rest of his beer in one sip and pushed the glass out in front of him when he was done. "And I am not. I'll do another, if you'd be so kind."

This time, it was Walt who laughed. "He is, and he ain't. I like that. Yeah, me too. We're all full of shit in here… and we also ain't. I'll drink to that." He took a deep drink, finishing the beer, and ran his tongue around his lips. Then he stood. "I should probably head back to work. Good to meet you, Peter. My wife's never gonna believe I met you. George, I'll see you later." Still shaking his head, he turned and walked out of the bar.

George took the empty glass from Peter, filled it, and set it back down. "You're all right, writer. Your burgers should be about done. I'll go check."

"Thanks. I was just fooling around, though. Truth is, I really don't know. The books I wrote were just stories I wanted to tell, so I told them. I know they're about *something*, but the answer never seems to be the same when I try to explain it, so I honestly just figure I don't know. Does that make sense?"

"I get what you're saying…" George said, turning away. "And I don't."

Peter laughed. "Fair enough."

George picked up the bag of hamburger buns he'd put on the table a few minutes before, then went back through the swinging door. For a brief second, the sound of sizzling meat escaped, but it was abruptly cut off as the door settled into place on its double-action spring hinges.

Peter sat back in the bar stool, crossing his arms. Unfed, the jukebox had shut off, but the silence of the bar was peaceful. Dim, warm, closed-in, and strangely—if not eerily—familiar,

Dale's Tavern reminded Peter of a giant pregnant belly, Big Mother's womb gestating drunken offspring and birthing them out onto the streets of Gilchrist. He smirked at the absurdity of the picture conjured by that comparison. Then he glanced into his glass and watched the bubbles slowly rise to the surface and pop. It was almost hypnotic to watch.

A few minutes later, George returned with a basket of burgers, and damn it if he hadn't been telling the absolute truth. Each was roughly as big around as a tea saucer, and they really were the best burgers Peter had ever tasted—and probably the largest, too. Both went down far too easily, and onions or no, he suspected he would be tasting those burgers right up through midnight as he lay in bed, one hand tucked behind his head, stomach acid nipping at the back of his throat.

When he was finished, Peter leaned back and rested his hands atop his swollen stomach, patting it contently. "I think you're going to have to borrow a wheelbarrow from someone to get me out of here. I'm stuffed. I honestly don't think I can move."

George was topping off a saltshaker, holding it at eye-level for precision. "They're good, aren't they?" he said in a measured voice, eyes watching the salt closely as it streamed out of the container and into the shaker, careful not to spill any.

"Dangerously so. My compliments to the chef." Peter pretended to tip a hat.

"Well, I don't know that I'd call myself a chef, but a good burger, I can do."

"No argument there," Peter said. "Whatever you're doing, I'd keep doing it."

"That's the plan. Except on holidays." George screwed on the top of the saltshaker and put it next to the three others he had filled.

"You said there's a lake around here? Is that right?" Peter asked. An idea had come to him; slowly at first, but over the course of an hour or so, it had grown to something he was starting to seriously consider.

"That's right. Lake Argilla. Locals call it Big Bath, though. Beautiful place."

Peter leaned forward, elbows on the bar. "I was hoping maybe you could help me with something. Maybe point me in the right direction. It'd be a lot easier than me having to search it out for myself."

"Sure," George said. "I'd be happy to help. What is it?"

Peter told him.

3

Leo Saltzman, owner of Saltzman Real Estate, stared down at the freshly shined tips of his Weejuns. The dress pants bunched around his ankles pooled over most of them, but the tips, he watched tap up and down as he sat in the dense heat of the small bathroom in the back of the office. He checked his watch and sighed. It'd been twenty minutes and still no movement. That was the longest he was supposed to sit there. Doc Barrett had told him any longer than that, and he would end up giving himself hemorrhoids, or *piles*, as his wife liked to refer to them. And making things worse, the castor oil the doctor had given him had failed to get his plumbing flowing properly again. The day was shaping up to be a bust. If nothing was moving yet, it likely wasn't going to budge. Not today, anyway. Leo picked up the bottle of castor oil on the radiator, unscrewed the cap, and finished it off for good measure. He'd been advised to take two to three tablespoons on an empty stomach, but Leo Saltzman was a man who believed in doing things right or not doing them at all. Why take two tablespoons with no food when he could take five times that amount with a hearty breakfast of bacon, eggs, coffee, and home fries?

The bells he had attached to the front door of Saltzman Real Estate jingled, and for a moment the sound of a passing car filtered in. Leo perked up, twisting the cap back on the oil in a hurry and setting it down on the radiator. "I'll be right with you." Then under his breath: "Shit. Lord of Timing, you sure do know how to screw me."

"Hello?" a voice said. "Anybody here?"

"Yeah, I'll be right there. One moment." Leo stood, frantically pulling up his pants, tucking in his shirt, and buckling his belt. "Have a seat, and I'll be right with you. There's cold water in the bubbler if you're thirsty. Help yourself. It's a hot one today. Gotta stay hydrated."

He went to the sink and washed his hands, and instead of using a paper towel, he ran them wet through his hair, the tips of his fingers pausing to inspect the growing bald spot at the back of his head. He caught himself in the mirror. His chubby round face was red and glistening, his upper lip beaded with small dewdrops of sweat. He pulled a paper towel off the sink, wiped it over his face, then adjusted his tie.

Leo was exiting the bathroom when the first signs of trouble hit him. It was what he'd been waiting for; it had just arrived at the wrong moment. *Thank you, Lord of Timing.* "Sorry to keep you wait—oooh. *Wooobaby!*" He stopped dead in his tracks, legs locking, as he stepped out into the office. A sharp pain shocked his gut, and he clutched it with two hands. Something inside shifted and gurgled. He looked across his office and saw a young man leaning over the Styrofoam model of the strip mall, hands in his pockets.

The man straightened. "You all right?"

Leo winced and rubbed his big belly. "That last cup of coffee isn't sitting right." He laughed nervously. "I'll be fine. Sorry to keep you waiting." Moving cautiously, as to not further disrupt what was happening in his bowels, he went around the desk in the middle of the room and over to the model. "You like that?"

"What is it?" the man asked.

"That's my baby. We're building a strip mall across town." Leo spread his hands out as if presenting a headline. "Saltzman Village. You like the name?"

"Is it yours?"

Leo stuck out his hand. "Leo Saltzman. Pleasure to meet you."

"Peter Martell." The man shook his hand. It was a strong grip, but somehow delicate at the same time.

"So what can I do for you, Peter Martell?"

"George sent me over. He said you might be able to help me find a place to rent for a few weeks. I was thinking about spending a little time in town."

Leo's eyes turned up as he ran the name through his head. "George... Bateman? Here, let's take a seat. I think better from a seated position." He gestured to the desk in the middle of the room, and they went over and sat down.

"I'm not sure about his last name. He works over at Dale's Tavern," Peter said. "I just met him a little while ago when I stopped for lunch. I told him I was thinking about renting a place, and he suggested you. He said you handle most of the real estate rentals in town, that I should talk to you if I was interested."

Leo nodded. "Oh sure, Georgie Bateman—don't tell him I called him Georgie, he hates that—but he's who you're talking about. He owns Dale's. His dad left it to him when he croaked. Nice guy… George, not his father. Dale Bateman was a prick. George is wrong about one thing, though." He grinned, a smile full of big polished teeth.

"About what?"

"I handle *all* of the rentals in town." Leo laughed. "Not just *most.*"

"So I take it I came to the right place, then?"

"That you did, Peter. Now what did you have in mind? I have a few things I can think of right off the top of my head that are available if you're just looking for a vacation rental. That is what you said, correct—that you wanted a place for only a few weeks?"

"That's right," Peter said. "I was told there's a lake around here."

Leo leaned back, lacing his fingers over his stomach. "Uh-huh. A beautiful one. Lake Argilla. Most people call it Big Bath, though. It's got loons… and I don't mean crazies." He laughed again, but stopped when another cramp twisted his insides. "*Wooodoggy.*" He winced, holding his side and taking thin breaths. "That was a good one."

Peter leaned forward, a worrisome look in his eyes. "You sure you're okay?"

"Yessir. I'm fine and dandy." Leo forced himself to sit up straight. "Don't you worry about old Leo. It takes a lot more than a little bellyache to derail *this* train."

Peter seemed to regard Leo's sweaty face for a moment. Then, hesitating, he went on: "I was hoping to find something on the lake if that's doable. Something quiet."

"Okay. Something quiet on the lake." Leo brought a hand to his chin and started tapping his lips with his finger. "Is it just you... or do you have need for a family-sized space? You know—multiple bedrooms, a big yard, a dining room? That kind of place? I only ask because your options go way down for waterfront properties. There's only a couple."

Peter glanced away, then back to Leo. "It'll only be my wife and I. I'm really just looking for somewhere to relax for a little while, maybe get some work done. It doesn't have to be anything fancy or big. Just a place to sleep and cook dinner and maybe read a book outside and watch the sunset. That's what I'm looking for."

"Okay. I see," Leo narrowed his eyes and nodded. "What kind of business are you in, if you don't mind me asking?"

"I write," Peter said. "When I can find the words, that is."

"A writer? Like a novelist?"

"I've written a couple of novels, yes."

Leo's generous features lit up, and he clapped his hands together in front of his chest. "I knew it. The moment I saw you, I knew there was something clever about you."

"Is that so?" Peter said. "I didn't know clever had a look."

Leo raised his right hand. "Honest to God. I knew it. And I felt it in your handshake, too. I'm good at reading people that way. It's a gift, I guess you could say. You know, I actually think I have the perfect place for you. Excuse me just one second."

"You mind if I grab some water?" Peter looked over his shoulder at the watercooler against the wall.

"No, no, help yourself. I'll be right back."

Leo stood and waddled to the back of the office, hitching his khakis higher up on his wide backside as he went. He grabbed the rentals binder, then returned, stopping briefly along the way to ride out another gurgling cramp. When he sat back down, he flipped through the binder, found the listing he was looking for, and set it in front of Peter.

"There." He tapped the page. "Take a look and let me know what you think. It's a steal, too, at only sixty dollars a week. It's a little small, but it's right on the water and even has its own private dock with a rowboat. In fact, you might actually be interested to know that another writer, a real well-known famous guy, stayed in the very same place a few years back. I forget his name." Leo started tapping his front teeth with the tips of his fingers, something he did when he was searching his memory. His wife told him it was an unsightly habit.

"Declan Wade," Peter said, flipping through the pictures of the little lake house glued to the binder pages.

"Yeah, Declan, that's it. I suppose Georgie already told you," Leo said, disappointed.

"He might've mentioned it," Peter said, not looking up. He studied the pictures a moment longer, then closed the binder and slid it back to Leo.

"Well, we don't get much excitement around here, so when something does happen, everyone likes to be the one to bend an ear about it." Leo leaned forward on his hairy forearms. "So what'd you think of the place? Is it what you're looking for? I know it's tough to judge from a few pictures, but I thought it'd give you the general idea and set us on the right track."

Peter laughed, shook his head, then leaned back and crossed his legs, running a hand over his face.

Leo's brow furrowed. "Not quite what you had in mind? That's all right. I have others. But if it's only that you have some doubts about the accommodation, you have my word that the place seemed to suit Mr. Wade and his writing needs just fine.

And I'd say that if you're looking for peace and quiet, then I don't think you'll do any better than—"

Peter held up a hand. "I'm sorry. It's not that. The house looks perfect, actually."

"I guess I don't follow. What's the matter, then?" Leo asked.

Peter's face darkened, and he sat forward, one elbow on the desk as if to impart a secret. "Do you ever get déjà vu, Mr. Saltzman? Like really strong déjà vu?"

"Of course," Leo said agreeably. He didn't know where the writer was going with this, but he went along out of sheer curiosity. "Doesn't everybody?"

"You'll probably think I'm crazy for saying this," Peter went on, "but when I drove into town a couple hours ago, I felt like I'd been here before, which I'm certain I haven't. It was the strongest spell of déjà vu I've ever experienced."

Leo leaned back, hands behind his head. "Oh, I don't think that's strange at all. Small towns are like that. Most people grow up in a tiny place like this, then go on to live in bigger cities, live bigger lives, and often forget the places they came from. Then when they stumble into a town like Gilchrist some years later, all those buried childhood memories and feelings come creeping up at the sight of something familiar but forgotten."

This was so much bullshit, but Leo was good at saying what he thought needed to be said to finalize a deal.

"Maybe. I don't know. I'm sure you're right. My imagination does have a tendency to run away with itself from time to time. It's a hazard of the job, I suppose. But just a moment ago, when you went back to get that book to show me the house, I knew exactly what the place was going to look like before I ever laid eyes on those pictures. I knew it right down to that porch swing. I'd swear to that in a court of law. It felt like more than just simple déjà vu." Peter pinched his temples and laughed again. "You must think I'm nuts, huh?"

Leo smiled, shaking his head and giving the look of an understanding friend. "On the contrary. I think you're a man who needs a few weeks of vacation. Maybe what you're feeling is fate pushing you back on track. Maybe it's the Lord's way of telling you to take a break before *you* break. Sometimes we work too hard, plain and simple."

"I'm not a very religious man, Mr. Saltzman. But today, I'm feeling like maybe you're on to something. Let's do it," Peter said, rubbing his hands on the armrests of the chair. "I just hope my wife will be happy about this when she finds out. This is kind of a surprise. It's been a while since either of us have gotten away from it all, and I thought we could both use it."

Leo waved a hand at Peter. "I'm sure she'll be delighted. Once she sees that first sunset on the lake, breathes in the fresh air, you'll have to beg her to leave when your time's up. I'm sure of it. You want to go take a look at the property before you commit to anything? It's only a couple miles away."

"I don't think that's necessary, do you? It's not as though I'm buying the place. I'm sure it'll be fine."

Leo didn't argue. If the fella wanted to skip the tour, that was just fine and dandy with him. It would save some gas. "All right. A man who knows what he wants. I knew I liked you, Peter. I'll go grab the rental agreement for you to sign, and we can get this done."

"Sounds good," Peter said.

Leo pushed himself up, went to a filing cabinet in the back of the office, and pulled out a fresh copy of the agreement. Five minutes later, after he'd filled in all the important specifics on the blank lines, he handed the agreement over to Peter.

"Go ahead and look that over if you'd like. When you're ready, you can sign down the bottom there. I already filled in the date and everything else." He pulled a pen from his breast pocket and put it down in front of Peter.

Peter picked it up, inspecting the wood body of the pen. On the side, SALTZMAN REAL ESTATE had been branded into the grain in small letters. "This is quite a pen."

"You like it? Keep it," Leo said with an air of casualness.

"I couldn't. This looks expensive. What is it—oak?"

"Cherry," Leo said, bobbing back and forth in his chair proudly. "I made it."

Peter's eyes widened, a frown of approval touching his lips. It was the look Leo loved to see. "Made it?"

"That's right," Leo said. "I lathe the bodies myself and buy the ink inserts. It's a little hobby of mine. I have a small shop in my garage at home where I do it. Just a couple of tools and a heap of scrap wood. You don't need much."

"That's impressive," Peter said, knocking the pen against his thumb knuckle. "In that case, I have no problem keeping it. Thank you."

"Don't mention it. Yeah, I like to keep my hands busy." Leo made a gesture similar to the one card dealers made in Las Vegas when they're being changed out. "Idle hands are tools of the devil. That's why I decided to develop the mall, too. Gotta keep busy."

Peter signed the form. "I imagine the devil has a lot of those."

"A lot of what?"

"Tools," Peter answered implacably. "I'm sure he's got a lot of tools." He pushed the rental agreement back to Leo and pocketed his new pen. "He's got a lot of work to do, doesn't he?"

"Well, I wouldn't know, Mr. Martell. I try and stay out of his affairs."

"Of course. Ignore me. I was only being cynical. That seems to be my nature these days," Peter said. "So when do I pay you? I'd like to get in there as soon as I can."

"I was just going to get to that," Leo said, his face brightening at the talk of money. "I'll need the security deposit—that's two hundred dollars, which you'll get back, provided you don't burn the place down—and the three weeks rent up front. The owners have had trouble in the past with people staying and then not paying, so they like for me to collect payment before I hand over the keys. I hope that's not a problem."

"Not at all." Peter reached inside his jacket and pulled out a checkbook. "What's the damage?"

Leo calculated the total, and Peter cut a check for the amount. Then Leo pulled a small leather bag—almost like a shaving kit—from his desk drawer and fished out a set of keys with the address 44 Lakeman's Lane written on a cardboard key fob. On a piece of office stationary, he wrote down directions to the house, in neat capital letters (the man had remarkable penmanship): FOLLOW MAIN ST. TO INT. OF LINEBROOK RD. LEFT ON LINEBROOK & FOLLOW ABOUT TWO MILES, OR UNTIL YOU SEE ARGILLA RD ON LEFT. LAKEMAN'S LN IS A QUARTER MILE ON RIGHT. #44. HOUSE IS NAMED SHADY COVE.

"The house has a name?"

"The owners like to do that around here. Kind of like naming a boat, I guess. Yours is Shady Cove. Here're the keys to the castle and the directions that'll bring you there. They pick up from this office, so as long as you remember how to get here, you'll find Shady just fine." He slid the keys and scrap of paper across the desk to Peter. "You can stay there tonight if you'd like. It's yours for the next three weeks starting this moment. Just cleared out two days ago. Actually, come to think of it, you're mighty lucky. Shady never seems to be open on this short notice. Usually books through Labor Day starting back in February. Looks like the stars aligned just right for you, my friend."

"I guess the universe gets what the universe wants." Peter folded the directions and put them in his pocket. Then he picked up the keys. "Is that it?"

Leo sat forward, shrugged, and tented his fingers. "That's it. Easy, wasn't it? No sense in making things more complicated than they need to be. You wanted something, and I had it. Basic business. Oh, and don't forget this." He slid Peter's driver's license across his desk.

"Basic business—I like that," Peter said, and picked it up. "Tell that to my publisher. Thanks."

Leo smiled and shrugged. "What can I say? I like a happy customer." He grabbed a business card from the little holder on his desk and handed it to Peter. "This is for you. If when you get up there, you find you need something, or something's not working properly, feel free to give me a call, and I'll take care of it myself or send someone who can. There should be a list of numbers taped to the fridge, too: police, fire, all the important ones. And Sue Grady will stop by to tidy up for you, mow the lawn, and haul your trash away to the dump. You'll like her. Interesting gal. Don't try to tip her, though. She hates that, and I pay her plenty."

"I appreciate it."

"Don't mention it. I just hope you enjoy our little town for the next few weeks," Leo said.

They stood and walked to the front of the office together. Peter stopped to fill his cup of water at the watercooler and eyed the strip mall model again.

"Pleasure to meet you, Peter." Leo stuck out his hand when they reached the door, and the two shook again. "Perhaps I'll see you around town sooner than later. You know where to find me. Stop by anytime."

"Take care, Mr. Saltzman," Peter said, and walked out.

"Please, call me Leo."

Over his shoulder, Peter said, "Don't forget to keep those hands busy, Leo."

Leo stood in the doorway a moment, his hand in his pocket, feeling the check and watching the writer walk across the street. It wasn't a lot of money, but it was a sale, and that was all that mattered. He was smiling about that when a terrible cramp seized his gut and doubled him over.

"Sweet Moses! This is it. This is the big one."

He reached up, locked the door, and flipped the sign around to read CLOSED.

4

Sylvia hadn't moved all day. The little square clock she kept on her vanity said it was a quarter past three. She didn't have the energy to get out of bed. Her mind was still thick from the tranquilizers she'd consumed the night before. She had felt Peter press his lips against her cheek as she pretended to sleep, then heard him leave around late morning. He hadn't tried to wake her. Lying on her back, propped against her pillow, she looked to her right. The sheer window curtains breathed in and out in the lazy afternoon breeze. She smelled cut grass and saw the tops of the trees at the far side of the property swaying against a hazy blue sky. She heard cicadas buzzing. Cars drove by every so often, their tires sticky on the hot asphalt of the road. The sound made her thirsty.

She blinked slowly, feeling detached, as if her head were a balloon floating away from her body. She turned away from the window and looked up at the ceiling. Her eyes focused on a small brown water spot where the paint was starting to bubble.

If my arm was long enough, I could reach up and peel away that paint with my fingernail, she thought. *I could just push the tip of it into that bubble and strip it back. And what would be behind the paint? What would be waiting there for me to see? Something rotten? Gray flesh?*

Sylvia put the back of her hand over her mouth, catching a thin roll of flesh between her front teeth. She bit down hard until she tasted blood, then pulled her hand away and looked at the little welt on her skin, indented with her teeth marks. It dripped blood down to her wrist.

This is going to be easy.

She pulled the sheets off her legs. The white silk nightgown she was wearing suddenly felt restricting. She looked down at her toes, saw them wiggle, but didn't quite understand that they were her feet. She saw them but could not comprehend them. They looked unusual and not her own. In fact, she realized her entire body didn't seem to belong to her. A divine warmth surged through her, and her mind descended into darkness, as if dragged down from a great below.

Sylvia sat up, turned, and hung her legs off the side of the bed. The balls of her feet brushed the hardwood floor. It was warm, and she could feel tiny granules of grime and dirt hiding in the grain of the wood. But like everything else she was experiencing, it seemed distant.

Sylvia stood and slid the straps off the gown and let it pool at her feet. She stepped out of it. Naked, she walked out of the bedroom and down the hall and into the bathroom, driven by a singular thought. She picked up the glass beside the sink, filled it with water, and returned to the bedroom. She sat on the edge of her bed and stared at the floor. She started picking at the side of her thumb. An hour passed. Perhaps more.

Eventually she stood and walked to the full-length mirror on the far side of the room. She regarded herself. Her ribs showed. She was pale. Her breasts were perky but starting to sag off to the sides. Gentle slopes with large dark nipples. She ran her hands down her stomach, over her tangles of pubic hair, then around to her buttocks. She did it without thought, as if seeing things from a distance, as if she were looking through the wrong end of a set of binoculars and seeing it all happen from some faraway place.

She turned away from the mirror, went to her bed, and lay down. Staring up at the ceiling, her eyes refocused on the water stain.

5

By the time Peter returned home, it was getting dark and had begun to rain. He'd been gone since ten o'clock that morning. He squinted and checked his watch. It was three minutes of seven, and he was a little drunk. After leaving Gilchrist, he'd stopped off at the Blue Shade Lounge in downtown Concord to celebrate signing the rental contract. A few weeks away at a lake house was just what he and Sylvia needed. He had high hopes that she might even be a little excited about the prospect of getting away for a while. It felt right. This could be the thing to knock them back on track.

He turned off the car and stepped out, eyeing the house. Not a single light was on inside. The screened windows looked like milky eyes. He ran up the driveway, jacket pulled over his head to shield against the rain, and opened the side door on the garage. Sylvia's car was there. She should be home, unless she'd gone out with a friend. But he had to admit that lately she didn't have many friends, and the ones she did have didn't seem to interest her.

He went to the front door, unlocked it, and entered the house. The air was stale and calm; it felt used up.

"Syl, you home?"

The only sound he heard was a lonesome slow drip of water coming from the back of the house. He knew it immediately. He went across the dining room, into the kitchen, and shut off the faucet. It did that sometimes, if the cold-water valve wasn't shut off all the way.

The sink was full of dirty dishes. That had been happening a lot lately. There had been a time when his wife would have sooner died than let the house fall into disarray. But that version of her had all but vanished the day their son died. He understood, but he missed that Sylvia sometimes.

"What the hell did she do all day?" Peter said under his breath, annoyed. He reached into his pocket and felt the keys to the lake house. That calmed him some. It was a source of change, an escape. He looked around, didn't want to see the mess anymore, and went upstairs to take a shower.

Standing on the landing at the top of the steps, he stared down the hall. The bedroom door was partly closed, the way his wife kept it when she was napping. Peter sighed. Sylvia was still sleeping, probably hadn't even been out of bed yet. *Don't be upset with her,* he thought. *This isn't her fault. You're both in this together.*

The hallway was silent. "Sylvia, you up? I have a surprise," he said, starting toward the bedroom.

When he got to the door, he caught a glimpse through the

three-inch crack. He could only see the foot of the bed. His wife's bare legs were side by side, pencil straight, and on top of the quilt. They were still. *Everything* was still. It was too silent. Something was wrong, and a cold shiver ran up his spine.

(*something wrong something wrong*)

Peter opened the door and went into the room. "Sylvia? You awake—"

The first thing that registered with him was that she was naked. Instinctively, his eyes scanned the room, searching for more that was out of the ordinary. Her nightgown lay on the floor... beside the bottle of pills. The cap was on the nightstand next to an empty glass. A few small things that added up to a quick understanding. He covered the remaining distance to the bed in a panic and picked up the bottle of Equanil.

It was empty.

"Oh no, Jesus Christ. What'd you do, Syl?" He sat beside her on the bed and tried lifting her up, his forearm behind the neck. He slapped her cheek softly but firmly. Her head lolled back, limp. Her lips parted, mouth slacked open. A small gasp of breath croaked in her throat.

He let her fall back against the pillow. With his thumb, he pushed open her eyelids—first the right, then the left. They stared blankly into space. He didn't know what to do. His entire life, he'd been certain he was a person who could act with a level head under intense pressure, but he found that he was useless. He was searching his mind for the next move, the proper thing to do, but it simply would not come.

He stood up, needing some kind of an abrupt physical action to ground himself. He was standing with his hands on his hips, looking down at his wife, when it struck him in a morbid way that for the first time in a long while, she looked at peace. He wanted to curl up next to her in bed and hold her, smell the sweet skin of her neck. But he just stood there, staring, vision blurring as hot tears began to well in his eyes.

Check her pulse, dammit, an internal voice spoke up.

He sat back down and pressed two fingers against her neck. He found nothing and tried a different spot, looking for her main artery. Nothing again. He continued moving his fingers around the curves of her neck, searching for a pulse, but he couldn't find one. He realized he didn't have a clue where the heck the artery was. Sure, he knew it from having a rough idea of his own body, but that was different. With Sylvia, he was searching blindly. Then a sickening realization struck him clear and sharp like glass: *Either I can't find her pulse, or there isn't one.*

"No, come on, Syl, wake up!" He grabbed her shoulders and shook her, angry that she would try to abandon him. Her teeth knocked together, making a horrible chattering sound. He picked up her hand, held it tightly in his, then slid his fingers to her wrist and searched there. "Please, you can't leave me. I'm sorry... I'm so sorry."

And as he felt his entire world slipping away from him, a faint beat touched the tips of his fingers at her wrist. It was hardly anything, but it was there. It was a soft, slow stroke: *tap... tap... tap.*

But it was there.

6

Peter stood outside the door to his bedroom as Charles Zaeder, the Martells' family physician, took Sylvia's blood pressure for the third time in an hour. His leather medical bag sat open at the foot of the bed. Sylvia hadn't yet awoken, but she had shown promising signs of responsiveness, which Charles had said was a good indication she would make it out of the woods okay. He had, however, recommended she go to the hospital, but Peter had declined unless it was absolutely necessary. Charles, with a great deal of reluctance and disapproval, finally backed off.

Charles released the blood pressure cuff and put it back in his bag. His stethoscope, he wrapped loosely around his hand and stuffed in the pocket of his coat. He ran a hand over his tightly cropped white beard, looked down at Sylvia for a pensive moment, then picked up his bag and headed out into the hallway, where Peter was waiting.

"Will she be all right?" Peter asked, glancing past Charles to Sylvia. He had dressed her in her nightgown before the doctor arrived. Looking at her brought up a rush of grief. He rubbed the back of his neck, shaking his head.

"She should be okay. I pumped her stomach before she could digest it all," Charles said. "Her blood pressure is low but stable, and all her other vitals are normal, but you need to keep an eye on her." He hesitated. "I'm far more concerned with her mental state, to be honest. I would like to reiterate that it's my professional medical opinion that you have her admitted, Peter. I really think it would be for the best. Just for a few days. It's no mystery what happened here. She should be taken in for observa—"

"Please, Charles, we went over this already. I don't need to hear it again. I know you're right, but I can't put her in a hospital. I don't want her to wake up in a place like that. She's been through enough already. She made a mistake. That's all it was."

He cringed hearing himself try to sell that lie. No mistake had been made.

"You *do* need to hear this. It could have been a lot worse. I don't know what dosage she ingested, but lucky for her, it wasn't enough to kill her... it was close, though. Next time it most likely will be, if she really wants it. And there could very well be a next time." Charles dialed it back. "Look, I know you and Sylvia have been through a lot, and clearly it's taken its toll. But this isn't something you should try to sweep under the rug. That's all I'm saying."

"Do you actually think I don't know that? No one is sweeping anything under the damn rug."

"I'm only giving you my honest opinion."

"Okay. I'll note it, but can we please just..." Peter bit his lip, shaking his head. "Listen, I just rented a quiet little place on a lake about fifty miles from here. I had been planning on surprising her tonight. I think it's exactly what she needs. And there I'll be able to watch her. I know it's not a hospital, but I think it's what's best for her."

There was a pause, and in it, Peter and Charles looked at each other, eyes searching.

"She could be a real danger to herself."

Peter squeezed his temples, losing patience. "Charles..."

"All right, all right, I won't mention it again. Just promise me you'll keep a close eye on her. You have to, Peter."

"You don't have to keep telling me that. She's my wife. Don't you think I want what's best for her? You need to trust me. Sending her to a hospital would only make things worse. She needs a break, not a hospital stay. She's seen enough doctors to last her a lifetime."

"I know. You and Sylvia are friends, and I only want what's best for you both. And it's clear I'm not going to convince you otherwise. So if you say this is what she needs, I'll trust you,"

Charles said earnestly, putting up a hand and surrendering the point he was trying to make. Then, changing gears, he asked, "How have things been going with Dr. Carlson? Have you and Sylvia seen him recently?"

Peter glanced at Sylvia, then back to the doctor. "Yes. To be honest, I get the feeling that's why this happened, actually."

"What do you mean?" Charles folded his arms.

"We had an appointment yesterday, and things didn't go well."

"What happened?"

"He said he doesn't know what's wrong, only that one of us might be infertile. Or both of us. Or neither," Peter said. "He doesn't really seem to know much beyond the fact that we can't conceive at the moment. So we're no better off than we were six months ago."

"That's what he said?"

"He said he can't find anything wrong with either of us and that we should continue to try, but that after this long, there could be an underlying reason. But it's a reason he doesn't know, so a lot of help that is."

"I understand how frustrating it can be to have more questions than answers. But yours is not entirely bad news, if you want my opinion. Sometimes no news *is* good news."

"That's what the other guy said." Peter let out a long sigh. "This is killing her, and I don't know what to do. Noah was everything to her. Now he's gone, and all she wants is to try again—to start another family—but it isn't working. *Nothing* is working, and she thinks God is blaming us for letting our son die. She thinks we're being punished."

"Oh, that's nonsense. She must know—"

"I know, I know, she has to know that it's no one's fault. It was an accident. The stars just aligned perfectly that night to take our son," Peter said with a parroting tone, not meaning to come off as rude; or maybe he did. He was exhausted, and the alcohol buzz he had tied on earlier had since fallen away to a dull, throbbing headache. "Sorry. I'm a little overtired. It's been a hell of a day, to say the least. I think I might make some coffee, if you're interested."

Charles checked his watch. "A little too late for me, thanks. It'd keep me up, I'm afraid."

"She'll be okay," Peter said abruptly. "I'll keep a close eye on her. You have my word. I've already taken her medications and hidden them." He hadn't, but he reminded himself to do it once Charles left. "I'll talk to her in the morning. You'll see, this whole thing will blow over. And I'll call you in a few days and give you an update. I think a few weeks away from this place is all she needs. We both need it."

"Well, let's hope you're right," Charles said without enthusiasm.

Peter put his hand on the doctor's shoulder and began leading him away. "I'm sure you want to get home now. It's late."

Charles stopped and looked at him, eyes narrowed. "How about you, Peter? Do you feel okay?"

"I feel fine. Why? Do I not look it?"

"Just thought I'd ask and make sure," he said, seeming to study Peter.

"Been a long day, Doc. That's all," Peter said. "Maybe I'll skip the coffee and just go to bed."

"Maybe that's a good idea."

The two of them descended the stairs, and a few moments later, Peter was waving from the front door as the doctor's black Buick backed down the driveway, headlights making little prismatic halos in the low fog rising up off the road. He stayed and watched the car's taillights stop and hesitate at the intersection at the end of Preble Avenue. They flickered a few times, then turned left and were gone, swallowed by the night. The rain had slowed to mist. The night was somehow cool and warm at the same time. He reached into his pocket and felt the keys to the lake house.

Peter went inside and up to his office. He needed make a call. But first, he stopped to check on Sylvia. She was sleeping soundly, snoring lightly, wrist bent beside her head on the pillow.

7

After what might've been the fifth ring—Peter wasn't entirely sure; he'd lost count midway through the second—there was a click, then the sound of someone clearing their throat. "It's late. Somebody better be dead or trying to give me money," the voice said.

It was a tough voice. Thick and unapologetic. Tom Landau spoke in much the same way a bulldozer toppled trees. And that was, perhaps, the reason Peter had liked the man so much after meeting him only once and for but a brief moment during a dinner party a friend had been hosting. Tom was honest in the most basic way: he didn't know how to lie even if he'd wanted to. There was never any bullshit to see through with him. And that was why Peter had contacted him the day after their first encounter and asked Tom to read his first novel and, if he liked it, to represent him. Three weeks later, Peter had himself an agent.

"Tom, it's me," Peter said.

"Pete? You were supposed to call me hours ago. I figured we'd talk tomorrow."

"Yeah, I know. I apologize. I got sidetracked," Peter said. But what he was thinking was: *Isn't that just about the biggest fucking understatement of the year.*

"Well, anyway, how'd the meeting go?" Tom asked. Then more quietly, he said to someone else: "Everything's fine, Joan. It's Pete."

"It went as expected," Peter said. "Everything got signed, if that's what you mean."

"Those greedy bastards didn't change anything on the contracts, did they? We had them just the way we wanted them. Everything was perfect and agreed upon. But I wouldn't put it past those shyster pricks to go ahead and try to sneak something in last minute. That's why I should've been there. Dammit, I knew it."

There was the sound of shifting on the other end of the line, the scratch of a flint being struck, then a long pause while Tom pulled a drag off his cigarette. Peter could picture him doing it, the same way he always saw him do it—eyes closed, head at an angle, enjoying the near-instant rush of nicotine being dumped into his bloodstream—whenever they met for drinks or at his office in Cambridge to discuss a project. More often than not, their meetings were nothing more than thin excuses to get drunk in the afternoon.

"Calm down, they didn't change anything. It was everything we discussed last week. Just let me know when they send the check."

"I always do, don't I?" Tom took another drag off his cigarette. Then, his voice taking on a more comfortable tone, he asked, "So did you miss me today?"

"I know you like to think that writers can't make it an hour without an agent to hold their hand, but I can handle signing my own name a few times."

"That's right." Tom laughed and made a pleased sound of agreement. There was also a soft hissing in the receiver, which Peter knew to be the sound of smoke jetting from Tom's nostrils.

"Listen, Tom, I need to give you a heads-up about something."

(*my wife tried to kill herself, we can't have a baby, and our life is falling apart*)

"Uh-oh. I don't like the sound of this already. Your tone's all wrong."

"I rented a lake house over in Gilchrist." Peter picked up a pencil and started mindlessly scratching it on a piece of paper on his desk. "Sylvia and I will be leaving for a few weeks on Sunday, and I won't be reachable."

"Gilchrist? Where the hell is that?"

"Fifty miles or so west of Concord. It's barely a speck on the map."

"And they don't have telephones there?" Tom said dubiously.

"That's not what I meant."

"I don't follow—why will you be unreachable, then?"

"I don't want to be disturbed," Peter said. "I'll call you with the number when I get there, but I don't want to hear from you or anyone else unless it's an emergency. Don't take it personally or anything, I just need the break. I need to cut the tether for a little bit."

"A break? Is everything all right?" Tom coughed and cleared his throat again. Peter could hear that Tom's posture had stiffened with concern. "This is a little abrupt, not that you need my—or anyone's—permission to take a vacation. I just want to make sure that everything is okay."

"Everything's fine. I promise," Peter said. "Sylvia and I just need a little vacation, that's all. We haven't had some time away from home since... well, it's been too long."

There was a moment of silence on the line.

"Maybe you two *could* use this. You're right. Go get centered, if that's what you need," Tom said, seeming to understand. Then, changing tones from sympathy back to business before things became too sentimental, he added: "But don't forget about your deadline. We agreed to have a polished draft of the new book to Kingston by the end of September. That's a short six weeks out, my friend. And I don't think I need to remind you that publishers don't take kindly to missed deadlines. They could ask for their advance back, and I'm sure you'd hate to have to part with that money."

"That's not going to be a problem, Tom. You worry too much. It's bad for your heart. The first draft is finished. It just needs some tweaking." Peter glanced down at the stack of manuscript pages sitting next to the typewriter on his desk.

"As usual, I'll feel better when it's in my hands and I'm reading it," Tom said.

"Soon enough, I promise."

"I have no doubts," Tom said.

"None? I hardly believe that."

Tom laughed. "A few, but not about you. When do you and the missus plan to go AWOL?"

"I was hoping to leave Sunday morning. Get an early start."

"Well, if anyone deserves it, it's you, Pete. You're one of the good ones, my friend. Don't forget that. I'll wait to hear from you."

"Calhoon's when I get back?" Peter asked.

"First round's on me," Tom said. "Take care now, and tell Syl I send my best."

"Yep, same to Joan. Talk to you later."

Peter was still doodling on the scrap of paper when he hung up the phone. He looked down at what he had written: *I've decided to go.*

It was something he did often. When he needed a push, sometimes he would write down the thing he was unsure of, as if in doing so, he was setting his decision in stone, committing to it. He even had a little slogan that went along with it: *When in doubt, write it out.*

He looked at what he had written once more and nodded to himself. Dr. Zaeder's concerns for his wife had been justified, but Peter felt this was the right choice. She needed a change, not a hospital. And so did he.

Chapter Three

RICKY OSTERMAN

1

Hooch Collins, whose real name was actually Christopher Collins, stood on the sawed-off tree limb fifty feet above the lake. He was wearing nothing but his soaking-wet underwear. His doughy body glistened gold and red in the setting sun. His dumb-wide moon-face shone out over the water like a beacon of bad ideas. In one hand was the beer he'd somehow managed to carry with him up the shoddy two-by-four ladder, which the generation of teenagers before him—perhaps even his own father—had nailed into the side of the giant oak tree, probably during a summer much like this one. In the other hand was the knotted end of the rope swing.

Grace Delancey watched the whole scene, the lump of disquiet steadily growing in her throat. Why had she agreed to come? She hated Ricky and Hooch. Their entire vocabulary consisted of nothing more than grunting, belching, swearing, and referring to girls as *wool*.

"Don't be such a chickenshit, just go," Ricky Osterman yelled up from the ground.

He, too, was standing around in his wet underwear and drinking a beer. His physique was much more athletic than Hooch's. His arms were long and sinewy, his back broad and striated with muscle. The skin on his shoulders and chest was spattered with large freckles that matched his dirty-red head of hair and made him look perpetually in need of a bath. His nonthreatening facial features—a small, flat nose; unremarkable, wide-set green eyes; and a soft jawline—suggested a person whose true nature often went unnoticed until it was too late. Grace suspected as much, anyway. That might've been the real reason she didn't like him. Something about him was dangerous.

"I don't see *you* up here," Hooch said.

"Quit pulling your pud, and I will be. Me and your fat ass can't be on that branch at the same time. It'd never support us both. Maybe lay off the Twinkies, chunko."

"Go piss up a rope, Ricky." His face sort of stalled, perhaps realizing he was, in fact, holding an actual rope.

"I got a better idea. You just need a little motivation." Ricky searched the ground, found what he was looking for, then cocked his arm back and fired the rock at Hooch. It whizzed by him, narrowly missing his thigh.

Ricky had been a decent pitcher before he'd quit the Gilchrist High School varsity baseball team last year. He'd never been much of a junk thrower, but man, could he throw straight smoke when he wanted to. Even when he was a freshman, the senior classmen didn't dare crowd the plate when he took the mound. Mitch Shepland had once made the mistake, and Ricky had sent him to the hospital with a fractured cheekbone. Ricky had never even blinked, not even when Mitch spat out four of his teeth onto home plate as he crawled around on the ground, dazed and mumbling incoherently. An example had needed to be made.

"Quit it, asshole," Hooch said, his face sobering. "That ain't funny. You want me to break my neck?"

"That's the point, fucko. We're gettin bored down here. We want a show." Ricky cackled.

His laugh ripped the air like a rusty chainsaw. The sound made Grace's skin crawl. As if he sensed this, Ricky glanced in her direction and grinned, exposing two rows of small yellowish teeth.

Lay off the cigarettes, Grace thought. *Blech!*

She and Beverly were sitting on the telephone pole near the water's edge. Sometimes kids stole the old poles from the utility department and brought them out to Big Bath to use as floats to drink beer on at night. The skilled ones, Grace had heard, were able to maintain balance well enough to have sex on them. She supposed if a couple positioned themselves properly, it might be possible, but what did she really know? She was still a virgin. She didn't want to be. It wasn't like she was saving it for her wedding night or anything, but she wasn't putting up fliers or taking out ads in the *Gilchrist Chronicle*, either. It would happen when it happened.

Her friend, on the other hand, seemed as though she couldn't do it fast enough. Beverly had expressed her desire to not enter high school a virgin. It was on her Summer of '66 To-Do List. And so was Ricky. Beverly was the reason Grace was there. She'd only come as a favor. Grace couldn't even begin to understand Beverly's crush on Ricky, but her friend wanted her there for support. Grace knew the real reason Beverly had asked her: Grace evened up the teams, two on two. Not that she would ever consider being with either one of those boys. Not only was she not in a rush to have sex... she wasn't desperate, either. And Ricky and Hooch were G-R-O-S-S.

Just like the boys, Beverly was stripped down to her underwear. She had a towel draped over her shoulders and was smoking a Viceroy she'd stolen out of her mother's purse. She was puffing on it, trying to look cool. Her dark hair was wet and matted and hung down in clumps, sticking to the cups of her padded bra. They'd all gone swimming except for Grace, who wasn't about to undress in front of two guys she could barely stand to be in same car with, let alone strut around in next to nothing. No, Grace was in a skirt and blouse. Dry. And she was absolutely happy as could be about that.

"Ain't that right, ladies?" Ricky said, wiping his forearm across his chin. "Don't we want a show?"

"You want a show?" Hooch called down to Ricky. "I gotta take a leak. Open up and say ahhh."

Ricky laughed derisively and shook his head. "What a weirdo," he said to the girls, as if trying to sell himself as the good guy.

Beverly took another clumsy drag off her cigarette, fingers shaking as she inhaled. She coughed out the smoke. "Come on, let's see what you got, Hoochy. Swing for it," she yelled, sounding forced. She picked up her beer and took a small sip. She turned to Grace. "Have some," she said softly.

"You're kidding, right? My dad would lose it if he smelled that on my breath. It's bad enough you're blowing smoke all over me." She scooted away.

"It won't kill you, Grace. Just a little sip. It's not like you're gonna get drunk."

"I don't want any, Bev. Knock it off." She looked up at Hooch, shaking her head. "He's going to hurt himself. This is crazy. That's really high up."

"Relax, they're just having fun. You ever thought about trying it yourself?" Beverly said snidely.

Grace knew it was the alcohol talking. Beverly was showing off. It annoyed her, but she understood it. People just wanted to be liked.

"Yeah, Gracie, have a little fun," Ricky, who'd been eavesdropping, said. "Your daddy ain't here. You afraid the chiefy is gonna come arrest his own daughter?" He smirked at her.

"It's Grace, not Gracie," she said. "And your friend will kill himself if he swings from up there. The water's too shallow. Just thought you should know."

"Wouldn't that be a sight. I'd pay to see it." Ricky looked up. "Hey, Hooch, she thinks you're gonna die. Maybe you should come down," he said sarcastically.

Hooch flipped him off and tossed the beer can over his shoulder. "Nothing can kill Hooch Collins!" he yelled, then howled like a wolf and beat his chest with his free hand. His howl echoed across Big Bath.

"You want next? You ain't got wet yet," Ricky said to Grace. "I bet you'd like to get wet. You look like you could use it." He winked at her. "I can take care of that."

"No thanks, I'm fine," Grace said, her tone flat but not intimidated. "That's a heck of an offer, though. The girls must go crazy for it."

She winked mockingly at Ricky to return his gesture and show him that he didn't scare her.

He scowled and narrowed his eyes. *You smart-mouthed bitch*, they said.

Beverly nudged her. "Grace, you promised to be nice," she whispered. "He's only kidding."

Grace looked at her and rolled her eyes. "Oh, come on.

What're we even doing out here?"

Beverly gaped at Grace. It was silent friend-speak that meant: *Please just give me a little longer, then I'll owe you forever.*

Grace sighed. Friend-speak translation: *Fine.*

Ricky came closer, not giving up. He wouldn't be silenced that easily. "You don't know how to swim, is that it?" He stood in front of the girls, and throwing his head back and pushing out his crotch, he chugged the rest of his beer. With a loud belch, he tossed his empty beer in the lake.

Beverly giggled.

Why is she laughing? Grace thought. *It wasn't even funny.* Though, once again, she supposed she understood.

"How lovely," Grace said.

"Like what you see, do ya?" Ricky gyrated his hips, laughing.

Wet, his underpants were nearly transparent. She didn't want to, but curiosity got the best of her, and Grace glanced. She looked away quickly, her stomach fluttering. It was one of those cases where someone says not to think about purple elephants, then *whammo!* your head is full of purple elephants.

Ricky shifted his attention, having had the final word.

"Jesus Christ, go already," he said across his shoulder, and spun around. He went back to the base of the tree and started yelling up at Hooch. "Go, or I'm comin up there to throw you off."

Once more, curiosity got the best of her and Grace caught herself looking at Ricky's butt. She could see all the muscles moving together as he mounted the tree ladder and squatted on the bottom foothold, letting one arm hang behind him like an ape. She was in no way attracted to him, but there was something about his lithe movement that drummed up a strange feeling inside her. She turned away from it.

"Here I come," Ricky said.

"I dunno, I think I'm too high," Hooch said uneasily.

"Yeah, and too stupid." Ricky let another blade of sharp, rusty laughter rip.

"You sure people actually swing from up here? I've done it from the low branches before, but…" Hooch trailed off.

He was starting to resemble a frightened cat stuck in a tree. The five or six beers he'd put away might've helped him find the courage to get up there, but they weren't quite enough to make him forget he had a fear of heights.

"All the time. You're fine. Now hurry up." Ricky jumped off the ladder and started searching the ground again. He found another rock and fired at Hooch for the second time. This one bounced off the trunk with a hearty *klunk!* right beside his head.

"I mean it, knock it off, Ricky." Hooch spat at Ricky, leaning over to watch its descent. But the blob of saliva dispersed on its journey down and was lost.

As he tried to straighten, Hooch lost his balance. One hand was holding the rope; the other was reaching blindly for the tree trunk to steady himself. It was too late. He was going down one way or the other.

"Here he goes, ladies and gentlemen," Ricky said, his voice taking on showman's quality.

Hooch wrapped his arms around the rope and leaped out over the water, feet finding a knot on the rope. He came straight down at first, but at about the halfway mark, the rope found tension and Hooch swung out over the lake in a wide and wild arc. He was screaming and laughing the whole time. Mostly screaming. When he reached the apogee, he let go and tucked into a cannon ball. He hit the water with a loud slap and sent a geyser of water thirty feet into the air.

Ricky cheered. Beverly cheered. Grace watched the place where he'd hit as the whitewater from Hooch's entry calmed.

Hooch didn't surface. A few seconds passed. Twenty. Still no Hooch.

Beverly didn't look so amused anymore. "Ricky, is he okay? Where is he? He should be up by now."

"Eh, I'm sure he's just messing around. He's fine," Ricky said, and went to check for another beer.

Grace stood and went to the water's edge, starting to kick off her shoes. She was going in after him. Maybe she didn't like Hooch, but she didn't want him to drown, either. "I told you it was too shallow, you moron."

She hiked up her skirt and waded in. The water was warmer than she'd thought it would be. "Chris?" She looked in the direction where he had landed. She could see boulders under the shallow surface, any one of which he could've smacked his head or back on when he'd landed.

"Don't call him Chris. He hates that name," Ricky said casually, searching through a rusty bucket of empty cans. "Only one left." He pulled out the last can of beer. "We're all out. Gotta make a run before they close."

Grace waded out a little farther. Her skirt was wet now. Panic was starting to squeeze her gut. She looked back over her shoulder at Beverly.

"Do you see him?" Beverly asked.

"No." Then to Ricky, she said, "Are you going to do anything or are—"

"*Blaaargh!*" Hooch launched himself out of the water about ten feet in front of Grace, arms waving wildly. "I'm the Creature from the Black Lagoon." He had covered himself in mud and was grinning, white teeth shining through.

Grace screamed, and smacked a handful of water at him. "You jerk! I thought you…"

"What?" Hooch said, the humor fading from his face.

Ricky laughed. "I told you he was just messin with you." He kicked the empty bucket over, spilling the cans. He opened the beer he'd found and started drinking it.

Amusement returned to Hooch's face, and he started toward Grace, arms out straight like a zombie. "Come to me, my love."

Grace turned around and stomped out of the water. "Screw you," she said, feeling an equal mix of anger and embarrassment.

She yanked the towel off Beverly's shoulders, sat on the telephone pole, and dried off her legs.

Beverly sat beside her. "They were just fooling around, Grace."

"Uh-huh, I know." Grace didn't look at her friend.

"Why're you so upset? It was only a goof."

"I thought he was… Can we just get out of here? I wanna go home."

Beverly started to answer, but Hooch and Ricky came to a decision for the group.

"Your turn," Hooch said to Ricky. "Climb on up, mister brass balls." He blew a snot rocket into the water.

But Ricky was already putting his clothes back on, slipping on a boot. "Gotta boogey, my man. We're outta beer, and the store's gonna close soon."

"Oh man, already?" Hooch said.

"Yessir," Ricky said.

Hooch slicked his hair back with both hands. "What're we waiting for? Let's go."

This was a subject that required no debate. Out of beer? Have to get more. It was practically the natural law of male teenage life.

Hooch trudged out of the water, rinsing the mud from his body as he went. When he made landfall, Grace noticed he had a long, thin gash on the top of his foot. It was bleeding, but he didn't seem to feel it. He got dressed in a hurry, and so did Beverly.

Grace just wanted the evening to be over. She wanted to go home. It was the last time she would ever do a favor like this for her friend.

Ten minutes later, they were all packed in Ricky's car again. The stale scent of lake water and damp towels mixed with the ugly smell of beer breath. Grace disliked the car almost as much as she did Ricky and Hooch. But it wasn't so much the car itself she didn't like. It was the way Ricky drove it: fast and loud. Dangerously.

One day, he would hurt someone. Or worse.

2

Elhouse and his wife, Gertrude (Gertie to those closest to her), never had delusions of retirement. It simply wasn't in the cards for them, and they were just fine with that. They ran a farm and never had children who could take over, so the work was what they had. But it was honest work, and it was an honest life. They both agreed on that. Not that they ever said as much out loud to each other, but it was a thing that never needed discussion. That was just the way it was. It was understood. And it was good. A shared rule born out of forty-five years of marriage. Contentment, Elhouse had learned, lived not in the words spoken to one another, but in the moments where they were not necessary. In the comfortable silences of a life spent together.

Even as they got along in years and their age crept up through their fifties, then their sixties, and now found them both spry and gray in their seventies, they never entertained the idea of not working. Of not tending and cutting the hay. Not raising the chickens and cleaning the coops. Or planting corn. And why should they? Both were in good health, and both wholeheartedly agreed that keeping active and busy had seen to that. As Elhouse's father had always said: *The day you retire is the day you start dying.* And with every season that passed, those words seemed to gather more weight. A person needed a purpose, Elhouse believed, a reason to plant one's feet on the floor come sunrise, and since neither Gertie nor Elhouse was ready to start dying, retirement wasn't an option.

They did, however, enjoy taking their evening walks. It might've been the closest thing to a recreational activity they had.

Their farm was on fifteen acres of flat land on the outer edge of Gilchrist near Big Bath, and their house sat at the front of the property along Waldingfield Road, a narrow, dirt access road that began off Route 2 and cut through to downtown Gilchrist.

"You about ready, Gert? Daylight ain't waiting on you," Elhouse said over his shoulder, and went back to what he was doing.

He was sitting on the front steps of the porch, lacing up his boots. If he didn't make sure they were tight, he would get blisters again, and then he would have to hear his wife tell him all about it, especially if it caused them to cut their walk short. She liked to get in five miles, which meant walking in the direction of town until they reached Gould's Creek, then turning back. Two and a half miles each way. That was what

Elhouse referred to as his wife's "Long-haul Backbuster." He could do it, sure, but he was just as satisfied walking to the fallen elm, sitting for a few minutes and having a pipe of Cavendish, then heading home. His route, full circuit, was just shy of three miles, and that sat far better with his feet and back than Gertie's five. He had found that hers left him sore, and also had them walking back in the dark this time of year, and he didn't like that. The narrow road was dangerous after dark, especially during the summer when the kids took to getting drunk up at the lake, often turning Waldingfield Road into their own personal drag strip on the way back to town.

The screen door opened and clapped shut behind him. "Ready when you are," Gertie said.

Elhouse pushed himself up and faced his wife. "My, my, my, Mrs. Mayer, don't you look like beauty's finest hour."

He was in the same dirty overalls and cotton shirt he had worn all day, but his wife had changed into a dark-blue house dress and cinched her gray-white hair back into a ponytail. She looked twenty years younger, Elhouse thought.

"Oh, stop it, Elhouse," she said, playfully abashed. She took the railing and came down the steps. "If you think I'm leaving the house in filthy chore clothes, you better think again. Just because I live on a farm doesn't mean I'm an animal."

They both laughed.

Then Elhouse repeated what he had said: "I meant it… a beautiful vision you are."

"You tie your boots right this time? I don't want to make it halfway and have to start listening to you complain about blisters."

Elhouse wiggled his feet, looking down at them. "Just did. Military knots, guaranteed by the good old US of A."

Gertie smiled, and they headed out of the driveway and down the road in the direction of town. As always, she set the pace, and tonight she walked slowly but with a steady, measured gait. Elhouse recognized her five-mile stride. His back wouldn't be spared this time, and that was okay. It was never that bad once they were into it.

3

They reached the creek just as the sun went mute in the sky. That meant they had roughly forty-five minutes before full dark, less than that in the thickly wooded parts of the road, which made up most of it. Gertie's pace had gotten them to the Gould's Creek Bridge in less than an hour, and that was good time. Elhouse's back and feet were barking, but it was nothing a few Blue Ribbons couldn't handle when he got home. And at least he didn't have any blisters.

He looked over at his wife. Gertie was leaning with her back against the bridge railing, her eyes closed and her face looking up to the darkening canopy of trees. She breathed in deep through her nose and smiled, just taking it all in.

"Nice, ain't it?" Elhouse said in a reflective tone. He was chewing on the end of his unlit pipe, his forearms resting on the railing as he leaned over and watched the water ten feet below.

Gertie didn't respond, but he hadn't expected her to. It was one of those comfortable silences that would say all they had not to each other.

A leaf, bobbing and listing in the water, passed under the bridge, and Elhouse followed it up the creek until his eyes lost sight of it. After that, he just watched the creek snake away, listening to the hypnotic burble of shallow water running over rocks. He watched where the creek bent and disappeared into the darkening woods, and just let his eyes relax. He stared into the shadows, trying to see beyond them. He did that for thirty seconds or so. A minute. Maybe two. Eventually he lost track.

"I love the way it smells out here," Gertie said, breaking her husband's trance. "It reminds me of when I was a little girl."

The air was cool in the woods around the creek, but it was still sticky with a strange, chilly humidity, like a damp cellar full of organic scents. And a faint smell of smoke.

Elhouse looked away from the dark pocket of the woods he'd been staring into. "What's that, now?"

Gertie lowered her head, opening her eyes and looking at Elhouse. "You fall asleep on me? I sure hope not. I don't think I could carry you back."

"No, just thinking."

Gertie turned around and put both hands on the railing. Then she put a foot up on the lower crossbeam and rocked back slowly, moving like she was in the prime of her life, and maybe she was. "I said the smell out here reminds me of when I was younger. Always does."

"Yeah?" Elhouse said, distracted. "How so?"

"I don't know. I can't put my finger on it exactly. Ain't you ever smell something that makes you think of a thing—a time, a place—you forgot about... or that you didn't even know you'd forgotten?"

Elhouse worked the pipe to the other side of his mouth using only his lips. It was a practiced move. "What the hell are you talking about, woman? I think this fresh air's gone straight to your head." The truth was Elhouse knew exactly what she was talking about, and he didn't know why he had denied it.

She sniffed, amused. "Oh, you know what I'm saying. I'm sure you do."

"I don't know."

"Yes, you do. That's okay," she said matter-of-factly, a smile touching her lips.

Elhouse rubbed the side of his face with a flat hand, his eyes moving from his wife back to where the creek disappeared around the bend. He suddenly became aware of a strange sensation of being watched. He kept staring into the woods, and he was certain he felt something looking back. That feeling came with an uncomfortable sense of dread. Like something in his world was out of alignment.

"We should head home. It'll be night soon." He slapped his neck. "Buggers are bad tonight, too." There hadn't been a mosquito; he just wanted to leave that place before the growing feeling inside him had a chance to become full-sized.

Gertie looked at her husband, reading the wooden look setting on his face. "Okay, let's go. Is it your back or your feet?"

Elhouse forced a smile. "Little of both, I guess."

"All right, I suppose that's enough for tonight."

Gertie sidled up alongside Elhouse and took his arm as they began their walk back.

They were less than a half mile from home when the sound of a racing engine cut through the quiet of the woods, shattering their peaceful evening. It started far-off at first, but in an instant, the noise was on top of them, everywhere, heading in their direction. After a few seconds, it came into view. The car fishtailed around the long bend a hundred yards up the road, its headlights wild and pitching, bobbing up and down over the shallow potholes. At normal speeds, that hundred yards might've seemed like a great distance, but the car was not traveling at normal speeds. The engine was grinding at full throttle. A rooster tail of dust billowed out from the car's rear tires.

"Watch yourself, now, Gertie," Elhouse said. "It's that goddamn Osterman son of a bitch. I'm gonna kill im."

They shuffled to the shoulder of the road and stood in the brush and tall grass on the edge of the steep embankment that dropped off the road.

Panic burst whitely in his gut. The Osterman kid was really flying. He didn't look like he even had control of the car. Elhouse stepped in front of his wife.

Ricky either didn't see them, or he didn't care. The car was headed right for them. It couldn't have been more than a hundred feet away. The headlights blared yellow. The black car screamed in their direction, engine ripping. It was still breaking loose in the dirt, but it straightened out and Ricky goosed it, the intake taking a huge gulp of air.

"Slow down!" Elhouse yelled, shaking his fist at the car, as if that would do any good against the two tons of steel and rubber barreling toward him at seventy miles per hour.

"I don't think they're stopping. Now move it!" Gertie tugged on her husband's arm, trying to pull him down the embankment. Her words were hardly audible over the roar of the engine.

They tumbled down the embankment right as the car sped by, one tire riding the shoulder, narrowly missing them both.

From inside, someone yelled, "Fuck outta the way!" and cackled, then threw something out the window. As Elhouse fell, he saw a beer can tumble across the road. The car was full of kids.

Elhouse lay in the brush at the bottom of the embankment for a few moments, staring up at the fading evening sky behind the canopy of trees, listening as the chug of the engine and the screams of the teenagers disappeared down the road. The summer insects became the only sound again, and the air fell still.

Gertie was breathing beside him. He sat up and looked at her. "You okay? I'm gonna kill those bastards. I swear, if it's the last thing..." He looked after the car, shook his head, and turned back to his wife.

She blinked rapidly, eyes searching for something, as if she were waking up from a deep sleep. "I'm all right... I think."

"It was Nate Osterman's boy again."

Gertie tried to sit up and winced. "I think I twisted my knee."

Elhouse helped her position herself, then slid her dress up and looked at her leg. Her left knee was already starting to swell, and a small cut on her shin was weeping blood. There was also a knot over her eyebrow that would likely bruise.

"Yeah, I think you might've knocked it good. Prolly sprained it," Elhouse said. "Goddamn idiots. Nearly killed you. They been drinking out at the lake and tearing up and down this road drunk all summer. I'm sick of it. I told Corbin, but he ain't wanna do nothing about it."

"Oh, it's okay. I don't want to make it into a big to-do."

"No, it isn't okay. We're lying down in a ditch. Ain't nothing okay about that."

"Gettin all worked up about it won't do any good, now will it? Nothing we can do about it. Boys will be boys. Don't you remember racing around when you first got your license? No sense in getting some kids in trouble over a little accident." She touched her knee softly and grimaced.

Normally, Elhouse admired her willingness to find the best of any situation, no matter how one-sided it was. But this time, her optimism nearly made him blow his stack.

"What're you going on about, woman? That weren't no accident. He almost killed us both. He prolly would've if we didn't get outta the way."

"Oh, don't be so dramatic."

Elhouse bit his tongue; it wasn't worth getting into an argument now. He got to his feet, wiping off the seat of his overalls, and offered his hand to Gertie. She took it and he pulled her up, putting his arm around her waist and taking the weight off her bad leg.

"Let's just get you home so we can tend to that knee," he said.

She took a hobbled step. "All right. Get me bandaged up, and I'll be right as rain tomorrow."

"Woman, you're staying off this leg until it heals. None of your tough-as-an-ox stuff. You want it to get better, you rest. Let's go. Easy now."

They made their way up the embankment and were back on the road, Gertie intact but with a new limp. Elhouse looked in both directions, then down at the crumpled beer can on the side of the road. Suddenly, as if something had called his name, he turned and glanced over his shoulder.

"Something wrong?" Gertie asked.

His eyes lingered long on the deep darkness spreading in the woods as night fell. Something was out there. Watching. He could feel it in his heart.

"No," he said. "Thought I heard a deer, maybe."

They headed in the direction of home, their pace slow, but together steady.

4

"What's the matter with you?" Grace yelled, once she was out of Ricky's car.

They were parked in front of the liquor store. A woman and her young son glanced at the commotion as they passed by, but kept on going up the sidewalk. They stopped to turn around and gawk once they reached the corner. A man pulling boxes from the bed of his truck stopped what he was doing, too.

"What?" Hooch said, and shut his door. "He was kidding around. Relax."

But Hooch didn't sound like he believed his own words very much. It sounded more like he was trying to convince himself of it.

Beverly, arms folded, went toward Grace. "Grace, calm down. It wasn't a big deal. Let's just forget about it, okay? He won't do anything like that again."

"Are you serious, Bev? Yes, he will. He's a psycho. I'm not getting back in that car."

Ricky got out and looked at Grace from across the roof of his car as she stood in the street, her fists clenched at her sides. "Beer? Booze? What'll it be? I'm buying," he said, grinning arrogantly.

Grace snapped, sidestepping Beverly so that Ricky knew she was speaking to him and only him. "You could've killed them, you jerk!" She had never been so angry in her life, and she wanted him to feel stupid. It was the only way she knew how to fight back, even though she hated stooping that low.

"Yeah, but I didn't," Ricky said dismissively. He shut his door, lit a cigarette, then rested his arms on top of his car and stared at Grace. "You wanna get over it and move on? We can keep having a fun time." He hesitated, then smirked at her. "But you don't gotta act like a bitch just because your dad's the law around here. Un-bunch those panties, Gracie." He stuck out his tongue and wiggled it suggestively.

She stomped her foot, feeling silly for doing it. "You're a psycho, Ricky. You think I was having fun with you today?" She laughed at him. "Oh please. Forget it. You think you're so cool and funny, but you're nothing but a loser. I bet Chris doesn't even like hanging out with you." She looked at Hooch. His face was stalled with surprise. "He only does it because he thinks he has to. He's afraid of you because you're crazy."

Ricky's face went dark, his eyes sinking deep. "You better watch your mouth. You don't want to mess with me, Gracie. You don't know what I can do. I—"

"What're you going to do? Are you going to beat me up, Ricky? What a tough guy you are, beating up a fifteen-year-old girl." Grace looked at Beverly. "I'm sorry, Bev, but I'm leaving. Are you coming?"

Beverly looked over her shoulder at Ricky and Hooch. Then back to Grace in a sincerer tone, she said, "Grace, don't you think that maybe you're overreacting just a little? I mean, he said he was only joking."

"Bev, if you get back in that car, then you're making a mistake. I hope you can see that."

Grace turned around, holding back tears. They weren't tears of sadness; they belonged to her rage. In her mind's eye, she continued to see that old couple diving down the embankment, trying to get out of the way. She couldn't bring herself to believe that no one had been hurt. And it was all because Ricky Osterman had wanted to look so cool and show off. God, what a jerk.

People like him were the cancers of small towns, and it was only a matter of time before his black heart metastasized. She doubted any of what she said would have an effect, but saying it to him had felt good. For that reason alone, it had been worth it.

As she walked away, she heard Ricky and Hooch both start complaining. "Oh, come on. You don't gotta go, too. Just stay. We'll behave. Gahhh! There she goes."

Grace thought they were talking to her for a moment, but then came the sound of footsteps running up behind her. "Hold on, Grace," Beverly said, out of breath. "I'm coming with. I'm sorry."

5

Elhouse got Gertie set up in bed, her knee elevated on a pillow, a cloth with some ice as the cherry on top. She refused to let him call the doctor, said it was a waste of money and, most importantly, a waste of time. She would be fine. It was only a scratch.

Elhouse stood beside the bed, looking down at her with a pensive darkness in his eyes. "You gonna be all right? I still have some chores I gotta finish up. It's hardly past eight o'clock."

"Elhouse, go on now and stop doting. You ain't the type. I told you three times already that I'm fine." Her gray hair was let down and covered the shoulders of her white nightgown. After forty-five years of marriage, he still thought she was the most beautiful woman in the world. "Just hand me my book, and I won't be a bother."

Elhouse leaned downed, pressed his lips to his wife's cool forehead, and kissed her. "I'll be back soon to check on you."

"It's over there on the chair." She pointed. "Under the quilt."

Elhouse went over to the wicker chair in the corner of the room and grabbed Gertie's copy of *Breakfast at Tiffany's*. It wasn't her kind of book, but her sister had read it a few weeks back and had promptly made a long-distance call from Denver raving about it, so Gertie felt inclined to keep up.

"Any good?" Elhouse asked, handing it to her. He didn't care, but it was something to say.

She nodded with apprehension. "I don't understand why this Holly doesn't just get a job. Foolish. Hard work is how you get what you want. No other way."

Elhouse tried to light up his face, but what was on his mind overwhelmed any artifice he could muster. "I wouldn't know," he said, his feet turning toward the door.

She made a content sound and cracked her book. That was his cue to leave.

Elhouse went downstairs and out into the front yard. It was just about full dark. The night was calm. No breeze, only insect chatter. The faint sound of cars driving on Route 2 in the distance. The air held the faint smell of smoke. He'd noticed that a lot lately. It always seemed to be there. Perhaps it always had been.

He headed toward the barn, needing to do something to take his mind off what had happened this evening. Because right now he wanted nothing more than to grab his shotgun from the upstairs closet, hop in his truck, and drive on over to Nate Osterman's house to give that bastard's son a scare so good the kid would have to change his underwear.

I might even do it, too.

He knew he wouldn't, though; he wasn't a violent man. Some men were, but he wasn't. Instead, he would settle for changing the oil in his tractor. It needed to be done anyway. Maybe by the time he finished, the angry knot in his gut would have unwound a bit. Maybe then he could think about calming down.

He went to his workbench and grabbed a couple wrenches, a new oil filter, and an old bucket he used for catching the dirty oil. He could do the job in fifteen minutes when he was in a hurry, but tonight he wanted to take his time, give the anger flowing through his veins a chance to die out.

The John Deere tractor was a reliable old machine that'd served him well over the last twenty years. He was a firm believer in the idea that if a person takes care of a piece of equipment, then it'll return the favor.

With a sigh, he dropped to one knee and put down all his supplies. Then he slid a little stool over and took a seat. His back was a little sore, but not all that bad considering the night he'd had. If he'd been hurting, that might've been the last little push he needed to send him on over to have a word with the Osterman kid.

Elhouse pushed the bucket under the tractor's oil pan, and with the wrench, he loosened the drain screw. He backed it out with his fingers, and the dirty oil started drooling out. With a rag, he gripped the oil filter and gave it a hard twist. It came loose. When he removed it, more dirty oil poured into the bucket.

He sat there and watched the engine give up its lifeblood for a good five minutes. When it was down to its last few drops, he screwed on the new filter by hand, careful not to strip the threads. Then he put the drain screw back in. That done, he stood and went to his workbench. He tossed the old filter in the garbage. He was about to grab the fresh engine oil when he heard the front door to the house slam shut across the field.

Elhouse walked out the barn doors. He had to squint to see

at night. Gertie was walking across the backyard, heading toward the woods behind the house.

"Gertie, where in God's name are you going?" he said, a half-shout.

She didn't seem to have heard him. He noticed something else, too: she wasn't limping. Her gait was slow and steady... if she had a gait at all. The nightgown hung so low, it covered her feet, sweeping over the grass. She looked like an apparition gliding through the night.

Elhouse blinked hard, twice. Then he called to her again, but once more was met with silence.

He glanced up at the bedroom window—the light was still on—then back at his wife as she moved farther away from the porch light and was slowly swallowed up by the dark. The moon made her look as though she were faintly glowing. Or maybe it wasn't the moon at all.

He rubbed his eyes, convinced the strange aura he was seeing around her was due to his cataracts and nothing more. Dr. Barrett told him that might happen—that he might see "halos," especially at night. This was the first time he had actually noticed it, though.

Elhouse started after her, a fast-paced walking stride. She was a good hundred feet ahead of him.

"Hold on now, wait a second," he said.

Gertie kept moving until she reached the tree line. She stopped and stood motionless on the fringe of the woods.

Elhouse came up a moment later. He stopped ten feet away from her. A shallow stream that ran along their backyard acted as a barrier between his property and the town's woods. The water separated him from his wife. Somehow she had managed to get on other side of it.

"What're you doing up and about?" he asked, catching his breath. "You're s'posed to be in bed. You walk through the damn stream?"

She didn't answer.

Her back was still toward him, and for some reason, he was scared for her to turn around. Whatever was there—whatever he would see when she did—would not be her. He knew this in a deep place inside, but he couldn't bring himself to believe the instinct, and so he wrote it off as something conjured up by his imagination.

Still, the idea had legs, and it was starting to take hold. A sense of unreality washed over him, and the cold jaws of terror were reaching up from his subconscious and starting to bite down on the back of his neck. His palms were prickly. His mouth was going dry. A warning siren started to wail inside his head, but he ignored it. Suddenly the entire moment had the feel of some bizarre dream.

"What on earth are you looking at? Ain't nothing out there, Gert," he said, his voice taking on an unsure tone.

He stepped down into the stream. Cold water rode up over his boots, soaking the bottoms of his pant legs. He watched his wife's back the whole time, unable to explain why he was approaching her the same timid and cautious way he might a dangerous animal.

"Hey, are you okay?" he asked. But what he really meant was: *Is that really you? Say something—anything—so I know it's you.*

He looked her up and down. It was hard to tell for sure in the dark, but he didn't notice any water on the bottom of her nightgown. He dismissed it. She'd probably just lifted it as she went across. No big mystery there.

"Come on, dear," he said, reaching out to touch his wife's arm, as if doing so would ground the strangeness of the situation and end it all.

But there was nothing to grip. His hand passed right through a frigid space. And when it did, the thing that looked like Gertie finally turned and faced him.

6

Elhouse stood at the end of their bed, looking down at Gertie as she slept. It was as if he had just been dropped there by some invisible hand of God. He had no idea how he had ended up in the bedroom. He couldn't recall coming inside or walking upstairs. The last thing he remembered was changing the oil on the tractor. Everything between that and how he had gotten here was a black sheet.

He glanced down at his feet. They were soaked and caked in black mud. Then his eyes found the bedside clock. It was a quarter past ten. He had gone out to the barn around eight o'clock to work on the tractor. That meant almost two hours of the night were missing from his memory.

He wiped a hand over his mouth. Something bitter touched his lips when he tried to lick them. His tongue was like sandpaper.

What happened to me?

His whole body was crawling with restless energy. He couldn't remember the last time he had felt so worn out. It was like he had a bad hangover… but different. He felt dirty inside, as if something had reached in, hollowed him out, and left something rotten and sick behind. Every bit of him hurt, felt used and tired.

There was something in the back of his mind, too, something new that hadn't been there before. A tiny green spark floating in a sea of black. He couldn't look directly at it and see it, but he sensed that it was there. It had the feel of an unfinished thing, a chore he had forgotten he needed to do but would eventually require doing. He recognized that the idea of it was the source of his restless feeling. A part of him understood he was bound to the green spark now—beholden to it.

Elhouse looked down at his wife. The moonlight printed the shadow of the windowpane across her face.

He undressed slowly, stripping down to only a T-shirt. His underwear was soiled. He hoped it was just water. He balled them up and stuffed them under the bed to deal with in the morning, then put on a fresh pair.

Jesus, what had happened—*was happening*—to him? Maybe he was in the throes of a stroke.

He sat on the edge of the mattress for a moment, looking down at his bald legs in the moonlight. Hair hadn't grown on them for years, and his skin itched and burned tonight. For some reason, that was okay. It was as it was supposed to be.

He held out his hand, studying it in the moonlight. It didn't feel like his own. His arms broke out in gooseflesh as the temperature in the room dropped. Or maybe it'd been cold the whole time. He could see his breaths. There was a smell: smoke and mildew. He had smelled it before, and recently, but he could not recall when. Something was in the room. He knew it as sure as he knew anything, but he was not scared of it because whatever it was, the thing was also the spark, and now so was he. The green thing in his head grew a little—and so did that feeling of purpose, that forgotten chore.

He had a strong sensation that he was sinking, being digested by an endless pit of darkness and despair.

I have to fight it. I have to… I…

Elhouse got into bed next to Gertie and lay down. She stirred and rested her hand on his chest. A battle raged on inside him, and something wicked and powerful was jockeying for control of his soul.

He reached up and put his hand on top of hers. Her skin was soft. He knew every ridge on the landscape of her body, every bump—*every bone I'd like to snap*—and wrinkle. That's what marriage is all about sometimes. It's about wandering in each other's fields until there isn't a single stone left unturned.

Half awake, Gertie whispered softly, "Everything all right, dear? You're absolutely freezing."

He hadn't cried since his mother's funeral, but he wanted to now. "Go back to sleep, Gert. Everything's fine."

But of course it wasn't.

He kissed her hand—*want to bite it*—and she patted his chest, then rolled onto her back. Her wrapped knee was sticking out of the covers. The bandage was starting to come unraveled.

Images of sharp objects flashed in his mind. Ugly, horrible images of ripped flesh and twisted faces struck with the look of shrieking pain. A giant colorful thing. A mask of bone. A green spark. He breathed slowly and stared up at the ceiling.

Sleep seemed an impossible thing, but eventually something like it overtook him. He dreamed darkness was falling down on him, enshrouding him. And in the folds of the shadow, the greenest eyes he had ever seen were watching him. He watched them back, became lost in them. They were inviting. They promised so much. He swam in them and felt himself dissolve.

The green spark grew inside him until it became everything.

7

On the other side of town, Ricky was sitting alone in his father's garage. The lights were out, save for the small fluorescent above the back workbench. The rusty sign on the front of the shop read OSTERMAN AUTO & TOWING in dingy red lettering. The small square cement-block building sat alone on an acre of gravel out on Pollock Road. Most of the acre was stacked with junked cars his father used for spare parts. The shop was his old man's pride and joy. Not that there was much to be proud or joyful about. The entire operation consisted of one old tow truck, which always happened to be in need of its own repairs, and a few oil changes here and there during the week. Maybe someone might stop in to have a headlight fixed or a flat patched or ask about a whining alternator, but that was about it. For anything more expensive or more important, a person who knew any better found their service elsewhere. It was no secret that Nate Osterman was a drunken hack whose honest business days were behind him.

Ricky had a key to the back door of the shop that he used to let himself in when he didn't feel like going home, which was often. He and his father didn't get along so well, and his relationship with his mother wasn't much of a relationship at all. There could've been something there had things worked out differently when he was younger, but things hadn't. As far as Ricky was concerned, things never worked out differently. Not for him, anyway.

He was five years old when his mother had her accident. He remembered some of it—bits and pieces like shards of a broken something he'd never truly known to begin with. He remembered yelling from upstairs. A loud crack. A crash. Then his mother wasn't upstairs anymore, and it was silent, and his father was coming slowly down the steps. His mom was at the bottom of the staircase, her head bleeding and eyes open, staring through him. She wasn't moving. No response. Silence. Slow footsteps getting louder. Another crack, this one across his face. Ricky was sent to his room with a burning cheek, tears hot in his eyes. Soon after, from his bedroom window, he saw a car pull up and park in the driveway. He recognized the man who got out. It was a doctor. The very same one he had gone to see three weeks before to have his tonsils taken care of, where he had been promised ice cream after they did a quick procedure.

The doctor came to the front door, carrying a little black bag. There were muffled voices from downstairs, and eventually the doctor carried Ricky's mother out and placed her in the backseat like a fragile porcelain doll. Ricky remembered the taillights as the car pulled away. They looked like the eyes of a giant monster, and his mother was caught in its mouth.

Barbara Osterman was gone for a little while after that, but she returned a few weeks later. She wasn't the same, though. No doubt about that. She hardly spoke anymore. And when she did, her flat, almost childlike voice made Ricky uncomfortable and sad. Sometimes she would look at him and smile. Then her brow would wrinkle, and she would turn away from him as if she didn't know who—or what—he was anymore. Most of the time, she never got off the couch, unless it was to make meals—usually burned—or to wash Nate's dirty duds in the sink. She just sat there dully, smoking her Chesterfields, one after the next, filling the ashtray while she knitted lumpy, uneven sweaters for family members Ricky had never met.

That's the entirety of the memory. But as he got older, the full picture slowly revealed itself, through both gained wisdom and firsthand experience. Ricky might not have been the smartest kid, but he understood well enough that his father had more than likely tossed her down the stairs that day. And Ricky hated him for it. If it weren't for his old man, Ricky might've had a relationship with his mother. Ricky might've known what it felt like to actually be loved by someone.

He hopped off the stack of tires he was sitting on and spat across the room. A big glob of phlegm landed on the window of his father's small office. He finished his beer and sent the bottle against the cement wall. It smashed and sent shards of glass flying everywhere.

He laughed. But when he realized there was no one there to see it, the grin faded.

Buncha pussies, he thought.

He was drinking the rest of the beer they'd picked up after leaving the lake earlier. He had been under the impression they were all going to party and get wasted. He thought maybe he would even get to dip his tip, if the girls loosened up enough. But what should've been a fun night turned out to be a bust. Everybody had left him. The broads had split once they got back downtown. And Hooch had left shortly after, leaving Ricky alone with half a case of undrunk beer and his racing thoughts.

It was all that uppity one's fault, the chief of police's daughter. She was such a goody-goody, and Ricky hated that. All day she had been judging him, thinking she was better than him, better than everyone. That alone had been bad enough.

But what had really done it, what had really put the pin in the party pig, had been what had happened outside the liquor store. That had killed the mood... and, in the process, his chances of getting laid. That numb cunt. Who did she think she was? He couldn't believe she'd screamed at him that way, and in public. What had she called him? A psycho? What the hell did that even mean? He was only goofing around. He wasn't actually going to run anyone over; he had only wanted to get a laugh. It was funny, wasn't it?

The icy internal voice, sharp and rusty like an old, trusty straight razor, spoke in his head: *But you did want to hit them. You wanted to feel their bones crunch under your tires, hear their screams mix with the sound of the engine, then be overrun by it. Hear their love die. That's good. That's very good, Ricky. You didn't kill them, but you could've. It was your decision. You are the judge of who lives and who dies.*

The dark thing was in his head again. He was thinking about taking life. Killing. It'd been on his mind a lot lately, but he'd been trying not to look at it. Sometimes he took a peek, though. For a while—since the first one—he'd had the beast on a leash pretty well. But like most wild things, it wouldn't stay caged forever. And like most wild things, sometimes it escaped and fed.

He had killed before. Only once. Well only one human, anyway. There had been dozens of animals. The stray cats and dogs. Birds and squirrels he plucked off the tree with his pellet gun behind his house. And of course, the experiments he did out in the woods in that old pump shed.

The girl was six years ago, three weeks after his twelfth birthday. And to say he hadn't been planning to kill her might've been inaccurate. He hadn't planned to any more than a wolf plans to kill a rabbit, but if one crosses its path, nature takes over. Nature always took over. So, no, Ricky hadn't planned to, but he had felt that it would happen in an undefinable way. The feeling was not something he quite understood. It was just there, like a black hunk of lead in his chest. Always heavy. Always there.

The day he became a murderer, Ricky had been down at Silver Bridge, burning ants with a magnifying glass he had stolen from Tedford's Hardware. It was a hot Saturday afternoon. He had spied a real busy colony of carpenter ants and was going to town on them, frying the little buggers as fast as he could catch them. Usually he had to stun them first with a firm press of his thumb to get them to stay still long enough for him to bring the white dot of death into focus over their little black bodies and set them alight. They would start to smoke almost immediately. He had liked the smell. It had been sweet but a little bitter, too.

He was midway through what must've been his twentieth execution when a shadow fell over him and darkened the anthill.

He looked up, squinting. "Hey, what gives? Move it. You're in my light."

He couldn't see who it was at first. His eyes were throwing spots from staring at the focused light of the magnifying glass. He could only make out a small silhouette standing in front of him.

"Whatcha doing?" a girl's voice asked. There was something unsettlingly tough in the girl's tone. The silhouette squatted down.

Ricky shielded his eyes to get a better look. He recognized the girl, had seen her around town on occasion, but he didn't know who she was. She had dark shoulder-length hair that was done into ponytails. Around her neck was a thin silver chain with a small letter M hanging from it. She was wearing denim overalls and, underneath, a white shirt with the sleeves rolled up past the elbows. The shirt was dingy with dirt. *She* was dingy with dirt.

"I'm makin em pay, that's what." He blinked hard, trying to clear away the spots floating across his vision.

"Makin em pay?" the girl asked, confused. "For what?"

"I don't know," Ricky said. "Them being there and me being here, I guess. That's good enough, isn't it?"

"Oh," the girl said, and picked up a small twig beside her and started flicking through the charred remains of the insects.

Ricky could tell she didn't understand. No one understood.

"Can I try one?" she asked.

"No, get lost," he said, feeling like his world was being invaded. He liked to do this kind of thing alone because the sensation it drummed up in him was one that made him feel a little funny in places that made him uncomfortable. "This isn't for little bitch brats, now beat it... or else."

The girl dropped the stick on the anthill and stood abruptly, hands on her hips. "Hey! You shouldn't talk like that, or I'll tell on you."

Ricky regarded her. She must've been a year or two younger than him.

He stood. "Now wait a second. I didn't mean it." He reached out, grabbing the girl's arm. Hard. It was thin, and he knew he could snap it if he wanted. And he did want to.

"Ow, you're hurting me, let go!" the girl yelled, flapping her arm up and down like a wet rope as she tried to pull away.

Ricky let go, grinning. "Relax, would ya? You wanna try one? I take back what I said. Here." He held out the magnifying glass to the girl. She was rubbing her arm, looking at him untrustingly. "I'm serious. Take it." He wiggled the lens like a piece of bait, which, of course, it was.

After a moment, the girl's face warmed, and her forehead ironed out, the toughness returning. "Let me see it," she said, and took it.

She squatted back down to where the ants were hustling and bustling around their flattened anthill.

"The trick is, you gotta stun em first," Ricky said, watching the girl. His stomach was fluttering with excitement. "Find one, then press your finger down on it. That makes it easier to keep em from moving."

"Uh-huh, I can do it," the girl said dismissively. She was already fixated on the anthill, trying unsuccessfully to chase the insects around with a poorly focused point of light.

Ricky stood over her, continuing to watch. She looked so small. So weak. So his.

Them being there and me being here, he thought. And following that came the first time he ever heard the sharp, cold internal voice that sounded a little like his own, but also different: *She threatened you, Ricky. She's gonna tell everyone you hit a girl and were down here killing ants all alone and playing with your little wee-wee. She'll tell everyone your secret. She'll tell everyone what you are, and then they'll know. And we can't have that. No we cannot.*

The voice should've startled him, but it didn't. It was like receiving a phone call from an old friend he'd been waiting to hear from for a very long time. He didn't know what was about to happen. But some part of him inside—the dark thing—was pulling the strings now, moving for him. And it felt good.

His eyes scanned the ground. He spotted what he needed sitting beside the metal drainpipe behind him.

"I can't get them to stop running away," the girl said, frustrated. Her eyes were glued on the ants, her tongue peeking out from the corner of her mouth in a show of determined concentration.

"Keep tryin. You'll get one," Ricky said.

He took a slow step backward, dropping down silently and picking up the rock. It was jagged, about the size of a baseball. It fit in his hand perfectly, as if he were meant to hold it.

Then he was standing over her, rock in his hand, watching the girl timidly try to catch the scurrying insects. She was too slow. And he could tell, as tough as she tried to act, she was too scared to touch them. He doubted she would even be able to figure out how to work the magnifying glass properly, if she did catch one.

He looked around. The street was empty. Not a house for a quarter mile in either direction. No kids riding up to take a jump off the bridge and into the Gilchrist River. He spotted the girl's bike. It was leaning up against a tree at the end of the little parking shoulder. She must've ridden there alone.

The dark thing showed him what to do. Showed him how good it would feel. So he did it, never thinking twice. The wild thing inside sank its teeth in and tasted human flesh for the first time.

Ricky brought the rock down as hard as he could on the back of the girl's head. The solid *clunk!* sounded like a small, hard pumpkin crunching. A high squeal popped out of the girl's mouth but was abruptly cut off as her face landed in the anthill. The insects started to crawl into her hair as she lay there motionless, eyes open and staring. They looked just like his mother's had when she'd been at the bottom of the stairs after her accident.

Ricky stood over the girl for a moment, the rock still in his hand, watching the blood ooze out of her and mix darkly in the dirt, the ants avoiding the growing spill. He looked down and saw his pants sticking out in the crotch. It felt good. The dark thing inside hadn't lied to him. It told the truth.

A part of him wanted to drop his pants and do what he'd recently discovered he could do to himself when his penis went stiff that way, but a more instinctive, self-preserving part of him kicked in. He needed to hide the body and get the hell out of there before someone came and saw him standing over a dead girl.

He went to the river's edge, cocked his arm back, and tossed the rock as far as he could. It splashed into the river fifty feet out.

He went back to the girl, nudging her thigh with his foot. Her body moved limply. "Hey… hey, you… you awake?" He kicked her a few more times with the scuffed toe of his ratty Chuck Taylors.

She didn't answer.

He bent down, yanked off her silver necklace, and stuffed it in his pocket. Then he picked up the magnifying glass. The handle was covered in the girl's blood, which he could smell. He threw that in the river, too. It flew through the air like a boomerang, curving on its downward descent, and landed a little farther out than the rock had.

Next, he had to make a decision about the body. There seemed to be two obvious choices: hide her or roll her into the water and let the current take her down the river. His initial gut instinct had been to stuff her in the drainpipe and cover her with brush, but the dark thing had advised against that. The dark thing showed him the way—the river. It might look like an accident that way. Hidden in a drainpipe would rule out any doubt of what had happened. If he dropped her in the water and left her bike leaning against the tree, it might look like she'd come out to the bridge and perhaps fallen over the edge while playing. Probably hit her head on a rock.

He grabbed the girl by the ankles and dragged her to the water's edge. She was heavier than he'd expected. He rolled her into the river and, with a long branch, pushed her body far enough out to let the current do its job. He stood and watched with black fascination as she disappeared under the bridge. He thought she looked very much like a piece of river trash and nothing more. After a minute or so, he lost sight of her.

Ricky turned and kicked loose, dry dirt over the blood on the ground until it was no longer visible. Then he left and went downtown to enjoy a hot dog and a root beer float at Woolworth's.

Three days later, the body of eight-year-old Madison Feller was found caught in a fish ladder over in Sawyer Falls. At the coroner's inquest, her death was ruled an accident.

8

Ricky looked around his father's garage. His beady, weasel eyes blinked slowly as he turned away from the memory of the Feller girl, trying to quell his rousing friend. He didn't feel like feeding it tonight. But it was too late. He had thought about it too much, and now the dark thing was taking hold of him. And it was hungry. Usually he could sense when it was going to wake up from its hibernation. He could feel it much in the same way he could feel the air sharpen and become charged with dangerous energy as a powerful summer thunderstorm approached. But not this time.

This time, it had hit him without warning. He wondered if, perhaps, that had been Grace Delancey's fault, too. Had she rattled the wild thing's cage? Undone the latch and allowed it to escape? Maybe she'd known about his dark thing and wanted to see it. Maybe she hadn't even been yelling at *him* outside Duddy's Liquors; she'd been yelling at *it*, trying to coax it out into the light. It *had* been the dark thing's idea to scare the old couple on the side of the road, after all.

Well, if that bitch wanted to see his shadowy friend, he would show her. Then she would really have something to scream about. His temples started to thud with red anger. He wanted to hurt Grace Delancey more than he had ever wanted to hurt anything before.

The voice spoke from the shadows of his mind: *We'll take care of her, show her she isn't any better than anyone, Ricky. Not tonight, though.*

"Okay," Ricky said flatly to the empty garage.

There was nothing he could do about Grace at the moment. She was, after all, the police chief's daughter. That would take more consulting with his dark thing to make sure he got it right. But it was still hungry. Tonight, he would have to feed his dark friend some other way. A temporary fix.

He squinted and rubbed his temples. "How?"

I'll show you.

At first he didn't know what he was going to do. Then he did. The idea came to him prepackaged, as if he had been thinking about it forever and already had all the details worked out. Sometimes things happened that way, he thought. You don't know something at all, and then you know it completely. Like how he hadn't known what he was going to do to Madison Feller six years ago, and then he had known exactly what he would do to her.

Ricky grabbed the chain off the ground and put it in an old milk crate. The chain was a good length and a heavy gauge. It was fitted with clevis slip hooks at both ends. His father's shop was full of towing equipment like that, so he would never notice anything missing.

Hanging on the beam beside Ricky were two chain binders. He would need those, as well. He put them in the crate with the chain. Then he left the garage and put everything in the backseat of his car. He got in, fired up the engine, and drove away from Osterman Auto and Towing. Turning right at the intersection, he headed in the direction of Waldingfield Road.

Ten minutes later, he was driving the same dusty road he had sped down earlier that evening, when the night ahead had still held the promise of a good time. Before the police chief's daughter had spoiled everything.

Oh well. This would be a good time, too.

A half mile before the access road that led down to the back side of Big Bath, Ricky stopped. He sat there on the side of the road for a moment, looking at the backs of his hands, listening to the engine rumble. He had never noticed how capable his hands looked before. They could do anything they wanted if he had the will. And he did indeed have the will. Now more than ever.

Hurry, before anyone sees you parked here, the voice said. *If someone drives by and spots your car, then we're shit out of luck, Ricky. This doesn't work with witnesses.*

Ricky stepped out. He grabbed the chain and the binders from the backseat. The chain, he draped over his shoulder, leaving one end to drag in the dirt behind him as he walked to the large oak tree a few feet off the road. He carried the binders, one in each hand, walking stolidly, a vessel with a hardcoded purpose. When he reached the tree, he let everything clatter to the ground with a loud but satisfying sound. The sound of important work.

He picked up one end of the chain and completed a full loop around the base of the tree about a foot and a half off the ground before attaching it to itself with the clevis hook. He took the chain in both hands and yanked it to make sure the hook had a good bite. Then he began walking the chain across the road to the other side. He found another tree a few feet off the road. It grew at the edge of the embankment, which dropped nearly ten feet. He did the same as he had done around the oak.

Heavy under its own weight, the chain sagged across the road. It was stretched at an angle: the second tree he had anchored to wasn't directly across from the first. Having the chain at an angle would work better, though. The dark thing confirmed it.

He went back to the oak and grabbed one of the binders off the ground. He slid the hooks onto the chain and laced his fingers over the steel lever arm. He leaned back, dug his heels into the dirt, and pulled down with all his weight, snapping the arm in place against the chain and tightening it stiff.

Ricky picked up the other binder and banged it against the taut chain, testing the tension. It moved slightly, but slightly was too much. He carried the second binder to the other side of the road and repeated the process, until the length stretching between the two trees held so much tension that it could've been a solid piece of steel.

He went out onto the road and stood at the chain, admiring his work. It came up to just above his knees. He lifted his leg and rested his foot on it, shifting his weight forward. It didn't budge.

Ricky lit a cigarette on the way back to his car. He started it, did a U-turn in the middle of the road, then drove slowly up Waldingfield until he spotted a trailhead where he could pull his car in and hide it.

He shut off the engine, got out, and found a few fallen branches to lean against the back of his car. Then he walked the four hundred or so yards back through the woods until he found a good vantage point to watch the action.

Waldingfield wasn't a busy road by any means, but on a Saturday night, people returning home from a night out in another town used it as a shortcut from Route 2 to downtown Gilchrist. Ricky did it all the time. Mostly, only locals knew about it. A random person driving down the highway wouldn't even see the road entrance if they didn't know to look for it.

Ricky was hoping it would be someone from Gilchrist who came along, maybe even someone he knew well. It would be more satisfying that way. He would be able to see the aftereffect it had, the same way he had heard all about how heartbroken everyone was when Madison Feller turned up dead in the river. His favorite part had been how the girl's father had fallen apart. How he had insisted her death wasn't an accident and hung those silly fliers on all the telephone poles around town. How no one had believed him. How everyone had said he was just a drunken lunatic. Then—the cherry on top—how the guy's wife had split on him and left town.

The anticipation of injecting a new dose of death into the town was so sweet, Ricky could practically taste it. He cleared away a spot on the ground, sat, and waited, arms resting on his knees.

From where he sat on a low hill looking down over the scene, he couldn't quite make out the chain strung across the road, but once his eyes adjusted a little, he could see the back of the big oak tree and the black line of the chain looped around its massive trunk. He hoped the chain would hold. He remembered the feel of it in his hands: it was thick enough, so it ought to work just fine.

Ricky began to whistle "When the Saints Go Marching In," tapping his toes in the dirt to add accompanying percussion. While he waited, he reached into his pocket and pulled out a Double Decker MoonPie, his absolute favorite. He unwrapped it and took a big bite. *Screw those dumb dames*, he thought. This might be the greatest night of his life.

Time washed away for him, and he became a fixture of the night—a part of it, not a foreign thing in it. The whole experience was enjoyable. He felt like he was sitting at the movie theater, eager for the curtains to draw back, the projectors to kick on, and the show to start.

And then, as if some higher power had heard his thoughts, the show did start.

He had eaten his MoonPie and was halfway through his fifth cigarette when the sound of an engine approaching rose up in the woods. After a moment he could make out the crunch of tires driving over gravel. The dawning and shifting glow of headlights flickered in the distance through the trees.

"We got a fishy." Ricky grinned. He dropped his cigarette and smashed it out with the heel of his boot. He squatted up onto his haunches. His chest was tightening with excitement. His breathing doubled along with his heartbeat. He felt his scrotum tighten as he became aroused. Flashes of Grace Delancey strobed in his head.

He could see the car clearly. It was a hundred feet up the road, coming from the direction of Route 2. The driver shifted up. It must've been doing at least thirty miles per hour. Ricky could see the chain illuminated by the car's headlights, but that was only because he knew where to look.

A moment before the collision, all the air and sound went out of the night. Ricky watched it all happen in silent slow motion. Then, like sound waves catching up to a firework explosion, the road erupted in a deafening cacophony of destruction, and everything sped up.

The driver never even had time to hit the brakes. The front left of the car hit first. Metal and glass squealed and crunched. Something tumbled up the road a short way. The car lurched right, guided by the angled chain, and careened down the embankment and into the woods with a loud crash, rolling over onto its side, then its roof.

Ricky's eyes widened. He wiped his hand over his mouth, stood, and went toward the road. He paused at the tree line, scanning left, then right. He walked across to the edge of the embankment and looked down at the overturned car. One wheel spun idly and wobbled on a damaged axle. Steam hissed from the radiator. The headlights were empty silver bowls. The entire left front end of the black car was completely crumpled in. The windshield was gone, save for the jagged fragments still stuck in the bite of the frame.

"Anyone in there?" Ricky said.

No one answered.

"Say, you all right? That was one hell of a crash, pal."

In the moonlight, he could see the rough shape of a person bent at strange angles upside down inside the vehicle. It looked like a man. Whoever it was, the figure wasn't moving.

Ricky started down the embankment, but stopped abruptly. *First things first*, the dark thing reminded him. *We'll have time for a souvenir after. Now cover your tracks.*

He turned and looked over his shoulder. The chain was still stretched tight across the road. He went and released both the binders, then undid the chain from the trees and dropped everything into a pile at the foot of the oak. If anyone came along at that moment, he could duck behind a tree and they would keep on going, giving him time to finish up.

Looking down at all the equipment, he decided he should've brought the milk crate along with him. It would've made it easier to carry everything back to his car. He could've used it as a seat, too, kept his ass from getting damp in the dirt while he had waited for his show to start. Why hadn't his dark thing thought of that? Why hadn't *he* thought of that?

A frail voice—this one completely external—called out, startling Ricky as he considered this lapse in foresight and what it meant. "*Heeelllp.*" One long gurgled word.

He went over to the top of the embankment to see someone crawling out through a busted window in the car. Ricky pursed his lips and rubbed the side of his face. "Shit."

He ran to grab one of the heavy steel chain binders, then shuffled down the hill until he was standing over the man. It reminded him of how he had stood over Madison Feller in her final moments.

"Marion," the man whispered, and coughed. He was crawling slowly toward nothing, simply moving instinctively away with the last of his strength, hoping to find some sort of deliverance that would never come. If there was one thing Ricky was certain of in this world, it was that people always moved away from pain and in the direction of release. It wasn't a choice; it was simply the stock wiring.

"Hold still," he said, stepping over the driver, legs straddling him. "Hey, I know you, don't I?"

He bent down to get a closer look. Ricky recognized the man, and it was hardly a man at all. It was the kid from the drugstore... Dan Metzger. Dan had been a senior in high school when Ricky was a freshman. Something in the crash had opened up Dan's neck three fingers wide, and blood drooled out steadily in spurts from the gaping wound. Ricky could actually hear the arterial spray spattering the dry leaves on the ground. The sound was steadily slowing.

"Help... me," Dan said again, his bloody hand creeping forward and trying to find purchase on the ground.

"Sure thing, pal," Ricky said, and laughed.

The chain binder came down. Then it came down again. And again. Three savage blows. Dan let out a pathetic *guffawww*. Warm blood wet Ricky's face. The hard vibration echoed in his arms, stinging his hands and wrists, and then it faded to a satisfying tingle. It was like striking a halfway-rotted tree stump.

He straightened and dumped the chain binder beside him in the dirt. He was breathing heavily, licking his lips. He tasted metal.

The dark thing spoke to him: *You are the judge because you are here and they are there. You decide, Ricky.*

"I am the judge."

Ricky wiped his hand over his face. He reached down and grabbed Dan's wrist, searching it. He found nothing. He checked the other. Bingo. He removed the watch and held it up to the moonlight. It sparkled dully where it wasn't black with blood. His second souvenir.

In the distance, another engine rose up in the night, interrupting the moment. It was heading his way. He stuffed the watch in his pocket.

Ricky picked up the binder, then hurried to the oak tree. He gathered everything in his arms as quickly as he could. He couldn't see any headlights, but he could hear the chug of the approaching vehicle getting closer.

He scrambled into the woods, the whole time thinking about the thing he had heard tumble up the road when the car first struck the chain. It didn't matter, though. He would leave it there, same as he had left Madison's bike leaning against the tree.

This was just another horrible accident. Tragic.

Chapter Four

THE METZGER KID IS DEAD

1

The brunette giggled. Her bright-red lipstick stretched into a smile as she slid her hand over the man's thigh and up into the crotch of his blue jeans.

Her name was Sandy. His was Jim.

"You like that?" Sandy said. "It feels like you do." She moved her hand to his belt and unbuckled it. Then she unbuttoned his pants and slid down the zipper. He already had an erection. She took it in her hand.

"Yeah, I do." Jim grinned, keeping his eyes on the road. "I like that a lot, as a matter of fact. Keep going." He turned down Waldingfield Road and pressed his boot down on the accelerator. The truck almost broke free on the gravel for a second, but he backed off the gas and kept the Chevy straight. He laughed, pulled the pint of whiskey off the dash, and took a swig. "Damn, you're good. Almost cracked us up."

Sandy giggled again. It was a sweet sound. "Turn your lights on and slow down, then. You fixing to kill us out here?"

"It's fine. You just worry about what you're doing, honey. It's a damn fine job."

She smiled proudly. "This ain't nothing. It's not even my favorite."

"Your favorite?"

"That's right."

"And what's that, then?" Jim had an idea what was coming, and it made the spit in his mouth thicken in anticipation.

Sandy pulled her hair back, gathering it in a ponytail and holding it there with a purple elastic thing. "Well, I don't want to ruin the surprise, darlin."

"I like a good surprise. Want a little something to wet your whistle first?" He tilted the bottle of whiskey in her direction.

"After," she said, "to wash it down."

Jim capped the bottle and tucked it under his thigh, behind his knee. "Suit yourself." He clutched the wheel with both hands as she started working him again. Then she slid farther across the bench seat, leaned down, and took him in her mouth. "Sweet-fucking-Christ, girl. Someone taught you good." He pressed his head back against the cab of his truck and tried to keep his eyes on the road, moaning every time he hit a pothole… perhaps even aiming for them. The ones he could see, anyway.

About two minutes into it, Chuck Berry came on the radio with "Johnny B. Goode."

"My lucky day," Jim said, reaching over Sandy's head and turning up the volume. "Maybe the kid's a nigger, but he sure can play the shit out of that guitar."

She stopped and sat up. "You say something?"

"Yeah… no… nothin. Keep going." He reached over and grabbed the back of her neck, pulling her head down. "Don't stop."

"Knock it off." She smacked his arm off her. "I don't like that."

Jim's brow wrinkled. "Don't like what?"

Sandy folded her arms and pressed her back against the passenger-side door. "Don't force me. It ain't right."

"Okay. Jesus. I'm sorry. I didn't mean nothin about it."

"I know you didn't, but I still don't like it."

"Look, I said I was sor—" *Thunk!* The whole truck jolted. Something scraped and tumbled along the undercarriage and got spat out the back. "The fuck was that?" Jim skidded to a stop, both feet on the brake pedal.

Sandy lurched toward the dashboard, but she put her arm out in time to catch herself. "Jesus-jumped-up-Christ! Take it easy." She pushed herself back in her seat and looked at Jim. "You hit something."

He let out a long breath and loosened his grip on the wheel. "No shit I hit something."

"I told you to turn your lights on. I knew you was gonna get us in an accident."

Jim turned to her and scowled. "Quiet," he said, and slid the shift lever into park. "Wait here." He opened the door and stepped out, buckling his pants. The whiskey he had stored under his leg slid to the edge of the seat, but he caught it and tossed it back on the dash again.

He shut the door.

Sandy looked out the back window. "I can't see anything. I don't like it out here."

Jim followed her gaze. There was only blackness. Without averting his eyes, he reached in through the window and flipped on his headlights. Behind the truck, everything washed a deep red from the taillights. In the middle of the road there was a long piece of bent metal. "Hell is that?"

"Can we just leave it and get outta here?" Sandy turned to him, her face pleading. She was scared.

Jim ignored her and walked around to the back of the truck. He kicked the piece of metal, then crouched down to inspect it. "Ain't from my truck, anyway," he said. "At least I don't think so."

"What is it?" Sandy asked, leaning out the window. "A deer? You hit an animal or something?"

"No, it ain't no deer." Jim stood. He reached into the breast pocket of his flannel and pulled out a crumpled pack of Camels. "It's a piece of a bumper… I think. Looks that way."

"A what?"

"A bumper… a car bumper. It must've fell off someone's car when they hit a pothole. That's what I figure." He removed a cigarette from the pack and lit it with his Zippo.

"Can we go, then?"

"Yeah," Jim said, "I'm just gonna move it off the road. Stay in the truck. I'll be right there." He took a hard drag off his cigarette. Then he secured it tightly in the corner of his mouth, bent down, and picked up the mangled bumper in both hands. It was heavier than he'd thought it would be. Or it might've been the fresh sex running through his veins, weakening his muscles.

"Hurry up," Sandy said. "I don't feel like getting murdered out here tonight."

"Stop talkin and you won't," Jim said, annoyed.

Smoke drifted up from the cigarette and stung his eyes as he walked the bumper to the side of the road. When he reached the edge, he twisted at the waist and hurled the piece of debris as far as he could down a small embankment. It tinkered and thrashed through the brush, eventually coming to rest somewhere Jim couldn't see. He took the cigarette out of his mouth, and without the orange glow of the ember blaring below his eyes, he could see.

At the bottom of the hill was a wrecked car rolled over on its roof, the front smashed in. Beside the car was the dim silhouette of a body splayed out on the ground. By the size of it, it looked to be a man. Whoever it was, he wasn't moving.

"What the hell?" Jim said under his breath. He shuffled down the embankment, gravel sliding underfoot, avalanching to the bottom in a thin rustle. "Hey, buddy, you all right?"

"What're you doing?" Sandy called after him.

"Hold on a moment, would you? There's somebody down here." Jim reached the bottom of the hill and went over to the body. "Hey... can you hear me?" He knelt, poking the man's shoulder. Jim's knee landed in something wet, and from there he recognized the face of Danny Metzger in the pale moonlight. "Holy Christ!" He jumped up, and for a moment he was frozen, unable to tear his eyes away from what he was seeing. Then something inside him cracked a whip, and he scampered back up the embankment to his truck.

Sandy was leaning on her forearms, hanging out of the window when Jim got back up on the road. Her face was bound into an anxious knot. "What? What is it?"

Jim yanked open the door, reached for his whiskey, and took a long pull off the bottle without offering an answer.

"What was it? What's down there?" she repeated, now sitting bolt stiff and staring at Jim, her hands clamped together between her knees.

He looked at her, catching his breath and wiping the back of his hand across his mouth. He capped the bottle and tossed it on the seat of his truck before climbing in. "How old are you?" he asked her, turning down the radio.

"Why?"

"Never mind *why*. I asked, didn't I?"

"Nineteen. What's that got to do with anything?"

Jim put the truck in drive. "Nothing. Just asking."

Sandy glanced at him, then fell back in her seat as he stepped on the gas and tore ass out of there.

2

The Gilchrist Police Department had a fly problem. Sick yellow ribbons of flypaper, swollen with stuck corpses, hung from the station ceiling like the forgotten streamers of a sad celebration.

Corbin Delancey had been following a particular fly since it took flight from the rim of his Coke bottle. It landed in front of him on the woman's breast. He blinked his wide blue eyes slowly, watching it laze about her body. Its movements were measured but chaotic, in the perfectly natural way it was designed to move. It sat on her nipple, twitched its head along the axis. It moved to her armpit, then to her stomach. It tasted her naval and went south from there.

Corbin released the breath he'd been unconsciously holding. The woman's name was Susan Denberg—August, 1966's *Playboy* centerfold.

There was a knock on the front door of the station. The screen door clattered against the jamb, the flimsy eye-hook lock rattling on the frame. Corbin could see the sound and all the familiar elements that made it up.

"You in there, Chief?" a man's voice said urgently. "There's been an accident."

Corbin flicked his hand at the magazine page and shooed the fly off Susan. He opened his desk drawer and filed the *Playboy* away. "Yeah, just a sec. Who is it?" He glanced at the clock. It was almost eleven o'clock. As was often the case, he was the last person at the station. Randall Buchanan would be in shortly to take the night shift, but until then, all problems were still Corbin's to sort out.

"It's Jim. There's some kind of accident out on Waldingfield Road. I just come up on it ten minutes ago."

"Jim? Jim who?" Corbin answered. From his desk, he couldn't see around the corner.

"Jim Krantz, sir."

"Hold your horses, Jim Krantz. I'm coming." Corbin stood, hitched his pants, and dropped the half-drunk bottle of Coke into the wastebasket beside his desk. He crossed his office and went out to the station lobby.

Jim was standing in the doorway, hazy behind the screen. Corbin knew the boy's father, Dick Krantz, and thought now more than ever that Jim was a true product of the man's loins, despite what others said behind Dick's back. As a featureless silhouette, Jim resembled his father a great deal: tall, thin, and long-waisted, he carried his weight hard on the backs of his heels. They shared the same bones. And his voice, an octave higher and rich with youth, held the same tone and inflection. Corbin had never noticed any of that before, but he'd never really thought about it all that much, either.

When Corbin came through the swinging gate, Jim stepped back from the door. The porch light revealed a sweaty, nervous face. "There's a car accident. It's real bad. I think it's Danny Metzger."

"You *think*?" Corbin stepped into the doorway and pushed open the screen door with his elbow. He looked beyond Jim at the idling truck in front of the station. A pretty candy-faced girl turned and peered out the window. Corbin stared at her. She smiled half-heartedly, then started chewing the side of her cheek and looked away.

"Yeah. It's hard to tell," Jim said. "He must've been going real fast."

"You got company, do ya?"

"Yeah… yeah, she was there with me. She'll tell you about it, too." Jim glanced at his truck. He dipped his hands into his pockets nervously, then brought them out and folded his arms across his chest. "I'm tellin you. The car's over on its roof down in a ditch. There's lots of blood. I ain't never seen so much before."

Only half listening, Corbin glanced down at Jim's knee. "Blood like that?" he pointed at the dark red circle on the kid's pants.

Jim looked down. "Aww, Jesus, that's what it was. I was kneelin next to him, seein if he was alive."

"Is he?"

"Well, I didn't take a pulse or nothin, but he didn't look alive."

Corbin leaned in closer and sniffed. "You been drinking tonight?"

"No." Jim wiped a hand across his mouth. "Maybe a little. But I'm okay to drive."

"Looks a little young for you, Jim. What're you… must be almost thirty now, that right? You're a little old for high school girls, don't you think?" Corbin moved out onto the porch and let the door slam behind him. He was a tall, slightly overweight man in his mid-forties, with a full head of sandy hair that showed no traces of gray.

Jim backed up, giving Corbin his space. "What? No. She ain't no high school broad. She's nineteen." He scratched his head. Then, with a confused lilt in his voice, he tried again: "Say'd you hear me, Chief? I said there's been an accident... I mean it. You should get out there. I think the Metzger kid is... well, I think he's dead."

"Who is she, then? She don't look familiar."

"I don't know. Just some girl I picked up at Dale's. Her and a couple of her friends... from Sawyer Falls, I think." Jim paused, and there was an atmosphere of silence between the two men. Then, cautiously, he said, "Listen, if you want, you can follow me and I'll show you where I come up on the wreck. You'll see what I mean. It's just a ways up Waldingfield, before Elhouse Mayer's place."

Corbin looked at Jim, a steady gaze that could cut. "Sounds like I should probably go have a look, then, don't you think?"

Jim's face went stupefied. "Yeah... yessir. That's what I been tryin to say. You need to come have a look."

"All right, let's go have us a look."

3

Corbin knelt beside the overturned car, looking in through the shattered windshield. He stood, moving his flashlight over the body lying in the dirt. He sighed and ran the tip of his tongue across the back of his front teeth. It was bad.

"Shit," he said under his breath. He'd harbored hopes Dick Krantz's boy was exaggerating, but if anything, Jim had *under-sold* it.

"See, it's just like I said. Bad, ain't it?" Jim stood at the edge of the embankment, smoking a cigarette. "I ran a piece of the car over about twenty feet that way." He pointed up the road in the direction from which they'd come. "It looked like a bumper. I threw it off the road near where your cruiser's parked now. Didn't want no one else to run it over. If you look, you'll see where it landed. It's there."

Corbin pointed his flashlight in that direction. "That way?"

"Yeah," Jim said, flicking his cigarette to the ground and stepping on it.

"And it was just sitting there in the road?"

"Yessir."

"You find anything else?"

"Not a thing. That was it. Well, there was little bits of glass maybe, but nothing big," Jim said. "Must've hit something in the road."

"All right, get back in your truck," Corbin said. "You and the girl go on now. I'll take it from here. In fact, maybe you should bring her home. It's probably past her bedtime, street lights being on and all."

Jim scowled, eyebrows pushing together. "Well, hold on a sec. Am I gonna get any sort of recognition for this? Name in the paper? I mean, I *am* the one who found it."

Corbin flashed his light in Jim's face.

Jim put his hand up and shied away. "I'm only wonderin."

Corbin said nothing and didn't lower the flashlight.

"That a no?"

The silence grew thick.

"Okay, then. Never mind, Chief. No harm in askin," Jim said. "You know where to find me if you need me." He walked back to his truck and drove off, the candy-faced girl looking out the back window as the taillights disappeared down the road.

Corbin walked up the hill to his cruiser. He grabbed the radio through the window. "Randy, it's Corb. You in yet?"

There was a pause.

"Just walked in, Chief. What can I do you for?"

"Better get the whole thing going. We got a situation out here on Waldingfield. A bad one. Got a body. Better call Buck Ryerson at the funeral home, and Doc Barrett, too."

"What should I tell those fellas?"

"Tell em to head out this way and bring the cadaver wagon. They won't miss me. Car's in the middle of the road." Corbin paused. "See if you can't get a hold of a photographer... Virgil Gillespie's always up for it. He works nights at the newspaper. Tell him I need a scene photographed."

"What type of situation we talking, Corb?"

"Car accident, looks like." Corbin glanced back at the kid laid out in the dirt, a sinking feeling of dread starting to fill his stomach. "Maybe try to get a hold of Billy and tell him to meet me here if he ain't busy. He was looking for overtime anyhow."

The radio crackled. "Car accident?"

"Yeah." He surveyed the scene again. "It's a mess. And Randy?"

"Yeah?"

Corbin sighed. "It's Danny Metzger, so keep that under your hat for now. I don't want the whole town to find out before I have a chance to contact his family."

"The drugstore kid?"

"Uh-huh."

"He's dead?"

"Barring some sort of miracle, I'd say so. I'll wait for Hank to pronounce it, though."

"Oh man. Okay."

"Jim Krantz found the wreck, so I'm sure it won't be long before he tells anyone who'll listen, but I don't want it coming from our station."

"I understand."

"Also, can you do me a favor and call Meryl at the house? She'll be expecting me home any time now. She'll worry if I don't show."

"Sure thing."

Corbin dropped the radio back on the seat and scratched deep in the curves of his neck. The humidity made his skin itch, especially on days he shaved too quickly. Today was one of them. He looked side to side, from one dark end of the road to the other. Both directions were pathways to the abyss. Corbin wiped the back of his hand over his mouth. Susan Denberg was a thought in his mind. Sweet, but far away.

He went down the hill to the body and washed his light over the stillness of it. Kneeling, he patted it down. Then he searched for a pulse, just to be thorough, but found none, as he had expected. The doctor would confirm it.

There was a wallet in the pocket of the kid's jacket. He took it out, opened it, and slid out a driver's license: Daniel Metzger, Gilchrist, Massachusetts, Born 7/9/1945.

Poor kid was dead at twenty-one, his whole life ahead of him.

He shut the wallet and tucked it into his breast pocket. Pushing up into a squat, he flashed his light into the overturned car again. It was full of bits of glass and debris.

Corbin stood, then went and sat on the grade of the hill. He found the handkerchief in his pocket and wiped it across his forehead and over the back of his neck. He cleaned his hands with it, removing the sticky smears of blood that had gotten on him when he patted down the body.

The night was calm, fully in the shadow of the day. A chorus of insects serenaded the woods with alien sounds. Corbin's breaths slowed and became deeper, each one breathing life into the moment. The atmosphere grew electric. The hairs on the crown of his head itched and felt as though they were standing on end. Corbin stared into the darkness of the woods. And for a moment, he was sure something was staring back.

4

Jim took Sandy to the boat launch at Big Bath after he left the scene of the car wreck. He wanted to finish what they'd started in his truck. At this time of night, the place would be empty, tourists nestled in the beds of their lake-house rentals, slumbering away on cheap beer and too much grill food. It was a good place to park and fool around with a date when he wanted a little privacy and didn't have anywhere better to go. He had done it all through high school, and not much had changed for him since then. He still lived at home.

"Where the hell're you taking me?" Sandy asked. She no longer looked like the girl who'd had a few too many beers at the bar and was looking for a good time. "I think I've had enough excitement for one night. Can you just take me home?"

Jim pulled up to the boat ramp and shut off his truck. The lights went out, but he left the radio on at a low volume. Mood music.

"Home? You want to go home? You kidding me? Look at this damn view, girl." He slid across the bench seat, sidling up next to Sandy. Her arms were folded tightly across her chest, and she was tucked in the corner of the cab, looking disinterested in anything Jim had to say or offer. "You want to spoil a thing like that? When was the last time you seen something this pretty? Not as pretty as you, though."

The moon was rising over the lake. The water was a plate of glass, and the moon was a crisp picture reflected in it. In the surrounding woods, the peepers were peeping and the crickets were thrumming at full throttle.

Jim tried to brush aside a curl of hair that had fallen across Sandy's face. She pulled away. "Take me home, please. I'm not in the mood anymore. The dead guy on the side of the road kind of killed it for me. And it's late now. My parents are gonna kill me."

"I don't even know where the hell you live," Jim said.

"I told you earlier. Sawyer Falls."

"That's two towns over. I ain't drivin that far."

She turned to him, her face clouding over with a mix of confusion and outrage. "What the hell were you planning on doing, then? Were you just gonna leave me on the side of the road after I'd sucked you off?" She laughed without humor. "What a true gentleman you are."

"If I ain't no gentleman, you sure as hell ain't no lady. That's for damn sure." He leaned away from her and stared out the window at the lake, working the inside of his cheek with his tongue.

There was a moment of hostile silence in the truck, where neither Jim nor Sandy knew what move to make next. Jim finally couldn't stand the tension and went first.

"Look, I'm sorry. I'll take you home." He slid a little closer and licked his lips, his tone dropping to a man trying to sweet-talk his way back into a failing deal. "But maybe you just make it worth my while first. Then I'll take you anywhere you want to go. Hell, I'll drive you to the damn moon, girl. Just don't leave me hangin, that's all." He reached over, put his hand on her thigh, and slid it up her skirt toward her warmth.

"I said no! Get off me, jerk!" She slapped him and tried to

push him away. His fingers grasped for her underwear and tried to pull them down. "Stop it!"

"Just real quick. C'mon, girl." He fell on top of her with the full weight of his body and pressed his mouth against hers. Their teeth met in an awkward, grinding kiss. She bit down on his bottom lip. Hard. He pulled back and clapped a hand over his mouth. There was already blood running down his chin. "You bit me. What the hell? I wasn't tryin to... I wouldn't... You *bit* me. Fuckin Christ, girl. You're a damn lunatic."

Sandy didn't say anything. She opened the door, got out, and started walking back the way they had driven in.

Jim got out of the truck and spat blood in the dirt, carefully touching his lip with the tips of his fingers. It stung and throbbed at the same time. "Where the hell're you going? You plannin on walkin outta here?" he yelled after her. "Look, I'm sorry. I'll give you a ride."

"Don't follow me," she said, and just kept on walking.

"Yeah, don't worry. I won't." Jim stood there a moment, listening to the frogs and the insects, gently running his tongue over the bleeding tear on his lip. "Fuckin crazy bitch," he muttered to himself between thin winces of pain.

He didn't follow her. The crunch of her footfalls in the gravel and the pale glow of her moonlit silhouette slowly faded, then vanished into the night. He never saw her again.

He reached into his truck and found the bottle of whiskey he had stashed under the seat before. He uncapped it and took a sip, trying to avoid his lip. He failed. The alcohol lit it on fire. It was a glassy burn.

"Shit." He sighed. "So much for a good night."

He shut the door, took the bottle around to the front of his truck, and leaned up against the warm grill. The radio was a soft murmur in the background. The Moody Blues were playing "Go Now." Between sips of whiskey and glances at the moon, he listened to the music play against the sounds of the lake and the woods. By the time the song was over, the bottle was empty and he was seeing double.

He threw the bottle against one of the big slabs of granite that lined the boat ramp, stumbling to the side when he lost his balance. Glass smashed, and the sound echoed across the water.

"Gotta go see a man about a mule," he slurred, turning and walking to the tree line beside his truck. There was a dumpster with tall grass and weeds growing up around it. He went behind it, unzipped his fly, steadied himself, and started to urinate. "Yup, that's a good mule you got there, sir. I surely would like to take er off your hands." He laughed at his own joke.

Then something happened. He had finished and was zipping up when someone began calling to him softly, almost a whisper. "James... *Jaaames*. What's wrong, James? Are the girls teasing you again, darling?"

It was coming from the woods beyond. It was too dark and the woods too thickly settled to see anything beyond a few feet. He squinted, but the moonlight revealed little besides the vague bark detail of a few close trees.

"Who's there?" he said. "Sandy? That you, girl? Look, I'm sorry about... well, if I..." He didn't finish the thought because he knew in a scared part of himself, where the dread was starting to knot and grow, that Sandy was long gone.

"James," the voice said again. And it was a gentle voice. A woman's voice. But there was a strange quality to it, as if she were speaking through a long metal corridor from some faraway place.

"Come on out!" Jim shouted. His hand reached around to the back of his belt, where he kept a five-inch Buck knife in a leather sheath. He slid it out, the blade winking in the moonlight. "Either you come on out, or I'm gonna come in there and *drag* you out. You hear me?"

"You're bleeding, James. Who hurt you?" The voice sounded a little closer.

He took a step forward into the tree line, fighting the instinct to turn around, get in his truck, and rip ass out of there. No one else was around. The girl with the sharp teeth had left him, but still, he felt as if he had something to prove, someone to impress. Then something hit him, an association so long-buried and clouded over by booze that he realized with startling clarity how long it had been since he'd thought of her. *James.* Only his mother had ever called him that. To everyone else, he was Jim, or occasionally Jimmy. Even his father didn't call him James. In his old man's opinion, it was the sissy version of his name.

His mother had died five years ago, though. Brain aneurysm. One minute, all three of the Krantzes were eating chicken-fried steak at the dinner table and talking about how Jim needed to clean out the basement to help out around the house more if he was going to live there rent free. The next, Lori Krantz went facedown into her mashed potatoes and never said another word to anyone again. That was the day James learned just how fast and fragile life could be, how it could turn on a dime before you even had a chance to say goodbye, or even finish your thought—or mashed potatoes.

"I mean it. You don't want to test me." He took another step into the woods, the sweat from his palm starting to make the knife handle slick.

Behind him, the radio in his truck squelched a burst of static. He turned around, startled. His headlights flickered. On. Off.

On. Off. Dim. Off. The radio let out another loud metallic *squink!* His heart was racing, and a panicky sort of innate survival instinct was starting to reach through his haze of drunkenness and tell him to go.

Go now.

When he turned back around, his mother was standing right in front of him. She was hovering a few inches off the ground in the middle of some giant dark cloud. And around the edges it shimmered like a million tiny diamonds. But the cloud wasn't a cloud. It was an opening, a parting of some cosmic curtain.

"I'm here now, Pickle," she said sweetly. That was what she used to call him. One day when he was a child, he had eaten roughly three dozen and gotten sick all over the living room carpet.

She reached out and brushed his cheek with her hand. Her skin was cold and rough. It smelled smoky and rotten. But it didn't matter.

James was frozen in disbelief. "Mom? What're you... how... I..." So many questions, but none of the answers seemed to matter. She had all the answers to everything. She *was* the answer. Looking into her deep-green eyes, which had been brown when she was alive, he felt an overwhelming sense that everything would be all right. If he just went to her, Mommy would make it all better. So he went to her. He dropped the knife and stepped forward into her open arms, tears brimming his eyes. He loved her. He missed her so much.

She shushed him the way a mother does to calm a frightened child. "James, my sweet little Pickle, come here and let Mother make it all better. I can take all the pain away. Listen to my words. I only want to help you. Will you listen to your mother? Will you do what she says?"

"Yes. Of course," he said. Or perhaps he'd only thought the words.

He fell forward into the void. And as the blackness enfolded him, he could see the figure was not his mother at all. It was something huge, with a brightly colored face. They were somewhere else now. The colors swirled and shifted on the creature's face. James wanted to float in them, to let them wash all over his body. But most of all, he wanted to obey.

5

Corbin watched as the tow truck dropped into gear. The rear end shuddered and bucked. Wheels scraped on loose gravel, slipping and catching on the grade of the hill. They found purchase, and the truck lurched forward. The rusty length of chain attached to the wreck tightened, pulling the overturned Ford off its roof and onto its tires as the truck breasted the hill and climbed back up onto the road. The wrecked Ford Custom righted and settled, shedding shrapnel to the ground in a chorus of shrill sounds. Then it was still.

No more than twenty feet away from the tow truck, Hank Barrett, Gilchrist's local physician, was loading Danny's body, covered in a white sheet, into the back of Buck Ryerson's Buick hearse-ambulance combination, with the help of Buck. Virgil Gillespie, the photographer, had already come and gone.

"What now, Chief?" Billy Porter asked. Billy was a third-year officer in his mid-twenties. He was of average height, with a slender, athletic build and a smart face that didn't always match his personality. He scratched the top of his head, looking back toward the hearse. "Kid's head was nearly gone. I ain't never seen nothing like that before." He burped, covering his mouth with his forearm, then dropped it with a shameful look in his eyes. "I don't usually get sick like that. I just ain't never seen—"

"You'll be fine," Corbin said. "Shake it off."

Billy's eyes dropped for a moment but quickly lifted. "None of this don't make no sense. The road's so narrow. He'd have to be going real fast to get mangled that way, and maybe not even that would be enough. What do you figure happened?"

"Probably was going real fast, as you said," Corbin said, not quite buying his own words. "We've had some complaints about kids speeding up and down this road, coming from Big Bath, all boozed up. It was bound to happen sooner or later."

"Yeah, but those are high school boys, Chief. Danny was older. I heard he'd just graduated college and was about to start school to be a pharmacist. I can't imagine..."

Corbin looked at him, understanding where the train of thought had been heading. "I know. It doesn't seem right he'd be out getting drunk and racing around like that. People make mistakes, though, I guess."

Hesitating, Billy said, "I suppose."

Corbin pinched his lower lip between his thumb and index finger, the way he did sometimes when he was thinking. "I'm hungry. You hungry? I think there's an apple in my cruiser. Go up and fetch it. And tell Buck and Hank they can head out when they're finished."

Billy looked at Corbin with a dumb-flat expression, then blinked twice. When Corbin didn't look back at him, he headed up the hill to do as he'd been asked.

"How much more time you gonna need, Corb?" Nate Osterman yelled down as Billy went past him, walking up. Nate was standing up on the road at the back of his tow truck, hands tucked into the pockets of his grease-stained coveralls.

"Give us twenty, then you can haul it away to the station," Corbin said across his shoulder. "Until then, I don't want to hear a word."

Nate didn't respond, only ran a hand over his head and went back and sat in the cab of his truck.

Nate Osterman was a drunk who, more than likely, had been halfway through his nightly case of beer when he got the call to come out. Chances were, he was itching to get back and finish off the other half, if he hadn't already been doing so in his truck.

Corbin sighed, then clicked on his flashlight and swept it over the car and the ground around it. The dirt near the car and where the body had been lying was scored with deep gouges, likely made by the car as it careened down the embankment. Then something occurred to him. The marks on the ground made a connection in his mind. It was a simple thing, but that was the way it worked in real-life police work, not like it did in fictional police stories. The simple details always revealed the most. It was the little things that were easily overlooked.

He walked a few feet up the hill until he could see the surface of the road. He flashed his light on the ground, searching. There had been a little bit of traffic from their cars coming and going, but nothing that should've hid or erased what he knew should be there.

"What're you looking for?" Billy asked as he returned.

"You find my dinner?" Corbin asked, not looking at him. He was focused on the road, slowly walking along the embankment, halfway up it.

"Yeah, I got it," Billy said, minding his footing on the hill's loose terrain and digging in his heels. "Just an apple? That what you call dinner?"

"Meryl's got me watching my figure. Says fruit's good for

me. Bring it here. Say, Billy, does it strike you as odd that there ain't a single skid mark in the dirt? Just these strange little diagonal marks." He turned to Billy and took the apple. "Seems to me like this fella must've hit something *in* the road, since I don't see any signs he veered off and clipped anything on the shoulder."

"Not sure I follow, Chief."

"If it was something in the road that he hit, why the hell didn't he put on his brakes before running into it? Anything that'd cause a wreck like this one is something a man would see coming, I'd think… drunk or not."

"Yeah," Billy said, sounding unsure. "That makes sense to me, I suppose. If it was a coon or something, I wouldn't go putting both feet on the brakes or cutting the wheel into a ditch. But a deer? Sure, that can do some real hurt to a car. I'd try to avoid that."

"Me too." Corbin continued along the embankment. He couldn't find a single sign that Danny had even tried to stop. But there also wasn't anything to suggest that he had hit an animal, either—no blood, no hair… no corpse. Although he knew if the car had struck something big enough to cause an accident like this one, there was a good chance it could've taken off running into the woods. It probably wouldn't get very far before succumbing to its injuries, though.

Corbin shuffled down the hill and inspected the front of the car, specifically the grill. No trace of hair or blood. It didn't look like the vehicle had struck anything with a pulse. In every accident he had seen involving an animal, it had left traces behind on the car, usually tufts of coarse hair, almost always on the grill.

"See anything?" Billy asked.

Corbin straightened and turned around, flashing his light at Billy. He finally took a bite of the apple. "I see a car accident that don't make a lot of sense. And lots of blood." He moved the light down to Billy's feet. "You're stepping in it."

"Aww jeez." Billy took a quick step back, checking the bottoms of his boots.

Corbin could smell the mineral scent of the blood in the dirt, mixed with the oily undertones of spilled gasoline from the car. There was another smell, too, one that had been only faintly present when he'd first arrived but had since become more pronounced. It smelled almost like wet ash and spoiled meat.

He took another bite of his apple, then cocked his arm back and threw the half-eaten fruit into the woods. "I hate apples. They hurt my gums."

Billy didn't say anything to that; he was still trying to get the blood off the bottom of his boots, scuffing them in the dirt and checking with his flashlight.

A door slammed up on the road and an engine started. Hank was standing at the top of the embankment. "We're going to get the body back to the funeral home, if you don't need us anymore."

"Yeah, you two can get on out of here," Corbin said. "I'll meet you there soon. Maybe give the coroner a call and let him know he'll have to meet us at Buck's."

"All right," Hank said, then turned and went back to the hearse. He got in, and Buck drove them both away.

Corbin glanced around, looking at everything but seeing nothing. He felt in a daze. The whole thing didn't sit right. As far as he should be concerned, it was a simple car accident. Open and shut. Sure, there would be a difficult call to make to the kid's parents, but after that, it would all be behind him. So why couldn't he shake the feeling that there was something more to this?

He went back to the embankment and carefully made his way up it. He started walking along the shoulder, searching for anything out of the ordinary, some small detail that didn't quite belong, anything that might speak to how the kid's car ended up upside down and in a ditch without a single sign that he'd touched the brakes. He didn't know what he was looking for, only that he would know it when he saw it.

Maybe it had been a stroke or a heart attack. The kid was young, true, but stranger things had happened.

As it turned out, what he was looking for was on a tree nestled in a thicket of brush a few feet off the shoulder. There was a peculiar pattern in the side of the tree's bark—indentations of some kind. He went up to it to take a better look. The mark started at the side of it and wrapped around the back all the way to the other side. The side facing the road, however, was free of markings. He touched a piece of the flaking bark near one of the oddly shaped indents. He pushed down with the tip of his finger. It was damp and slightly spongy. The exposed tree flesh was fresh, not gray and hardened with time. The wound was recent.

"Billy, come have a look at this," he said. "Quit worrying about your shoes."

Billy, still fixated on the blood on his boots, stopped wiping his soles in the dirt and came up the hill. "What is it?"

"Look." Corbin painted the spot on the tree with his flashlight. "What do you make of this?"

"Make of what?"

"These marks," Corbin said. "They look new, don't they?"

Billy leaned in closer and touched the scored bark with his finger. "Yeah, they're pretty fresh, I guess. Maybe a piece of the car hit it. Didn't you say that Jim found the bumper in the road?"

"Yeah, but I don't think it's that," Corbin said. "It looks like something was wrapped around the tree… tight. Take a look at how the marks go almost all the way around."

"What the hell would be wrapped around it?" Billy asked.

"I haven't a clue," Corbin said. "Wait here a second."

He went to the other side of the road and started searching. At first he looked directly across from where he had found his first little out-of-place detail. Sometimes he thought of them like small fingerholds, each one bringing him farther up the mountain.

He started to make his way down the road, heading in the direction away from town. Once again, it didn't take long. The second tree, which was at an angle from where Billy was still standing, was much larger than the first and had a thicker skin of bark, but the markings were visible on it just the same—a ring of odd imprints three quarters of the way around. And like on the other tree, the side facing the road was strangely free of the marks. Only that wasn't exactly accurate. The section where the bark was left untouched wasn't squarely facing the road; it was facing the other tree.

"Ain't that interesting," Corbin said under his breath, then clicked his tongue against his teeth. He flashed his light to where Billy was standing next to the tree across the road. Billy had returned to wiping off his boots in the dirt.

"You about done, Corb?" Nate Osterman asked, leaning his head out of the tow truck. "I wouldn't mind gettin home soon. It's gonna be a bear pullin that wreck up this embankment. You seen how steep it is."

Corbin lowered his flashlight and looked over at Nate. "All right, go ahead. Hook it up and bring it to the station. Randy will unlock the gate for you when you get there. You can take it around to the back lot."

"Appreciate it, Corb." The truck's door squealed open and Nate hopped out, a beer can clattering to the ground behind him. He picked it up and tossed it back in the cab of the truck, attempting to conceal it.

"I'm going to pretend I didn't see that," Corbin said, his tone that of a fed-up teacher dealing with a habitually unruly student. "And I'm going to ignore it because I know you'll hold off on getting completely pissed until you haul my evidence back to the station. Do we understand each other? No more drinking. We got one car accident tonight, and I don't need another."

Nate rubbed the back of his head, refusing eye contact. "I ain't had but the one—"

"And it better be the last one," Corbin interrupted. "You hear me?"

"Yeah, Corb, whatever you say," Nate said, sounding very much like a scolded child.

"Good. Now go on and get to it." Corbin went back across the road as Nate set to work hooking up the wreck.

"You see anything over there?" Billy asked when Corbin returned.

When Corbin was a kid, he and his brother used to play army games in the woods behind his house. Sometimes, when they were really getting into it, they would try to set small booby traps for each other. His brother's favorite used to be to use a piece of their father's fishing line to tie a tripwire across the main path behind the house and see if Corbin would stumble into it. That was the first thing that had come to

Corbin's mind when he saw those markings on the trees: someone had tied a tripwire across the path. But it was just a wild hunch. Too early to be sure.

Corbin looked at him. "No," he said. "I didn't find a thing."

For now, he would keep his hunches to himself.

6

It was almost four o'clock in the morning, and Corbin hadn't slept in nearly twenty-four hours. He was standing in the basement morgue of Buck Ryerson's funeral home, sipping a cup of weak black coffee while Hank finished looking at the body from the car wreck. Satisfied, he pulled the sheet back up over the kid's waxy, pale face.

A call had been placed to the county ME, and Danny Metzger's parents had been notified. They had already come and gone, making a positive identification of their son. Mrs. Metzger had fainted when Hank peeled back the white sheet and she saw her boy lying there with his Silly Putty skin and a caved-in skull. Hank had draped a towel over the worst parts, but he couldn't hide it all.

Carter Metzger, who owned the local butcher shop, had tried to remain strong—and he had held it together at first—but eventually he broke down in tears. When they left, they had been in no better shape, and Corbin really felt for them. He couldn't imagine having to bury a child.

Hank went to the small sink and washed his hands. "I don't think you need a doctor to tell you how this boy died. His head was crushed. And if that didn't do it, the injuries to his neck would have. His carotid and his jugular were both severed. So take your pick. Must've been going a sight over the speed limit, if you want my opinion."

Henry "Hank" Barrett was a man of generous height and girth, with leathery sun-cured skin. He was in his mid-sixties and wore square dark-rimmed glasses and a military crop of silver hair.

"Something's not sitting right with me." Corbin was leaning against a steel support column in the center of the room. He yawned and rubbed the heel of his palm into each of his eyes, one at a time. A fountain of lights flashed behind the lids. The coffee wasn't helping any, but he hadn't expected it to.

Hank looked across his shoulder as he washed his hands. "Why? What's the matter?"

"I wish I knew. It just feels… wrong, I guess."

"Well, seems clear to me, but I won't tell you your job." Hank picked up a towel above the sink and started to dry his hands. "Want another opinion, this one as your personal physician?"

"No. But I get the feeling that won't stop you," Corbin said.

"Go home and get some sleep. The autopsy will give you an official cause, if they decide to do one. They might not since he was practically decapitated and it looks pretty obvious that it was a car accident."

"All right." Corbin sighed. It wasn't the cause of death that didn't sit right with him; it was the accident itself. "Will you excuse me a moment? Coffee went right on through."

"Don't let me stop you," Hank said.

Billy Porter was sitting in a desk chair by the door, pale-faced, hat in his lap, when Corbin turned around. He had almost forgotten Billy was there.

"I never thought a car accident could do that to a person," Billy said tonelessly, eyes avoiding the body on the steel table.

He pulled a pack of Clark's Teaberry gum from his pocket and popped a piece in his mouth.

"Yup, it's a bad one," Corbin said.

Billy looked up at him. "Sorry, Chief."

"You won't get sick again, will you?"

"No, I'll be fine… promise. Caught me by surprise earlier. That's all it was."

"You sure?"

"I'll be fine."

Corbin scratched the side of his face. "Okay. I'll be right back."

He walked out into the hall, opened the bathroom door, and went in, closing it behind him. He locked the door and went to the sink. Turning on the faucet, he caught a glimpse of himself in the mirror. Below his eyes looked like crescents of deeply bruised flesh. Bending down, he christened his face, then patted it dry with a paper towel. He brought a handful of water to his mouth, rinsed, and spat. That done, he dipped two fingers into his breast pocket and pulled out the Benzedrine inhaler. He hated having to use it—it felt like some sort of cheater's last resort—but duty called, and the coffee wasn't pulling its weight. He removed the cap and put the end of the inhaler to his nose, pressed a finger against his open nostril, creating a seal, and breathed in deep, head angled back. His skin immediately flushed warm, especially the tops of his ears.

Corbin switched the inhaler to the other nostril and did that side, evening himself off. His pupils widened as large as gun muzzles, the light in the bathroom taking on a vivid, electric edge. The boost the inhaler gave him felt good, but it was a counterfeit, hollow kind of energy that felt all too much like an imposter of the sleep he really needed. It worked in a pinch, though; he wouldn't argue that.

He slid the inhaler back into his pocket and looked in the mirror again. His face had drained to the pallid color of the porcelain sink. His stomach was coming up. He bent over the toilet and vomited dark, yellowish liquid, a mixture of stomach bile and the half cup of coffee he had substituted for a real breakfast.

7

Billy regarded the shape under the sheet as he sat alone in the morgue, hands clasped anxiously atop his knees. Hank had excused himself a moment ago to make a phone call to the coroner's office, leaving Billy with the stiff. His eyes were glued to it, agape with that disgusted and horrified look of fascination that always seemed to be saved for those who want to look away but cannot, held hostage by their own morbid curiosity. He tried to find something else to focus on, but the machine of his imagination was already winding up, running away with itself and firing horrific ideas into his mind's eye.

The scenarios came, each one hardening the knot in his gut a little more. *What if it sits up? What if it isn't dead? What if that's actually me under there, and I'm dead but just don't know it? What if the sheet moves… just a little, then a little more, then a lot? What if…*

He slid his feet out a few inches in front of him and started tapping the toes of his boots. Deliberate sound always seemed to push away fear. Like how sometimes, when he was kid, he would take extra-loud footsteps on the stairs when his mom had asked him to get something from the attic. Or how he would cough really loudly when he switched on the light. Maybe if he gave the scary things time to hide, they would appreciate it and not feel obligated to terrorize him.

He laughed to himself. It was one of those desperate laughs that was really supposed to show anything that might be watching that he wasn't afraid. "Jesus, Bill, get a grip, would you?" he said. A regretful thought followed: *It's already bad enough I puked in front of everyone.*

Billy wished he could take back that part of the evening. It'd been so embarrassing. Corbin had been nice enough about the whole thing, but once the other guys—especially that prick Dave Blatten, who'd been a bully in his youth and had carried the act right on into adulthood—got wind of the news, it would be all hands on deck. He would never hear the end of it.

God, he hated Dave. But he had good reason to.

He sighed and stopped rubbing his hands on his knees. He removed the gum he was chewing and stuck it under his chair. It was a bad habit he had been trying to break since childhood. He didn't even realize he was doing it half the time. Growing up, he used to get yelled at for sticking it under the coffee table in their living room.

The overhead lights dimmed and flickered, the fluorescent bulbs crackling. Billy looked up, startled. The temperature in the room had plummeted, too. His breath was coming out in small wisps and breaking apart in front of his face. The lights gave another series of flickers and pops. Then they went off. It was dark, but enough streetlight filtered in through the windows to leave everything a shadowy orange. The hollows of the room grew very deep very quickly.

"Little Willy William, you want a piece of haaard caaandy?" a voice called out. "I got the hard stuff for you. Just don't tell your mother I let you spoil your appetite. Don't tell annnyone."

Little Willy William? The only person who used to call him that was... He didn't want to think about it. But that voice, it was different than he remembered it, but he still recognized it. This version of it sounded muddy and rotten, as if it'd traveled through a clogged drain.

"Jesus Christ. This is not happening," he whispered, looking around frantically, waiting for something to show itself. The logical part of him told him that it had to be a person, someone playing some kind of joke—*but how could they know?*—while another more suggestible part of him offered a far more terrifying explanation than any rational idea he could come up with on his own.

"Want to get under the covers and plaaay?" the voice croaked again. "Just don't tell Mommy and Daddy. Don't tell anyone, or I'll cut it off."

Billy closed his eyes, his jaw starting to tremble. In that moment, he was ten years old again.

Then everything stopped, and the room fell away to a deafening silence as if a giant glass bell jar had been placed over him. The only thing he could hear was the thick pulse of blood in his ears and the shallow whine of his panicked breaths.

"Just a taste, it's okay," the voice whispered, filling the eerie silence. Somehow it had come from behind him, even though his head and back were against the wall. A surge of adrenaline snapped him into action.

He opened his eyes and stood up. "Who's there?" he said, feeling foolish. But feeling foolish didn't seem to make the fear any less terrifying—or any less real. "This isn't funny." He tried the light switch beside him, but it did nothing.

He heard the dry, soft scratch of stiff cloth being dragged across something rough. He looked at the body on the table ten feet away from him. Where Danny Metzger's groin would be, the sheet was standing at attention. "Popping a tent," he and his friends used to call it when they were kids. Something was slithering under the sheet. Not slithering. The whole body seemed to be writhing slowly, gyrating at the hips. A hand, gray and bloated with clotted flesh, dropped out from underneath the sheet. It had a big gold ring on the pinky finger. Billy would've bet his life that if he looked closer, he would see the little blue Masonic Square and Compasses symbol on the ring, just like his uncle Lonnie used to wear.

The voice returned, this time with a mean, angry edge to it: "Get the fuck over here, boy, and take what I got to give you. And if you tell, I'll kill your mommy and your daddy. Then I'll cut yours off and put it in a blender."

"Stop it!" Billy cried, and a single sob escaped his mouth like a gob of pudding.

The hand became animated and moved down the body, starting to touch itself in bad places. It started moaning sick sounds of gross pleasure and taunting him.

"I'll cut yours off, I'll cut yours off, I'll cut yours off..." There was a pause—a terrifying moment of silent hostility. "Then I can give you mine!" the voice shrieked.

Billy didn't remember tearing his eyes away or going for the door, but now he was looking down at his hand as it fumbled with the doorknob.

8

Corbin was coming out of the bathroom when there was a loud bang, followed by a high-pitched squeak and a rattle as the door to the morgue flew open up the hall, crashing against the wall.

Billy burst out in a hurry, looking around frantically like a man trying to figure out where he was. He spotted Corbin, straightened, hitched his pants, and seemed to gather himself.

"Everything all right, Billy?"

Billy was breathing heavily, his hand pressed over his forehead. "Yeah. Yeah, I'm... I'm fine," he said, standing in the middle of the hallway. He turned and looked into the morgue through the open door. He went over and shut it.

"You sure?"

The kid hesitated, stuffing his hands in his pockets.

"I thought you said you'd be fine."

"I'll be all right," Billy said. "That room gives me the creeps."

"Yeah. I don't like it much myself. Let's get out of here."

"We done?"

"Yeah, for the night. I need to get some sleep. You should do the same."

9

Meryl was sleeping when Corbin came in. He took a seat on the chair in the corner of the room and unlaced his boots before slipping them off one at a time and gently setting them on the floor beside the dresser. He looked at the alarm clock on his nightstand. It was 4:57 a.m. He was exhausted and could still feel the dirty energy of the Benzedrine in his system, but it didn't stand a chance against the sleep he needed. He removed his clothes until he was wearing only his boxer shorts and a white cotton T-shirt with yellowed armpits and a stretched-out neck. He caught his reflection in the mirror on the wall. There was something sad about the picture. His belly stuck out farther than he had remembered. It'd gotten bigger over the last couple of years as his metabolism finally started to dig in its heels. The ass of his boxers sagged, making it appear as though he might be wearing a giant diaper beneath. His legs were skinny and pasty. The anemic morning light only added to the grimness of it all. He looked like a character out of a Russian novel he'd never read.

Sunrise was still an hour away, but already the sky was a dark bruise. The birds had started their morning routine. Corbin sighed, and crossed to the windows on the far side of the bedroom. They faced east, looking out over his backyard. There was a small fenced-in garden, a little twenty-by-twenty lot near the back, where he spent many a day off tending to a small variety of crops. Mostly he grew tomatoes, corn, and squash, but this year he'd added cucumbers and carrots. A gopher had managed to sneak in under the chicken-wire fence, but for two nights, Corbin had sat out there with his .22 rifle, a case of Budweiser, and a sack of beef jerky until the trespasser showed up and he plunked the darned thing right between its beady little eyes. The carrots had stopped going missing after that.

He pulled down the roller shade on each window to keep the sun from blaring in when it came up. He shut the curtains, too, adding a second layer of defense. If he was lucky, he would be able to get at least five good hours of sleep before he had to get back to work. He didn't even want to think about that at the moment, but it was impossible not to.

He got into bed and lay on his back, arms behind his head, fingers interlaced. He was thinking about the kid's mangled body. That wasn't an image he would soon forget.

Then Meryl slid over to him and put her hand on his stomach, and he wasn't thinking about any of that at all. "Tough day?" she asked softly, never opening her eyes.

"Tough day," he answered.

"I'm sorry," she said. "Get some sleep. I'll make you breakfast and coffee when you get up." She slid her hand farther down and slipped it into his boxer shorts. She took him in her hand gently and drifted back to sleep holding him. She did that often, and Corbin thought it was just about the funniest thing in the world. He kissed the top of her head. Her hair smelled of lavender soap.

Corbin closed his eyes, and he was asleep.

Chapter Five

SHADY COVE

1

Peter and Sylvia were on the road by seven o'clock in the morning on Sunday. The car was packed full with groceries and suitcases. On any other vacation—this was really more of a convalescence of sorts than a vacation—alcohol, and lots of it, would have been a standard provision. But he hadn't brought any. It was going to be a sober three weeks while they were there. Time to touch down and get grounded. That included abusing prescription medications, which meant Sylvia was no longer in charge of her Equanil intake. Peter had scoured the house and found every bottle he knew of on Friday night, even the ones he knew she thought were superbly hidden. He was rather surprised at how well she'd taken it when he told her he wouldn't allow her to self-administer her pills anymore. She would get one pill every four to six hours as needed, and he would make sure she actually took them so she couldn't squirrel away too many nuts and then take them all at once.

They passed into Gilchrist just after eight o'clock. The sky was a tall and clean electric blue. Not a single cloud. It was going to be a hot day, but the air held the dry edge of autumn six weeks out—the kind of weather a high-pressure system brings when it decides to park itself over New England at the tail end of summer. Sylvia was staring out the open window, hands folded in her lap as they passed the sign welcoming them to town.

ENTERING GILCHRIST Inc. 1889
MAYOR EARLY CRAWFORD WELCOMES YOU TO THE
TOWN OF GILCHRIST. STAY AWHILE,
YOU'LL LOVE IT HERE.

Since having that strange dream a few nights ago, Peter had found himself turning the bizarre details over in his mind at odd moments. Usually it was after seeing something that reminded him of it, like the elderly man in line at the grocery store yesterday. That had drummed up recollections of the aged reflection of himself. And then there was the hose at the gas pumps that had reminded him of those oily snakes. Or the stoplight that had looked a little too much like that brooding red sky. It was always little things, the artifacts of everyday life. His mind was waiting to latch on to any excuse to remind him of that dream. And every time it did, a trace of free-floating anxiety drifted in its wake.

Seeing the sign welcoming them to town had drummed it up this time.

Gilchrist, he thought. *The snakes whispered it to me. Why?*

His palms started to sweat, and he began to squeeze the steering wheel a little tighter... then a little tighter.

"You okay?" Sylvia asked.

He looked over at her. "Huh?"

"Your face is a little gray." She reached over and touched his arm.

And when she did, Peter was hit by a bright flash followed by a scream that was abruptly cut off. The feeling was vaguely familiar—a distant cousin to the other knack he had for finding things he had no business finding when they were lost. But it was also a very different feeling. Truth be told, he had never experienced anything quite like it, and he was glad when the sensation faded.

He looked over at her. "I'm okay. I should've eaten before we left. I'm starving."

"That makes two of us," Sylvia said. "How much longer?"

"We're almost there." Peter cleared his throat. "I'm pretty sure, anyway."

Sylvia didn't say anything more, but she slunk down in her seat with a content look on her face. She seemed to have brightened and smoothed out in the last twenty minutes or so, as if some invisible hand had tuned the internal strings of her spirit. She inhaled deeply, let it out as a sigh, and leaned her head out the window, her face angled up to the sun. She closed her eyes as the wind ran through her hair. Before they had left, she'd let it down, doing away with the tight updo she'd been fond of for so many years. Now silky ribbons of her auburn hair swam around her face, kissing and whipping the shoulders of her white blouse. She looked the way she had when he'd first seen her in the college library a decade ago. They both had attended the University of Massachusetts Amherst, and she'd been wearing a white blouse that day in the library, too. In his mind's eye, the image of her sitting at that huge library table, stacks of books surrounding her, and chewing on the end of a pencil, was as clear as anything he'd ever seen.

"The air reminds me of something," she said, dropping her arm out the window and letting her hand ride the wind up and down.

"The smell?" He watched her face flicker in the bars of sunlight as the road narrowed.

"Yes," she said, her eyes still closed.

"Me too," he said.

Peter knew exactly what she was talking about. He had smelled it the first time he had visited the town, and he smelled it again now. It was the faint smell of woodsmoke. It reminded him of the fall and itchy sweaters. And suddenly that powerful nostalgic feeling returned. The feeling that he had spent a lifetime here.

2

Lakeman's Lane was a scabby dirt road with a grassy crown between two tire paths that'd been worn to deep ruts over the years. Rocks and twigs plunked the undercarriage of the Dodge. The car dipped and rocked as Peter carefully navigated potholes, occasionally bottoming out. Every so often a driveway would appear on the right, and on some tree near the entrance a small wooden sign would be hung, always with a name painted on it.

Eventually they came to a large tree with a sign that showed a faded number 44 painted on it. Peter stopped the car in the middle of the road. Below the number were two words: SHADY COVE.

"I think this is it," he said, leaning forward and squinting at the sign. "Home sweet home."

"I don't see a house. Where is it?" Sylvia sat up, peering around.

It was cool and gloomy on the road. The sunlight couldn't penetrate the thick tree cover. A pleasant lake breeze rustled the canopy overhead and passed through the car. The name Shady Cove made sense.

"From the pictures I saw, it's right down on the water. My guess is it's set back off the road a piece." All of the land on the right side of the road slanted down at a steep angle and went on for about two hundred feet before flattening out near the bottom and meeting up with a dark, sandy shoreline. "We can go explore the property once we get settled. The guy said there was a boat. Maybe we could take it out... if you feel up to it."

"Don't do that," Sylvia said, not angrily but firmly.

"Do what?" Peter said. He knew exactly what she meant, though; he had heard it himself as the words left his mouth.

"Don't treat me like that the whole time we're here. If that's what this is going to be, you walking on eggshells around me, then you can take me home now. What's the point of getting away from it all, if you're going to be carrying it with you the entire time and waving it under my nose?"

"You're right. I'm sorry," Peter said. But he thought, *Cut me a little slack, okay?* He thought, *I deserve at least that; it wasn't you who came home to find me at death's door, having taken a fistful of pills.* He thought, *You didn't have to search me for a pulse to make sure I was still alive.*

Peter blinked and shook his head. He needed to put those kinds of things out of his mind. They were infectious thoughts that led far too easily to something like resentment, and deep down he knew it wasn't right to blame her. It had been her choice to do what she had, but it hadn't necessarily been her fault.

He turned into the driveway and drove down the winding grade. In the distance, beyond the trees, slate-colored water reflected the sun. It twinkled in the morning light. After another twenty seconds or so, they came around a sharp curve, and the house appeared. It looked exactly like the pictures in Leo Saltzman's binder. Actually, better.

Peter parked in the small crushed-stone shoulder at the front of the house and cut the engine. He opened the door, got out, and stretched. Sylvia did the same, hands pressing against her lower back as she pushed out her breasts. Immediately they were surrounded by the stock sounds of lakeside living in the summer: insects, birds, little scurrying mammals, a small motorboat purring across the water, and wind soughing through the trees.

"It's private," she said, her tone suggesting that could be a good thing.

"It's great, isn't it?" Peter said. "Look at that view."

Shady Cove sat on top of a hill. It was a simple one-story, rectangular design, with dead pine needles dusting the roof, gray weathered-shingle siding, and a large porch that wrapped around from the lake side of the house all the way down the long east side. Because of the hill, the shorter portion of deck that overlooked the lush greens and gray-blues of Big Bath was on tall four-by-four stilts. There was a love swing suspended on chains and covered by a section of partially screened-in porch—a place to watch thunderstorms pass across the lake. A set of railroad-tie steps met the deck stairs and wandered away to a small yard that sloped down a gentle hill and leveled out to meet a crust of shoreline. It was their own little lake beach, about sixty feet wide. The water was gently lapping. Right before the yard dropped off to silt, exposed roots, and sand, three Adirondack chairs sat in a scattered semi-circle around a little teak table. The trees had been cleared away on this part of the property, and the sun splashed bright on the grass and the little beach. On the far right side of Shady Cove's piece of shoreline was a narrow pier, which jutted out about twenty-five feet into the water, where a rowboat was overturned on a large square dock.

He fished around in his pocket and found the key with the little cardboard key fob attached to it that had 44 Lakeman's Lane written on it in blue pen. He held up the key and shook it.

"Shall we go have a look?" he said.

Sylvia shut the car door. "Grab a few bags of groceries. We should put them away. It was a long drive."

Peter glanced at his wife. She wasn't looking at him. Her head was on a swivel, her eyes appraising everything. He could see the ideas firing in her mind as she tried to situate herself in this new environment, trying to position the template of the life she knew over the three weeks she would spend here.

Dr. Zaeder's words echoed in his head: *Just promise me you'll keep a close eye on her. You have to, Peter. She could be a real danger to herself.*

He knew that was true. He didn't believe for a minute that what she had done to herself had been any kind of accident. But he also couldn't deny that there seemed to be a new glow about her. Though a stranger might not recognize it, something about her had changed. There had been a small but perceivable shift out of the black. He had heard stories of people using suicide as cry for help or to get attention, people who pulled the punch at the last moment with no real intention of ending anything. Maybe that was what she had done: taken just enough of her pills to elicit a scare and push their relationship in the direction it needed to go in order to mend. Maybe that was her way of trying to get them unstuck. His idea had been to rent a lake house and take a few weeks off from their daily routine, which had worn to a rut; hers had been to ask for help in the only way she thought she could.

You don't really believe that, do you?

He went to the backseat and loaded up his arms with grocery bags. Then they were walking down a short stone-dust path that led from the little parking space to a red door off Shady Cove's porch. The path was lined with tiger lilies that had started to bloom like tiny orange trumpets.

Sylvia plucked one, smelled it, and put the flower on the porch railing.

Maneuvering with his arms full, Peter managed to open the screen door and prop it ajar with his leg while getting the key into the lock. He had to work it from side to side a few times, but eventually the pins aligned and the key turned. A gentle shove with his knee opened the door with a chirp and a squeal. He went in and was immediately hit by a wall of stuffy air. He was standing in a small mudroom, the walls pegged with wooden dowels to hang coats, hats, beach towels, anything else that needed hanging. Two rowing oars stood in the corner. There was a milk crate on the ground, with a dusty bag of rock salt and an old rusty coffee can in it. Beside the crate was a stack of yellowed newspapers tied neatly with twine. On top sat a box of wooden matches alongside two bottles of lighter fluid and a bag of charcoal briquettes.

"Must be a grill somewhere," Peter said, looking over his shoulder at Sylvia.

She followed him in, the screen door shutting behind her with a rattle. Her eyes continued to take stock of everything. "When was the last time they rented this out?"

"The guy told me it's booked most of the summer usually. We were actually pretty lucky to get it on such short notice," Peter said. "I'll open some windows. We'll get some fresh air in here. It's stuffy. That's priority one. Sound good?"

Sylvia folded her arms, cupping her elbows. "I'll take care of the windows. You just unload the car. I like to get everything put away. I hate when a place feels unsettled."

"Agreed," Peter said. "You do that. I'll handle this."

He walked up a short hallway until he found a big double-wide doorway on the right that opened into a kitchen and living room. It was one giant room separated by a narrow countertop that doubled as a breakfast bar and a couple of stools. A sliding glass door, framed by navy-blue curtains, looked out over the lake and offered egress to the back portion of the deck. A bay window above the kitchen sink looked down over the yard.

Sylvia fiddled with the latch on the sliding door, then pulled it open. The curtains breathed in as a lake breeze ran through the screen. She stood there a moment, hands on her hips, looking content. Peter watched her. He couldn't remember the last time she'd dressed down to blue jeans and a plain cotton blouse, but he could recall exactly how attractive he'd always thought it was when she did. He'd never been one for makeup and fancy clothes, although those kinds of things had made their way into their life slowly over the last decade. With her red hair and her blue eyes, she'd always been naturally beautiful.

She turned away from the door and set about opening the windows as Peter started putting away the groceries. He had grabbed the perishables first. The hamburger, steaks, chicken, milk, eggs, and cheese all went in the refrigerator, which was spotless and smelled of lemon-scented cleaner. Taped to the door of the refrigerator was a list of emergency phone numbers, just as Leo had promised.

"Where's the bedroom?" Sylvia asked.

Peter wheeled around. "Your guess is as good as mine. Check across the hall. I saw a few doors over there." He pointed to the doorway that had led him to the kitchen.

"What's that?" she asked, nodding to the piece of paper on the fridge.

"A few phone numbers, in case we need them."

"Oh. Okay," she said simply, and disappeared out of the room.

Peter heard a door open, then came the squeal and shudder of more window sashes being thumped and pushed open. Probably she was using the heel of her palm. He thought about it for a moment and realized his wife's new energy and focus might be a result of her freshly minted sobriety, same as his. The deal was he would give her the Equanil when she needed it, but it occurred to him that she hadn't asked for any in the two days her medication had been under his control.

This was a good start, Peter thought. Things felt… they felt *right*.

The place was cozy. Wood-panel walls covered in paintings of landscapes. A bamboo couch with flowery upholstery. Two deep leather reading chairs. A small dinner table in the middle of the kitchen. A novelty duck-shaped clock above the refrigerator. A bookcase stuffed with worn paperbacks. The bottom shelf was dedicated to rainy-day time-killers: a few jigsaw puzzles, a Monopoly board game, Scrabble, and a few decks of playing cards in a small wicker basket.

He went to the sink, ran the water for a few seconds, grabbed a glass from the cupboard, filled it, then smelled it. The water had a metallic, mineral scent to it. He took a sip. Not too bad.

He dumped out the rest and put the glass on the counter. He was leaving the kitchen and heading back to the car to get the rest of their stuff when he turned the corner and saw a person peering in through the front door of Shady Cove.

3

She had her wide pink face pressed against the screen and her hands cupped around her eyes so she could see inside. "Howdy, howdy. Anybody home?" she said with a big-toothed smile when she spotted Peter coming up the hallway. Her voice was enthusiastic and quick.

"Can I help you?" he said.

The woman backed away from the screen, scratched her nose with the back of her hand, and sniffled. "You the Martells? You must be. I'm Sue… Sue Grady. I work for Mr. Saltzman. I take care of all the properties he manages." She opened the door and held it ajar with her sturdy body, putting one foot up on the wooden threshold. She couldn't have been more than five feet tall and was wearing a khaki short-sleeve work shirt, olive shorts, wool socks, and a pair of heavy work boots. She resembled a mix between a park ranger and a scoutmaster. "Just thought I'd pop in to meet you. See if you needed anything," she said. "But by the look of things, you're just getting settled."

"Nice to meet you. It's Peter." He extended his hand, and she met it. Hers was a firm, jittery little grip.

156

"Likewise, Peter. You just go right ahead and call me Sue. I wouldn't have it any other way." She went up on her toes a little and tried to look over his shoulder. "You have a wife with you, ain't that right? Leo said it was a married couple staying the next few weeks."

Peter laughed politely. "Yeah, my wife and I." He turned his head, speaking into the house. "Syl, you want to come meet Sue."

"Who?" Sylvia's voice carried from inside Shady Cove.

"Sue Grady. She takes care of the place. Come say hello." Peter turned back to Sue and smiled. She smiled back, her generous face bunching in the cheeks. Her front teeth were huge, each the size of a piece of Chiclets gum.

There was a beat of silence. Then Sylvia came out of one of the bedrooms and up the hall. She was holding her hands out, fingers spread as if they were covered in something. "Who?" she repeated, wiping her hands together.

Sue took another step forward and was standing in the mud-room now. The screen door shut behind her. "Howdy, howdy. Sue Grady, ma'am. I take care of the place." She extended her hand.

Sylvia brushed hers off on the thigh of her blue jeans and offered it to the caretaker. "Sylvia," she said, then added: "Martell. Sorry, I got a little dusty."

"A pleasure, ma'am. Just wanted to make sure you folks were getting along all right. I was saying to your husband only a moment ago that it looks like I caught you as you were showing up. Leo said he wasn't exactly sure when you'd arrive, so I've been driving by every so often, wondering when I'd see you. Looks like I hit the jackpot today."

Peter looked at his wife. "Leo's the realtor who rented me the place," he said to her. "Sue works for him as the caretaker. He was a real nice guy."

"Yup. Nice fella," Sue said. "We go way back, Leo and I."

"Thank him for me, will you?" Sylvia said. "The place looks great."

Peter regarded Sylvia. There was something different about her. He couldn't so much see it, not on the surface, but he felt it like a warm energy buzzing out of her. He had spent the last forty-eight hours since her "accident" practically glued to her hip, and he hadn't noticed it at all then. It hadn't started until they had driven into Gilchrist.

"Happy to. He'll be delighted," Sue said. "Anyway, I won't keep you, ma'am. It looks like you were in the middle of something when I darkened the doorway. I'll let you get back to it."

"Just opening windows," Sylvia said. "It was a bit stuffy when we first arrived."

"Oh, sure, that'd be the case. I keep all the windows shut between houseguests in case it rains. We get some pretty fantastic storms here in the summer months. I'm sure you'll catch at least one before the season departs. Still got a few ripe weeks left." Sue tilted her head as if a thought had struck her. Then she said, "Which reminds me—do you have any kids with you? Because if the sky starts to go bruisey, best to get em inside. Lotsa branches come crashing down in the yard when the wind picks up good."

Sylvia smiled uncomfortably, her gaze shifting down to the floor. Peter could sense that she had just recoiled back into herself.

"No," she said, "it's just us."

"Oh. No need to worry, then," Sue said, her chubby face brightening. "But do yourselves a favor and heed the same warning. I'd hate to have to call Chief Delancey and tell him he needs to send somebody out here to scoop your brains up off the ground because a tree shook something loose on one of you." Sue wrapped the side of her head with her knuckles, making a hollow knocking sound.

"I think I'll go wash my hands. Nice to meet you, Mrs. Grady," Sylvia said in a low voice. "I'll make sure we aren't too much trouble." She turned and walked away.

"Sue's fine. No need for formalities around here," she said after her, standing on her tiptoes and peering over Peter's shoulder. "Just enjoy yourselves."

"You know, I'm curious, is there a grill somewhere?" Peter asked, trying to change the subject. "I noticed charcoal and lighter fluid in the mudroom. I was going to poke around and look for one, but I figure if you're here, you might be able to save me a little time."

Leo had said Sue was an interesting woman, and Peter now understood what he had meant.

"There sure is," she said. "Follow me and I'll show you. It's around back. There's a few other things I'd like to run by you, too, if you don't mind me bending your ear a bit." She wheeled around, opened the door, and was already outside before Peter could respond. He followed her until she stopped at a pair of rusty trash cans around the side of the house. She was standing with her arms folded, legs in a wide stance. "We got raccoons around here. They're nosey little buggers, and they'll sure as Sam make a mess if you don't take a few extra precautions. That's what these are for. Use em." She reached down and plucked a black length of bungee cord that was strapped over the top of one of the trash cans.

"No sweat," Peter said. "We have the same problem at home, except we use a rock on the lid. Does the job just fine."

Sue narrowed her eyes, seemed to hesitate a moment, then said, "Well, these ain't your city coon. These are smarter. You bet. You put a rock on the lid here, they'll just push the whole darned thing over. Then whadya got? A mess, that's what. And guess who Leo sends to clean it up? So use em." She plucked the bungee again. This time harder. It slapped like a heavy snare.

"You have my word," Peter said, holding up a hand as if to pledge an oath. His tone was playful, bordering on sardonic. "When does the garbage truck come?"

Sue laughed and snorted. "Are you crazy? No garbage truck can make it down this road. Wouldn't that be a sight. No, I come Mondays to haul your trash to the dump. Leo shoulda told you that."

"You're right. He did. I forgot."

"Uh-huh. I also come by every Tuesday morning to mow the lawn and do any other yard work that needs doing."

"That's good to know. Thanks."

"Uh-huh. Grill's this way." Sue started down a worn path of beaten grass that sloped along the back of the house toward the lake. She continued speaking as they went: "I offer laundry service, too, if you're interested. If not, there's a small Laundromat downtown. Sunshine Cleaners. Some people don't like the idea of a stranger folding their unmentionables. I won't be offended should you happen to feel that way. Most folks do."

"I'll keep that in mind. It might be helpful," Peter said. "I'm not the modest type." He watched her as he trailed behind, studying how she moved. He'd been doing it his whole life—studying people, their behavior, their mannerisms, and the details of their existence. The habit wasn't a conscious decision; it was simply the way he was wired. It was the reason some stranger he'd sat next to in a restaurant or on a bus might end up becoming a character in one of his books. That had happened before.

Sue's calves were wide and muscular, webbed with fine threads of purple spider veins, especially on the backs of her knees. He couldn't tell if she was forty-five or sixty-five. Her hair was well into the transition from brunette to gray, her skin rough and loose, but she moved with the sprightly gait of a younger woman. She looked like she might have large breasts, but in her work shirt, they appeared flattened.

"Okay," Sue said, turning the corner as she reached the end of the house. "Here it is. A little rusty, but it works just fine."

She had stopped and was standing underneath the section of deck that overlooked Big Bath. It was mostly steep-angled terrain that slanted down away from the house and eventually met up with the backyard and the shoreline. There was, however, a narrow two-foot berm of flat grade abutting the foundation of Shady Cove that served as a sort of natural shelf for storage. There were only three things there: a stack of firewood, an overturned wheelbarrow with a flat tire, and a Weber kettle grill.

"If you run out of charcoal or fluid, you can pick up some more at the hardware store. You know where that is?"

"I think so. Tedford's, right?" Peter remembered parking in front of a hardware store when he'd first come into town.

I wouldn't mind one of Dale's Delights right about now, he thought, instantly developing a yen for one of those greasy burgers and an ice-cold beer. He licked his lips and tried to turn away from the idea of alcohol. It was a slippery thought that could easily snowball and then get away from him.

"Tedford's, that's right. Good. Alrighty. I think that about covers it." Sue rubbed the back of her hand across her nose again, leaving a shiny streak of snot, which she wiped on her shorts without hesitation. It was an almost childish action.

Peter tried to pretend he hadn't noticed, avoiding immediate eye contact. "I appreciate you stopping by to check on us, Mrs. Grady," he said. "I get the sense we're in good hands."

"Sue," she said flatly, checking her hand. "If my mother crawls out of the grave, you can call her Mrs. Grady."

"Sue, that's right. Sorry."

"No bother. I'll get outta your hair now, let you and the missus enjoy the place and get settled. It's shaping up to be a nice day." She started back up the hill, and Peter followed. When they reached the top, she hooked left and stopped near the front door. "My number's on the refrigerator if you need me. Don't hesitate to call," she said. "Anything else I can do for you while you got me here? Speak now or forever hold your peace."

"I think we're all set at the moment," Peter said.

"That's my cue, then," Sue said. "Take care, Mr. Martell. Same to the wife." She turned and trudged up the path.

Beside Peter's car was her beaten-up old truck, faded yellow with patches of rust. The bed was full of tools and a pile of dead branches. She opened the door and, with a little hop, wedged herself behind the wheel. The truck started with a cough of smoke, and she backed out of the driveway.

Chapter Six

A SUNDAY MORNING IN GILCHRIST

1

Fayette Pynchon was Pastor Pynchon of Our Savior Lutheran Church of Gilchrist until he suffered a stroke. Two actually. The first had been a minor one. It happened during a Sunday morning mass as he was giving the sermon. His hands were firmly planted on the pulpit as he scanned the room pensively, reciting the word of God. Then his words just sort of became slurred gibberish, and he continued to preach the gibberish with conviction, unaware that anything was wrong. It sounded like porridge falling out of his mouth. Slowly, in the pews, the eyes of all God's children filled with worry. Mouths scowled, a mix of disgust, fright, and confusion. A light murmur. Then Pastor Pynchon got woozy, passed out, and pissed his pants.

Pearl Lynch stood and shouted, "Praise the Lord!" She thought it was some strange brand of evangelism and wanted to make sure she was a part of it. Not until Hank Barrett rushed to Pastor Pynchon to provide care did she realize it wasn't part of the sermon. She sat down quietly, chin up, fanning herself and checking from the corners of her eyes to see if anyone noticed. They had.

The second stroke came for Fayette six months later when he was taking a bath and listening to the Red Sox beat the Yankees on the radio. It was his sixtieth birthday. His wife found him nearly drowned when she went to bring him a beer and trim the hair on the back of his neck the way he liked her to with the straight razor his father had left him. She dropped it when she saw his head half submerged in the water, his terrified eyes staring up at her, a scared semi-consciousness locked inside a paralyzed and failing body. The razor cut her toe right through her sock when it came down. She has a scar from it that she's only showed her sister. Hank Barrett also saw it, but that's because he stitched it up.

Suffice it to say, the days of preaching and sermons were behind Fayette. Nowadays he spent most of his time in a wheelchair on the porch, painting with oil paints.

This morning, Fayette was looking rather worried—more than the usual slack-faced partial paralysis gape—as he ate his breakfast of oatmeal, orange juice, and dry wheat toast. He was at his post on the porch, his latest work in progress in front him on the easel Gale had bought for him after he had shown an interest—and some actual talent—for painting. Dr. Barrett had suggested Fayette take up a creative hobby, in hopes it might help retrain the parts of his brain that had been damaged. It seemed to be working. His speech and his upper-body motor skills had improved steadily over the last eighteen months or so. Nothing close to a miracle, but enough for hope to rear its clever little head.

He had something on his mind today. A dream had struck a chord of unease somewhere deep inside him. The painting was an attempt to capture the vision that had played on the silver screen of his mind as he slumbered away in a fevered sleep.

"That's a peculiar one," his wife said as she sat down beside him in the rocking chair and sipped her coffee. "What is it?"

Fayette turned to her slowly, bottom lip wet and shiny, mouth still working on his last spoonful of oatmeal. He spoke slowly, almost sounding drunk, sometimes stammering. "I don't nuh-nuh-know. It's an odd one... isn't it?" He set down his spoon and wiped his mouth with the heel of his palm.

He had been a handsome man before his health betrayed him. Tall, slender, hazel eyes, a square jaw, a hard nose, and short dark hair that'd since turned a silvery white.

Gale set her coffee down on the little table between her and her husband, then leaned in closer, studying the painting. "This one's different than your others. It might be your strangest one yet. What is that thing? It looks like some sort of monster, Fay. Ick!"

Fayette sort of half shrugged. "It was a dreab I had last night." He had tried to say *dream*, but sometimes his words came out "wonky," as his wife would say.

"More like a nightmare," she said. "It gives me the willies just looking at it. I don't like this one." She looked at him. "No offense. Just maybe not one for above the mantel."

"I don't like it, either," he said, looking back at the thing he had spent the last four hours working on. He had woken Gale at five o'clock in the morning and asked her to set him up downstairs with the porch light on. He did that sometimes, and she always seemed happy to oblige. If she wasn't, she hid it well. "But I had to m-mmm-paint it. I couldn't h-huh-help it."

The painting wasn't completely finished, but it was as finished as it was ever going to be. He was sick of looking at it.

There was something upsetting about it, something that chilled his heart. What he had created was a crude offense against the normal order of the world.

Some hulking, grayish humanoid thing was holding a man in its massive, sinewy hand. The creature had a bald welted scalp with tiny wisps of hair. Its face was a brightly colored swirl that looked almost like a Greek comedy mask with a gleeful yet sinister grin smeared on it. But the mask might not have been a mask at all. At closer look, it almost resembled colored threads of bone growing out of its face. The creature seemed to be a part of the abstract forest behind it, entangled in tree roots and limbs, emerging from a dark cloud of shadows where all definition disappeared into thick smears and globs of black paint. It looked like something pulled directly from the mind of a schizophrenic.

Some of this Fayette could see simply by looking at what he had put down on the canvas. But a lot of it he knew because he could feel the horrifying nature of the thing. It was one of the clearest feelings he'd had in a long time. And when he closed his eyes, he could see the image of his dream as clearly as if he were in it once again, as if he were so close to something terrible but also separated by an infinite space between.

"Take this inside," he said to his wife. "I don't wamp to suh-see it anymore. I don't like it. Throw it away."

"I said it gives me the creeps, Fay. I didn't say you should send it out with the garbage."

"I'd rather not look at it… if you don't mind."

"Are you sure that—"

Fayette reached up and squeezed the sides of his head as if he had a headache. And that might've been because he felt one coming on. "Please just get it away from me, dammit."

"Okay, settle down, I'll take it away," Gale said. "Somebody wake up and step on a thorn today?"

She plucked the painting off the easel, then carried it into the house. Fayette sat in the stillness of the late morning, watching the woods behind his house, imagining them full of abstract trees that were really more like tendrils rising out of the earth. And that thing with the colorful face—he thought about that, too.

2

He had gone somewhere. It was a cold, foul place. The wet basement of the universe. Awful things live there, and he had been hollowed out.

Jim Krantz prowled up the road, with an expressionless face. He took slow, deliberate steps. His skin burned and itched. It was all okay now. Mother said so.

In the distance was a house with a garage. And in the garage, a man was doing something. He knew the man and went toward him. The man had what he needed. It was a ring in his pocket.

(*get the ring*)

Somewhere deep inside him, Jim cried out into the void: *Help me! Let me go!*

His mother's voice, soft and sweet, responded: "I am helping you. And you are helping me, Pickle. We are together now. I will take care of you. Just let me show you what it's like."

Jim crossed the street and headed toward the house. It was all some paralyzed dream. He was merely a passenger.

3

Leo Saltzman spent the better part of the morning out in the woods looking for good specimens to lathe in the little shop space he had created out in his garage. It was his side hobby, and if he was bold enough to take his own opinion of his work, he was actually pretty good. And if that wasn't enough, the fifty or so pens he had turned on the machine had all been well received by those who had gotten them as gifts. Mostly he gave them out for Christmas or as a promotional product for his real estate business. But on occasion, especially once word spread around Gilchrist that he was creating some beautiful craftsmanship—which he thought of as artwork, and why shouldn't he?—he would get a special request. Usually it was for someone who wanted to have something made for them or for a friend. More than a few times, though, it was a wife looking to have something commissioned for a husband as an anniversary present. That seemed to be a popular trend.

This morning, he had found a great piece of elm burl that he would be able to cut into at least a half-dozen nice pen blanks. The burl he had found was beautifully figured, rich with deformed grain. Deformity was a good thing, he had learned, when it came to woodworking.

He was thinking about doing one for that writer who had just rented the place out on Big Bath. Something better than the one he had already given him. Something more personalized. It was all about making connections. Do something nice for a fellow like that, a fellow who probably has—or will have—the kind of money that can afford a second home someday, and maybe he remembers the name Leo Saltzman when he starts looking to purchase a lake house of his own.

Leo was thinking about this as he ran the chunk of burl through his band saw to cut it into pen blanks, each eight inches long and one inch wide. With those made, all he had to do was drill holes for the brass inserts, lathe and polish the wood, lacquer it, then insert the twisting pen mechanism and press it all together in his vise. Voila! He would have a gorgeous custom pen better than anything a person could find in a store. One of a kind, too.

A tap on his shoulder startled him. He wheeled around and his wife was standing there, dressed in her Sunday church clothes.

"Jesus Christ!" Leo said. He reached over and shut off the saw. The electric motor came to a stop. "How many times, Helen? How many times have I told you not to sneak up on me when I'm working with these tools? They're dangerous."

He lifted his plastic safety glasses so they were resting at the peak of his forehead.

"Leonard Saltzman, if you take the Lord's name in vain with me one more time, you can spend the rest of your days out here in the garage with your tools and your pens. Let's see how you like that."

"All right, all right, let's not lose our tempers. I apologize. You scared me, is all. I only got the ten fingers, and I'd like to keep em all, if I can." He held up his hands and wiggled all of his pudgy, hairy-knuckled little fingers for his wife.

Helen smiled, but the expression didn't touch her other features. "I forgive you. But it isn't me you need to worry about, dear." She gestured toward heaven with one pointed, rigid finger, and her face took on the sanctimonious look of a Sunday school teacher scolding a child who had dared to question the existence of God.

Leo rolled his eyes. He had been raised with religion, but it had faded through his adolescent years. If he hadn't married a devout woman, he might never have set foot in a church again. "Well, what is it? I'm working," Leo said.

"It's almost time for church," Helen said. "I won't be late."

"What time is it?"

"Just after ten."

"Okay. Give me fifteen minutes, and I'll be ready to go." He was wearing a pair of sawdust-covered coveralls, but underneath he already had on his church clothes. Maybe he wasn't a devoutly religious man, but he wasn't stupid enough to ever make them late for church, either. And it wasn't God's wrath he was worried about. "I want to try out one of these blanks real quick and see how the wood turns on the lathe. This is some beautiful grain. Have a look for yourself." He handed Helen one of the blanks he had just cut.

She turned it over in her hands, didn't really seem interested, then handed it back. "That's nice."

"You're darn right it's nice." Leo scoffed.

"Ten minutes," she said, turning and heading back toward the door, which led into the house. "God won't wait on us."

"Fifteen. I want to see how the grain shows after a turn," Leo said after her as she closed the door and went inside.

He took one of the blanks, the worst of the bunch, and got it ready for the lathe. He had bought the Craftsman from Sears three years before, about a week after the woodworking bug started to bite. It was a twelve-inch, one-horsepower machine. One of the best lathes they had in the store. It was a little more power than he needed, but it did the job well, and if he ever decided to take on some larger projects, its one-horsepower electric motor would easily handle those, too. Somewhere kicking around in the back of his mind, he had designs on building his own dining-room table, lathing the legs himself and everything. But for the moment he was sticking with pens. These days, the strip mall kept him too busy for larger projects.

He loaded the blank onto the mandrel and secured the whole thing in place on the lathe. He dropped his safety glasses back over his eyes, checked to make sure he didn't have any loose clothing that could get sucked in—that was the biggest warning the salesman at Sears had given him—then flipped the switch on the side of the machine. It wound to life with a mean whir, the spindle quickly accelerating the mandrel and the wood up to twelve hundred rpms, turning the whole thing into a blur.

He grabbed the rounded cutter tool off the workbench and set it on the tool rest. He brought it carefully toward the blur until he made slight contact with the turning wood, and flakes of sawdust started to spit up, covering his hands. He slid the tool to the left, running it along the waxed tool rest in even, smooth passes, slowly rounding down the wood. Each time, he took a little bit more. It was a slow process, but that was what Leo liked about woodworking. It was relaxing. It was so different from his day job, which was often stressful and, as of late, had been causing him some severe bowel distress. When he was turning a piece of wood, his mind was completely in the moment.

As he was making what he thought might be his final pass on the lathe, a shadow fell over him as he stood there hunched over the spinning wood. His first thought was that his fifteen minutes were up. Helen was probably behind him again, about ready to start yelling that they were going to be late for church. Leo was still hanging on to this idea, even as the strong, peculiar odor of wet smoke washed over him and the air around him cooled.

He started to turn around, but something violent slapped down on the back of his neck and began to squeeze. It was a cold hand. Leo had never felt strength like that before. Whatever—or whoever—it was could've crushed his neck if it had wanted to. The power was there.

On the floor behind him, he could see a pair of dirty engineer's boots caked in black mud.

"What the hell?" Leo cried. "Let go of me!"

He shrugged his shoulders up and tried to bring his head down, attempting to shirk the hand gripping the back of his neck. He felt very much like a frightened turtle trying to retreat into its shell. He dropped the cutting tool on the ground and managed to turn his head to the side just long enough to see Jim Krantz, Dick Krantz's boy, standing there. He didn't know him very well, maybe enough to say hello in passing was all. So he couldn't for the life of him figure out what the hell Jim was doing in his garage, let alone why Jim would be assaulting him. The best guess Leo could conjure was that the kid was drunk and confused about where he was. But something told him that wasn't it. Jim didn't look right. His eyes. God, those eyes.

Something is wrong. Something is very, very wrong.

"Jim, what're you doing? Let me go. What's the matter with you?" Leo struggled to break free, but it was no use.

Jim just stood there, a dead look on his scowling face, his alien green eyes revealing nothing. The grip on the back of Leo's neck tightened. He thought he heard a crunching sound and felt fingernails dig into his skin. He saw a bright flash of twinkling white light in his periphery. His hands reached up wildly as he tried to free himself from Jim's grip, but the strength was quickly draining from his body. Then Jim was pushing him down, down and down and down, pushing his face toward the mean whir of the spinning lathe. He hadn't shut it off. Now he tried to. His hand gave up the task of prying at the viselike grip on the back of his neck, instead fumbling for the switch on the back of the machine. His vision was starting to blur. There was a bitter metallic taste in the back of his throat.

"Stop! Stop it! Why are you doing this?" Leo pleaded. "Helen! Helen, help! Call the police! Get help."

The thing that was Jim Krantz reached down, grabbed Leo's left wrist, and twisted the arm behind his back before he could turn off the lathe. His wrist snapped with a crunch. Leo screamed in agony.

He kept waiting to hear the chirp of the door that led into the house, waiting for Helen to somehow come to his rescue. But what could she really do? What could she do except watch? No. It was best she didn't have to see this. Leo stopped screaming because he knew it was coming. He couldn't stop it; he was too weak. He didn't know why it was happening, only that it was.

He closed his eyes. He could feel the soft cool tickle of air coming off the spinning piece of wood still firmly clutched in the lathe's claws. He could smell the scent of freshly turned elm. He could smell that smoky smell, too. It was coming off the thing behind him that looked like Jim Krantz. In his final moments, Leo Saltzman knew that whatever it was, it wasn't human. It was no longer Jim. He could sense it wanted death. It wanted suffering. It wanted pain. It wanted to…

Leo's bottom lip hit first, and it got sucked between the wood and the tool rest. He cried out. The hand on the back of his neck moved to the back of his head and pressed harder.

4

Helen Saltzman finished doing the dishes, shut off the sink, and dried her hands with the towel on the counter. She hung her apron on the hook beside the refrigerator and checked herself in the mirror. When she was finished applying a fresh coat of lipstick, her eyes darted to the clock on the wall. It was twenty past ten. They had ten minutes to make it to church. Maybe a little longer. Usually mass started about five minutes after it was scheduled, so they would make it in plenty of time. It was a five-minute drive to Our Savior Lutheran.

With the water off, she could hear the machine still running out in the garage, which meant she was going to have to go rally the troops. The singular *troop* was more accurate, as they'd never had kids, and so the Saltzmans weren't quite an army.

She hated that Leo made her nag. He complained about it constantly, and she could tell he resented her for it. In her experience, it was a simple thing: if he did what she asked, then she wouldn't have to pester him. It was so simple, yet so completely impossible. It was marriage. Twenty-five long years of it. But she had every intention of twenty-five more. They weren't the perfect couple, but they worked. They loved each other. And that was fine and good. It was how it ought to be.

Helen grabbed the car keys out of the little bowl sitting on the hallway credenza and prepared to nag one more time. She went up the hall to the door that led into the garage. She paused for a moment, her hand resting on the knob, as a chill ran up her spine and seemed to travel farther north and caress her cheek. Later, she would think that maybe this cool touch on her skin had been her husband kissing her goodbye one last time. This idea would help her through a lot of sleepless nights, but it would keep her up many more.

She opened the door…

5

The Saltzmans' neighbors, Bob and Dotty Zeller, called the police when they thought they heard screams coming from across the street. When Bob went over to see if something was the matter, he found Helen cradling her husband's bloody body in her arms. She was sobbing, rocking him back and forth like a child, her hand trying to support a head that no longer had anything resembling a face. The walls, the ceiling, the floor—they were all covered in a fine spray of blood and hunks of flesh. One of Leo's lips was stuck to the tip of his own shoe. It looked like a bloody slug.

The lathe was still spinning away. Bob reached behind it and shut it off. Finally the motor stopped shrieking.

But Helen continued.

6

Dave Blatten sipped his coffee—black—then set it down on the dashboard. He was in his police cruiser parked on the side of Town Farm Road out near Nipmuc Station, Gilchrist's coal-fired power plant. Sitting at the breast of a hill, he could see the chimney stacks peeking above the sun-kissed tree crowns ahead. The stacks were billowing white smoke against the clean cerulean sky. As a child, he had always thought of them as cloud machines. He came here sometimes in the morning, when there wasn't much going on, and thought about that exact thing, usually with a faint smile on his face. And if it wasn't on his face, he was at least thinking about a smile.

Sunday mornings were usually slow. A lot of folks were attending the eight o'clock mass or getting ready to go to the ten thirty mass. Those who weren't religious were probably still at home eating breakfast. Or perhaps they were doing the yard work they had put off on Saturday. The Sunday-morning shift, from six o'clock to three o'clock in the afternoon, was Dave's favorite shift. Sometimes he could even get a nap in, especially if the Patriots were playing a one o'clock game and everyone was home, glued to their televisions. He hated to have to miss it, but he could usually catch it on the radio, and that was just fine. Besides, Sundays meant overtime, and the extra pay certainly didn't hurt, not with the way his wife spent.

Dave took a Marlboro out of the pack on the seat beside him, slid it behind his ear, and pushed in the car's cigarette lighter. He looked down at his wedding ring and wriggled it with his thumb. It was starting to get tight. If anything ever happened between him and Sarah—not that it ever would, because he firmly believed the part of their wedding vows that had gone something like: *until death do us part*—he would likely have to cut the damn thing off. He had put on a little weight in the last few years, and it was starting to round out his small five-foot-eight stature. *Paunchy* was what his mother used to say about his father. Dave Blatten was getting paunchy. Like father, like son. He was even starting to show signs of the trait that afflicted all Blatten men by the age of thirty: a receding hairline.

Between his legs was a paper bag with an assortment of fresh donuts. It was such a cliché, but damn it if they weren't the best complement to a cup of black coffee. While he was waiting for the lighter to pop, he reached in and pulled out a piece of a glazed cruller he had picked up from Marty's Donutland earlier that morning. He dipped it in his coffee and promptly shoved it in his mouth. A few drops of coffee dripped off the hunk of donut and fell on the thigh of his pants.

"Goddammit!" he said through a mouthful of sugar-glazed pastry. Sarah had just cleaned the damned things. He scraped at the two dime-sized stains with his thumbnail and gave up when he saw it was doing nothing to help. He picked up his coffee again. It was hot.

She'll just have to wash them again, he thought between sips. That was her job, wasn't it? To take care of her husband? To obey? Lord knew she didn't contribute much else around the house. The sex had been stale between them for the last year or so, too. He didn't like that.

He was contemplating what this might mean, when out of nowhere, a dog started to bark right beside his open window. *Rooof! Garooof! Roof-roof! Grrrr-Garooof!*

"What the fuck," Dave said, startled. The little jump scare caused him to spill half the scalding hot coffee down the front of his shirt. "Awww shit! What the... Mother of Christ!"

With two fingers, he held the wet part of his shirt away from his skin to keep it from burning him further. He looked to his left, beside himself with rage. The dog was standing in the middle of the road. A dim whine replaced the bark as it turned its head at an angle—the universal sign of canine curiosity. Usually it was because a nose had smelled food of some sort. In this case, donuts.

"You lousy little mutt. What're you doing all the way out here? You get loose?" Dave said, the anger in his voice a controlled simmer.

He stepped out of the car and tried to wipe away some of the coffee with a handkerchief he kept tucked above the sun visor. Once more, it was useless. Sarah would have her work cut out for her when he got home. He was damn sure of it. He balled up the handkerchief and tossed it back inside his cruiser.

"Just my goddamn luck." Behind him, the dog whimpered, and his attention shifted. He looked at it, eyes narrowing. "And who the hell are you?" he said, a baleful grin spreading across his face.

The dog was a black Labrador retriever. No collar. If it belonged to someone, they probably didn't know it was missing. If they had cared about it in the first place, then it would've been wearing a collar and tags. He supposed it could've gotten its own collar off somehow, maybe gotten it caught on a tree and managed to shake and yank free. But that seemed doubtful.

Dave dropped to one knee. The dog whined, barked, took a cautious step forward, then back again. "Come on, fella. I won't hurt ya. You hungry?" He reached in the cruiser and pulled a chunk of his glazed cruller out of the bag, then tossed it in the road a few feet from Black Dog.

Black Dog went to the food and scarfed it down greedily. Closer now, Dave could see that the animal was covered in mud, its coat far from groomed. There were a few burrs stuck to its tail. The vigorous wagging was no match for the tiny barbs. They would stick to him until someone was kind enough to remove them.

"Good boy, Black Dog. That's a good boy," Dave said, talking in silly dog-speak. "You want some more?" He grabbed another hunk of donut and dropped it right in front of him.

Black Dog hesitated a moment, its wide tongue hanging out as it panted. Then it came across the northbound lane and started eating the pastry no more than a foot from Dave. He was still down on one knee. He reached out and started petting Black Dog's head, then around its neck and behind its ears.

There was a springy pop inside the car as the cigarette lighter finished juicing itself up and ejected. He reached in with his right hand as his left continued to scratch Black Dog. And as the wayward mutt was finishing up the donut crumbs on the asphalt, Dave lifted the dog's head in his hand and pressed the glowing hot cigarette lighter into the tip of its nose.

It yelped, yowled, and whimpered, whipping its head from side to side as if trying to shake some invisible thing off. Its claws tick-tacked like hard pieces of plastic against the blacktop as it scurried away. Dave stood, pulled the Marlboro from his ear, and lit it with the still-hot lighter. He was quite pleased with himself. The dog was already running off back into the woods, occasionally stopping to rub its nose in the dirt.

Dave laughed, then yelled after it: "Burns, doesn't it? You don't like it very much, do you?" He looked down at his shirt once more. "Stupid dumb dog." Once more, he yelled after it: "I'll send you the cleaning bill!"

The dispatch radio in his cruiser burped static. "You there, Dave?" It was Evan Connor on dispatch.

Dave watched the dog for another second or two before losing interest. He leaned back in his cruiser and grabbed the radio. "Yeah, this is Blatten. Go ahead."

"We just got a call. Something's going on over at Leo Saltzman's. You might want to go check it out."

"Saltzman? What happened?"

"Not sure. Dotty Zeller called a moment ago to report she and her husband heard screaming coming from across the street."

Dave hesitated. He was resting his arm on the roof of his cruiser, looking around at everything and nothing all at once. "I'm all the way out near Nipmuc. Isn't there anyone else who can take this one? The Saltzmans live on the other side of town."

"Nipmuc? What're you doing out there?"

"I was doing a drive-through of the area and spotted a stray. I was trying to help the damn thing, but it ran off on me."

"Want me to call animal control and send Walter Deacon your way?"

"No, it's fine," Dave said. "Hey, what about Porter? Ain't he on shift? Why doesn't he take the call? I'm sure wherever he is, it's closer than I am now."

"He's off this morning. It's just you at the moment. Sorry, Dave."

"Fuck," he hissed, his finger off the talk button. Then, into the radio, he said, "All right. I'm on it."

He tossed the radio back in the car, following in after it. He started the engine, cut the wheel hard, and did a U-turn in the middle of the road, tires skidding on the dirt shoulder, then squealing briefly on the pavement. Leo Saltzman better be dead or dying, he thought. This was supposed to be his quiet Sunday-morning shift. First the dog, and now this. Could his day get any worse? What in the hell had he ever done to deserve this?

7

Billy finally gave up trying to get a hard-on and collapsed on top of Sarah Blatten with a frustrated sigh. While his face was in the pillow, Sarah patted his back gently as if to tell him it was all right, that it happened to all men from time to time. Nothing to worry about.

"Everything okay?"

"Uh-huh," he groaned into the pillow.

"That a yes?"

He nodded.

"Are you worried about Dave coming home? He's supposed to be on 'til this afternoon, and he never comes home early."

"I know," Billy said, his voice muffled. "I'm not worried about him."

She giggled. "Can you imagine his face if he walked through that door right now? Oh, I bet he'd be so mad." She giggled a little more.

Billy lifted his head, resting his chin on her shoulder. "Mad? Naw. Why would he be mad?"

"Do you think he'd shoot you?"

"Not if I shot him first."

"You'd do that?" Her eyes brightened. If this was a joke to her, it didn't show.

"Try and stop me." He wasn't entirely sure if he was joking, either.

A part of him wondered if that was the reason he always insisted they met at her place and not his: the thrill of the confrontation and the explosive potential of where that might lead. He didn't really think any shots would be fired—Dave was a hot-tempered bully, not a murderer—but he did anticipate a series of events that might end in divorce. And that, he suspected, was the only way he would ever end up with Sarah. He knew it was selfish, but he also knew that she would never leave her husband on her own. So maybe in this case, selfish was okay. He just wanted to protect her.

Dave had hit her before. Billy had seen the bruises on her neck and arms and the dim shiner under her eye from where an open-hand slap had landed. She had denied it at first, of course, but eventually she had told him all about how Dave had been mad that she hadn't filled up the gas tank in his truck after she had borrowed it to go visit her mother up in Portland. It'd taken every ounce of Billy's self-control not to intervene, but Sarah had insisted he not. So he hadn't.

Sarah kissed his neck, slowly tracing her fingers up and down his spine. "You're my hero, William Porter."

"Is that what I am?" he asked.

"Yes."

"I don't feel much like one right now," he said, and started to roll off her.

"Not so fast. Where's my hero going?" She grabbed him below the waist and gave a few gentle tugs, trying to get things going. "I want to do this for you. I'll go slow." She dropped her voice to a more seductive tone. "Slow is good... don't you agree?"

He sighed again.

"What? What's wrong?"

"I don't think I can do this today. It's not you." He rolled off her and lay on his back, draping a forearm across his eyes in shame. "I'm tired is all."

But it wasn't really shame he felt at the moment. Not exactly. He couldn't get what had happened in Buck Ryerson's funeral home earlier that morning out of his head. He couldn't remember the last time he had even thought about his uncle. The whole thing had left him buzzing with an unpleasant feeling of disquiet.

(*want some hard candy, kid?*)

Had it all been in his head? Of course it had. He didn't even want to consider what the alternative might mean. He had probably just been overtired. Hell, he was still tired. He had hardly slept in the last twenty-four hours, that's all. What had happened in the morgue had just been some kind of nightmare.

Sarah sat up and pulled the sheets over her breasts. She lit a cigarette, took a long drag, and blew two streams of smoke from her nose. "I know. I don't take it personally. You're usually straight out before I've even touched you. I'm not worried. Well, maybe I am about what's going on up there." She pointed to his head. "Something's been on your mind since you showed up."

He peeked at her from beneath his forearm. "It's that obvious, huh?"

"Women's intuition." She smiled.

Billy dropped his arm and looked at her. God, she was beautiful. Dave didn't deserve her.

"Anything you feel like sharing?" she asked.

"Really, it's nothing. Just work stuff. There was a car accident last night," he said, sitting up against the headboard. "You know Danny Metzger? He's a bit younger 'an you and I."

"I do, sure," she said. "His father and my father worked together at the slaughterhouse for a time. I think they still have the occasional beer down at Dale's. Was he hurt?"

"You could say that," Billy said. "He's dead. It was a mess. I've never seen anything like it." Something haunted touched his voice. "Never want to again, neither. I..." He stopped himself, deciding there was no need to tell her about how he had gotten sick when he had first seen the body. It made him look weak, which he wasn't. He just hadn't been ready for it.

Sarah's eyes widened, and her mouth dropped open as slow as a rotted door on rusted hinges. She crushed her cigarette out in the ashtray beside the bed. "Dead? What happened?"

"I just told you... a car accident. He flipped his car on Waldingfield Road last night."

"Was anyone else...?"

"No, just him. Looks like he was alone, poor kid."

"How?"

"Prolly just going too fast."

"Was he drunk or something?"

"Might've been. Not really sure, to be honest. They'll test his blood and find out." Billy's eyes went serious, and he pushed himself up even straighter. "It's hard to think about. I never thought this sort of thing would bother me so much, but I guess it does."

Is that really what's bothering me? he thought. *Or is it the other thing I don't want to look at?*

She put her hand over his and gave it a gentle squeeze. "I'd think you were strange if it didn't bother you, Billy."

He looked at her.

"Oh, I feel just terrible now," she said, seeming to change gears. "I feel so foolish. No wonder you're distracted. And here I am, being so... I'm sorry."

"It's fine. Really," Billy said. "You didn't know. I think I just need to go home and get some rest. It was a long night."

"How 'bout I make you some breakfast first? How do eggs, toast, and coffee sound? I have some potatoes for home fries, too."

"You don't have to do—"

"No, I do. I'm afraid I must insist. One way or another you're leaving here satisfied," she said, giving him a playful look. "Otherwise you might make a gal feel completely useless, and I can't have that. I do have my pride, you know."

Before he could refuse again—and he really didn't want to refuse again—he was looking at her naked body standing at the foot of the bed. Her arms were raised as she gathered her dark-blond hair into a ponytail. A blade of morning sunlight coming through the window caught the side of her face and gave her an angelic glow. He studied her small breasts, the perfect curve of her waist and butt, and her pale smooth skin.

She sat down on the bed, grabbed Billy's white undershirt off the ground, and put it on. She turned and gave him a smile. "Mind if I borrow this for a bit?"

"Go right ahead," Billy said, leaning back and lacing his hands behind his head. For a split second, if he pushed away all other thoughts and kept his mind entirely in the present, this felt like a life that might actually be theirs and no one else's. This was *their* home. He was lying in *their* shared bed. It was *his* wife about to make him breakfast.

"How do you like your coffee?" she asked, furthering the illusion.

"Milk and sugar."

"And your eggs?"

"Over easy, I guess. Or scrambled. Make it a surprise."

"Okay, comin right up," Sarah said, and winked at him. "I'll bring it here so you can enjoy a nice breakfast in bed. That always used to cheer me up when I was kid."

Wearing only his undershirt, she left the bedroom. A few minutes later, Billy heard the sounds of cooking start up in the kitchen. It was comforting. Yes, this was a nice little taste of what could be. What *should* be.

But the fantasy didn't last. Reality crept back in as he stared up at the ceiling, listening to the fake sounds of home. And with it came all the worries. All the realizations that this wasn't his life. That he was only stealing another man's place for a while.

He grabbed his pants off the floor and got his pack of gum from the pocket. He popped a piece of Teaberry in his mouth and started chomping, trying to pound and grind the flavor out of it. For as long as he could remember, that had been his habit.

It was something he did, almost to the point of compulsion, to release anxious energy. He supposed there were worse things than chewing gum when he was upset. He didn't drink. Most of the men he knew did, but he didn't.

After a few minutes, the smells of cooking started to find his nose: toast, coffee, and fried potatoes. He started to feel a little silly about sitting there under a bedsheet, completely naked. Apparently sex wasn't in the cards for him, so what was the point of being all dressed up in his birthday suit with no party to attend?

He got up and put on his clothes, sans the undershirt he had on loan to one Sarah Blatten, then lay back down. A copy of *Field & Stream* sat on the bedside table beside him, along with a stale glass of water, a bottle of aspirin, and a tube of Brylcreem. It had to be Dave's side of the bed. Billy picked up the magazine and found an article on how to catch late-season bass. He wasn't much of a fisherman, but he thought he might like to be someday.

Halfway through it, he heard the soft sound of bare feet patting up the hall. He hadn't realized how powerful his appetite was until Sarah appeared in the doorway with the tray of food she had made for him. It made sense, though—he had puked up his dinner last night and hadn't eaten anything since.

"Hope you're hungry," she said as she crossed the room.

"Look at this," he said, dropping the magazine on the bed. "I must've died and gone to heaven. I'd swear it."

"I love cooking, but Dave says I'm no good." She handed Billy the tray, and he took it carefully. The coffee was steaming, and he didn't care to see what it might feel like dumped on his lap. He set it across his thighs and made sure it was stable.

"I'm sure he has no idea what he's talking about," he said. "It smells mighty fine to me."

"Should you tell him that, or should I?" Sarah said with humor, and went to sit at her vanity, still wearing nothing but his white T-shirt. She started putting on makeup.

Billy's attention switched to the food. His stomach grumbled in anticipation as he took a sip of his coffee. "Hot, hot," he said, realizing he still had gum in his mouth. He took it out and got rid of it, then ran his tongue over the burn on his lip.

"You okay?" Sarah asked, distracted.

"I couldn't wait to taste it."

She laughed softly. "Well… how is it?"

"I'll let you know when I'm done. Coffee's hot, though. That's a good start."

Sarah continued to do her makeup. And between bites of eggs and toast—rye wasn't his favorite but still quite capable of hitting the proverbial spot—he stole glances of her while she got ready for another long day of sitting around the house and being Dave Blatten's unappreciated wife.

By the time he was cleaning up the yolk on the plate with his last bite of toast, he knew he loved her. He always had.

8

Laura Dooley and her son were playing. He was six years old and loved Sunday mornings because Mommy let him come into her room and play Cave Explorer in her bed while she got dressed. It was his favorite game. What he liked most about it was that it always turned into hide-and-seek. So really it was two games.

That wasn't the only reason he was so fond of it, though. He liked it because, before his father had died of a harp attack—

heart attack, his mother always corrected—they used to play it, and it reminded him of Daddy. In fact, Daddy's the one who showed him how to be a cave explorer and how to search for lost treasure under the covers of the bed, which Jake Dooley, the boy's father, had always called the Blackwater Mines. And when he said it, he'd always used that spooky voice that Kevin thought was funny but also a little scary.

Daddy had shown him other things, too. He had shown him how to use his other eyes. He said there were lots of people like them in the world. Some were born with it, and some acquired it. But they all had one thing in common: they had special equipment. Daddy said it was kind of like x-ray vision... only different. Mommy didn't have it, but that was okay because Kevin did, and he could use it to help her when he needed to, like when he had helped her win at bingo once when they'd needed money to repair the car. But he knew that had been wrong. She had told him so, too. She hadn't been mad, of course—she had laughed and giggled as they skipped back to the car through the church parking lot that Saturday—but when they got in the car and shut the doors, she had told him they shouldn't have done it. Still, they had celebrated with ice cream and pizza, so he figured it must not have been all that bad.

Laura was brushing her hair, watching in the mirror's reflection as Kevin knelt on the bed in his favorite pajamas: the bright-red ones with the fire engines. He was about to crawl headfirst under the blankets to head into the caves and see what gold treasure he could find. He wanted to find something nice to give to Mommy.

"I'm going in," he said. "It's gonna be the longest *exedition* ever."

"You think you can dig up something for Mommy?"

He nodded. "I can try. What do you want?"

"Hmmm. I don't know." She narrowed her eyes as if to mull it over. "How about something shiny. Keep your eyes peeled for diamonds and rubies. Mommy likes those. But don't stay down there too long. I don't want to have to come find you. It's awfully dark in those caves. And if you do"—she turned around and made a snarly face, lifting her hands and hooking them into claws—"the monsters might smell you and get hungry for children."

"Not if you have one of these," Kevin said, and adjusted the hairband he was wearing around his head. It was his pretend headlamp, the kind cave explorers wore. "The monsters hate the light. It banshees them."

Laura's face returned to normal, and her posture straightened. "You mean *banishes*, sweetie?"

"That's what I said—it banishes them."

"Okay, kiddo. Good. I have mine right here, too," she said, and picked up another headband that was sitting beside her.

"Okay, Mommy, I'm going esploring for treasure. The monsters won't get me. Don't worry."

He sucked in a huge breath, puffed out his cheeks, and dove headfirst under the covers. He started working his way down into the caves, which, of course, were located near the foot of the bed, where the sheets were tucked in and the space got tight and claustrophobic. When he reached the end of the mattress, where everything was cool and constricting, he turned his body ninety degrees and started crawling lengthwise along the foot of the bed. It was so quiet down there, and he could barely see. The only thing he could hear was the sound of his own breathing. In his pretend world, the caves were vast echoing chambers and his headband illuminated the whole place.

Kevin continued slowly inching along the foot of the bed until he reached a corner. Then he managed to turn himself around and start doing a second pass back. That was when the monster came for him.

"We smell children," his mother said. "We want *fooood*." Only in that moment, she was not his mother; she was the monster.

Kevin started to crawl faster under the covers, going back and forth and zigzagging as fast as he could to avoid being caught in the monster's grip. It was on the bed now. Its claws kept coming down on top of him, sometimes catching him briefly, squeezing his ribs and tickling him. Whenever that would happen, the monster would say, "I've got you. You're mine, and now I will eat you up."

But Kevin would always get free and crawl away to the opposite side of the bed, trying to hide among the ripples and bunches in the thick quilt. Or at least blend in with them. That was around the time the cave exploring game usually turned into hide-and-seek, when his goal would change from hiding to making a break for safety. He would try to make it out of the caves once the monster started to really close in on him, once it began to attack and catch him more and more frequently. When the time was right, he would scurry out from underneath the covers, run out of Mommy's bedroom, and hide somewhere in the house. And when the monster did sniff him out, it would make him French toast and bacon and let him watch an hour of television. Kevin loved Sundays. And Kevin loved the monster.

He was curled up in a tight ball, hiding on the very edge of the mattress beneath a giant heap of blanket, when he sensed an attack coming. His position had been found. This would be the last attack before he fled for the laundry room in the kitchen and hid behind the ironing board or maybe underneath a pile of dirty laundry.

"I smell you, child. You can't hide from *me*," the monster said in a gravelly voice. "Fee, fi, fo, fum."

Kevin took off crawling. He was scrambling as fast as he could for the head of the bed, where he would ascend the caves and burst forth into daylight. The hairband slid off his head, but he didn't care; he wouldn't need it once he was out of the caves. He felt the monster bounding across the bed, trying to get a hold of him. Then something rather peculiar happened, something that had never been a part of their game before. As if the space around him had just opened up, he was no longer in a small place. It was still pitch-black all around him, but the feeling of being confined had disappeared. The air was cooler, too. Not just cool, but frigid. The smell of something burning, the smell of smoke, became so strong it made his eyes sting.

Is something on fire? he thought. *Stop, drop, and roll. Stop, drop, and roll...*

He continued crawling toward the top of the bed, his hands clawing out in front of him, grabbing fistfuls of the sheets, waiting for one of his frantic hands to find the opening and break free into familiar space. Mommy's bedroom should be there waiting for him. But it never came. He kept going, moving faster and faster. Now he was completely up on his hands and knees, charging toward where he thought the head of the bed should be. And it should've been there. But it wasn't. The blankets were no longer on top of him, enfolding him. Where was he? Where was the top of the quilt? Where was the quilt at all? He couldn't get out.

His lungs ached. He was running out of breath. Panic was overtaking him.

"Mommy? Mommy, where are you?" he cried out. His words echoed—but not as if he were in a cave. The reverberation seemed to stretch on to infinity, building into a violent crescendo that sounded like a million tiny metallic shrieks.

He couldn't feel his Mommy on the bed anymore. He couldn't hear her pretending to be the monster. Where was she? Better question: Where was *he*?

9

Laura was kneeling on her bed in her bathrobe, chasing her son around as he crawled back and forth under the covers. Every so often, she would pounce on top of him and tickle him through the quilt, then let up and allow him to scurry to another corner and hide there. He loved playing, and she supposed she did, too. Having an excuse to act like a child once the responsibilities of adulthood had sapped away her silly side was one of the better parts of being a parent. Although sometimes she had to remind herself that twenty-three wasn't that old. It just *felt* old because of the turns her life had taken.

Now she was looking at a giant lump in the corner of the bed, where she knew Kevin was hiding. Any moment now, he would make a break for it and crawl out from under the blankets, giggling and squealing with joy before going to hide somewhere in the house. The laundry room was his favorite.

"I smell you, child. You can't hide from me," she said, starting toward him. "Fee, fi, fo, fum."

The shape under the bed started to move, and she fell on it, prepared to give the tickling to end all tickles. Something was wrong, though. She wrestled with the blanket for a moment, trying to find a body beneath it to grab, a set of ribs to tickle. But there was nothing. Somehow he had slipped through her arms and gotten away, crawled behind her. She pushed herself up and scanned the bed, her mood sobering. There were a few lumps under the blankets, but nothing big enough to be her son. Still, she patted her hands down on top of them, deflating each one, just to be sure.

"Kevin, kiddo, where'd you go?" she said, confused.

This was the first stirring in her that something wasn't quite right. It was a small feeling, as if a single icy hair had been dragged across the back of her neck. He had probably already snuck out of the bed and gone to find a hiding spot in the house. That must be it. Another part of her thought maybe it was more than that, though. Maybe it had something to do with her son's strange gift. The same one her husband had possessed.

"Ready or not, here I come," she called out.

Half an hour later, after she had searched every single place—inside and out—she came to the realization that she was in an empty house. Her son had simply vanished. All that she had found was the hairband he'd been wearing.

10

George Bateman was opening the bar for the day. He had already picked up the ground beef and a couple pounds of thick-cut bacon from Metzger's Butchery. Carter wasn't there to shoot the breeze like he usually was. The kid running the shop this morning, Kip Clap, told him Carter had a family emergency. Apparently his son had been in a car accident the night before. A bad one. Kip didn't know whether he was okay or not. So George bought the meat, then went on down the road to the bakery and picked up a half dozen sleeves of freshly baked hamburger buns. That was all he would need for the day. He ran a simple operation.

He liked to buy his ingredients fresh each morning. That was what made a Dale's Delight cheeseburger so damn delightful. The toppings, too—onions, tomatoes, lettuce, cheese, and cucumbers for his wife to make her famous pickles—those were all locally sourced from farms within Gilchrist County lines, when the seasons permitted, of course. He didn't have a fancy menu, no list of entrees and appetizers for customers to choose from. It was only burgers and fries down at Dale's Tavern, the way his father, Dale Bateman, had always done it.

And it worked. People kept coming back to eat, so he kept making the food the same way it had always been made. He firmly believed, as his father had, that the secret to succeeding in any venture was to do one thing and do it well. That way, the hard work had a far better chance of paying off. In the case of the tavern, he was right. He wouldn't change a thing for as long as he owned the place. If he and Mrs. Bateman ever had children—and there was always the idea kicking around in the backs of both his and his wife's minds that they still might someday, even as they both approached forty—then he would make sure his son or daughter understood the golden rule of business: don't mess with success. On some level, he wondered if that was the exact reason why he and Beth never tried harder for kids when they were younger, before the idea started to seem less and less realistic.

George checked the wall clock hanging above the juke. It was just after ten.

I got time, he thought. *That's one thing I know I have—time. And right now this is my time. I like that I can hear the clock ticking. The front door is locked, and everything stays out until I invite it in. That's power, isn't it? Hearing the ticking if it's only that I have to listen hard enough? Not letting others drown out the details? If I keep this time, this place, for me and just me, isn't that power? Isn't that important?*

He turned away from the clock, listening to it count off the seconds, and wiped down the bar top with a damp rag.

In an hour or so, he would turn on the deep fryer to get the oil warmed up and ready for french fries. He hand-cut those himself, of course. Grew the potatoes in his own backyard, too. During the winter, he had to outsource some of the produce, but he didn't think there was any shame in that. He couldn't control the weather.

Sundays at Dale's Tavern didn't usually pick up until around one o'clock, when the late-lunchers and the early drinkers started to get a hankering for whatever fix scratched their itch, whether it be bourbon or a beer and a burger with a basket of fries. Even then, the traffic stuck mostly to regulars on the Lord's Day.

Benny Feller was usually first through the door. That was a given on most days, not just Sundays. He was of the latter group, the early drinkers, and his itch was scratched with vodka. Usually he took it in a pint glass, mixed with a small splash of orange juice. And although he called it a screwdriver, it was pretty much all screw and no driver. He would do about three of those over the course of two or three hours, slowly sipping it as his eyes glassed over more and more. Then at around three o'clock, he would get up to finally use the bathroom and stumble sideways into the jukebox. At that time, George either had to ask him to leave or kick him out. He knew it wasn't exactly the right thing to do, letting the guy get all soused and then turning him loose on the streets of Gilchrist. But he felt bad for him. He had been a mess ever since his daughter died. And if George didn't serve him, Benny would just go to another bar or the liquor store. Benny was getting drunk one way or another, so why not at least let him spend some time among the closest thing to friends and family he had, even if it was only for a few hours?

11

Benny Feller awoke in the woods behind Agway Lumber out off Northgate Road, which was on the south side of Gilchrist. That wasn't anything unusual for him. Neither was the gaping black hole in his memory. He regularly paid for his poison in large chunks of lost time. It had been that way since the drinking had gotten heavy. And the drinking had gotten heavy about a year after his wife left him, which was about ten months after Madison died.

That was six years ago.

He sat up, eyes burning, mouth dry, and glanced around. He rubbed the sleep tightness out of his face, blinking hard and stretching his mouth. His bottom lip, chapped and dry, cracked and started to bleed. He wiped the blood on the sleeve of his shirt. He was only forty-seven years old, but this morning he felt like a dying man in the final act of his life.

"Holy hell," he said, his voice a low rasp.

He needed a moment to get his bearings. He picked up a pint of vodka that was sitting on the ground beside him, found it empty, and tossed it aside.

No luck today, he thought. *The gods stopped smiling on me long ago… if they ever did smile.*

He got to his feet, his joints groaning, and wiped the pine needles off his knees and butt. The crotch of his blue jeans was damp. He looked down to discover he had pissed himself. "Well, ain't that just great," he said, looking up at the sky. "What I ever do to you? Huh?"

He would have to go back to his trailer and change his pants before starting in on the day's drinking. First stop, of course, was Duddy's Liquors. He had to get something strong in him before the shakes set in and his whole body went all squirmy and nervous the way it did when he started to dry out. But more importantly, he wanted to get a drink in him to keep away the weirdness that existed in Gilchrist. The stuff nobody else could see. Booze seemed to remedy that, too. It kept what he called his "freaky antenna" turned off.

He found a bent cigarette in his pocket and lit it. The world was spinning, but everything slowed with each draw of nicotine.

How did I end up here?

It was a good question, one that he asked himself often. Sometimes he meant it quite literally, especially when he had to actually figure out where the hell he was. Most times, though, it was something he felt deep in a small pocket of sober rationale he still had tucked away in a dry part of his brain. In that place, he felt it not as an actual question but more as a longing for something different than what his life had become. Around his heart, like a piano wire slowly cinching, the feeling would come and sit, aching like dull glass in his chest, until he pushed it away with something strong.

So how had he ended up here? This morning, as something close to sobriety nipped at his heels and the morning sun blared in his face, he supposed the answer was simple: he had lost his daughter, and nothing had been the same since. Losing Madison had derailed his life in a way he had never seen coming. His wife's, too. The end result was that their marriage simply couldn't handle the added weight of losing a child, and everything had just fallen apart.

In the wake of the tragedy, his wife, Donna, had wanted to move on with her life, and she felt the only way to do that was to move to Florida, where she had family who could lend her the emotional support she needed. It was also a place where, every time she went outside, she didn't have to be reminded of what had happened. A place where she didn't have to hear her husband constantly talking like a madman about how he didn't think it had been an accident at all.

(*why can't you just accept that our Maddie is gone, Ben? why? why? why?*)

In Florida existed a life where his wife didn't have to walk the downtown strip and think about how one Sunday morning two months after Madison's death, drunk, grief-stricken, and in his underwear, he had wandered the streets, raving about how his little Sweetie Pie had been murdered by a masked beast he saw in his dreams. She didn't have to see Chief Delancey and be reminded of how he had been the one to bring her husband home that day and walk him to the front door, drunk and sobbing about murderers and monsters.

That, so far as he could tell, had been the tipping point: his talk of dark things from a strange dark place. It had made him sound fit for a padded room.

He wasn't crazy, though. Not at all. A drunk? Sure, you bet. He wouldn't deny that. But crazy? No way. His daughter's death had been no accident. He didn't know how he knew it, but he did. It was a strange sensation, as if the universe were whispering into his ear. There was a dark channel broadcasting through Gilchrist, something he had always sensed. And after Madison's death, an antenna had been switched on, and he could pick it up more clearly. He could tune in to the hidden frequency and sneak a peek into another plane of existence. But what he saw there was nothing good. It was hell. And in that hell, some terrible thing with elephant skin stalked the town of Gilchrist behind the thin veil of reality. He had seen its true form in his dreams. It was an ancient puppeteer—a timeless abomination corrupting the natural order of the universe, leeching off it like a parasite.

It had pulled strings, taken his daughter, and drunk in his grief and his anger to feed. The universe had whispered this to him, and the knowledge had become wisdom. If there was one thing he had learned after all that had befallen his life, it was that the universe truly did speak to those who listened.

Squinting, Benny walked out to the road, greasy hair tangled with flecks of dried leaves and pine needles, trying not to think about the freaky antenna stuff. It always made his blood run like ice water and left a pit of despair in his stomach. But he couldn't resist.

He tossed the cigarette into the road, then reached into his pocket and pulled out a silver pocket watch. He popped open the face, but he wasn't checking the time. It had stopped working in its intended way years ago. Glued to the inside of the cover was a picture of Madison. Staring up at him was her sweet smile. Her hair was in pigtails, the way she had liked to wear it. He touched the fading photograph with the rough tips of his fingers. He closed his eyes and thought of her laugh. He thought of the way she always used to smell of watermelon lollipops, the ones the doctor gave her after check-ups. He thought about her tough little attitude and the way she would scrunch her face into a point of exaggerated disdain, hands balled into loose fists and planted firmly on her hips, when she was frustrated or wanted to be taken seriously.

Sometimes, baby, I think you would've saved me from myself, he thought sadly. *I sure as hell wasn't perfect, but you gave me reason. You were my boundary, the line I wouldn't cross. Sometimes, I wonder if I should just—*

Benny heard soft giggling coming from the woods across the street. He recognized it immediately. It was Madison's laughter, but there was a mean, antagonistic quality to it. Laughing *at* him, not *with* him. It was as if by thinking about her, he had bled the memory of his daughter out into the world. He kept his eyes shut, knowing what he would see when he opened them. It would be the gray-skinned thing from his dreams. It was pulling strings again. Taunting him.

It wants a snack, he thought, and the idea sent a shiver up his spine.

Madison's voice called to him: "Daddy, come play with me. I want to show you where I live now."

He closed his hand around the watch and cleared his mind, trying to push every ounce of sadness and anger from his heart. He would give the parasite nothing to feed upon. That was what it wanted: his despair. He had been thinking big sad thoughts.

Benny opened his eyes, prepared for the worst. And it was, in fact, the worst. His daughter was standing thirty feet away on the other side of a low rock wall that ran along the edge of the woods. She was beckoning to him and smiling, wearing the same clothes she'd had on the last time he had seen her alive… the clothes she had been wearing when they had fished her body out of the Gilchrist River. Blood was dripping down the side of her head. Her overalls were wet and covered in black moss.

"Come on, Daddy. I miss you. Don't you want to be with me?" Its voice turned mean. "I know you do."

Benny stood there, his face a stony outcropping, seeing the horror but refusing to feel anything. It wanted his fear, his sadness, his anger… it wanted something black.

"It's not you," he said coarsely, his words catching in his dry throat. "My baby's gone."

It giggled again. "Don't be silly, Daddy. I'm right here. I've always been right here… watching you."

"No," Benny said coldly.

The Madison Thing turned and ran behind a tree. He couldn't see its face anymore, but he could see a bloody shoulder sticking out and a hand gripping the side of the bark. The fingers were unnaturally long, thin, and slick… almost batrachian.

It continued to giggle, the mean tone deepening further. "Come and find me, Daddy."

Benny clutched the watch, thinking about the picture inside, trying desperately to fill his heart with love and happiness, thinking of the good times, not the bad.

"I won't feed you," he whispered, closing his eyes. "Find someone else's strings to pull." He finished the thought internally: *Can't you see I won't dance for you? Why won't you leave me be?*

"Daddy, you should've protected me," it said.

He opened his eyes and glanced up as cold, rotten breath bathed his face. It was a mixture of sewage and wet ash. Terror seized him, and he stumbled backward, dropping the watch and falling hard on his butt. The heels of his palms scraped across the asphalt and started to burn and ache.

"Mother of God," he said, his skin icing over.

Towering over him was a grotesquely deformed version of his daughter. She looked like a giant rubber doll whose limbs had been stretched out by a greedy child. She must've been eight feet tall. Her arms looped down to the pavement, skin pallid and crisscrossed with dark veins. She still had pigtails, but her hair was black and thick like burnt straw. And the face was no longer a likeness of his daughter. It had been replaced by the awful face of the puppeteer behind the veil. It had deep black eyes and flat lips that lined a toothless maw. The colors of its face moved, shifting and shimmering in the same way an oil slick floating on top of water does when the light hits it right.

It was sickening to look at, but even harder to look away. It leaned closer and seemed to sniff him.

It's tasting me, Benny thought.

He wanted to get to his feet and run, but he was frozen in place, half terrorized and half hypnotized by what he was seeing.

The Madison Thing stared back at him. Then its mouth dropped open, unleashing a horrible high-pitched shriek. The figure seemed to grow another ten feet, and it descended toward him, the mouth becoming a gaping black cave that would swallow him whole. The screaming filled his head, rattling his brain. In the background, he was sure he could hear that mean-spirited giggling.

He closed his eyes, covered his head, and curled up into a ball in the middle of the road, waiting for whatever was about to happen to just be over.

"Just kill me already! Stop toying with me!" Benny yelled, pleading. He waited for pain. He waited for death.

Instead, the shrieking sound began to change shape. What had started out as an otherworldly, wraithlike howl became a familiar sound he recognized. He opened his eyes in time to see that the Madison Thing was gone and a car was headed right for him. It was skidding to a stop, smoke trailing from its squealing tires. He saw the undercarriage growing and thought he would soon be catching an up-close glimpse as he tumbled beneath and was spat out the back, bloodied, gouged, and as limp as a rag doll.

This is it, he thought as the car barreled toward him.

He pushed himself up just as the chrome grill of the car came to a stop six inches from the tip of his nose. He spotted a splattered fly stuck to the Cadillac's bumper.

The driver opened the door and hurried out, hustling around to the front of the car. It was Early Crawford, the long-standing mayor of Gilchrist, and his gourd-shaped face was a deep shade of angry red. He was in his Sunday church clothes—a gray plaid blazer and a pair of slacks. When he saw that it was Benny Feller, the anger seemed to fall away to something like sympathy.

"Ben? What'n the Sam Hill are you doing sitting in the middle of the road? I almost ran you flat as a hotcake," Early said.

Benny gazed around, eyes wide, as he gathered his faculties and looked for traces of the horror he had just witnessed. "I... uh..." He scratched his head, scanned the ground, and found his pocket watch. "I s'pose I fell, that's all. I dropped my watch." He grabbed it and tucked it away in his pocket. He started to get to his feet but winced.

"I see," Early said doubtfully. "Here, don't hurt yourself." The mayor offered his hand, and Benny took it reluctantly.

Early Crawford was in his late sixties, but he still had a grip like a bench vise and a stocky, athletic build that was perfect for this kind of heavy lifting. Even at his age, he still managed to make it out to Boston every year to run the marathon. Benny felt Early's strength as the man hauled him to his feet.

"Thanks," he said, not meeting the mayor's eyes. "Didn't mean to scare you."

"You look like you're in rough shape. Everything all right?"

"I'm okay," Benny said.

"What're you doing all the way out here?" Early leaned against the hood of his car. He saw a fleck of road debris on the paint and rubbed it off with his thumb.

"Just taking a walk. Clearing my head, I guess."

"A walk, huh? Downtown's a good five miles up the road. That's a heck of a walk."

"I know," Benny said. "I have a lot on my mind. Anyway, I should be going. Take care, Earl."

He turned to leave, but Mayor Crawford's hand shot out like a snake and caught Benny's arm.

"Whoa, whoa, hold on a moment. Why don't I give you a ride back to town? You don't want to walk all that way, do you?"

Benny glanced down at the hand, then up at Early. The look on the old man's face was of sincere concern.

"No, that's—"

"It's only a lift, Ben. You don't need to read into it any more than that… neither of us does," Mayor Crawford said, letting go of Benny's arm. "Now don't be stubborn. Get in. I'm gonna be late for church if I stick around here any longer."

Benny looked around the area again, searching the dark hollows of the woods, looking for a masked face grinning out at him. He didn't see one, but thought he might if he looked with his heart, not with his eyes.

"All right," he said. "I'll take a ride."

They got into Early's car. Jazz played on the radio.

"Where you headed?" he asked as they headed up the road. "You feel like joining me for Sunday service? That's good for clearing the mind, too. *I* think so, anyway."

"Not today," Benny said.

"Okay. Not today," Mayor Crawford repeated. "There's always tomorrow, though. Don't forget that."

They drove the rest of the way without speaking. There was no tension between the men, only John Coltrane on another strange Sunday morning in Gilchrist.

12

Corbin pushed his scrambled eggs around the plate, occasionally taking small bites. He had managed to get a few hours of sleep, but it wasn't enough. He felt foggy. His stomach raw. Eyes burning. He had work to do, though. Things he needed to sort out.

He would have to take a sniff of Benzedrine. Without it, he wouldn't be able to function today. He touched his breast pocket and felt the inhaler.

You don't need it, you want *it.*

Meryl was at the stove making a second pot of coffee, and Corbin studied the curves of her outline. She was a beautiful woman, short with a firm behind and breasts that had remained perky beyond breastfeeding. Her face was effortless. She was the kind of woman whose attractiveness was found in the ease with which eyes could linger on her without meaning to.

"Where's Grace?" he asked, setting down his fork. He took a bite of toast and washed it down with the rest of his first cup of coffee. "I feel like I haven't seen her for days. Think she remembers me?"

"You've been busy. That's the job." Meryl came and sat down at the table as the coffee percolator took the flame. "She's still in her room. On the phone, I think. One of her friends—Beverly—she called twenty minutes ago."

"A little early for phone calls, isn't it?"

"Not that early. It's ten o'clock," she said. "It's fine. Just a couple girls gabbing about boys. You didn't sleep enough. You're cranky."

Corbin rolled his eyes, then leaned forward on his forearms. "Boys? What does she care about boys?"

Meryl let out a sniff of laughter, as if to say: *Oh please. Where the heck have* you *been?* But what she actually said was: "She's fifteen, Corbin. Don't you remember what we were like at that age?"

He did, and it made him dislike the idea of his daughter caring about boys even more. He didn't even want to consider what it meant on so many different levels.

He pushed back from the table and patted his belly, even though he had hardly eaten a thing. He didn't want Meryl to worry about him. "Maybe *you* were like that. Not me. I was a damn saint. A virgin 'til our wedding night. Anyone tells you different, and they're lyin.'" He winked at her as he stood and grabbed his hat off the back of the chair.

"You have to go already?" she said, her eyes following him up.

"Duty calls… and calls and calls," he said jadedly, putting the hat atop his head and tipping the brim, a wide, tired grin painted across his face. He could feel himself trying to mask his own uneasiness with humor. He knew Meryl could see right through it. But she would be kind enough not to say anything about it, for the same reason she hadn't called him out for not really touching his breakfast.

"Want me to bring lunch down to the station later?" she asked, grabbing his plate and taking it to the sink. "Better than junk on the go. Besides, you can't eat greasy food every day. It's not good for your stomach."

"Tuna salad sandwich?" Corbin asked.

"Tuna salad it is."

He went to his wife and gave her a kiss. As he turned around to leave, she patted his bum gently. Then he was standing outside in the driveway, listening to a lone cicada buzz somewhere off in a treetop. He looked over his shoulder at the house… at his home. He needed to head to Elhouse Mayer's farm to have a talk with him about Danny Metzger's car accident—and possibly more. He sensed that it was going to be a dark day, but he needed to start somewhere.

His eyes wandered up to his daughter's bedroom window. Thinking about her made the corner of his mouth twitch with a faint smile. She always made him feel better. She really was a great girl. He had certainly lucked out in that department. When Grace had first been born, all of his friends had joked with him about how much of a handful she would be, especially when she became a teenager, and he had always suspected that their predictions would probably come true. But it simply never happened. There was the occasional argument, sure, but more times than he cared to admit, the fault was his own.

As far as he was concerned, God had given him a good one. And if today was going to be a dark day, he thought maybe he should brighten it a little first.

13

"He almost killed them," Grace Delancey said into the phone. She was lying on her stomach, propped up on her elbows with her legs crossed behind her at the ankles. She moved them back and forth slowly in time with the cadence of the conversation as she doodled on the notebook in front of her in pencil. She was drawing a flower—a daisy.

Beverly was on the other end of the line. Her voice came through reedy. "He was just playing around. Ricky's a good driver. He never would've hit them. It was just a gag, Grace. You really let him have it downtown, jeez. I've never seen you so mad."

"Ricky's crazy… and he was drunk," Grace said. "It could've happened by accident, even if he *is* a good driver. Anyway, I don't know why you like hanging around with him and Chris. All they do is smoke cigarettes, hang out at the lake, and see who can burp the loudest."

"I kinda like Ricky," Beverly said, her voice taking on a guilty tone. Then it switched to one of secret excitement. "There's something… I don't know… dangerous about him."

Grace recalled the look that had come over Ricky's face when he spotted the couple walking down the road as they were driving back toward town to get more beer. An intense storm had formed instantly on his face. His features had darkened, and his eyes had glassed over. He grinned a clownish smile. *Watch this. I'm gonna make them shit their drawers*, he had said as he stomped on the gas pedal and pointed the car at them. The rest had happened so fast that it was all a blur. She just remembered Ricky's hyena laugh as they drove by, and Hooch throwing a beer can out the window.

Grace blinked, pushing away the memory. Something about it made her stomach sour. "You can say that again. He could've really hurt someone yesterday. Running people off the road into a ditch isn't what I call a gag." She paused. "Do you think anyone saw our faces? I think my dad knows that guy."

"Your dad's the chief, he knows everyone. Don't worry so much." There was silence for a moment, and then Beverly giggled. "He's cute, don't you think?"

"Eew, yuck! Ricky Osterman? Cute? He smells like an ash-tray. And his teeth… Does he even know how to use a toothbrush, you think?"

"They're not that bad." Beverly sounded defensive, border-line offended. "Everyone who smokes looks like that."

"So what?"

"So I think I want to start, actually. I've been practicing, stealing my mom's. We should get a carton and hide them somewhere. We can split it."

"Double yuck. Cigarettes are so gross," Grace said. "Why would you want to smoke?"

"Little Grace Delancey, she likes the rules," Beverly mocked. "Just because dear old dad is police doesn't mean you can't have fun every once in a while."

"How is driving around getting drunk and smoking ciga-rettes fun?"

"God, you're such a square, Grace. Lighten up, or boys will never like you. Next year is high school, and I don't plan on being left out."

"Why're you being so nasty?"

"I'm not. I just don't want people to think I'm boring. Is there anything worse than being *boring*?"

"Dating Ricky Osterman or Chris Collins."

The girls both laughed.

"Okay, okay. I didn't mean to be a jerk. Forget I said any-thing," Beverly said. "Ice cream later?"

"That sounds nice. Just you and me?"

"Promise. No boys. Ricky and his friends can get their own milkshakes," Beverly said.

"Can you believe the summer's almost over?"

There was a bang, then a hollow clatter outside her widow.

Grace slid to the edge of her bed and saw her father's face appear outside her window. "I'll call you back."

"Okay."

Grace hung up the phone. "Dad? What're you doing out there?"

"Hi, baby," her father said. "I brought you flowers." He held up a sagging bouquet of dandelions and smiled her favorite smile. "Can you spare a moment for an old man like me? I feel like I haven't seen you in ages."

Grace laughed, then went to the window and opened the screen. "Of course I can."

Her father handed her the dandelions and leaned forward on the windowsill. "Who was that on the phone? I didn't mean for you to hang up. I just wanted to say hi."

"It's okay. It was just Beverly," Grace said, smelling the dandelions. They had a sweet, bitter smell she didn't mind.

He raised his eyebrows and nodded, making a funny face. "Oh. Okay then."

"I know you don't like her."

"I didn't say that," her father said, showing her his palms.

"You didn't have to." Grace went to her dresser and set the dandelions down. "You're a terrible liar. I hope you know that."

"Well, I don't have a lot of experience in that area, so I suppose I'll take that as a compliment. What're you doing today?"

"Finishing up some summer reading. I might grab ice cream later."

"Okay, well, be safe," he said, then hesitated. "I was thinking maybe you and I could catch a movie sometime before school starts? The drive-in over in Heartsridge. You choose the movie, and I'll treat. We'll even bring your mother, if she's nice."

Grace sat down at her vanity and started combing her hair, watching her father in the reflection of the mirror. He was drumming his fingers nervously on the windowsill. "Sure, Dad, I'd like that. *Fantastic Voyage* is coming out. I bet it'll be super."

"Never heard of it. Love story?"

"Science fiction."

"Oh. Aliens. I didn't know you liked that stuff. But even better."

Grace shook her head, amused. "You going to work?"

"Affirmative. Duty calls. I just wanted to say hello and bring my special gal some flowers."

"Some weeds, you mean?" Grace laughed.

"I always heard it was the thought," her father said. "Buncha nonsense, huh?"

"They're wonderful. Thank you."

"Anytime," he said. "I'll see you later. Shut the screen so the flies don't get in. Love you."

"Love you more, Dad."

Her father descended the ladder and pulled it away from the house. Then she heard his cruiser start up, followed by the sound of him backing out of the driveway and heading up the street. She listened until she couldn't hear him anymore.

As far as fathers went, she had a good one.

14

Ricky Osterman checked the oil and then dropped the hood of his car. It latched shut with a solid *clunk*. The black Chevrolet Biscayne was powered by a 409 big-block V8 he had salvaged, rebuilt, and installed himself the summer before. No doubt about it, she was a fast machine. He could lay a strip of rubber a hundred yards long with the tap of a toe on the accelerator. *When it screams, the girlies cream*, he would joke to his friends.

Really, he only had the one—Hooch. But Hooch always laughed, so Ricky kept saying it.

He lit a Lucky Strike, and pulled a comb from the pocket of his blue jeans. Looking in the reflection of the driver-side window, he ran it backward through his greasy red hair until a satisfied grin curled his lips. In the reflection, the spray of freckles on his nose and cheekbones were hardly visible. He hated his freckles. The cigarette smoke wandered up into his eyes and caused him to squint. He thought it looked cool.

"I am the judge," Ricky said under his breath. "And I decide."

Ricky was still buzzing from yesterday. He was already hearing about it. His father had been called out to tow the wreck.

"Ricky, what in the hell did I tell you?"

Speak of the devil, and he shall appear.

His father was standing behind him, nursing a morning beer. He was wearing his favorite coveralls, the ones with the words Osterman Towing written in faded red cursive across the back. The grease stain on the right shoulder looked like Florida.

"I don't know. What'd you tell me, Pop?" Ricky said in a cold, flat voice. He was still regarding himself in the window's reflection, tucking strands of hair behind his ears. He could see his father standing there, eyeballing him. He didn't like it.

I am the judge.

"I told you to mow the damn lawn yesterday," Nate Osterman said, taking a step toward Ricky. "That skull of yours too goddamn thick to understand one fuckin thing I tell you?" There was a beat of silence. "Well, answer me."

"Guess so. Must've gotten it from you." Ricky straightened, turned to his old man, grinned, and tapped the side of his head with his index finger.

I decide…

Nate glared at his son, letting out a quick, belittling laugh. "Oh, I see—you're tough now. All grown up because you just turned eighteen. Is that it? You're the top fuckin dog now? Don't have to listen to anyone because you're a big bad adult? Well, big man, you ain't top dog around here." He drained his beer, eyes locked with his son's, then crumpled the can in one hand and threw it at the hood of Ricky's car... at his baby. "Remember that while you're mowing the fuckin lawn today, big shot."

Ricky followed the can's arc and watched as it bounced off the shiny black paint, leaving a spattering of beer foam across the top of his hood and on the windshield.

His head whipped back around to his father. Lips sneering. Teeth clenching. "What the fuck's the matter with—"

Nate wound up and smacked Ricky across the face with an open hand. The old man's palm and fingers were thick and rough with callouses. It felt like being hit with a brick. There was a flash of white. The left side of his face went hot. His ear rang. Warm blood leaked from the inside of his cheek onto his tongue. He loved the taste. He loved the pain.

Ricky might've been tall and wiry, but his father was bigger. He had the same height and strong physique, but his muscle was padded by an extra seventy-five pounds of brutish blue-collar flab that could easily be put to work. Ricky could fight, and in fact had never lost in his life, but he wasn't foolish enough to go toe-to-toe with his dad—not if the fight was fair. The old man would knock his dick in the dirt. Pride is one hell of a motivator, and Nate would never let his own son best him.

"You slapped me." Ricky laughed and spat a mouthful of blood on the ground.

"I'll hit you like a man when you are one, Richard." Nate turned around and crossed the yard to his tow truck, his broad, lumbering back like that of a gorilla's. When he reached the door, without looking in his son's direction, he said, "Cut the grass, shit-for-brains. Or I'm towing the car into the goddamn lake when I get home. Try me."

Richard? Nobody calls me that. He's just asking for it. Oh man, he doesn't even know what I could do if I wanted to. He's here because I let him live.

Ricky glanced at the eight-pound splitting maul sticking out of the chopping log next to the woodpile. It hadn't been sharpened in years. Even better. His father was only twenty feet away. He could be on him before he even knew what happened. Ricky could bring the dull ax right down on the crown of his head. His mother was likely in the back parlor, knitting and staring at the wall, and wouldn't hear a thing. No one would ever know. Maybe Nate Osterman finally got fed up with his no-good son and wife and split.

Split, split, split, split! The ax will split. It will bash and crack. I am the judge, and I decide. I wield the ax. I am the split, and I am the bash, and I am the crack of his skull.

Ricky didn't have any memory of moving from where he had been standing beside his car, but now he was at the pile of firewood beside the shed, hand folded around the ax handle. The fire was burning inside him again. Warmth in his veins.

The opportunity for judgement passed. His father had already reached the end of the driveway in his truck. He hesitated a moment, then went right, kicking up a great plume of pale dust as his truck dipped and rocked down the gravel road, tow chains jingling like sleigh bells.

Ricky unwrapped his hand from the ax, then went back to his car and wiped off the beer. When he was finished with that, he went into the shed to drag out the lawnmower.

15

Peter and Sylvia were going for a walk down Lakeman's Lane. Peter wanted to get the lay of the land. The plan was to do a circuit around Big Bath, sticking as close to the shoreline as possible, then head back to Shady Cove and make an early lunch—or a late one, depending upon how long their trek took them. Maybe they would even take a row on the lake, if Sylvia was up for it. She seemed in good spirits. They had only been away from Concord for a few short hours, and already it was as if they had left much of their misery behind. The immense weight from before was gone. At the very least, it had lightened.

Coming to Gilchrist had been a gamble, a last-ditch effort to extricate themselves from the rut their lives had fallen into, and in Peter's opinion, it was working. Since the first moment he had driven into town, something had told him this was where they needed to be.

They were only ten minutes into their walk when the boy in the red fire-truck pajamas came running out of the woods and into the road, tears and snot soaking his terrified and confused face. He was drenched with sweat, his hair matted.

He paused in the road, looking around wildly. He spotted the Martells and ran to them. His bare feet were black with dirt.

Peter glanced at Sylvia, his brow gathering a mix of worry and bewilderment. Before he could say anything to her, the boy reached him. Peter dropped to one knee and held him by the shoulders. The kid was trembling, and his lips were blue. He was ice cold. When Peter laid his hands on the kid, he had a brief sensation of touching something charged with the cleanest, whitest electricity—something pure. But the sensation went away as quickly as it had come.

"Hey, buddy, you okay? You lost?" Peter asked.

"I wuh-wuh-want m-my mm-uh-mommy." His words were punctuated by thick sobs. Spittle stretched between his lips. Small bubbles of snot bloomed and popped from his nostrils.

Sylvia leaned down, hands clasped between her knees. "Do you live around here?" she asked, her voice taking on a maternal sweetness that Peter had not realized until that moment he missed so badly.

The boy looked at her, blinking. He immediately seemed more at ease when she spoke. "I don't know," he said, and wiped an arm under his nose. "I think so."

"Okay. Let's start with something easier," Sylvia said. "What's your name?"

Peter watched his wife. There was a sympathetic yet confident look on her face. At once, he was filled with sadness. He had forgotten what a wonderful mother Sylvia had been... and would've been. How caring. The feeling overwhelmed him.

"Kevin," the boy said.

"Kevin?" Sylvia repeated back to him. "Okay, now we're getting somewhere. I like that name. Kevin what?"

"Duh-Dooley," he said with a thin sniffle. Then, as if repeating something he had practiced before, he followed it up with: "I live at three-three-three Mishell Road in Gilchrist, Massachooketts."

"Okay, sweetie, that's good. Do you live with your mommy there?"

Kevin, scratching the corner of his eye with a finger, nodded.

"I'm sure she's worried sick about you. Do you think you can—?"

A squirrel scurried up a tree in the woods beside them. Kevin whipped his head around, terror seizing his body. Peter, hands still on his shoulders, felt every muscle in the boy stiffen. He looked at Sylvia, concerned. Her face returned the worry. What the hell had scared this kid so thoroughly? What had he been running from?

"Hey, look at me. It's okay. It's just a little squirrel. It can't hurt you," Sylvia said, bringing Kevin's attention back to her. "What are you scared of? There's nothing out here that can hurt you. You're safe."

Peter, seeing that his wife had the situation well under control, took his hands off the boy and stood. "The number for the police is back at the house. Let's head back there. I'll give them a call. It's a small town. I'm sure they know his parents."

Kevin looked at Peter curiously, then to Sylvia as if checking with her.

"You'll be okay," she said. "Want me to carry you? You look tired."

Kevin nodded. "My feet hurt. I didn't want it to get me."

"That was very brave of you," she said, leaning down and picking him up.

He wrapped his arms and legs around her, resting his head on her shoulder.

"All right, let's go. We'll go call your mommy." She sniffed the boy's hair. "Are you camping with your family?"

"N-No."

"You smell like smoke. Was there a fire somewhere in the woods?"

He nodded. "It was a cold fire."

"A cold fire? Okay."

"Maybe someone is burning brush," Peter said. "I've been smelling smoke since we got here."

"I know, me too."

They were about to head back to Shady Cove when Peter saw the bottom of the kid's feet. "Jesus, Syl, look at his feet."

"I can't see. What's the matter with them?" she said.

"I didn't want it to get me," Kevin repeated again, his voice a tired whisper.

"He's bleeding," Peter said. "I think he must've stepped on something."

But it was more than that. They were bloody and raw. And they weren't cut. They looked blistered and worn—as if the boy had been running for a very long time.

Chapter Seven

FIRE

1

When Corbin arrived at the Mayers' farm, Elhouse was walking toward his barn. The old man was carrying a gas can in each hand, headed toward his house. He was moving along at a healthy pace for his age, too. Corbin shut off the engine and stepped out. In the distance, Elhouse's wisps of white hair looked like a nest of smoke settling atop his head. When he spotted the police cruiser, he stopped and put down the cans, using his hand as a visor to get a better look.

Corbin stretched, hitched up his holster, and waved at Elhouse. He didn't wave back. He just stood there and stared, one arm hanging at his side. That tickled Corbin the wrong way. The two knew each other well enough. They weren't close friends or anything like that, but they weren't strangers, either. They had shared more than a few beers down at Dale's, talking about this and that.

"How goes it? Hot enough for ya?" Corbin said, a low shout across the hundred feet or so of field that separated them.

"Sorry to just drop in on you like this. I wanted to ask you a couple questions, if I could. Had a car accident a couple miles up the road last night. Any chance you heard something…" He realized Elhouse probably couldn't hear him anyway.

Elhouse just stood there, hand curved over his eyes. Corbin wasn't sure why he thought so, but he had the idea Elhouse was agitated. He was standing still, yet somehow the old man seemed to be twitching all over, almost as if he were emitting some kind of dark radiation—fine black filaments that floated on the air, expanding endlessly outward, an extension of his body. He couldn't see them, but he could feel them and knew they were there. A cold dread tightened his chest.

Corbin started toward him, but then the radio in his car hissed, and Dave Blatten's voice came through panicked and fuzzy: "Chief, you on yet? I got a real mess over here at the Saltzman house."

Corbin stopped, held up a finger to Elhouse, then doubled back to his car.

He reached in through the window and answered the call. "Yeah, Dave, I'm here. Any chance this can wait? I'm smack in the middle of something."

"Leo Saltzman ain't no longer with us, Chief."

"Jesus," he said, his finger off the call button. He looked around for a moment, wiped the back of his hand across his forehead, then responded. "He's dead?"

"As a doornail."

"You sure?"

"Yeah… yeah, I'm sure, boss."

"Well, what the hell happened?"

"Had himself a bit of an accident in his garage, I guess."

"You gotta give me more than that," Corbin said, irritated. "What kind of accident we talkin?"

"The goddamn idiot…" Dave must've heard himself or remembered he was addressing a superior. He started again. "Poor fella went face-first into his lathe. Not much left of his face. I figure he tripped… or maybe his tie got caught. I don't know. He used to make them pens, remember?"

"Is his wife there?"

"Who do you think found him?"

"Christ. All right, I'll be there shortly. Find something to cover the body. There's gotta be a tarp around there some… where…" He took his finger off the call button. "Holy hell." It was a whisper of horror and shock.

In the distance, Elhouse raised a gas can over his head and doused himself. Corbin saw it happen, but he didn't understand it right away. For a moment he thought maybe they were cans of water, not gasoline, and that the old man was hot and trying to cool off. But even that didn't make sense; it was just his brain trying to align with some sane explanation. Corbin felt the blood in his face drain away as what he was witnessing registered.

Elhouse dropped the can, then turned and walked across his yard and into the barn. Corbin caught a whiff of the gasoline as it carried upwind.

"Oh my God." He started after him, dropping the radio.

When Corbin reached the barn, Elhouse was standing in front of his hay baler, holding a box of matches. He had one pinched between his thumb and forefinger, poised on the strike strip.

"Get out of here, Corbin," he said.

"Tell me what's going on." The gas fumes in the barn were so strong, they made Corbin's nose burn.

"I know why we're all here," Elhouse said, his lower lip trembling, eyes unblinking. "It's worse than you can imagine."

"I don't understand what you mean, Elhouse. You're makin me awfully nervous with them matches. Why don't you put em down? Think you can do that for me?"

"It made me hurt my Gertie," Elhouse said. "God forgive me." He clenched his jaw and groaned, and for a split second Corbin could've sworn the old man's eyes shifted from blue to green and then back again. If he was imagining this, it was one hell of a vivid hallucination.

"What happened to Gertie?" Corbin said. "Where is she? Is she in the house? Dammit, Elhouse, what's going on? Talk to me. I don't understand."

"You *will* understand. Everyone will. It harvests what it sows. Can't you feel it everywhere… watching? Right around you, all the time? It's been here all along."

Corbin took another step forward, hands up, showing his palms. "Please, Elhouse, you don't have to do this. Where's your wife? You say you hurt her?"

"It wasn't me—you have to believe that. I wouldn't hurt her." Elhouse finally closed his eyes. "I'm sorry, I'm not strong enough. It wants more." Two giant tears gathered along the seams of his eyelids and broke free, streaking down his cheeks.

Corbin took another step closer to Elhouse, hand creeping back toward his gun. He was ten paces away. If he could get a shot off and hit Elhouse's arm, he would take it. "Now just wait a—"

Elhouse struck the match. There was a small spark, then a soft *whoomp*, and he went up in flames and began to scream.

"Elhouse, you goddamn lunatic!" Corbin looked around frantically, searching for something—anything. Behind him, parked outside the barn doors, was Elhouse's pickup. The tailgate was down. In the back, he spotted a heavy canvas tarp. He ran and grabbed it.

He spread the tarp open as he charged toward Elhouse, catching him in it like a net and wrapping him up. Flames licked up from his back and shoulders. The sour smell of burnt hair and flesh was overwhelming. An awful smell. His arms burned. He wrestled Elhouse up against a wall of stacked hay bales. They caught fire in an instant. Then, together, Corbin and Elhouse fell to the ground, Corbin on top of Elhouse. He started beating out the flames, tucking the tarp tightly around Elhouse to choke off the fire. Thick yellowish smoke billowed up, stinging his eyes. The smell and the taste made him want to throw up.

After about twenty seconds or so, Corbin pulled the tarp back. The flames had gone out, but the damage had been done. Elhouse's white hair was singed down to a bald and blistered pink scalp. His head was moving from side to side, eyes wide open. But that might've been because his eyelids had melted off. His ears certainly had. Where they had once been were two waxy lumps with small holes in them. His arms looked like two pieces of raw rolled beef. His chest pumped up and down in small, rapid breaths. He wasn't dead yet, but he would be soon if he didn't get to a hospital.

Corbin looked up. The stacks of hay were burning steadily. The flames had already reached the barn's crossbeams. He tried to slide his arms underneath Elhouse to pick him up, but he was hot to the touch and too slick with loose, burnt flesh that wanted to slide away like cooked chicken skin. Instead, he took Elhouse by the ankles, where the fire had hardly touched him, and dragged him out of the barn. The old man moaned incoherently the whole way out, gaped eyes rolling around like wild doll eyes.

Corbin dragged him until they were thirty feet clear of the barn. Then he hurried back to the car radio to call for help.

The whole time he ran, the old man's voice repeated in his head. The words flashed red and white, shrieking and blaring like a warning siren: *It made me hurt my Gertie… It made me hurt my Gertie.*

Corbin was afraid to know what Elhouse had done to her.

2

He had seen dead bodies before, but he had never seen some-one die. Later he would think that death happens fast. He would come to believe that this was one of the most terrifying things to understand about being alive.

Elhouse's breathing had slowed to a shallow whine by the time Corbin returned. The old man's burned hands were resting on his stomach, trembling. His fingernails were the cracked yellowish-brown of burnt biscuits.

"Just hold still," Corbin said. "We'll get you some help. Hang on. Can you still hear me? Nod if you can. Don't try to speak."

Elhouse's body radiated heat, like a hot hearthstone. Patches of cartilage were exposed on his nose. And the smell. God, that smell. It was the scent of something that shouldn't burn.

Elhouse's eyes seemed to search the air until they found Corbin's. Something like a dry croak tried to make its way out of his throat. All the while, the siren kept screaming in his head: *It made me hurt my Gertie… It made me hurt my Gertie.*

"It's okay. Don't speak. Just hang on now," Corbin said.

It looked like Elhouse tried to blink, but without eyelids his brow simply furrowed, and he swallowed with a loud, thick gulp. Corbin kept thinking that those sick green eyes were going to return at any moment and somehow swallow him up, but they never did. Elhouse reached up and wrapped his blistered hand around Corbin's wrist. It was a hot grip. He attempted to pull him down close, then said something unintelligible.

"Don't try to speak. Help is coming, you crazy bastard."

Swimming eyes stared up at him like giant tide pools. They were pleading. Elhouse pulled harder, his lips moving wordlessly as he tried to speak.

Corbin bent down.

"*Please... help... her,*" Elhouse said in a pained whisper. Then he let go and started coughing. After a few high, dry wheezes, what looked like a small lungful of black smoke came out of him. The smoke seemed to shimmer, as if its edges were crawling with fine blue webs of electricity. It drifted up, then broke apart in the air and disappeared.

Elhouse dropped his head back against the grass and lost consciousness. Corbin pressed his fingers to the man's neck to search for a pulse, but he couldn't find one. It was hard to tell through the thickness of burned flesh, but he knew Elhouse was gone. He knelt there a moment in shock.

It didn't last long. Things were happening fast around him. His gaze shifted to the front door of the house.

It made me hurt my Gertie.

He rose to his feet and ran toward the house. A slow jog was the best his knees would allow. When he reached the front porch, he pulled his gun. He didn't know what he would find in there, but given what he had just witnessed, it couldn't be anything good. There was a dangerous edge in the air. The entire place felt sick with it.

A loud crash exploded from the barn, startling Corbin. He glanced back over his shoulder. A section of roof had collapsed.

The thing must've been as dry as a bone to go up that quickly. A gust of smoke and sparks burst out of the double barn doors, curling upward once they cleared the doorway.

He went up the steps. The front door was open a crack. There was fresh blood on the jamb and the latch. A smudged handprint. A long smear on the porch, too.

"Gertie, you in there?"

No answer.

Louder, he called out, "Gertie, it's Chief Delancey... it's Corbin. I'm coming in, is that okay?"

The only sound was the crack and pop of the flames behind him. Then in the distance, he could make out the fire-truck sirens approaching.

He opened the door with his foot and stepped inside. The house was cool and dark. The shades were all drawn. Curtains closed.

His eyes adjusted quickly. He picked up a trail of blood on the carpet and followed it upstairs to the second floor, gun leading the way. He didn't know what he should be cautious of exactly, but he had a sense that there was reason not to charge ahead carelessly.

More blood had smeared the second-story hallway floor. Corbin could smell it in the stuffy upstairs air. Metallic. Sharp.

There were five doors in the long hallway. All were open except for the one at the back left. That's where he was heading; it was the one with blood on it.

His heart was starting to thump harder, faster. He didn't know what was waiting for him. Between the nearly decapitated body of Danny Metzger and watching someone he had known his whole life set himself on fire for God knew what reason, he couldn't be sure what to expect next. Whatever it was, the idea of it turned his stomach.

Bad things come in threes, he thought. *First the car accident last night, then Elhouse, now whatever this is about to be.*

He found a little morbid hope when he recalled the radio call he had taken from Dave Blatten about Leo Saltzman. Maybe that was the third thing. Maybe he would get lucky and open that door at the end of the hallway, and there Gertie would be, sleeping. Taking a nap. The blood? Oh right, that. Well maybe Elhouse had cut himself.

None of these hopeless ideas really counted for much. He didn't even begin to believe any of them. Because bad things didn't just come in threes; they came in ones, twos, threes, fours, and all the way up to infinity.

Corbin stopped outside the closed door and tried the knob. It was locked. He was about to call Gertie's name again when he heard an unmistakable sound come from behind the door. It reminded him of when he used to go hunting with his father. Two soft clicks.

A deafening blast ripped through the door, leaving a hole the size of a grapefruit. Corbin dropped into a crouch. The wall opposite the doorway was pocked with buckshot.

"Jesus H. Christ!" Corbin backed away from the door, but kept his gun trained on it. "Gertie, that you in there? It's Chief Delancey. What's going on?"

There was a short pause. Then a weak voice: "Corbin?"

"Yeah, it's me, Gert. Any chance I can convince you to drop that gun and step out into the hall?"

There was a thud followed by a strained groan. "I... I don't think I can. I'm hurt."

Corbin looked at the hole in the door, then at the holes in the opposite wall. "Help's already on its way. Now, are you planning on taking my head off if I come in there? I gotta tell you, I don't feel like a load of buckshot to the face today."

"No," Gertie replied meekly. She didn't sound so good.

"All right, I'm gonna hold you to that."

Corbin spotted a small mirror hanging on the wall beside him. He lifted it off the hanger and went back to the door. He held it in front of the hole to see into the room.

Gertie was sitting on the floor, leaning against a radiator, one hand pressed against her belly. A double-barrel shotgun was lying on the floor next to her. The front of her white shirt was dark maroon with blood.

Corbin decided to take his chances. "Okay, I'm coming in. Hold tight."

He reached his arm through the hole in the door, found the lock latch, and opened the door.

Gertie's head was bent back against the radiator, eyes looking down her nose at him. She tried to offer a smile but winced instead. "Hi, Chief. Hope you aren't mad. I didn't know it was you. I thought you were… I thought… well…" She flattened her lips, eyes closing for a long blink.

"Let's have a look at you, okay?" Corbin dropped to one knee beside her. "Where're you hurt? There?" He gestured to her stomach.

Gertie's hand was resting over a spot on her lower abdomen that appeared to be the source of all the blood. It was pooled around her on the floor, too.

"I think it's pretty bad," she said. "I can't feel my legs… my hands, either. I could barely pull that trigger. If you'd come a few minutes later, I wouldn't need a new door."

"All right, keep pressure on it. We're going to get you to a hospital, you'll be okay." He didn't know if that was true or not. He had no clue how badly she'd been wounded.

He looked her over but didn't see any other bad wounds.

There was what looked like bruising on her neck, though.

"Where's Elhouse? Something isn't right with him," Gertie said. Her tone seemed regretful and sad, despite the fact that her husband was likely responsible for her injuries—and likely the person for whom that double blast of buckshot had been intended.

"I don't know," Corbin said.

"You don't know?" she replied sharply. Panic struck her face at once, and she started to try to push herself up.

"Whoa, hold on, stay still."

"You don't understand. He's—"

"Gertie, take it easy. He's outside."

"Is he…?"

Corbin nodded. He looked at her, then away. "I'm sorry."

Her lower lip trembled, and her eyes swelled with tears, but she never cried. "I don't understand what got into him," she said, speaking to no one.

Corbin didn't understand, either. He had roughly a hundred questions he wanted to ask her, but it wasn't the time.

With another crash, a large section of barn collapsed. Corbin rose to his feet and looked. The flames were licking the sky, sending twists of smoke and sparks into the blue.

"What was that?" Gertie asked.

"The barn's on fire," Corbin said, never taking his eyes off the hypnotic blaze.

Gertie sighed.

Through the window behind her, Corbin saw the first fire truck turn down the long dirt driveway and head toward the burning barn. Thirty seconds later, Buck Ryerson drove up in the ambulance with Hank Barrett riding alongside him in the passenger's seat.

Chapter Eight

"YOU'RE LIKE ME"

1

Kevin Dooley sat on the edge of the kitchen counter at Shady Cove, drinking a mug of hot chocolate while Peter finished talking to the police on the telephone.

"Yep… Uh-huh… Kevin Dooley, he said… My wife's with him now. He's a little shaken up, some cuts on his feet… That's right—Mishell Road… I can ask him again if… Oh, okay, probably Mitchell, then… Oh, you do… Of course, I'm sure she's worried sick… It's Peter Martell… Yep, Martell, M-a-r-t-e-l-l…That's correct—Lakeman's Lane, number forty-four." Peter gave the phone number for the lake house and hung up.

Sylvia looked at him. "What'd they say?"

"They know his mother. They'll give her a call," he said, folding his arms.

"You hear that?" Sylvia said to Kevin. "Your mother's going to be here soon. The police will call her, and she'll come get you."

"Okay," Kevin said. "I hope she isn't mad at me."

"I'm sure she misses you like crazy, kiddo," she said. "I know I would."

A bitter thought followed, though: *What kind of mother doesn't know her child is running wild in the woods, wearing nothing but pajamas? I would never let that happen.* This thought was followed by a mean internal voice that cut like a knife: *No, you'd never let* that *happen. You'd just have him fall out a window while you drew him a bath.*

Her heart squeezed.

Peter, who had been standing silently with a look of contemplation stamped on his face, crossed the kitchen and took one of the stools at the counter. When he sat down, Kevin looked at him and giggled.

"What is it? Do I have something on my face?" Peter wiped a hand over his mouth playfully.

Kevin leaned toward him, slowly reached out his hand, and touched Peter's forehead with one finger. "You're like me," he said, and smiled.

"You mean handsome?" Peter glanced at Sylvia and smirked. "Apparently Mitchell Road is all the way on the other side of town, almost three miles away." Back to Kevin, he said, "How'd you get all the way over here, pal? That's quite a trip."

"I was playing esplorer," he said, and sipped his cocoa. "I found a new cave nobody's ever discovered before. But I had to run the whole time, though, because the monster was chasing me."

"Explorer? What's that?" Peter asked. "Were you playing it with your friends in the woods? Is that what happened?"

Kevin shook his head.

"What kind of monster was chasing you?" Sylvia asked.

Kevin shrugged. "I don't know, but it was big and had a bright face. Not like Mommy Monster."

Mommy Monster? Am I a Mommy Monster? A killer of children? Sylvia thought.

"Well, there're no monsters here." She looked at Peter. "Did we bring any first-aid supplies?"

"Yeah, I brought a few things. I put them in the bathroom." He pushed back from the stool. "I'll be right back."

Peter left the kitchen. Sylvia heard drawers opening. The medicine cabinet closing. Rummaging.

"How's that cocoa taste, kiddo? You like it?" she asked, leaning on the counter, her chin cupped in her palm.

Kevin nodded.

"You want some more marshmallows? They're my favorite." She popped one in her mouth and smiled.

Kevin nodded again, his face brightening a little.

She dropped in two more marshmallows before grabbing one of the chairs from the kitchen table behind her and taking a seat so that she could get a better view of his injuries. "Okay, I just want to have a look at your feet. We don't want to let them get infected. Is it all right if I take a peek? I used to be a candy striper."

"Candy stiper?" Kevin repeated.

"That's right. A candy *stri*per. It's like a nurse," she said as she took one of his heels in her palm and lifted his leg gently to get a look at the bottom of his foot. "So don't worry, you're in good hands. This won't hurt a bit. I'll just clean them off a little. Sound good?"

"Okay," he said.

She turned Kevin's foot over in her hand a few times, inspecting it. There was a fair amount of dirt and dried blood, as well as a strange black substance. She ran her finger along the side of the boy's foot, just above the arch. Something sappy, almost like tar, transferred off. She rubbed it between her fingers. It stunk, burning the back of her throat and nostrils like a whiff of acetone. It was a bitter, rotten smell. Damp smoke and putrefying organic matter.

Peter returned, his arms full of the first-aid supplies he had brought from the medicine cabinet at home and put in Shady Cove's bathroom. There were some Band-Aids. A wrinkled aluminum tube of bacitracin. Rubbing alcohol. Iodine. Gauze. Scissors. It looked as though he didn't know what to grab, so to be safe he had brought everything.

"This will have to do." He dropped the supplies on the counter. "It's all we have."

"Peter, can you get me a small bowl of warm water and a dish towel?"

He stood there with his hands on his hips, staring vaguely around the kitchen. He looked, Sylvia thought, rather handsome. It was a strange thing to consider given the circumstance, but she thought it just the same. And it had been a while since she had thought that about her husband. Well, that wasn't true. She had always thought Peter was handsome, but this was the first time since Noah died that she found herself attracted to him romantically. They'd had sex since their son died— it was part of the job when it came to trying for a second child—but there had never been anything particularly enjoyable about it. The physical contact was necessity, not sex. Not for her, anyway. And she assumed the same for her husband.

"Peter?" she repeated.

"Yeah," he said, and seemed to snap to. "Oh right, water and a towel. Got it." He went to the cabinet beside the sink, found a small soup bowl, and filled it with warm water. Then he grabbed a towel hanging on the oven handle and handed it to his wife. She took it, and Peter set the bowl down on the kitchen table next to her.

The phone was ringing.

"Mommy," Kevin said, as he sipped his hot chocolate. He never even looked up.

2

Kevin's mother arrived at Shady Cove less than twenty minutes after Peter hung up the phone with her. Sylvia could see her through the window. Dressed in a dingy bathrobe and slippers, she came shuffling down the path, a worried expression cramping an otherwise pretty but tired face. It was a mother's exhaustion. It was a mother's fear.

Sylvia headed to the door to meet her, while Peter played Go Fish with Kevin at the kitchen counter. He had given the boy his Red Sox hat to wear, and too big for him, it hung low over his eyes. He peered out beneath the brim, fanning through his hand of cards.

It was funny, she thought as she glimpsed the moment, how quickly the boy had gone from a terrified state to calm and carefree. Kids were good at letting go of painful emotions, she supposed. At that age, the emotion filter of the human mind is new and clean. No clogs. Feelings pass through and get hung up on nothing.

"Your mother's here," Sylvia said as she went past and turned down the short hallway.

Both her husband and the boy were so absorbed in their card game that neither seemed to hear her. "You got any tens?" Peter asked. "Nope. Go fish," Kevin answered.

Before she could reach the screen slammer, Sylvia saw the boy's mother opening the door. The two made eye contact, and the woman let go of the handle, looking apologetic.

"Hi—hello. I'm Laura Dooley, I just spoke with—I'm sorry, I don't mean to be rude, but is my son here? The man I talked to said forty-four Lakeman's Lane. That's this house, right? The sign on the tree back there..." She looked over her shoulder, then back to Sylvia.

"No need to apologize. That was my husband you spoke with on the phone. Come in, please." Sylvia pushed the door ajar, and Laura took it the rest of the way and came in. "Kevin's in the kitchen, walloping Peter at a game of Go Fish. He's perfectly okay."

"Thank you," Laura said.

Sylvia regarded the woman. Her eyes were puffy and red. She had been crying, and she seemed nervous. Maybe more than that, though: she looked scared.

The moment they entered the kitchen, Laura burst into tears at the sight of her son. It seemed to be a combination of sadness, relief, anger, and pure elation coming forth all at once.

Kevin looked up from his cards and dropped them on the counter. His arms went out to her. "Mommy!" he shouted, with a huge smile.

"Kevin, I've been so worried." She went to him and wrapped her arms around him. For a moment they were one. A big flowing mass of bathrobe and pajamas embracing. And when the initial reunion faded, she held him off her hip with one arm, lifting his new hat and checking all around his head for signs of injury. "Are you okay? Where did you go? You just disappeared. You were in the bed and then..."

"I found a secret cave, Mommy. It's so big. The biggest ever."

"Yeah? A secret cave?" She kissed the side of his cheek. "And where was this cave, explorer man?"

"The whole place, Mommy. Everywhere."

"The whole place?"

He nodded.

"Okay, sweetie, everything's all right now." Laura pressed her son's head against her chest and held him, her hand loosely covering his ear. She looked at Sylvia and Peter, who had moved together and were standing on one side of the counter. "I don't know what happened. I have no idea how he snuck away without me seeing. It was like he vanished. One second he was right there on the bed. The next… Where'd you say you found him?"

"He came out of the woods about a quarter mile up the road, I'd guess. Not far from here at all," Peter said, taking his hands out of his pockets and gesturing toward Lakeman's Lane at the top of the hill.

"I don't understand. Where did you go, little guy? And why do you smell like smoke?" She rested her face against her son's head, took a long breath in. Kevin was asleep. "Don't ever do that again, okay?" she whispered into the side of the Red Sox cap, and kissed him as she slowly rocked from side to side.

"He must be one heck of a runner. He covered quite a distance. Especially impressive, considering he was barefoot," Peter said. "His feet are a little worse for wear, but nothing a tough little guy like him can't handle. Sylvia patched him up."

Sylvia pointed to Kevin's gauze-wrapped feet. "I cleaned his feet a little and put some bacitracin on the worst of it. There was nothing but a few small scratches and blisters." Sylvia paused. "I hope that was okay. I didn't want anything to get infected, and I wasn't sure how fast this would get sorted out."

Laura was staring into the living room behind them, eyebrows pushed together, still turning something over in her head. "I'm sorry, my nerves are a mess right now. I can't focus," she said. "Thank you, really. You have no idea how grateful I am you found him. I'm just trying to replay what might've happened." She let out a humorless laugh. "Goodness, you must think I'm just about the worst mother in the world. I swear this has never happened before."

Sylvia suddenly found herself feeling guilty for her earlier thoughts about what kind of mother Laura must be. Sometimes accidents just happened. She, of all people, should understand that. The woman seemed genuinely terrified—and, likely, her imagination was showing her what *could* have happened if things had taken a worse turn.

Sylvia felt a swell of Noah grief try to rise up in her, but as it had been happening since she arrived in Gilchrist, it didn't break the surface. Instead it subsided, leaving behind only a strange warm buzz. It was a lot like her pills, but better. Cleaner.

My pills, she thought. *I really don't miss them at all.*

"Nonsense," she said. "These things happen."

"I appreciate that." Laura's eyes seemed to sharpen and clarify—normal order being restored to her life by slow degrees. "Listen, I can say thank you until the cows come home, but those are just words. On the phone, Peter mentioned you're renting this place. Is that right?"

"For the next few weeks, yes."

"Well, since you're new in town, I'd like to officially invite you both over for dinner. It's the least I could do. Consider it a welcoming gesture from our humble little Gilchrist, and a show of my appreciation."

"Oh," Sylvia said, her hand touching her chest, surprised. She looked at her husband.

He shrugged, a look that said: *I don't see why not?*

"I won't be offended if you say no, but I'd be happy to repay you both with a home-cooked meal. I'm sure he'd love it, too." She used her chin to point to her son. "I make a pretty good meatloaf. If you're undecided, think of it this way—you get to avoid a mess of dishes for an evening, and I get to clear my conscience. It's a win for all of us." She offered a sincere smile.

Now Sylvia saw that Laura wasn't just pretty; she was quite young, as well. Perhaps only in her early twenties, and with a six-year-old child. She wondered if there was a Mr. Dooley. She didn't see a ring, however, so she thought perhaps not.

"We'd be delighted," Sylvia said. "That's very nice of you."

"Great. How does tomorrow night sound? Unless, of course, that's too short notice. I'd completely understand if it was."

"It's perfectly fine," Sylvia said. "We got here a few hours ago, so it's not like we've made any plans. A home-cooked meal sounds great. What time should we be there?"

"Six o'clock?" Laura said, sounding unsure. "And nothing fancy. Wear something comfortable."

"Six is perfect." Sylvia found herself enjoying the idea of a casual meal with someone who, at first impression, seemed so very different from the kind of people she and Peter had spent the last five years of their life around. It was refreshing. She couldn't remember the last time an invitation to dinner hadn't come with the additional pressure of trying to impress someone, rather than simply enjoying the evening.

After plans had been made for the evening and directions to her house confirmed, the three of them moseyed to the front door of Shady Cove. Laura kept repeating how she couldn't understand how Kevin had disappeared to begin with. Sylvia had a pretty good idea about what had transpired, though:

Laura had most likely been dawdling around the house with chores—as people often do on Sunday mornings—splitting her time between that and entertaining her son. She probably played with him for a few minutes, went back to doing something else, and when she finally returned, Kevin was gone. Chances were he had slipped out of the house and gone exploring in the woods, eventually getting lost. Then maybe something spooked him, and he panicked and took off running. He didn't stop until he came out on Lakeman's Lane.

They were standing on the front porch.

"It's been nice meeting you both," Laura said. "I'm sorry it had to be under the circumstance it was. I'll bet half the town will have something to say about this once word gets around… and believe me, it will get around. That's one thing you can count on in Gilchrist—secrets don't stay secrets for very long."

"Well, they won't hear anything from either of us," Sylvia said, pretending to zip her lips.

Peter had his hands in the pockets of his jeans, starting to look bored. "Don't mention it. Nothing like a little adventure to spice things up. And as long as your meatloaf is as good as you promised, we'll hold off on sending you a bill for our services," he said, joking.

"Hopefully I haven't oversold it." Laura smiled, and looked down at her son. "I almost forgot, can I assume this is yours?" She took the hat off Kevin and tried to hand it to Peter, but he refused.

"It's his now," he said, "I gave it to him. I have about six more just like it at home."

Kevin's eyes were blinking. They opened. He squinted in the bright sun, looking confused. Laura set the hat back atop his head.

"Do you want to say goodbye to Peter and Sylvia? Maybe say thank you?" she asked him. "They're going to be coming over for dinner tomorrow. Doesn't that sound like fun?"

Kevin nodded, rubbing an eye with his little fist. "Thank you," he said groggily to Peter.

"My pleasure, sport. Take care of this, all right. It's one of my favorites." He tapped the brim of the hat. "We'll have to do a rematch of Go Fish sometime. Maybe tomorrow if your mom says that's okay."

"I could make an exception," she said. "Even though you nearly gave me a heart attack."

Kevin smiled, but he was fading quickly. He looked tuckered out.

"Hope your feet feel better, wild guy," Sylvia said. "No more exploring the woods without your—" But before she could finish the sentence, he stuck out both arms. At that, something familiar and pleasant rippled through her. Her eyebrows shot up, and her jaw slackened. She was caught flatfooted by both the gesture and the feeling.

"Somebody wants to give a hug," Laura said, teasing. Then to Sylvia, she added, "He must really like you. He's usually a little shy with goodbyes. I think you might have a new secret admirer."

Sylvia leaned in and let the boy wrap his arms around her neck. He still smelled of smoke and something else unpleasant. His little nose, the tip of it icy cold, pressed against the top of her ear as he squeezed her tightly.

His breath tickled as he whispered to her. Then it was over. Kevin let go, pulled back, and gave her a comforting little smile as he sat perched on his mother's hip. "Thank you," he said, and rested his head back against his mother's chest as he closed his eyes.

"You're welcome," she responded, rather late. She was trying to mask her trembling voice.

Later, this entire fifteen-second exchange would be reduced to something that felt more like a dream than an actual occurrence. But here, in this moment, it was crystal clear. And it was real.

By the time Sylvia regained her presence of mind, Laura was already walking back up the path to her car with Kevin in her arms. The driver-side door was still open and the engine idling. She had never shut it off.

Sylvia watched them leave, and as they drove away she became aware of a fading sensation—a connection to the boy. It was as if they had been briefly bonded together and were being peeled apart. And in the yawning rift, the words he had whispered in her ear hung suspended like a dying breath in the dark. Smoke letters floating in a sea of black.

3

"You don't look so good. Are you okay?" Peter asked when they returned inside.

"Give me a second." Sylvia went to the sink and got herself a glass of water.

"What happened to you at the end there? You hugged the kid and then looked like you were about to pass out," Peter said.

He was watching her as she sipped the water, one hand anchoring her to the counter. She could smell her breath mixed with the water in the mug. A cold, pondlike smell.

She closed her eyes. Her body hummed with electricity.

The boy's words were still echoing in her head. She needed a moment to process. Had she imagined it? Was it some sort of psychotic break? After all, she had tried to take her own life just two days before. *Yes, let's consider that for a moment, shall we.* Without any motivation that she could recall, she had swallowed her entire bottle of tranquilizers. She had little memory of the whole thing, only a vague sense that she had been compelled to do it.

She opened her eyes, looking into dead space above the sink. "Did you mention Noah to him?" she asked, turning to him.

Peter looked smacked by confusion. "What? To who?"

"To Kevin. Did you tell him about Noah, or say his name at any point?"

"No. Why would I?"

"Are you sure?"

"Yes, I'm sure. I'm positive," he said.

Sylvia tilted her head and cocked a doubtful eyebrow at him.

"What? I swear I didn't. That would be a little strange, don't you think? Telling a six-year-old about our dead son?" He laughed nervously. Then, sobering, he said, "I don't understand. Why're you even asking me this?"

"This will sound absolutely mad, I know, but when he hugged me goodbye just then, he whispered something to me." Sylvia hesitated on the punch line. "He told me he was sorry about Noah."

"What?"

"That's what he said to me."

Peter stood expressionless for a beat. A long beat. She expected a derisive laugh to come from her husband at any moment, but she got nothing like that, to her surprise.

He pulled a chair out and sat down at the table. It looked like a vital cord that had been holding him together at the seams had been pulled from his core stitching. He rested forward and clasped his hands.

"Are you going to say anything?" She sat down opposite him at the table, trying to find his eyes.

He lifted his gaze to her. "What you're saying doesn't make any sense," he said. "It's impossible, Sylvia. How the hell would a kid know that about us?"

"I don't know. But he did. He did know it. I could feel it." She reached her hand across the table and rested it on his forearm. It was tight. "I know you think I'm losing it—that I'm depressed or something—but I'm telling you what that boy said. I'm certain of it."

"Certain of what you *heard*, or what he *said*?" An accusatory edge bled into Peter's tone.

Sylvia withdrew from him, shaking her head. "Why on earth would I make something like this up? Of all people, I wouldn't expect you to be so skeptical."

"Now wait, hold on," Peter said. "I'm not saying he didn't say something to you—I'm sure he did—but maybe you misheard the words, that's all. You know what I mean?"

"I'm not mistaken. I know what he said, it was crystal clear."

Peter rubbed his hands over his face. "Okay. Okay. Let me start over... I believe you. I don't understand it, but I believe you. I'm sorry."

Sylvia was caught off guard. "You do?"

"Yes. If you tell me that's what he said, then I believe it."

Sylvia reached out and rested her hand on top of his. It was hot; his body always put out so much heat compared to her own. That was something she had always found oddly attractive about him. In bed on cold nights, she imagined Peter was her own little furnace keeping them both warm. She missed that feeling: skin against skin, him holding her, his arm draped across her chest, face pressed against the back of her head, toes tickling the bottoms of her feet.

"I'm not trying to convince you of something I've created in my head. I don't know how he knew it, or why I'm so sure he did." She hesitated, averting her gaze. "But I can understand how crazy I must sound. How silly it is."

"No, it's not silly," Peter said, and sighed. He assumed the look of a man who was about to unshoulder a burden of his own. "Can I tell you something?"

"Of course."

"I've had a feeling since I first came to this town. It's a little hard to explain. But it's like I've been here before. And I know I haven't been. I feel it so strongly, like I'm wandering through an old memory or something. I don't know." Peter scoffed at himself.

Sylvia laughed softly.

"What?" Peter said.

"You know, for a writer of make-believe stories, you sure do have a hard time with the fantastical."

"Am I missing something?" Peter asked.

Sylvia regarded her husband for a moment. She had never seen him look so vulnerable as he did right then. "Just because something doesn't make sense to you," she said, "doesn't mean it isn't real."

4

After nearly forty-five minutes of rearranging furniture to get things just right, Peter managed to turn the second bedroom of Shady Cove into a decent workspace. He was sitting at the small writing desk that had originally overlooked the backyard. He had moved it for his purposes, pushing it up against a windowless wall to avoid distraction. When he worked, he liked a dark room—all the shades drawn, all the doors shut, no music. Although since his son's death, he had made a minor adjustment to that routine and transitioned to keeping the door open. That had taken some getting used to. He had fought it at first, but the crippling case of anxiety that showed up every time he tried to close it finally made the decision much easier.

He was sitting in front of the Olivetti typewriter. It was his travel typewriter, and compared to the new IBM Selectric he had in his office back at home, it was an ancient machine, but it was reliable. Solid and steady. He had also used it to write his first two novels, so there was some sentimentality there, too.

He was chewing on the end of a red felt-tip pen as he read the last lines he had just written on the Olivetti:

Hilly turned her back on it all, the old question losing its shape against the new context of her life: Does God weep for the sinners, for the worst of them, for the ones who cannot be saved? Does God weep for any of us?

She wondered what it meant that she no longer cared to know the answers to these questions.

A decent end to a pivotal chapter, he thought. He leaned back, hands laced behind his head, and spoke to himself. "Not bad, but not great. You're trying a little too hard, Peter."

He would tighten it up on the next, and final, go-around. This was the fifth draft of a particularly fussy—but important— middle chapter that continued to feel clunky. He would go over it one more time, make his final tweaks, then type it fresh on the Olivetti again. If it still didn't sit right after that, then he would scrap it and come at it from a new angle from the ground up. Sometimes killing the tired thing and starting over with a new approach was best.

Isn't that what we're doing up here at a lake house—starting over? an internal voice suggested.

"Maybe," he answered himself aloud. "Or maybe trying a little too hard."

He took the page of copy from the typewriter and shuffled it together with the rest of the fifth draft of chapter fourteen of *Untitled Novel #3*. Normally he would let a fresh draft—whether it be a single paragraph or an entire chapter—sit for at least a day or two before attacking it with The Red Pen of Death as he liked to call it. But today he was feeling impatient and just wanted to get the scene finished so he could move on, or at the very least, accept that he would soon have to kill a darling. Understanding that invested time was in no way a valid excuse for saving a piece of writing that didn't work was perhaps one of the most valuable lessons he had ever learned. If it doesn't work, kill it. That didn't make it any easier, though. And it didn't mean he had to like it.

With his teeth, he uncapped the pen, turned it around, and reset it. Now it was armed.

He took a deep breath, trying to switch on his brain's more critical eye. The house was so quiet. He could hear the duck clock in the kitchen ticking away. The smack of his typewriter had sounded like an industrial invasion cracking the serenity of the lake with each key punch. The machine was resting now, though, and it was time to do the fine detail work by hand—the stitching and the trimming. But before he could get started on that...

He was supposed to keep a close eye on Sylvia while they were at the lake house. He didn't think that was quite as necessary as Dr. Zaeder had, not to the degree the doctor had suggested, anyway. She didn't need a babysitter. He didn't discount what had happened, but he also knew his wife, and she was perfectly okay so far as he could tell.

He leaned back in his chair, dipped his fingers underneath the shade, and lifted it. Sylvia was sitting in one of the Adirondack chairs in the backyard. She had changed into a thin pastel-yellow summer dress. She was drinking the iced tea she had made and reading a copy of *Catch-22*. It had been among the books on the bookshelf in the living room. It also happened to be one of her favorites.

Peter began to read chapter fourteen. Two lines in, he found his first typo. It was a real rookie spelling error: *definate* instead of *definite*. He went to strike a line through the misspelling, but the pen tip was bone dry.

"My luck," he said, scribbling it on a piece of scrap paper to get its blood flowing. Nothing. He licked it and tried again. Nothing.

He chucked the pen in the wastebasket beside the desk, then grabbed his briefcase to look for another. But before he even began to search, he had a clear recollection of the fresh pack of red Flairs he had bought from the drugstore the day before sitting on the dining room table back at his house. He had forgotten to pack them.

Flustered, Peter stood and pulled open the deep side drawer in the desk. It was packed with kitchen linens—placemats, tablecloths, and cloth napkins. He shut it with his foot, then tried the knee drawer. It opened a few inches and jammed. It felt full, wanting to sag forward. Through the narrow crack, he could see a messy nest of loose papers and other odds and ends. A junk drawer. Every house had one somewhere. Usually it was in a kitchen, but not always. He had just found Shady Cove's tucked away in an old writing desk in the back bedroom. Dollars to donuts, there was at least one pen in there somewhere. That would do for now; he could pick up more at the store later.

He hooked his fingers into the opening, sliding them along and trying to feel for whatever was causing the jam. After feeling nothing obstructing, he pushed the drawer back in and pulled it out again. It didn't work. He wasn't in the mood for this. He pulled a little harder, favoring force over finesse.

Something gave, and the entire drawer flew out of the desk, scattering its contents across the floor and around his feet. Right away he spotted at least two pens in the mix. One slid under the night table next to the little twin bed.

"Shit!"

Hard thumping started to pound at his temples. He wanted a drink.

Peter clenched his jaw, closed his eyes, and breathed. Opening his eyes, he put the now-empty drawer on the bed and knelt to gather everything that had fallen out. Junk drawer was right. And there was plenty of it. The paperclips would be the biggest pain in the ass.

And they were.

Ten minutes later, he had most of the junk back in its drawer. He had found three pens—two blue ballpoints and a red Flair felt-tip, just like his own. What were the odds?

He was finishing up the last of the cleanup when something caught his eye. The majority of the papers he was picking up off the floor and gathering together were blank. Some looked like old score tallies from one of the various board games in the living room. There were a few brochures for local attractions. An unsigned copy of the very same rental agreement he had signed. The owner's manual for the refrigerator. A Sears catalog. None of those mattered, though. What did, however, was the piece of high-quality bond paper. It was similar to the paper he used in his typewriter. In the top left corner of it, the initials DW were written in neat red handwriting. Next to the initials was a date: 3/1/62. And in the very top center, underlined, two words stood out in all capital red letters: GILCHRIST PROJECT. Dots connected: the red pen, the initials, the paper, the timeline. Declan Wade.

According to both Leo Saltzman and George "Don't-Call-Me-Georgie" Bateman, Declan had stayed in the house a few years back. Peter sat down at the desk and studied the paper. His hands were trembling with depraved excitement. It was a glimpse behind the scenes—a voyeuristic peek at a fellow writer's process.

He knew what he was looking at immediately, because he had scribbled out countless pages of his own that looked nearly identical in the same primordial way. They were early story notes for a book.

It was almost hard to believe they were the product of a supposed professional writer who sold millions of books to the masses. His own, he had to admit, probably never looked any more professional than DW's, though. One thing he had discovered was that there was no right or wrong way when it came to a writer's process. Just do what works.

5

The notes were on one side of the page, nothing on the back. Peter read through it three times, a feeling of unease growing in his chest as he saw the eerie parallels to his own current situation.

DW 3/1/62
GILCHRIST PROJECT

Haunted house? Been there, done that. Haunted town????
Haunted people??????? Better idea. We all have ghosts. Towns
have ghosts, secrets. Bloody roots.

Possible town name: Jackson Hill, Massachusetts. I wonder if
Shirley would notice or mind.

There is a "thinness" to the town, barrier breaking down,
something radiating through from another side. From where?
What caused it? Why here? This is the kind of place that can
get to you—that calls to you. A constant feeling of déjà vu. It
summons. Possible title?—It Summons or The Summons. Or
maybe just Jackson Hill. I don't care for any of these. Keep
trying, you'll get it.

What is it? A membrane between here and there. What's on
the other side. Can it be controlled or stopped? Is it just a dif-
ferent form of natural disaster? Something we simply haven't
seen before? Perhaps we haven't looked hard enough.

Could be a gishet. Remember Nana's stories? Do some research
on gishet. Death Harvester... now there is a title.

Possible plot line: A failing marriage saved, or destroyed, in
Jackson Hill. Catalyst for something else? Why is marriage
failing? What happened? How is town important (significant)
to them? Remember your dreams.

It's almost time for lunch. I think I'll make a couple hot dogs.

And that was all. A few story notes—a disorganized brainstorm, really—then, presumably, some thoughts on lunch. Hot dogs. But Peter was left feeling as though his flesh had just been shucked and he was sitting in the open air, raw nerves exposed.

"What's that?" Sylvia said, startling him.

Peter flinched, reeling around in the chair. "You almost gave me a heart attack. Jesus, Syl. I didn't hear you come in." He glanced back at the paper in his hand and put it facedown on the desk. "It's just some notes for a story idea I had."

He wasn't sure why he didn't tell her the truth.

"The way you were staring at it, you'd think you were reading your own obituary." She sat down on the bed and looked through the junk in the knee drawer Peter had yet to put back in the desk. She didn't really seem interested in it, though. It looked like a nervous distraction to disarm whatever it was that was hot on her mind.

"What's up?"

"Nothing's up. Just seeing how it's going in here." She had a curious, yet distracted, look on her face. "The story idea, is it something new you're working on?"

"Something old, actually," he lied. "Procrastinating, really."

"Not cheating, I hope," she said, smiling wryly at him.

"Huh?" He was taken aback for a moment, but then it hit him what she was referring to. "You remember that?"

It was something he had told her when they had first met. He had said how when he was working on a story, he had to stick with it until it was finished—a sort of literary monogamy. Only then would he turn his attention to other story ideas. To break this rule was akin to creative infidelity so far as he was concerned.

"Of course I remember." Sylvia squinted at something on the floor. She bent down to pick up a paperclip at her feet, then dropped it in the drawer. She wasn't wearing any shoes and had dry grass clippings on her toes. "What happened here?" she asked, gesturing to the drawer. "Looking for something?"

Peter turned sideways in the chair and draped his arm over the back, resting his chin on his shoulder. "The drawer jammed when I was looking for a pen. Don't know my own strength, I guess. I tried to get it unstuck, and the whole thing came flying out."

Sylvia laughed softly, then licked her lips. She slid back a little on the bed and tucked her hands under her thighs, letting her legs hang off the bed. She was staring at her swinging feet. It was a youthful, carefree look, one Peter hadn't seen on his wife since their first years together, before any of the bad stuff had infected them.

"How's the book? Good as the first time you read it?" Peter asked. "You looked peaceful out there by the water."

"You checking on me?" She looked up, took her hands from beneath her legs, and pushed some hair behind her ears. She gave him a cute little sideways smile.

"Admiring," he said, lying again. He *had* been checking on her, and he was pretty sure they both knew it.

Something odd was going on. Sylvia was giving off an air of unpredictability that made Peter a little uneasy.

"I like that better." She stood up and crossed the room. "It's nice out there. You should join me later. It's so stuffy in here."

"Maybe," Peter said, eyes tracking upward as Sylvia approached him. A sheen of sweat glistened across her chest, her cleavage. Her nipples, dark and small, peeked through the dress.

She stopped and stood in front of him, resting her hand on the back of his neck. "I'm bored."

He looked up at her, suddenly understanding why he felt that sensation of unease about her. There was an energy between them that he hadn't felt in a long time. It was both exciting and terrifying at the same time. A sense of something that should feel familiar feeling foreign and perhaps even a little dangerous.

"I have to run into town to get a couple things," he said. "Feel like taking a ride? I thought maybe when we got back we could make some lunch."

"Okay," she said, stepping one leg over his lap and coming around to face him. She gently positioned him so that he was sitting with his back squarely in the chair and she was straddling him. Her hands now resting on his shoulders, she leaned down and kissed him. Her tongue brushed the tip of his. She tasted like sweet tea.

When she pulled her head back and smiled, Peter could see down the front of her dress. Her breasts were small but perfectly shaped. His blood started to stir.

He was looking at her, a stupefied expression of surprise on his face. "Syl, are you sure you want—"

She pressed her finger against his lips and kissed him again before he could speak. As her lips slid over his, she took his hand and placed it on the inside of her thigh. She slid it farther up until Peter could feel her pubic hair brushing his knuckles. She wasn't wearing any underwear. He found her slick seam with his thumb.

Was she planning this? he wondered.

The answer didn't matter. She was unbuckling his belt. Fly unzipping. Hand reaching in. Taking him out. Their kissing became a war of tongues. She bit his lip. Heavy breathing building. She gripped him firmly, sliding her hand up and down his rock-hard erection.

She kissed his neck, then his ear. "I want you," she whispered.

He closed his eyes and buried his face in his wife's breasts, tasting her sweat. "Come up here." He slid his other hand behind her and squeezed. He pulled one of her breasts out and bit her nipple. It was salty. She moaned.

Sylvia let go of his penis, wrapped her arms around him, and sat down slowly until he was inside her. They were moving together, and the chair was scuffing the floor, its joints groaning and creaking. Then they were on the floor, rolling around, and scuffing themselves.

Eventually they took it to the bed, knocking the junk drawer onto the floor and spilling its contents for the second time.

6

Peter sat at the kitchen table, wearing nothing but his underpants, while Sylvia napped in the bed where he had left her. His body was buzzing with endorphins, but he had a headache. He popped two aspirin into his mouth and washed them down with orange juice as the phone receiver rang in his ear.

From the right angle, he could look across the hallway to the bedroom and see his wife's feet on the bed. It conjured up an unpleasant memory of when he had found her after she had taken too many pills. How he had only been able to see her legs through their partially open bedroom door at first.

"Yeah, hello." Tom Landau's voice came through on the phone.

Peter cleared his throat. "Tom, it's Peter."

"Hey, pal," Tom said cheerfully. "You miss me?"

Peter believed that everyone had at least one bad joke in their repertoire that they recycled too frequently—a sort of personal catchphrase. Tom's, when talking to Peter, had always been: *Did you miss me?* Even if he had been gone five minutes: *Did you miss me?* He wondered if Tom said it to his other clients, and supposed he probably did. He didn't care.

"Always, Tom. How's it going? I'm calling on a Sunday. That okay?"

Tom laughed. "Any time, day or night, is fine, Peter." He paused. "I have to be honest, I didn't think I was going to hear from you the entire time you were away. You make it to the place all right?"

"Syl and I just got here this morning."

"How's the lake? Nice? Hopefully you opted for a place with a good view."

"Beautiful. It's a great place with a great view," Peter said, watching his wife's feet slide down the bed as she stirred. "We're already making friends with the locals."

"That so?"

"Dinner invite tomorrow," Peter said, running his finger around the rim of his cup and flicking off tiny flecks of orange-juice pulp. "But listen, I need a favor."

"What's up?"

"I need you to work some magic for me," Peter said.

"Magic?"

"That's right."

"What kind of magic are we talking?" Tom asked. Peter could hear him light up a cigarette on the other end of the line. Then he heard the thin clatter of ice cubes in a glass.

A drink would be nice right about now, he thought, but gave the idea the slip before it could drag him down.

"The schmoozy kind. Agent magic. I want you to put me in touch with Declan Wade. Do you know him... or someone who does?"

"Do I know him?" Tom said. "I wouldn't be much of an agent if I didn't. Personally I don't really read his stuff—Joan does, from time to time—but the guy sells a lot of books, that's for sure. Why? What do you want with him?"

"Nothing important," Peter said. "Writer stuff."

"Is that all you're going to give me?"

"That's enough, isn't it?" Peter said.

"Should I be worried?"

"Not at all."

"Your breath reeks of bullshit, my friend."

"Then I'm speaking your language, aren't I?"

"Touché," Tom said. "I could make some calls and probably put you two in contact. It shouldn't be that hard. I won't be able to do anything today, but I'll see what I can do tomorrow."

"Good enough. Thanks, Tom."

"Yeah, yeah, that's my job." There was a brief pause. "But if someone asks what this is about, what should I tell them? 'Nothing important' might not be the best response to get results. Can you give me something? *Any*thing?"

Peter could tell Tom was just digging for info as to whether or not this was regarding a matter that would affect his bank account.

"Say it's regarding his Gilchrist Project."

"What the hell does that mean?"

"He'll understand." Peter said. "At least I think he will."

"All right. I'll see what I can do," Tom said.

Peter gave him the phone number to Shady Cove. The two said goodbye, and the conversation was over.

He stood and went back to the bedroom. It was perfect napping weather. A steady afternoon breeze had cooled the room to a comfortable temperature. Perhaps a front moving in. Distant boat sounds drifted in from across the lake. Wind chimes kissed lightly on the porch. Loose manuscript pages on the desk, held down by a box of paperclips, lifted and dropped with the wind.

Sylvia was sleeping in the nude and snoring softly. Her yellow dress was a pile on the floor, along with Peter's clothes. He lay down beside her and draped his arm across her chest, pulling her close. He fell asleep almost immediately.

But it was the thin, delirious sleep of a fever-struck mind.

7

Peter was in the woods. It was a mad but familiar place. Everything was burning. Bright colorful flowers grew out of cracked and swollen smoldering trees. But they weren't flowers at all. They moved. Quivered. Their fleshy petals puckered as if tasting the air. Despite the fire, the place was bitterly cold, and the air smelled of smoke and carrion decay. An icy mist permeated the atmosphere, tickling the tip of his nose as he moved through it. The sky was a low sea of churning black clouds. Silent bursts of red lightning strobed from the inner depths. It was a place of stored misery. He could feel the atmosphere pulling a charge from his heart, draining him slowly but steadily. And like a battery connected to a faulty circuit, if the connection wasn't soon severed, there would be nothing remaining but a dead cell.

But he wasn't ready to leave. There was something here that called to him.

Peter went toward a clearing up ahead. He was standing in the backyard of their house in Concord and looking at the back of their home in the near distance. Only, it wasn't exactly their home. It was a similar two-story shape, but there were elements of Shady Cove mixed in—a wrap-around porch that shouldn't exist and gray weathered shingles instead of the usual white lapboards. And surrounding the house like a castle moat were hundreds of massive orange tiger lilies, each ten feet tall, the flesh of which looked wet and membranous like all the other strange foliage that wasn't really foliage.

A narrow path ran through the tiger lilies and led to the house, where, as if waiting for him, there was a single rectangle of yellow light. Every other window was dark except for this one on the second floor.

You know what this place is.

He looked down at his hands and could see through them to the ground. Then he looked up at the house once more and immediately understood. It wasn't a matter of *what* he was seeing... it was *when* he was seeing. He knew this scene far too well. And he knew what came next. This was simply a new angle from which to watch the horror unfold.

A small figure was in the second-floor window. It was Noah, and he was banging on the screen, pressing his little weight against it. It wasn't going to hold. Peter started running toward him. He had to stop it. This time he had a chance to save his son. His lungs caught fire as he breathed in huge gulps of the sour air. He tried to scream his wife's name, but only a strange reverberated version of his voice came out, completely distorted. He had an idea that she needed to hear him, that if she did, it could change everything. He had to warn her of what was about to happen. Right now she would be in the bathroom, starting their son's tub time, and Peter himself would be in his office, writing with the door closed. One of them needed to know they had to save their son. *God, just go check on him. Please. He's about to...*

Noah kept knocking the screen with his tiny fists. It was all happening silently, but Peter could see that his son was giggling, having a blast, blissfully unaware of the tragedy he was headed toward.

Peter was passing through the tall tiger lilies, which whispered to him in unison as he ran by, but he couldn't make out the words. Then he could. It was a song. The flowers were singing "Can't Help Falling in Love" in a distorted version of his wife's voice. It sounded as if it were traveling down a long metal pipe. That was the song Sylvia always used to sing to Noah.

As he drew closer to the house, he saw something squatting on the roof like a gargoyle. It was a giant long-limbed creature with leathery skin and a shimmering face. Nothing of the earth that he knew. It wasn't moving. It was watching, a green glow emanating from its broad chest. The light throbbed like a heartbeat. And it was getting brighter and faster.

Whatever the being was, it didn't seem to notice him... or, if it did, it didn't care. It was just squatting on the roof directly above the window his son was about to fall out of.

An idea struck Peter like a two-by-four across the forehead: *It isn't just watching the tragedy... it is* guarding *the tragedy.*

The screen popped out of the window, and his son was falling. For the second time in his life, Peter could do nothing about it. He was too far away. He couldn't move fast enough. He dove, arms outstretched, eyes closed. His elbows and knees scraped against the ground. His hands grabbed nothing but cold air.

I'm sorry, Noah...

8

Peter sat bolt upright in bed, fresh tears standing in his eyes. A glaze of cold sweat covered his skin as his heart clicked in his throat.

"Noah... I couldn't..." he said, trying to figure out where he was. He scanned the spare room of Shady Cove that he had turned into a makeshift study. It was rushing back to him.

We rented a house in Gilchrist. Shadow Cove. No. Shady Cove. It's light outside. Afternoon still. We took a nap after we made love. It was good sex, not like before. I called Tom. I want to talk to Declan Wade about his time here, about the book notes I found. We were invited to have dinner tomorrow night with that woman... Laura Dolan. No. It's Dooley. Laura Dooley. Her son is Kevin, and there's something...

His wife's voice and touch grounded Peter further. Sylvia had her hand on his chest. She was sitting up sideways beside him. Her face was sweet and beautiful, compassionate. "You were dreaming. It's okay," she said in a soothing voice.

He looked at her and ran a hand over his face. "Yeah... I... I was."

"Must've been a good one." Her hand started rubbing him in small circles, calming him.

"That was so bizarre." He blinked hard a few times. "What time is it?"

"I think we've been out for at least an hour." She pulled the sheet up and covered her breasts.

Peter remembered her nipples in his mouth and tasting the salt of her sweat. If he wasn't so shaken up from his dream

(*that was no dream*)

it would've been a pleasant thought.

Sylvia's eyes drifted down. "What happened here?"

"What?"

She gestured to the sheets covering Peter's legs.

There were a few small spots of what looked like bright-red blood. He pulled back the sheet. Both his knees were scraped and bleeding. A chill went through his body as a cold claw closed around his spine. He covered them up, then checked his arms. Both forearms and elbows were scraped.

"What'd you do to yourself?" Sylvia asked.

I tried to save our son, Peter thought. But he couldn't bring himself to tell his wife that. It would be too much. Too hard.

"I don't know," he said, feeling a faint pang of guilt for lying. But it wasn't a lie. Not exactly. Because that would mean he believed that the implication of his wounds could possibly be true. "It must've happened when we were... you know." He wiggled his eyebrows in a way that made him look less like a young man in his thirties and more like a high school teenager who had just lost his virginity to the prom queen. "Battle wounds of love, I guess. They're not bad. I'll be fine."

"Let me take a look."

"No, I'm fine. Don't worry. Just a little rug burn. It was worth it."

She smiled, her cheeks flushing. "Maybe the floor wasn't the best idea."

"I'm not complaining." Peter's eyes went to where they had fooled around on the floor before moving to the bed. There was junk all over the place from when he had tossed the drawer aside. For the second time, he would have to clean it up. But it had been worth it. Both of them had needed that. Something about it had felt like a beginning.

"Me, either." She leaned in and kissed him.

God, her lips were soft. He couldn't understand how, for the past eighteen months, they had felt so stiff and uninviting. In that moment it was like everything between them was completely normal. He hoped it would last, that it wasn't just a one-time gift from whatever unseen force doled out such wonderful things.

"What're your plans for the rest of the afternoon?" Peter asked, swinging his legs off the bed.

"I think I'll go for a swim off the dock. I dipped my toes in the water earlier, and it's absolutely perfect. It's like bathwater. You want to join me?" Sylvia sat up, letting the sheet fall away from her breasts.

There was a freeness about her that Peter had forgotten entirely about. Whatever shift had occurred in her—in both of them—in the brief time they had been in Gilchrist, it seemed to be restoring that part of her. Or maybe it was just that for the first time in almost two years, they both felt a connection to each other that wasn't purely death and tragedy. The cold slab that for so long had sat stiff between them had finally begun to break down. Peter wanted to believe that it was owed to nothing more than a round of good and long-overdue sex. But he had an unsettling idea that maybe it was more than that. It was something he couldn't quite pinpoint, but he could feel it in his heart, too vague to identify.

His back to Sylvia, he looked at his knees again. It was the only thing that felt out of place, the little itch in the back of a throat that threatens to put a damper on a good time. It will either go on to become a rip-roaring case of strep or, with any luck, will disappear without growing into a problem. He knew one thing for sure, though: he had not sustained those scrapes from making love on the floor, from making love anywhere.

There was a little streak of what looked like black tar on one of the deeper cuts. It looked a lot like the stuff that he had seen on Kevin's feet. Peter rubbed his finger over his knee and smelled it. It had a sour, smoky smell.

"Everything okay?" Sylvia said, stealing Peter's attention.

"Yes," he said, looking over his shoulder and smiling. "A swim sounds great. I'll clean this mess up later."

They spent the rest of the day swimming in the warm waters of Lake Argilla, or Big Bath, as the locals referred to it. At sunset, Peter fired up the grill and made hot dogs and hamburgers. Sylvia made a salad. It almost felt like a normal life again.

Almost.

Chapter Nine

GOOD DOG

1

Around nine o'clock on Monday morning, Corbin drove to Gilchrist County Hospital over in Hammond to talk with Gertie. He had called ahead and was told they would be moving her to Massachusetts General Hospital at noon. He hated hospitals, and if he could've avoided going altogether, he would have. But he had questions that needed answers. Mainly he wanted to know what the hell had transpired at that farm for her to have been holed up in her bedroom with a shotgun, and for her husband of forty-five years to have attacked her and then set himself on fire.

Corbin's boots squeaked on the waxed linoleum floors as he walked down the sterile hallway to the nurses' station.

A short, wide woman in a white nurse's uniform was sitting behind the desk, filling out a form when he approached. "Can I help you?" she asked, continuing with her paperwork.

"I spoke to a Mr. Graves about an hour ago," Corbin said,

drumming his fingers noiselessly on the counter. "I'm here to see Gertrude Mayer. She was brought in yest—"

"*Dr.* Graves, you mean?"

"That's what I said, ma'am."

"Uh-huh. He's not here at the moment. And that patient is not able to see visitors. She's being transported shortly."

"I know that, ma'am… at noon, if I'm not mistaken. Boston, right?"

The nurse sighed and looked up. Her face changed from an irritated scowl to a look of retroactive apology when she saw he was in uniform. "I'm sorry, Officer. I didn't realize—"

"Chief… It's Chief Delancey, from over in Gilchrist." Corbin winked at her and gave a derisive little nod.

"Yes, of course. I'll go find him. I'm sure he's around here somewhere," the nurse said, her face a sheet of red.

"I'd appreciate that, if it isn't too much trouble."

"Not at all. Why don't you take a seat while you wait." She came around the station and went up the hall, disappearing through a doorway.

Corbin took a seat in one of the hard plastic waiting room chairs. He picked up a copy of *LIFE Magazine* and flipped through the pages. First forward, then backward. Then forward again. He did the same with copies of *Time* and *The New Yorker*.

He was about to pick up the copy of *Cosmopolitan* when a doctor came around the corner, carrying a clipboard. "Chief Delancey? Scott Graves. We spoke earlier."

A moment later the nurse returned to her work behind the nurses' station without looking in their direction.

"That's right. About Gertrude Mayer," Corbin said, dropping the magazine and getting to his feet.

"She's one lucky lady," Graves said.

"I gotta be honest, she didn't look so lucky when I found her."

"She took a deep stab wound to her abdomen and lost a fair amount of blood. It could've been a heck of a lot worse, though. Whoever attacked her managed to miss every major organ and artery. Have you caught the guy?"

Corbin folded his arms. "Didn't have to. He died."

"I see."

"Uh-huh. Doc, if you don't mind, I'd like to get to it," Corbin said.

"She's stable for the time being—we managed to stop the internal bleeding—but we're moving her to a facility that's better equipped to handle the surgery. She's this way," Graves said, and started up the hall. "But I'll warn you, she's been sedated. And I can't allow you to upset her. If I think that you're starting to put her well-being at—"

"I'm only going to ask her a few simple questions. I don't like this any more than you."

"No. I suppose not."

Graves led him around a corner and through a set of double doors. Gertie was in the last door on the left. When they went in, she was staring out the window. Her skin looked like wax paper.

She turned to them. "Hi, Corbin," she said weakly. She had an oxygen tube under her nose, and was attached to an assortment of expensive-looking machines that beeped and booped to the rhythm of her heart. "Have you come to arrest me?"

"Not unless you'd like me to," Corbin said, trying to lighten the mood. She smiled at him, but he could tell she didn't mean it. "No, Gertie, I just came to ask you a couple questions, if you feel up to it. Of course, if you don't think—"

"Do I look like someone who won't be okay?"

"No. You don't."

"So don't treat me like one. You want to know why I almost shot you," she said point-blank. "You've a right to ask."

"That's a good place to start, yeah." Corbin pulled up a chair and sat down beside the bed. "At the time, you said you didn't know it was me in the house. You were waiting for someone, though."

"That's right. I thought you were Elhouse," she said, as if it made complete sense. Her eyes went back to the window. Corbin could tell it wasn't that she didn't care—she just wanted to get the pain over with already. Like ripping a bandage off in one quick motion.

"So you wanted to shoot your husband?" he asked.

"I don't know if 'wanted to' is the way I'd put it."

"So how would you put it, then?"

"I had no choice," Gertie said, flattening her lips.

"I don't understand."

"That makes two of us, doesn't it?"

"Try and help me paint a picture here," Corbin said. "I saw Elhouse when I first pulled up, and he was acting real strange. He told me he'd hurt you. Is he the one who did this to you?"

She looked at Corbin and shook her head. "We were married for forty-five years, and the thing that attacked me yesterday was not my Elhouse. It might've looked like him, but that wasn't the man I married. I don't know what that was."

Two tears ran down the side of her face, but she didn't outwardly cry. Corbin looked at Dr. Graves to check the count. The doctor gave him a warning look.

"Was he sick? Had he been showing signs something was wrong? Anything?" Corbin asked.

"No. Nothing like that," Gertie said.

"Can you tell me what happened? Just help me understand. Forget the uniform. I want to know for my own peace of mind, if you can believe that. What in God's name went on over there? I'm trying to wrap my head around it and… and frankly, I'm having a tough time making any sense of it. I've known you both my entire life, and I can't for the life of me…" He trailed off, his point made.

"You're talking as if he and I both lost our minds. I was just defending myself. That's what went on," she said firmly. "Elhouse is the one who wasn't himself."

"What do you mean by 'wasn't himself'?"

"I mean just that… it wasn't him. I already told you that."

"Can you give me a little more to work with?"

She sighed. "When he came to bed Saturday night, something seemed different about him. That's when I first noticed it."

"What do you mean?"

"I don't know exactly," Gertie said, her tone taking on a frustrated lilt. "It's hard to say without sounding completely off my rocker. And the last thing I want is to spend the rest of my days in a looney bin, eating spoon food and staring out the window."

Corbin could tell she was scared and upset. Probably still in shock. He put his hand on the bed, not touching her, but leaving it there if she wanted something familiar to hold. "I promise you I don't have anyone waiting around the corner with a straitjacket."

"It was like he was there, but he wasn't there," Gertie said. "And I felt, maybe, like I was sleeping next to a stranger, I guess. I know that makes about as much sense as a Jell-O umbrella, but that's what it was like. I just thought he was still mad about the kids racing up the road. I figured that's what was on his mind and he'd be back to his normal self in the morning. I never thought... well..." Gertie stalled, her face racing with painful recollection.

"Was he back to his normal self in the morning?" Corbin asked, trying to push the moment forward. But he heard the foolishness of the question as it left his lips, and he immediately regretted asking it.

"What do you think? I'm here, and he's dead. Does that seem 'normal' to you?"

"I guess not, no."

Gertie folded her hands in her lap and started rubbing her thumbs together. This was hard for her. Perhaps the hardest thing—aside from being prepared to shoot her own husband—she had ever had to do.

"No, it was worse the next day," she said. "That man was up at five thirty on the nose every morning, rain or shine, for as long as I've known him. So when six o'clock rolled around and he hadn't come downstairs yet for his breakfast, I went to check on him." She swallowed hard. "He was just sitting there on the side of the bed... naked, staring out the window at the woods behind our house. And when he looked at me, I swear my heart went cold. His eyes were... they were green. But my Elhouse's are blue, like yours. That doesn't just happen."

A twinge of surprised dread fired off inside Corbin. He had seen those very same green eyes for a split second when Elhouse was in the barn. He had tried to convince himself it had been his imagination, but he wasn't so sure anymore. A part of him thought he should tell Gertie that maybe he had seen the same thing, but that seemed like too big a step into territory he neither wanted, nor knew how to navigate.

"Is that when all *this*"—he gestured to her lying in the hospital bed—"happened?"

"No. Eventually he came downstairs… dressed. But dressed funny. He had on dirty clothes from the day before, and his boots weren't tied. He hadn't showered, and he smelled. It was a funny smell. I don't know what it was… like burnt something. He didn't say a single word, just walked downstairs, looked at me for a second, then went out the front door and disappeared, trailing that awful smell behind him."

"Disappeared? Where?"

"He liked to work on the equipment when had something on his mind, so I figured he was in the barn and would talk to me when he'd worked out whatever it was bothering him."

"If I can interrupt, that's the second time you've mentioned he was upset," Corbin said. "What's that about?"

"I told you already—and I know Elhouse brought it up to you more than a few times this last year—but kids treat Waldingfield Road like a raceway. We were taking a walk Saturday evening and nearly got run over. It was Nathaniel Osterman's son. Elhouse recognized the car. Anyway, I tried to calm him down about it, but I could tell it wasn't something he would let go easily."

This bit of info made a strong case for Elhouse being involved in Danny Metzger's car accident. Maybe Elhouse, angry about being nearly run over, had snapped and set a trap to teach the local kids a lesson about speeding down his road. The Elhouse *he* knew wouldn't do that, but the version of him that Gertie was describing—the version that could attack the woman he loved and then douse himself in gasoline—might have been capable of such a thing. He didn't think it was an outlandish jump to make. But he couldn't ignore that it just didn't sit right.

It was like finding a puzzle piece that fits but only roughly: it'll slide into place, but only if you force it a little more than should be necessary, and only if you look at it with squinted eyes.

"I'll have a talk with Ricky, you have my word," he said. "I'll make sure that doesn't happen again. That boy is a royal pain in my rear, and his father isn't any better."

Gertie gave him a smart look that said: *How sweet of you, Chief, but let's not pretend* that's *what matters right now… or that it'll change anything.* Instead, she said, "You do that," and went on.

"A little while later I was hanging the laundry, and Elhouse came up from behind, scared the dickens outta me. I turned around, and he was standing there. He was trembling. Shaking all over. I'll never forget what he said. He said, 'I love you, Gertie. Now run and don't let me catch you no matter what… kill me if you have to.' And he was crying. I didn't understand what was happening. He was always such a sweet man, not capable of anything like this. I remember thinking that so clearly, even when he pulled the kitchen knife out of his pocket and stuck me with it. Those green eyes stared at me the whole time, never blinking."

Gertie wiped her tear-streaked cheeks, and when she did, the doctor cleared his throat and stepped forward. "I think that's enough for now. Mrs. Mayer really needs her rest."

"Like hell I do," Gertie said, as quick as a whip. "I'm finishing this story, then it'll never touch my lips again. Besides, if God had intended for me to die, I would've died in that house. It's not my time, so you can just hold your horses with all that worrying."

Dr. Graves put up his hand. "Okay," he said, and muttered something inaudibly. Probably something like: *I'm only a doctor. What do I know?*

Corbin glanced at him and watched the doctor slink back

against the wall like a child who had just been caught red handed stealing from the cookie jar before dinner.

"I managed to get away and run into the house, but he came after me quick. It was like being chased by a rabid dog. That relentless, sick mind that drives at a single confused idea until it has it in its teeth and doesn't know what to do with it but bite down. That's what it felt like. It's a bit of a blur after he stabbed me, but I do remember that I was on the staircase in the front hall, and he was on top of me, choking me, and the world was going gray. I think I was heading off to my big, final sleep, if you want to know the truth. Then that thing on top of me leaned in close, and I heard my Elhouse's voice tell me not to give up. He told me to fight. That part was him."

Gertie paused a moment. The room was silent. Her last words hung on the air.

"Then what?" Corbin finally asked. For a second he felt like he was five years old again, and he was listening to his mother tell him a bedtime story. Not a sweet story, but a story where he had to know what happened next.

"I fought," she said. "I jammed my thumbs into those nasty green eyes, and that thing let out an awful scream." She demonstrated with a pointed thumb, which she jabbed weakly out in front of her. "That's when I ran upstairs, grabbed the shotgun from the closet, and locked myself in the bedroom and waited. I was there until you found me."

Corbin sat up stiff in the chair but didn't speak right away. He didn't know what to say. If anything, he was more confused than he had been before walking in there.

Gertie looked at the doctor. "I didn't mean to speak curtly to you, Dr. Graves. You've been very good to me, and I appreciate it. Thank you."

"It's okay," he said in a subdued voice. "But I must insist you get some rest now. You need it before they transport you. You have surgery this afternoon."

"And I will, but would you mind giving Corbin and I a moment alone before I do? After that, I promise to do whatever you say. I'm too tired to put up a fight."

"Why do I get the feeling it doesn't matter what I say?" Dr. Graves said, then left the room and shut the door behind him.

"Corbin," Gertie said, "I know what I just told you doesn't answer much. In fact, I'd wager you probably have more questions than before you stepped foot in this room. Maybe you even regret coming. I'm sorry if you do."

Corbin, who had found himself staring absently out the window, looked at her with a blank expression. "I just don't understand. Why would Elhouse do something like this all of a sudden? People don't just lose their minds overnight and decide to start killing the people they love."

He remembered that he still had the unpleasant task of telling Gertie about how her husband had died, and it sent a pang of anxiety through his body. He couldn't keep that from her forever. He would just as soon forget about it himself. He could still smell the scent of burning flesh, as if it were coating the insides of his nose.

"My Elhouse didn't do this to me," she said. "He tried to save me as best he could. It wasn't his fault, and I don't blame him. Neither should you."

"You keep saying that it wasn't him, but I have to be honest, I just don't think I…" Corbin trailed off, dragging a tired hand down his face and breathing out slowly. He couldn't bring himself to finish the thought, but the word, once more, would've been *understand*. At that point, it seemed completely repetitive, like an old refrain he was sick of hearing.

"Yes, you do. You understand, Corbin, you just don't want to. I know you feel it. Probably always have," she said, as if stealing a glimpse inside his mind. She took his hand and gave it a gentle squeeze. Her skin felt like cool, damp clay. "You feel it here." She gestured to her chest with her other hand.

Immediately he thought about what Elhouse had said right before he struck the match and set himself ablaze. He had said something similar. He had said he could feel it everywhere... whatever *it* was.

"I'm afraid I don't know what you mean, Gertie. Feel what?"

She smiled at him. His poker face was terrible. "That's the problem, I think. Everybody wants to pretend there's nothing wrong. It's easier that way, I suppose. People hate the truth, Corbin. Facing it means having to do something about it—trying to, anyway—even if there isn't anything you *can* do. Sometimes you just gotta know when to run, I suppose. Remember that."

"Maybe the doctor's right. You should get some rest."

She ignored him. "Gilchrist hasn't ever felt right, and you know it. There's something... special about it, I guess you'd say. Not special in a good way, either. It's like there's some invisible wall between this place and another terrible place, and it has grown far too thin. The town looks good on the surface. But underneath... underneath, Corbin, you know it's far darker and meaner than most places. And I think it's that way for a reason."

"How much of this medicine did they give you?" Corbin forced a laugh, but she saw right through it like a spotlight piercing fog.

"It's okay to be scared. You should be. At least that means you know it's there," she said, her face a grave carving of off-white marble. "There is something horrible in Gilchrist, has been since well before any us were alive. I don't know how I know, but I do. I can feel it, like a black tide rising around my heart. It took my Elhouse and broke him. Turned him into a tool of the devil."

Corbin thought about something Elhouse had said back in his barn: *It harvests what it sows.* It had struck him as odd when he'd first heard it, but at the time, he had thought they were just the words of an unsound mind. Thinking about it now, though, it almost made him feel queasy. There was a dreadful truth hidden in those words that he could not quite comprehend, yet he could feel its weight pressing down on him.

What does it sow?

"I have to get going, Gertie," Corbin said. He could hear a little bit of shame mixed with the denial in his voice. "I hope you know how sorry I am. Regardless of what happened, Elhouse was a good man. I just wish I could make some sense of it."

"Yes," Gertie said, "he was. Now you go on and pray. Something tells me we all should."

Corbin pulled his hand out from underneath hers, stood, and headed out of the room. He stopped at the doorway and turned around. "Gertie, there's something I haven't told you yet. But I think I ought to. It's about how Elhouse… well, how he—"

"I'm tired, Corbin. Let me sleep now. What you have to tell me is something I don't ever need to hear. Do you really think it matters? He's gone."

"No," he said. "I suppose it doesn't."

2

On his way back to town, Corbin stopped on Waldingfield Road to have another look at the scene of the wreck. He needed to take his mind off his conversation with Gertie. It had left him feeling disrupted, as though someone had just taken his life, turned it upside down, and given it a violent shake. Now everything he knew and understood was out of place, and in some places, new things had been uncovered. Things he wasn't so sure he wanted to know.

He needed to restore some order. So he parked on the shoulder, shut off his car, and stepped out. He looked in both directions. No one was coming. He reached into his pocket and grabbed the Benzedrine inhaler, taking one hit in each nostril. His focus sharpened on cue, and he quickly dialed in on the big oak where he had found the second set of markings.

He went over to it and had another look. It had been completely fresh, still slimy, when he had first discovered it. Perhaps only an hour or two old. Now where the tree flesh was marred, it was already starting to dry out. He ran his finger over one of the more well-defined imprints and thought about a time two years back, when a bad storm had knocked down the large maple in their front yard, and he had used a chain to drag the biggest pieces into the woods behind his house. Reflecting on this as he stood on the side of Waldingfield Road, he had a pretty good idea what had caused the markings. The pattern and the shape were unmistakable in daylight, identical to what he remembered seeing two years ago. What he didn't know, however, was whether or not Danny Metzger had been the intended target. It didn't seem likely. There would be too many variables to control. Too much uncertainty. It would be like firing a cannon into a crowd of people and hoping to hit the right person.

Unless it didn't matter who was hit...

Another thought struck Corbin, this one carrying with it the full weight of what this all might mean: *And if it wasn't Elhouse who was responsible, then I have a murderer on my hands. Probably a local. Probably someone who knows the area.*

There was a deliberate cruelty attached to this whole thing, an oiliness that he could feel. And it didn't feel like Elhouse Mayer. And it didn't feel like any kids playing a prank that had paid out more than they had bargained for. It felt cold and mean and awful. Depraved.

You feel it here, Gertie had said, and pointed to her heart less than an hour ago in her hospital bed. And Corbin thought, maybe, he understood what she had been talking about more than he cared to admit.

The last time he had felt this way was when Madison Feller turned up dead in the river. It had been ruled an accident during the inquest, but that had never sat right with him. There had been no evidence to suggest foul play, but he remembered the same bitter, oily feeling. It was like being caught downwind of a raging tire fire. The air felt corrosive and sticky at the same time.

He glanced in all directions, slowly pinching and releasing the loose skin below his chin between his thumb and forefinger.

"Then what'd you do?" he said in a low voice as he worked out the scene in his mind. "Did you watch? You must've watched. You took the chain down right after it happened to make it look like an accident. You had to watch. So where's the best place?"

He turned and walked about a hundred feet up a gradually sloping hill until he was at the top and looking down at the road through the woods. They weren't thickly settled in that area. He could see his car and the faint markings on the back of the oak tree where one end of the chain had been anchored.

Taking a wide zigzagging path, he moved slowly back down the hill, eyes scanning the ground as he went. He wasn't sure what he was looking for but was certain he would know it when he saw it.

(*like a black tide rising around my heart*)

He was about midway down the hill when he spotted the Double Decker MoonPie wrapper a few feet away.

(*it took my Elhouse and broke him*)

He picked it up, looked at it, sniffed inside.

(*turned him into a tool of the devil*)

The package still held the faint, lingering smell of chocolate and marshmallow. The wrapper was fresh.

(*it harvests what it sows*)

It seemed like an odd place for someone to be eating a snack like that. Of course, it could've been littered out of a car and blown up there in a gust of wind.

Maybe. Maybe not. Or maybe he was blowing smoke up his own ass, bending the narrative a little too much.

Then Corbin spotted the little cleared-away spot of ground to his left, and the picture came into focus a little more. In the center of the little clearing of dirt, he counted five crushed cigarette butts. One was a little farther forward than the group and looked like it'd been stamped out under a heavy boot heel. It was still partially buried in the deep indentation. He picked them all up and studied them in his palm. Lucky Strike brand. "Luckies," the teenagers called them. Each one was smoked down to the filter. Nothing wasted.

Squatting on the hill, his eyes moved back and forth between the cigarette butts and the MoonPie wrapper. He could see it clearly—the *what* not the *who*. Someone had sat up on the hill, smoking and eating, and waited for a car to come along. Probably they hadn't cared who they hurt, so long as someone did get hurt. A random act of violence. They had watched the whole thing, and it'd been fun for them. Probably this wasn't their first time, either. When Corbin played the scene out in his mind's eye, the person watching was a faceless figure, a perfectly black shadow that smoked Lucky Strikes, ate MoonPies, and wore boots. That didn't offer a whole lot, but it was a start.

He spent another forty-five minutes searching the area, but came up with nothing else. He took the evidence he had found back down to his cruiser and got in. On the floor of his backseat was a lunch sack from the week before. He checked inside, and it was clean. No crumbs, no grease. He dropped the cigarette butts in, the MoonPie wrapper on top, and placed the bag on the seat beside him.

He pulled out the inhaler and stared at it. He dropped it back into his breast pocket and left. By the time he reached the end of Waldingfield Road, it was in his hand again. He tossed it out the window as he drove and heard it bounce off the asphalt. Then the sound disappeared behind him and was gone. There was something oily about that thing, too. He had always known it. He had always felt it.

3

Dave Blatten was sitting on the cedar sweater chest—the one Sarah had bought on a Sunday last summer over at Todd Farm flea market in Rowley—and tying his boots when he spotted the gum stuck behind the bedpost.

"The hell is this?" he said under his breath and crept toward it suspiciously. He reached behind the post and picked off the little white-pink wad. It was still tacky. He sniffed it. It smelled faintly of those Wint-O-Green Lifesavers he liked to suck on.

He examined the artifact. It didn't belong. It wasn't his, that's for sure. He didn't like the stuff; it hurt his teeth. Too many cavities, according to his last dentist appointment. Maybe it was Sarah's.

She was thoughtless sometimes, sure. Like the time she'd bleached his favorite shirt and ruined it. Or the time she had taken his truck to see that bitch mother of hers and left him with an empty tank. He had been forced to teach her a little lesson that time. As he saw it, she'd left him no choice in the matter. Her little oversight had made him late for his hunting trip, when he had been forced to stop off for gas on the way. He couldn't have that. He hadn't done anything mean to her, just a light slap upside the head like his daddy used to do for him when he didn't think. So yeah, maybe she didn't use her head from time to time, but she wouldn't do something so intentionally stupid and crass as stick a wad of chewing gum on their furniture.

And it was on *his* side of the bed.

His mind immediately entertained the blackest of thoughts, and a blade of panic sliced his gut, almost causing him to physically wince. Instead he clenched his jaw as his face bent into a scowl.

Would she...? Could she have...? Nahhh, not my Sarah, she wouldn't do that to me. That fucking slut! That dumb little whore!

Until death do us part...

"Sarah, can you come in here a minute?" he said, keeping his voice calm. Same as with the dog, he didn't want his tone to give him away. When trying to trap an animal, the last thing a person ought to do is make a bunch of sudden, aggressive movements. He subscribed to *Field & Stream*, and he knew those kinds of things from reading the articles.

"What is it?" She was in the kitchen, making lunch for him to take to work. "Can't it wait a minute?"

He looked at his wedding ring. "Listen, just come in here a sec. There's something I need to show you. It won't take but a minute. Then you can get back to makin my lunch."

When I'm done with her, she ain't gonna be able to make spit, let alone those stale Wonder Bread and bologna sandwiches she calls lunch.

There was the sound of a knife being dropped on the butcher block, then a pause as she hung up her apron, the one her grandmother had given her. God, she never shut up about that. Footfalls came up the hall. He could see it all. This was his house, and he knew all the sounds and routines that lived in it.

All, except, maybe one. This new one with its threatening little head peeking out.

He was rolling the gum into a perfectly round ball between his fingers when Sarah came into the bedroom. The petulant look on her face pissed him right the fuck off. Some wife she was to look at him that way when all he'd done was ask her to do a simple thing and come talk to him.

"I was making your lunch. Just what you asked, baby," she said, and ran her hair behind her ears.

Dave laughed, but it was a mean laugh. "A wife obeying her husband… well. Isn't that just so considerate of you, *darling.*" He accentuated the last word in such a way that made him sound like he was speaking through chewed stone. A vein throbbed in his forehead, sending a dull ache to the core of his brain.

Sarah's face twitched a little at the sight of him. "What's wrong?"

"Here I was, gettin ready for work, when I spotted something I just can't make any sense of. I thought maybe you could help me to work it out." Dave moved toward her with slow, deliberate motion. He was still eyeing the piece of gum between his fingers, rolling it in small circles. He held it up and closed one eye as if inspecting it. "You know what this is?"

His boots tromped on the floor as he crossed the room. It was a dreadful sound. The sound of impending doom.

"No. What is it?" Sarah swallowed hard.

Dave could smell that she was hiding something. Liars produced a scent, and the scent was bullshit. The room reeked of it. That and the other thing.

"Is it yours?" he asked, stopping right in front of his wife. He held up the suspicious artifact a few inches from her face. Her eyes even crossed a little, and he thought it made her look dumb.

"I don't even know what it is, so how could it be mine?" she said, backing away. She startled when her butt hit the windowsill and she realized she was cornered between the dresser and the wall.

"You don't know what it is? I mean, you *really* don't know what... it... is? Why don't you take a real good look, then."

"I am," she said. "It looks like Silly Putty. I don't know, Dave. What's the matter?"

"It's gum!" Dave yelled, his eyes deepening in their sockets. "It's fucking *gum*!"

"Okay, so it's gum," Sarah said, confused. "Why are you showing me gum?" She laughed nervously. "I don't understand, that's all. That's all. Don't be mad. I don't know what I did wrong."

"Well, it ain't mine," Dave said. "So why was it stuck behind the bedpost?"

"I don't know. I didn't put it there, if that's what you think. Is that what you're upset about? Do you think I put it..."

For a second Dave could see the jackpot lights flashing behind her eyes. As she began to understand, her face bleached white.

He reached over slowly and shut the door to their bedroom. "That's exactly the fuckin problem, ain't it? It's not yours, it's not mine... so whose is it, then?"

"I swear I don't know." Tears were gathering in her eyes.

The girl can't cook, Dave thought. *And she sure as shit can't lie worth a damn.*

"Oh, sweetheart—yes, you do," he said in a kind voice, and clicked his tongue at her. "And you're gonna tell me. You know why?"

She put her hands on his chest. He was a big man compared to her. "Dave, please—"

He grabbed both her wrists in one hand and pushed them away. "Because if you don't tell me who was up here chewing my"—he reached down and cupped her crotch hard—"gum, then I got no choice but to snap your little whore neck."

Sarah Blatten started to cry.

"No... no, please." She tried helplessly to go around him, but he shoved her back against the wall. Her elbow struck the dresser and knocked a bottle of her cheap Woolworth's perfume onto the floor. It smashed and splashed his boots. Now the place reeked of bullshit *and* roses. And the other thing.

"You take me for an idiot? You think you're gonna let another guy sample what's mine, in the bed we share, and I won't find out? How dumb are you?" His head tilted to the side, and his eyes stared into blank space for a second before finding hers again. "Or did you want me to find out? Is that it? Because I think maybe you did, and ain't that just a fine howdy fuckin do."

"It's not what—"

"Who is he, Sarah? Last chance before I gotta whoop it outta you. And I promise you it won't be a whoopin you'll soon forget. No sir." The false kindness had gone from his voice. His face was pulsing with wild anger. "How 'bout it? You gonna open up that mouth of yours and spill it, or you saving that tongue for your mystery man?"

"There is no one," she whimpered. "I swear, baby. Please, you have to believe—"

He grabbed her by the throat. "Well, okay. The hard way it is. Here, bite down on this. You're gonna need it. Open up now... come on. Don't worry, it's still fresh." He forced the gum into her mouth. First with his thumb, then with the heel of his palm.

Then he removed his belt, wrapped it twice around his hand, and kept his promise.

4

"The way I see it, someone set a trap," Corbin said to Billy as they ate their lunches in the back room of the police station. "He strung a chain across the road—like a tripwire, you follow?—and sat up there in the woods, smoking cigarettes and eating MoonPies like it was a goddamn Saturday-afternoon matinee. He watched the whole time."

"A trap?" Billy washed down his mouthful of ham and cheese with a sip of Coke, then wiped a hand across his mouth, missing some mustard on the edge of his lip. "You s'pose they knew

Danny would be coming that way? Seems as though that'd be awful hard to get right."

"I don't think it was meant for him at all. I think it was intended for whoever happened to come along, and it just so happened to be that boy's bad luck he was driving that road at that exact time. Could've just as easily been me or you. I don't believe it would've mattered one bit to this person. If for some reason he had a target on Danny's back, there're far simpler ways to go about it." Corbin crumpled the parchment paper Meryl had wrapped the sandwiches in, then dropped it in the wastebasket beside his desk. "No, I think this was something else altogether."

"Who'd do a thing like that? That's some bad stuff, Chief."

"Not sure. For a time, I thought it could've been Elhouse trying to teach someone a lesson, but I don't really buy that anymore."

"No? He came down here a few times to complain about kids speeding down Waldingfield. Makes sense, doesn't it? And after all that weirdness that went down at their house, I wouldn't put it past the old coot. It sounds like that man's tractor might've been missing a tire or two, if you catch what I mean."

Corbin caught what he meant and glanced at Billy. Thing was, he didn't entirely disagree, but he felt defensive of Elhouse. He was reminded of what Gertie had said: *We were married for forty-five years, and the thing that attacked me yesterday was not my Elhouse.*

He didn't exactly understand it, yet he respected it in the way a person respects any truth that's hard to believe.

The story already making its way around Gilchrist was, by and large, the truth: Elhouse had attacked his wife—for what reason, maybe only God would ever know—then somehow managed to get himself killed in a barn fire. There was no mention, however, of how the fire had started. Corbin had decided he was going to bury the detail of Elhouse dousing himself in gasoline and lighting himself up like a birthday candle. Gertie didn't need to hear about it, and neither did the town. It changed absolutely nothing. It only added acid to an already-churning pot. There had been three deaths in town in as many days, and people were starting to talk nervously among themselves about it, almost as if they feared it was catching.

"Yeah... yeah, I know what you mean. But it just didn't sit right with me. Not after I found this stuff." Corbin pointed to the cigarette butts and MoonPie wrapper arranged neatly on a piece of newspaper on his desk. "I know it could very well be unrelated—and I might be making jumps I have no business making—but I just have a feeling it's connected. And I've learned over the years that it's a bad idea to ignore what your gut gives you. We don't know nearly as much as we think we do. You'd do well to take that advice, Billy. Might save your life someday."

Billy nodded, then finally dabbed the mustard on his lip after finishing his sandwich and downing the rest of his soda. "So what now?" he asked, popping a piece of gum in his mouth.

"I'm not sure. I suppose we could go door-to-door and ask everyone if they did it," Corbin said. "We could stake out Virgil's Gas 'N Go or the General Store and see who buys MoonPies and Lucky Strikes. Or we could figure out who has access to chain. That ought to narrow down the list of suspects to around a thousand people or so, give or take a hundred."

"Okay, okay, okay. It ain't gonna be easy," Billy said.

"What I know is that there's a better than good chance we have someone dangerous walking around our streets. And we haven't a clue who he is, if he'll do this again, or if he's done something like this before. I'd wager my best Woolly Bugger he's got some sorta history." Corbin wiped an open hand across his mouth, then put on his hat and stood up. "Well, anyway," he said, and sighed.

"Heading out?" Billy asked, eyes tracking up.

"Gotta go talk to Ricky Osterman about his lead foot. I told Gertie I'd make sure he never sped down her road again, and I aim to make good on that. Do me a favor and put this evidence in the safe. It's all we got at the moment."

"I'll take care of it."

The phone rang on Corbin's desk as he was walking out from behind it.

He picked it up and cleared his throat. "Yeah, this is Chief Delancey." Worry and confusion mixed over his face at the sound of crying on the other end of the receiver. "Who is this?"

"Corbin, it's Sarah. I need to talk to Billy. Is he there? Oh please... please tell me he's there. It's important."

"Hold on, just slow down. You want to talk to Billy?" Corbin said. "What on earth do you want with him?"

"Please. It's important... I... I just need to speak with him. Please, Corbin, just put him on."

"All right, all right, take it easy. He's right here. Hold on." He looked at Billy and shook his head. He handed him the phone, palm covering the mouthpiece. "It's for you, I guess. Dave's wife. God, Billy, tell me you aren't that stupid."

Billy, still sitting, looked like the cat who'd just ate the canary. If the yellow mustard had still been on his lip, that would've added a nice touch.

"For me?" he asked sheepishly, and slowly got to his feet. "I... shit."

"I'd say shit is right," Corbin said. "And something tells me you just stepped in awfully big pile of it."

Billy took the phone. "Sarah?... Slow down. I can't understand you... What happened?... You told him? Oh jeez... No, all right... Wait—what?... He did?... That son of a bitch!... I'm gonna kill him!... It's him who should worry... No, he's not."

Corbin stood on the other side of the desk, arms folded like a disappointed parent, and watched Billy's face work through the corresponding emotions: concern, surprise, relief, a flash of something like happiness, then quickly to hot anger.

Corbin liked Billy. He was a good police officer and a nice kid. Of all the people in his department, he was the one Corbin didn't mind sharing a lunch and a chat with. They had even had him over for dinner a few times, and Meryl had said he seemed like a kind boy. Corbin could tell Billy had a good heart. But he was young and often a little too naïve for his own good. That was why Corbin had held off on promoting him. He wasn't ready.

Out front of the station, rubber screamed against road. A car door slammed. Then someone yelled: "Billy, you piece of shit, get the fuck out here!" Dave was hot under the collar about something, and Corbin could take a pretty good guess about what.

"I gotta go," Billy said into the phone. "No, it's okay, I'll be fine... Yes. Now pack a bag and get out of there. Go to your cousin's. I'll pick you up soon. I'm just gonna talk to him."

"Billy, listen to me, not in front of the station," Corbin said, but Billy was already storming out.

"I'll kill that prick," Billy muttered, his hands clenched into fists. He started opening and closing them rapidly.

Corbin had never seen the kid angry before in his life. There was always something unsettling, he thought, about seeing a person who was normally calm blow their top. It was a lot like watching a bomb go off in church.

He followed after him. "Shit. This is just what I need." He passed by Ray Stanski, who was working dispatch.

Ray looked at him dumbly and blinked without saying a word.

"Don't just sit there. These two assholes are about to go at it. Give me a hand."

"Yes, sir." Ray scrambled to his feet and around the radio desk.

Through the door, Corbin could see Dave standing in the street, pacing back and forth. His fists were tight white balls. The cruiser he had pulled up in was taking up three spaces, its door still open.

"*I'm* the piece of shit?" Billy said as he burst out the front door, almost tearing it off its hinges. He pedaled down the steps in a hurry. "What kind of a man hits a woman? You're pathetic. No wonder she's leaving you. I swear I'll make sure you never come near her again."

Dave stopped when he spotted Billy. He stared him down, then started toward him. No more than forty feet separated the two men. They were two violent storm fronts headed for each other.

"You ruined her," Dave said, eerily calm. "You had no right to break my home that way." He no longer looked mad; he actually looked sad. Something was off.

Corbin came out onto the front steps of the station. "Hey!" he shouted. "You two morons want to knock each other around, take it out back. You hear me? Not here, or I swear I'll crack both your skulls and suspend you without pay for a month."

Neither listened, but he hadn't really thought they would. If Billy had been up to what it sounded like he had been up to, then there was no stopping it. This particular fuse could not be unlit once it had been set.

Billy and Dave were closing the distance between each other, both pushing up their sleeves. Across the street, Immie Davenport—the biggest gossip in Gilchrist County—was walking by, but she stopped, her face locked in a show of appalled curiosity. The scene was simply far too juicy to ignore. Two kids had stopped on their bikes in the middle of the sidewalk and were watching, leaning on their handlebars and sipping milkshakes.

Corbin couldn't help but notice that Billy was outmatched by about fifty pounds, although he did have a couple inches on Dave. He didn't know if either man could fight, but if Dave was even halfway capable, he had the clear advantage. Corbin was reluctant to get involved, but he couldn't just stand there and watch like some dumb-eyed street gawker as two of his officers pounded the spit out of each other.

He was halfway down the steps when he saw the thing in the street, and it stopped him cold in his tracks. To someone watching, it might've looked as though he had just walked into an invisible wall. He nearly fell backward but caught his balance. He blinked hard. It had to be some kind of hallucination.

There was something—something big—standing behind Dave. It was maybe ten or twelve feet tall, with long arms that hung down to the ground, and muscular, avian legs. It had gray skin, except for the face, which was a dizzying, swirling blur of shimmering colors. The back of its head was covered in welts that seemed to flutter open and closed, and around which black tendrils of thick hair grew. The creature was just standing behind Dave, looming over him like a giant, ugly shadow. And he could see right through the thing, just how he could see through his own reflection when he stood in front of a window. It was there, but it wasn't.

Corbin only saw it for a couple seconds before it vanished. He glanced over his shoulder at Ray, who was right on his heels. "Did you just see...?"

He didn't finish the question because he already knew the answer. If anyone else had seen that hideous thing, there would have been screaming.

"Did I see what?" Ray asked.

"Nothing. Never mind. Just help me put a stop to this. I'll grab Billy. You get Dave."

The last thing that went through his head before things turned horrible was once more Gertie's voice from their conversation earlier that day: *It's like there's some invisible wall between this place and another terrible place, and it has grown far too thin.*

What happened next, happened fast.

At twenty feet from Dave, Billy spat out his gum and started raising his fists. Dave didn't raise his. Instead he widened his stance and brought his right hip back a quarter turn. Then at ten feet, he pulled his pistol from his holster and fired two shots into Billy Porter's angry, charging face.

Crack! Crack! The sound rebounded off the brick buildings and danced down Market Street, leaving a haunted wake behind it.

The onlookers on the street let out a collective gasp of stunned horror. A flock of birds took flight from a nearby tree, spooked by the gunshots. Mrs. Davenport dropped the bags she had been carrying. A stiff hand covering her mouth, she was silent with shock, each one of her eyes roughly the size—and color—of a cast-iron cannonball.

Billy reeled back, his legs folding underneath him. Then he crumpled into a pile on the ground like a wet towel. Bits of brain and skull were scattered on the street behind him. His right eye had exploded, and what was left hung out of its socket, still attached to a bundle of sinewy nerves and veins. Dave calmly stood over him, and fired three more rounds from his .38 into Billy's chest.

When the gun was finished barking, the street fell silent. The smell of cordite slowly permeated the air. Only it didn't smell quite like spent gunpowder. It smelled mixed with something sour and rotten.

For a few horrible seconds, Corbin could only stand there in shock, his senses taking a snapshot of the moment and searing it into his mind. His head did a dazed panoramic sweep from left to right, recording the scene.

The two kids on bikes had their jaws hanging open. One had dropped his milkshake, which was oozing out on the sidewalk. It was pink. Probably strawberry. Allan Shepard, a local CPA, was standing in the front window of his accounting firm across the street, hands planted on his hips. The Open flag hung listlessly over his door. The engine of the police car Dave had pulled up in was running. Its radiator fan kicked on with a loud whir.

Dave kept his place standing over Billy, his arm still extended and holding his revolver. He showed an indifferent face.

Immie Davenport finally started to scream, and it was her shrill cry that called Corbin to action.

"Jesus Christ Almighty, he's lost his mind. What the hell did he just do?" Ray Stanski said from behind him.

5

Dave could feel his heartbeat in his hand as he squeezed the pistol grip. It was thumping in his fingers. Sweat was starting to itch his palm.

"Drop the gun!" someone shouted.

Dave didn't focus on who had said it; he was looking down at Billy's dead body. He didn't think he had been planning to do that on the drive over. But somewhere between leaving his house and arriving at the police station, something must've boiled over inside him.

I had no choice, he thought. *What kind of a man would I be if I didn't defend what's mine?*

Someone repeated the command: "Drop the gun, Dave. Now!" And this time he recognized it as Chief Delancey's voice.

Dave turned his head and looked across his shoulder. The chief had his gun pointed at him. Ray Stanski was doing the same, but he looked nervous and pale—unsure of himself. Corbin looked plain furious, but there was also a hint of something like sadness in his eyes.

It felt odd to see the law from this side. In a matter of seconds, he had completely flipped his life upside down. And all it had taken was a few tiny flicks of his finger on a trigger. He couldn't decide if that was a terrifying or exhilarating thing to understand.

Ray leaned toward Corbin and said, "He only fired five shots, Chief. Gun's not empty, I don't think."

"I can count, Ray," Corbin said.

Immie was screaming, "He killed him. He killed him. I saw him do it. Oh dear God, he's killed him," over and over again.

"Goddammit, Dave, put your gun down. I won't tell you again."

Dave lowered the gun so that it was pointed at the ground, but he didn't drop it. He faced Corbin squarely, who stiffened his stance. "He ruined her," Dave said. "He might as well have killed her. Billy got what he deserved and nothing more."

"You didn't have to shoot him," Corbin said, taking a step toward him. "Jesus Christ, you didn't have to do that."

"People get what's due them." Dave nodded. "That's all this wa—" *Grrr... Garoof!* The sound startled Dave, and he looked to his right. "The hell?"

The dog he had found out near Nipmuc the day before was standing in the middle of the street. It was growling at him, its giant, sharp teeth bared. There was something different about the dog. It had strange, shimmering eyes that seemed to shift colors like two black pearls. The thing was huge, too. At least twice the size as he remembered it being. He didn't think Labradors could even get that big. Its mouth was dripping with silver slobber, and its coat was covered in something oily.

"What the fuck are *you* doing here?" he said, turning to Black Dog. "Didn't I already teach you not to sneak up on people?"

He started to raise his gun at the dog, but it leapt at him and sank its teeth into his arm. He felt the bones crunch, and his fingers went numb.

Dave dropped the revolver, fell onto his back, and started to shriek with pain.

6

"Holy hell, he just bit himself! Did you see that? Did you *see* that?" Ray said, horrified. He was pointing his gun at Dave, but the barrel was shaking. "Jesus, what's the matter with him?"

"I don't know," Corbin said. "But you're going to have to cover me, in case he reaches for that pistol. Can you do that while I put the cuffs on him?"

"Yeah… Yes. Yessir," Ray said, wiping the back of his hand across his forehead.

"Don't you take that gun off him, you hear? I haven't a clue what he'll do."

"It looks like he's havin a seizure," Ray said. "My brother used to get em."

"That ain't no seizure," Corbin said. "Just make sure he doesn't move for that gun. If he does, plug him. He just shot Billy Porter in the face. You don't forget that. If you and Dave was friends before, you ain't right now. Don't hesitate, because he sure as hell won't."

Dave was flopping around on his back in the street, screaming. It looked like he was wrestling some invisible thing. If he was faking it—which of course he was, because what other explanation could there be?—it was one hell of a mime act. The muscles in his arms and neck were corded with straining tendons. He was giving it his all. "Help, you assholes! Get this thing off me. Somebody shoot this mutt, for chrissakes."

But there was nothing there. There was no mutt. Only a grown man in the throes of some strange episode. He had bitten himself in the meat of the forearm hard enough to draw blood.

Across the street, Immie was still screaming. She had changed her refrain, though: "What's he doing? Oh Lord, why is he doing that? Why? Oh no, why? Dear God, someone stop him."

"Show's over," Corbin said, moving toward him cautiously. "Now get up. I'm going to cuff you and take you inside." He kept his eye on the revolver on the ground. It sat in a pool of Billy's blood.

Dave continued shouting and flopping as if possessed: "Kill it. Kill the fuckin thing."

Corbin looked down at Billy's mangled face staring up at him, thought about what a waste of a life it was, and lost any sort of patience he had left. "Kill what, Dave? What're you tryin to do here? Billy's dead, so let's go... now. I'll put one in you if you make me, and I won't lose a wink of sleep about it."

"Shoot it, asshole, what're you waiting for? Shoot it, shoot it." Dave flailed around on the ground.

The whole thing looked rather ridiculous, Corbin thought. For a man who had just murdered someone in the name of pride, he sure was acting like a desperate fool.

Dave shook hard, his legs spreading and stiffening, toes pointing up toward his head, then down away from him as if he were about to pencil dive. "*Gawww!* Stop! Nooo! Goddammit, no!"

He lunged his head up, brought the inside of his wrist to his mouth, and bit a chunk out with his teeth. Blood jetted from the wound and covered his face. He'd hit an artery.

"Get it off, get it off, get it off!" He howled in pain, his mouth a rabid maw, bits of flesh stuck in his teeth, blood turning his lips to a clown's lips.

Corbin stopped cold. This was something out of a nightmare—too bizarre to be real.

"Help me, Corbin. Help me," Dave pleaded. "God, please." His body jolted as if a surge of electricity had ripped through him. He grunted and snorted. "*Guurgh! Gawww. Breff.*" He took a bite out of his other wrist, pulling a mouthful of tendons and veins with it. Then he was waving his hands around wildly in front of his face as if defending himself, spraying blood every-where like a garden sprinkler.

He continued to scream, but they became muffled screams: he was chewing and swallowing, chin covered in spit and dark blood.

"Mother of God." Corbin made the sign of the cross and thought of that ugly thing he had glimpsed standing in the street behind Dave. It didn't make sense, but he knew it was somehow responsible for all this. And it wasn't finished.

Dave sat bolt upright, chest heaving, eyes bulging. He was drenched in his own blood. He turned his head to Corbin, his mouth dropping open. He let out a guttural cry.

Then there was a sickening crunching sound, like snapping celery, as Dave's jaw unhinged and opened impossibly wide, his skin stretching until it looked as though it would tear. He lifted an arm, made a loose fist, and pounded it into his mouth. His head jerked back as he stuffed his arm down his throat halfway to the elbow and started gnawing on it like a dog on a bone.

There was a single gunshot, a punctuation mark to end the horror, and Dave Blatten's forehead exploded. He slumped over sideways and was still.

Corbin wheeled around, his left ear ringing. The barrel of Ray's gun was smoking, and Ray's eyes were bulging. He was half-crouched in a firing stance and appeared to be in shock. The crotch of his pants was dark, and the stain was spreading down his leg.

"He was reaching for the pistol," he said, barely above a whisper. "I swear... I swear to God he was, Chief."

Corbin turned back around without saying a word. He hated to admit it, but he didn't care whether Dave had been reaching for his gun or not. He was only grateful the whole thing was over.

The scene looked surreal. It was eerily quiet. The only sound was the whir of the car radiator in Dave's police cruiser. Immie Davenport had fainted and was sprawled out on the sidewalk among her bags. The two boys on their bikes had gone, leaving a pink puddle of milkshake where they had been. People were starting to gather at street corners. Crowds were forming.

What in God's name is happening in this town? he thought.

The afternoon had started to grow dark to the west, and the wind began to change as storms rolled in.

Chapter Ten

DYNAMITE MEATLOAF

1

Peter was leaning forward and squinting. The windshield wipers were doing their back-and-forth dance but having a hard time keeping up. A storm front had rolled in earlier that afternoon, and the rain had kept on going right into the evening. He liked everything about this sort of weather—the wind, the rain, the thunder, the lightning, the premature darkness. It was cozy, he thought, so long as you weren't stuck outside in it without a place to go.

"Should we bring something?" Sylvia asked. "We could pick up a dessert. I hate showing up empty-handed."

When they came to the intersection where Linebrook Road met Main Street, Peter hesitated at the stop sign and looked at his wife. Neither of them had been dressed so casually for a dinner in almost ten years. It felt nice.

"I saw a bakery downtown when we came through. We can go check it out. We have time." He checked his watch. Laura

Dooley had invited them for dinner at six—it was only five thirty. "I think there was a drugstore next to it, and I wanted to grab a few things anyway."

He turned the car right, toward downtown Gilchrist, and found a place to park.

While Sylvia was next door, picking out a cake from Joyce's Bakery, Peter perused the aisles of Quints Pharmacy. He found a package of red felt-tip pens. They weren't Flairs, but they would do the job, just the same. He grabbed a bottle of aspirin, a couple extra toothbrushes, and a Johnson & Johnson first-aid kit.

On his way to the cash register, he spotted a metal-wire paperback rack. He glanced out the large display window of the drugstore. Outside, cars sloshed through the street. Thick thunder grumbled. Lightning snapped. People ran up the sidewalk, covering their heads with coats, while the more prepared carried umbrellas. He had his own writing to focus on, but if there was ever a night to dig into a novel, this was it. And he hadn't been particularly interested in any of the books at Shady Cove.

The top shelf of the drugstore rack was all Agatha Christie novels: *The Burden*; *Ordeal by Innocence*; *Cat Among the Pigeons*; *The Pale Horse*; *And Then There Were None*, which was often considered her masterpiece. Peter had read some Agatha Christie when he was younger and had enjoyed her books a great deal. They were fun stories, plain and simple. Good plot twists. Well-developed characters. Page-turning suspense. It was only in his college years that he had shifted away from books of that sort and moved more toward highbrow literary works. In the circles he wanted to be a part of, they read highbrow fiction like Salinger, Faulkner, F. Scott, and Hemingway. Somewhere along the way, he had gotten the idea that in order to be taken seriously, he had to read about and discuss serious things. And he had allowed the very same principle to affect—sometimes he thought *infect* would be a better word—his views on writing. But in the back of his mind, he had always felt that looking down upon any type of fiction was a rather silly idea. Yet he had done it anyway. The truth was, he never thought there was anything wrong at all with writing mystery, horror, or science fiction. So far as he was concerned, if the reader was entertained, the responsibility of the writer had been fulfilled. He had started writing in high school with that very outlook, but as they often do, priorities changed. Not that there was anything wrong with that, either. It was just a fact of life.

The middle shelf was a mix of Ian Fleming, Ray Bradbury, and Philip K. Dick. But on the bottom shelf, there was only one novel. It took up every slot in the row. Declan Wade: *Jackson Hill*.

Peter's chest fluttered. He remembered seeing the title on the notes he had found in the drawer. He picked up a copy and studied the cover. It was a brooding but simple design—black and red with the title written in large silver gothic letters. Below that, a small blurb read: "From the author of *Devil Incarnate* comes a frightening new novel of horror and suspense." Across the lower half of the cover was a white silhouette of trees against black.

He turned the book over and saw the author's picture in black and white in the bottom corner. Declan was leaning on his elbow, a closed fist resting against his temple. He had shortish gray hair and was sporting that clever smile Peter had seen before in magazine articles. He knew the guy was in his sixties and thought he looked pretty good for his age. Of course, the picture might've been an old one the publisher had recycled. They did that sometimes, especially with an author like Declan who put out at least one new novel a year.

Peter started to read the book synopsis for *Jackson Hill*:

Three years after losing their son to a tragic accident, Jacob and Sandra Thornhill are still unable to move on. In need of a fresh start, and compelled by strange dreams, the couple decide to move to the small New England town of Jackson Hill. But as bizarre events begin to unfold around them, they soon discover moving there may not have been their decision at all. A timeless being called a gishet has—

"That book was written right here in town, if you can believe it."

Peter looked up to find the pharmacist standing behind the counter. "I heard that. I take it that's that why you have so many copies. Am I right?"

"You are, indeed. It's a bit of a novelty around here, I guess you could say. It came out years ago, but folks still stop in to pick up a copy a few times a week. It's just to say they read it, I'm sure. Don't want to be left behind, you know. But if they'll keep buying them, I'll keep stocking them. Much as I don't care for it myself. Too violent for my taste."

"It looks interesting," Peter said, stepping to the counter and setting everything down. "Good weather for it, too."

"That it is. Should clear up by t'morrow." The pharmacist slid his glasses to the tip of his nose and regarded Peter. "I can't say as I recognize you. You renting up at the lake?"

"For three weeks. My wife and I."

"Gosh, it's nice up there this time of year, isn't it?" The pharmacist pushed his glasses back up.

"Love at first sight," Peter said. "Whoever rents it next might have to blow us out with dynamite."

A sweet smell hit him out of nowhere. It reminded him of the banana bread his grandmother used to make. Then it faded and was gone, a meaningless, passing detail.

The pharmacist laughed. "I suppose they might. Which place are you renting?"

"Same house this was written in, actually. Shady Cove." Peter gestured to the copy of *Jackson Hill* sitting on top of the first-aid kit. "That's what I was told when we rented the place, anyway. Don't hold me to it if I'm wrong and making a fool out of myself. Did I get greased?"

He knew it was true, though; he couldn't think of another reason Declan Wade's writing notes would've ended up in the desk drawer. Plus, the realtor, Leo Saltzman, had outright told him. Unless, of course, that was a tactic he used to bait people into renting the place.

"Uh-huh, that's the one," the pharmacist said. Then his face took on a look of sad regret. "You rent it through Leo Saltzman, by any chance?"

"I did, yes," Peter said. "Seemed like a nice guy."

"He *was* a nice guy. Darn shame what happened to him. I couldn't believe it, myself."

"What happened?"

"You didn't hear? No, I guess you wouldn't've. Jeez, I hate to have to tell you this, fella, but Leo died yest'dee. Had an accident in his garage."

Peter felt his jaw go slack. "Oh my God. How?"

"Not quite sure. Heard it was something with one of his

power tools. A real dumb-luck thing. Poor guy. Here one day, gone the next. Life's sticky that way."

"I only just met him, but…" Peter trailed off. He thought about how Leo had given him a pen and was struck by a far-off sadness for the man.

"I know. It doesn't make it any better," the pharmacist said. "Dyin is dyin, no matter how you look at it. His wife found him, too. I can't imagine." He shook his head and punched a few keys on the cash register. "That'll be nine dollars and twenty cents for all this. Need a bag?"

Peter nodded, distracted. "Yes. Thank you."

"Didn't mean to put a damper on your day, son. Maybe I should've kept my trap shut. I'm sure you could've gone your whole three weeks here without having to think about that. I apologize."

"No, it's all right. I'm just surprised, that's all."

"Well, you wouldn't be the only one," the pharmacist said, handing him the bag. "Been a strange week altogether. Must be some sour luck going around. It'll pass. Always does."

"I'm sure it will," Peter said.

He paid and then left, a sinking feeling in his stomach. It was funny, he thought as he ran up the sidewalk against the wind and the rain, how death can unsettle a person it had no business unsettling. He had only known Leo a few days, had spent a total of maybe an hour with the guy, and yet he genuinely felt disturbed and saddened that Leo had died.

When he returned, Sylvia was waiting in the car, a pink pastry box dotted with rain spots sitting in her lap. "I got a vanilla cake. Nothing fancy."

"Okay," Peter said, running a hand through his wet hair. He dropped the bag from Quints Pharmacy in the backseat, then started the car.

"Something wrong?" Sylvia asked.

"You won't believe what I just heard," he said, bewildered. "The man I rented the lake house from died yesterday. Some sort of accident."

"What happened?"

"I don't know." He looked at Sylvia and forced a smile. "It's fine. I don't mean to put a mood on the evening. It was strange to hear, that's all."

"What's so strange about it?"

"It's just, well, you would think you can sense something like that coming. You know? I mean, I sat across from the guy and chatted for almost an hour, and never once did the idea of him dying cross my mind. Death is a big and ugly thing. It's clumsy and loud, yet somehow it manages to be so damn clever and sneaky. It just doesn't seem fair."

Sylvia reached over and took his hand. "I know."

They sat there, saying nothing to each other while rain beat down on the roof of the car and thunder tumbled high above heaven. It was a pleasant and sad piece of time. And it was good. When they were ready to go, they drove.

2

As it turned out, Laura Dooley hadn't been lying about her meatloaf. It was so good, in fact, that Peter ate two helpings before finally having to surrender. Sylvia thought she had even seen him undo the top button of his pants to make a little room. The only other time she ever caught him doing that was at Thanksgiving.

He and Kevin had gone over to the living room to play a rematch of Go Fish, leaving just the girls at the kitchen table.

"More coffee?" Laura asked. "There's still a little left in the pot."

"That'd be great," Sylvia said. "Thanks."

"My pleasure." Laura topped off her cup. "So as I was saying, when my grandmother died, she left me the house and everything else she had. It wasn't a fortune or anything like that, but it's enough for me and my son… for now, anyway." She stirred sugar into her own coffee. "If it wasn't for her, I don't know what we would've done. Probably be living at the Willows."

"The Willows?"

"It's the trailer park across town."

"Oh," Sylvia said, her eyes drifting down for a beat. She felt terribly self-conscious about the face she may have inadvertently made.

Laura smiled sweetly, a look that said: *You have no idea, do you? But that's okay.* "It would've been awful to live there. The Willows is no place for a single mother, and I don't mind saying it. There's plenty of good folks there—don't get me wrong—but there are plenty of bad ones, too. Like anywhere."

Sylvia hesitated on the next question, but it was out of her mouth before she knew it. "What about your parents?"

Laura glanced away, then back to Sylvia. "They're dead."

"Goodness. I didn't mean—"

"No, it's perfectly fine. You wouldn't know that. Besides, it happened when I was only two years old. I don't even remember it."

"What happened to them?"

"My dad was a sick man. Schizophrenia," Laura said.

Sylvia became aware of a hard courageousness in the girl's demeanor—a girl who had been forced to grow up too fast. She also recognized, only because she had been through it herself, the stiff tone of voice that always seems to arise when a person begins to recite a story they've become tired of telling. Everything trimmed down to the barest details so as to get the information delivered as succinctly and quickly as possible.

"He murdered my mother. Shot her one night when she was sleeping, then turned the rifle on himself. He didn't leave a note or anything like that. It wasn't suicide… he was sick. It happened, that's all. My grandmother told me he should've been in a hospital." She wrinkled her nose and made an embarrassed face. "Are you sorry you asked?"

"No. We all have a past we can't control. But I am sorry that happened to you."

"That's nice of you to say. Thank you."

Sylvia cleared her throat and shifted in her chair. "How old are you, if you don't mind me asking?"

"Twenty-three. A little young to have a six-year-old, I know." She set the spoon on the table, then ran her finger around the rim of her coffee cup. "Now you can go ahead and ask me the follow-up. It's fine."

"What follow-up?"

"Sorry," Laura said. "But you want to know where Kevin's father is. It's okay."

"It wasn't my place to ask."

"You're very polite, Mrs. Martell. I like that."

"And you're very mature. We're both great, aren't we?" Sylvia winked at her and sipped her coffee with a smile. Then she added, "And for goodness' sake, don't call me that. I'm hardly ten years older than you."

"I'm sorry. You just seem so… I don't know… together, I guess."

Sylvia blurted out a single syllable of laughter. "I promise you I'm not. But thank you for cheering me up. I needed that."

Laura smiled, then went on. "His name was Jacob—Jake. He was a real special guy. Really smart and probably the kindest person you'd ever meet, I swear. We got married when we were eighteen. See?" She held up her hand and wiggled the appropriate finger. There was a thin gold ring with a small diamond chip on her wedding finger. "It isn't much, but we loved each other. And I think that counts the most. It could've been a bread tie or a Band-Aid, and I would've liked it just the same."

"What happened to him?"

"The doctors said he had a heart attack." The way Laura said it suggested she might not have agreed with the diagnosis. She crossed her arms and leaned forward on her elbows. "That was two years ago. Kevin took it hard. We both did."

"Wait. I'm a little confused. You just said you got married when you were both eighteen. Which means he was the same age as you."

"I know." Laura nodded. She understood where Sylvia was headed with this because it was where most people headed with it. "How does a healthy person in their twenties have a heart attack, right? And he *was* healthy. Hardly ever even caught a cold."

"I've never heard of such a thing."

"I hadn't, either. It never made sense to me. Sometimes I get the feeling we're just dying for something else's amusement." She shook her head and laughed at the last part.

"I know what you mean."

"Death never seems to make sense, does it?"

"No, it doesn't." Sylvia thought of her son, then of what Peter had said about death being sneaky.

"Anyway, what could I do other than accept it and move on? I realized that trying to find the reason in it wouldn't change a thing. Even if it was somehow justified, he's still dead no matter how you cut the deck."

"The doctors didn't find any kind of heart condition?"

"Nothing. Like I said, he was as healthy as could be. They said it was like his heart just stopped beating."

"What was he doing when it happened?"

Laura chewed at the side of her cheek, eyes distant. "He went out for a hike one afternoon to scout for deer tracks and never came home. I thought he might've spent the night out there. He'd done it before, said the best time to track deer activity was at night. But two days later, a couple hunters found him sitting up against a tree. He was gone. Happy world one day, upside down the next. But that's life, right?"

"There certainly isn't a shortage on surprises, especially the bad ones. I know that much," Sylvia said.

Tears had gathered in Laura's eyes, but she looked at peace. "We were going to see the world together. A little bit at a time. We were planning on leaving this place finally. He wanted to move to Texas, and I just wanted to get out of here. Anyplace else was fine with me. This town…" She shook her head a little as if shedding a thought. "Never mind. I sound like a bore. If I keep going, I'll probably scare you off. And you and your husband seem like fine people I wouldn't want to leave an impression like that with."

"Nonsense, I get it," Sylvia said. "Small towns are tough. I grew up in one myself. You reach a point where you just don't care to have everyone knowing everything about you. And when you reach that point, it's time to pack up and go."

"That's part of it, sure. But that's not what I was going to say." Something troubled touched Laura's face. "Mrs.… Sylvia, I hope you don't take this the wrong way, but I've lived here all my life, and I know Gilchrist is a great place to pass through or to spend a couple weeks up at a lake house forgetting your cares. But living here, you get to notice that a lot of bad things happen in town. More than seems normal. At least it feels that way sometimes."

Sylva was starting to get a clearer picture of Laura Dooley, and in that picture, she saw a reflection of herself. The girl had been stuck beneath a cloud of death her entire life, and now she couldn't help but see the world in dim, hopeless shades of gray. Tragedy, to her, was no longer a random part of life, but a symptom of something beyond her control. Sylvia knew firsthand that when it came to loss, finding something to blame was easy, if not necessary.

Laura had simply set her sights on the biggest target she could find—Gilchrist. And why shouldn't she associate death with the town she grew up in, when it was all she had ever known?

"Take it from me," Sylvia said, "it's easy to see bad when you forget what good looks like."

"Maybe." Laura brought her knees up to her chest, her heels resting on the edge of the chair. "Did you know five people have died in town over the last few days?"

"No, I didn't. Well, Peter told me the man he rented the house from passed away in an accident of some kind. I did know that. But five people? No. What happened?"

"From what I heard, three were accidents. But the other two were a couple of cops who got into it over a woman. I went to high school with them, actually. Now doesn't that seem like a lot to you, even a little strange? That's too much death for a small town like Gilchrist."

It did seem like a lot. But not all that strange. People had accidents all the time, and men fought over women every day; it was practically the oldest conflict in the history of the world. But Sylvia could see how filtering it all through a lens tainted by a lifetime of tragedy could make a person think as much. In the pitch dark, every unexpected sound is a ghost or a ghoul.

"He's good with Kevin," Laura said.

"Huh?" Sylvia looked up. She had drifted away in thought. She looked at Laura, then followed the girl's gaze into the living room, where Kevin and Peter were laughing and playing cards.

"Your husband—he's good with Kevin," she repeated.

"They do seem to be hitting it off, don't they?"

"Do you two plan on having kids?" Laura asked. "You seem like you'd be good parents."

Sylvia crossed her arms and cupped her elbows. "We were parents for a little while. We had a son. Noah. But he died."

Laura's lips parted as she drew in a breath.

"It's okay," Sylvia said.

She heard her voice shift into monotone as she began to tell Laura about the child they had lost. But for the first time since it had happened, she didn't feel sad as she told it.

3

"I think they're talking about us in there," Peter said, looking into the kitchen. He raised his eyebrows at Sylvia, who smiled at him and then returned to her conversation. Back to Kevin, he asked, "You have any threes?"

Kevin scrunched his face and fanned through his cards. He was wearing the Red Sox cap Peter had given him, and it was falling over his eyes again. "Hmmnn-no. Go fish."

"Wow. Nothing again?"

"Huh-uh." Kevin shook his head, pushed up the brim of the hat, and scratched his nose.

"You've been stonewalling me all night, pal. Are you cheating? I think you're cheating. No one in the history of Go Fish has ever been this good."

"I practiced all night."

"So that's your secret. Okay." Peter glanced back at the kitchen, saw that he wasn't being watched, and leaned closer to Kevin. "Hey, pal, can I ask you something?"

Kevin nodded, never lifting his eyes from his cards. "I know what you want to ask me."

"You do?"

"Yes, I don't mind."

"What do I want to ask you?"

Kevin squinted at his cards, as if he were looking through them, not at them. "When you hugged my wife yesterday," he said in a voice that sounded like he might've been trying to imitate Peter, "she told me you whispered her a secret. What did you say to her?" Kevin scratched his nose again and continued to arrange and rearrange his cards.

Gooseflesh broke out all over Peter's skin as an even blend of bewildered excitement and uncomfortable awe washed over him. "Holy sh… cow. How did you just do that?" Not only had the boy gotten it right, but he'd recited the question nearly word for word, using the same phrasing Peter likely would have used.

"I can see it," Kevin said casually.

"See it? How can you see it? I don't understand."

"With my other eyes." Kevin finally looked up from his cards. "It's like x-ray vision, only different. You have them, too."

"I have what?"

"Other eyes."

"I do?" Peter laughed uneasily. "Where are they? I only see the usual two when I look in the mirror."

Kevin stood and leaned across the coffee table. He spread his first two fingers into a V and touched them against Peter's forehead. "They're right here. I don't think they're open, though. Not all the way. My dad said most people have them, but they just never learn how to use them."

"Can you do it again? I mean, can you show me how you use yours again?"

"Uh-huh." Kevin cocked his head to the side as if thinking. "Want to see a trick?"

"Okay."

Kevin closed one eye, and his face steeled over in concentration. "Pick a number between one and a hundred."

"Really?"

"Uh-huh. I'll guess it."

"All right," Peter said, but he had a hunch it wouldn't be a guess at all. He closed his eyes and focused. When he had the thought held clearly in his mind, he opened his eyes. "I've got one. It's a big one."

Kevin's forehead bunched in a show of confusion. "Hey, did you cheat? What's an unkis?"

"What do you think it is?" Peter asked timidly.

Kevin concentrated again. Then, with an air of uncertainty, he said, "A cat? A big, *fat* cat?" He giggled.

Peter nodded silently. After a second, he found his words. "Unkis was my cat when I was your age. That's amazing. But how…?"

Instead of thinking of a number, Peter had conjured up a memory of his childhood pet—Unkis, a fat white tabby that used to sit oddly humanlike on the couch with its legs spread and one paw resting on its wide belly.

Sadness sprouted on Kevin's face. "He got hurt."

"That's right. My father..."

Kevin looked back down at his cards. "I don't want to see it anymore. Do you have any Jacks?"

The demonstration was over, and Peter understood why: if Kevin really could see what he thought he might be able to, then he could see that Unkis had died when he fell asleep behind the back tire of the family station wagon and Peter's father hadn't thought to check before leaving for work.

Peter was in shock. He shook his head in utter disbelief. "How is this possible?" A small, astonished laugh escaped him. "You did know about Noah," he said in a low voice to himself, and looked toward his wife.

He heard the words coming out of his mouth, but they didn't feel his own. Was this really happening? In any other place, at any other time, he would have found a way to explain it away, maybe even flat-out refused to believe it no matter how much evidence there was. Giving in to irrationality was an uncharacteristic sidestep for him, but he stepped anyway. Something about the town, about the boy, evoked a sense of verisimilitude that compelled him to let go of his conventions. Well, that, and people could only rationalize so much before having to accept the thing staring them in the face.

It was as if his life up until that very moment had been lived inside the circle of a spotlight, and someone had just brightened the bulb and widened the light to reveal a slightly stranger world that had once been hidden in the shadow beyond. And that someone was a six-year-old boy sitting across from him with a goofy, too-big Red Sox hat and an itchy nose. A boy who could seemingly look into his mind and tell him what he saw there, yet who also had trouble pronouncing certain big words. He was an astounding balance of ordinary and extraordinary.

Kevin nodded. "Yeah, I saw it. I didn't mean to. Sometimes I can't help it."

"And you told my wife that you were sorry about what happened to him when she hugged you goodbye," Peter said in a low voice. He wasn't asking questions; he was stitching together pieces of a bizarre quilt and beginning to see the full shape. But it was a shape he didn't quite understand. He thought of what his wife had said yesterday: *Just because something doesn't make sense to you doesn't mean it isn't real.*

"She was sad, and I didn't want her to be," Kevin said. "Was she mad at me for looking?"

"No, pal, she wasn't. Maybe just a little confused. But that's okay." Then, more to himself than to Kevin, he added, "I get the feeling you've confused people before."

Footsteps started their way. Creaking floorboards. The sound of a sink turning on.

Peter looked sideways across the room. Sylvia stood in the doorway, leaning against the jamb, arms folded. She yawned. Behind her, Laura was cleaning the dishes off the table, rinsing them and then stacking them beside the sink.

"Getting late?" he asked.

"It's only nine, but I'm exhausted. I can barely keep my eyes open." She sat down on the couch next to Kevin, who was focused intently on his hand of cards, even though the game had fallen away to more interesting things.

Peter checked his watch. "I guess we should call it a night. You don't mind if we finish this another time, do you, pal?"

Kevin shook his head.

Sylvia looked at him. Her mind was turning something over. Peter had a good idea what it was, and damn it if she didn't have a good reason to wonder it. She hadn't brought it up since their conversation the day before. She might have stolen the occasional glance in Kevin's direction, but nothing more. And Peter saw in her face that she already knew what he had just discovered about the boy. For her, there had never been any doubt. They had shared something special when she had hugged him goodbye at Shady Cove.

"Did you whoop him?" Sylvia asked Kevin. "Sometimes he gets a big head. It's your job to make sure it doesn't pop like a balloon."

He nodded. "Yes." Then he faced her and smiled. "I let him win one round."

Peter looked at Sylvia. "Hey, I'll take it. A win is a win."

"Well, I'm sure he appreciates your mercy very much," she said, her eyes pinned to Peter's.

Laura came into the room, shirtsleeves pushed up, hands reddened from hot dishwater. "All right, kiddo, it's someone's bedtime. I've let you stay up long enough, and the Martells need to get going. Say goodnight and goodbye." She scooped up her son and held him off her hip.

"Goodnight and goodbye," he said, and smiled. It was the smile of a normal six-year-old boy who had stayed up a little later than he was used to and was starting to crash.

"Go brush your teeth and get into bed. I'll be up in a few minutes to tuck you in. Okay, sweetie?"

"Okay, Mommy."

She kissed the side of his head and put him down. Peter and Sylvia wished him a good night. Then he scurried up the stairs. The night had been a pleasant one and, for Peter, an interesting one.

"Thanks for dinner," Peter said, standing on the front steps of Laura's house as she stood in the doorway to see them off. "I think you might've undersold that meatloaf. Best I ever had. I'd swear to it in court."

Laura smiled, folding her arms. "I don't know about best ever, but I do think it was one of my better ones. You got lucky."

"We should do it again," Sylvia added. "Maybe we could have you and Kevin to the lake house before we leave. We don't exactly have a lot going on these next few weeks."

"I'd like that," Laura said. Suddenly she didn't seem so young anymore—she looked like a mother. A seriousness glazed over her face. She glanced over her shoulder into the house, then back to them. "He must trust you both an awful lot. He doesn't usually let people see what he showed you."

Her directness threw Peter. "I uh... I'm not sure what you—"

Laura smiled. "He's my son. Do you really think I don't know?"

Peter passed a hand over his face. "To tell you the truth, I don't know what I saw. All I know is that it was truly remarkable." He looked at his wife to confirm what he suspected she already knew. "It was. You were right, Syl."

Sylvia nodded. "When he hugged me goodbye yesterday"—she swung her gaze to Laura—"it was like..."

"Like you were sharing one mind?" Laura said.

"Yes. That's exactly it," Sylvia said, her eyes growing wide. "I didn't want to bring it up before. I hope you don't think I was trying to keep anything from you, but it was just so bizarre. I didn't think I should say anything because I thought you might think I was completely crazy. I've never... I mean, how?"

"I don't know," Laura said earnestly. "But his father was the same way. I think some people just have it, the same way some people are born tall or short or blond."

Peter thought about how Kevin had touched his forehead and told him he had other eyes, too. "I promise you we won't say a word to anyone," Peter said, offering his sincerest tone. He meant it, too.

A small laugh escaped Laura's mouth, and her grin spread. She had considered this before, probably more than a few times. "That's nice of you to say, but do you really think anyone would believe you if you told them?"

"No," Peter said, "I suppose not. They'd lock me in the looney bin. That's what would happen."

"Besides, even if someone would believe you, you wouldn't say anything," Laura said. "Kevin knows who he can and can't trust. And if he trusts you, that means you're safe to him."

They all stood there in the cool silence for a moment. There seemed nothing left to say, so the Martells went to their car and got in. Laura stayed on the front steps and waved as they backed down the driveway. As they drove home to Shady Cove, Peter told Sylvia about what had happened during his game of Go Fish with Kevin. The whole time, she had a content look on her face. The look said: *See, I'm not crazy.*

4

The telephone was ringing when they returned to Shady Cove. The bell sounded like an alarm calling out from darkness.

"Who would be calling this late?" Sylvia asked, stepping slowly through the dark house. "Does anyone even have this number?"

"I don't know. Probably a wrong number." Peter flipped on the kitchen light and went to the phone. As he did, another thought occurred to him. When Kevin had been sitting in their kitchen yesterday and the phone had started ringing, he'd said *Mommy* before anyone answered it. He had known it was her calling. Peter once again shook his head in disbelief; he was still processing the strange information he had just been given. In some ways, the whole thing felt like a dream.

"Answer it, Peter. I'm going to take a bath," she said, and disappeared into the back bedroom.

Peter picked up the receiver. "Yeah, hello." There was no answer. "Hello, anyone there?"

"Sorry," a gritty voice said. "I was about to hang up. Didn't think anyone was going to answer."

"I'm here," Peter said. "It's a little late, but what can I do for you?"

"I'm trying to reach Peter Martell. I was told I could find him at this number."

"This is Peter. Who's this?"

"This is Declan."

Peter swallowed. "Declan Wade?"

"I think so. If not, I've been cashing the poor bastard's checks. I imagine he'll be righteously pissed when he finds out."

"Mr. Wade? Oh man, I apologize. I didn't know it was you," Peter said. "That was awfully quick."

"Don't say you're sorry. Wouldn't I be just about the biggest asshole if I was mad at you for not knowing it was me? We've never even met before. I know who you are, though. I read your first book… the Jupiter one."

"*Jupiter Place.*"

"That's it. God, I sound arrogant, don't I? I didn't mean to. The book was great is what I should've said. You're a fine writer. Intelligent. And intelligent can be boring. But yours wasn't."

"Thank you, Mr. Wade… I think."

"There's a compliment in there if you pick off all the gristly bits."

"I'm sure there is." Peter laughed. "I imagine you want to know what this is about. I was pretty vague with my agent when I asked him to put us in touch."

Declan's tone stiffened slightly. "All I know is I was given this number by Doreen and told you had some questions for me. Like I said, I knew who you were when she mentioned your name. And to be honest, I had a feeling I'd hear from you sooner or later, kid. If I was a betting man, I would've guessed sooner."

"I didn't realize you were expecting to hear from me," Peter said, slightly confused.

"I'm making assumptions. Let me back up," Declan said. "Are you a fan? What I mean is, do you read my books? I won't be offended."

"I've read *Gray Dawn*, but that's it. I actually just picked up another one today, which was why—"

"So you haven't read *Jackson Hill*?" Declan interrupted. "And that's not why you're calling me?"

"Well, no, I haven't read it yet. But that *is* why I'm calling you. At least I think so. I just bought it."

"You're confusing me, son," Declan said.

"Yeah, I'm afraid I'm a little confused myself." Peter pulled out a chair and took a seat at the kitchen table. He could hear the bathtub running, but his wife had become the farthest thing from his mind.

"So what's this about, then?" Declan asked.

Peter realized he hadn't quite thought everything through. He didn't know why he had wanted to talk to Declan. Those notes had strangely resonated with his own situation, but that had been nothing more than coincidence. Hadn't it? He wasn't so sure anymore. But what he was sure of was that he didn't want to come off as a complete, raving fool to someone influential enough to torpedo his career with a few well-placed phone calls.

"My wife and I rented a lake house in the town of Gilchrist. I believe you've heard of it. People around here seem to be of the opinion that you have."

There was a beat of silence on the other end of the phone. The dead air crackled with static as lightning flashed outside and painted the lake in snaps of blue. Thunder rumbled but never quite broke into a clap.

Then Declan said, "Let me guess… Shady Cove? Is that where you are?" A strange tone had crept into his voice.

"Yes. As a matter of fact, I'm here right now. Have been since yesterday. How'd you know that?"

"Let's call it a hunch." Under his breath, Declan added, "I knew this phone number looked familiar. I don't believe this. I really don't."

Peter kept going, not wanting to lose his focus—or his nerve. "I found some notes of yours… at least I think so. They looked like story notes for what appears to have become *Jackson Hill*. They were in a desk drawer at the house, scribbled freehand, and your initials were on them. Looked like really rough stuff."

Peter took a second to center himself. He could feel the words wanting to come out faster than he could think.

"And?" Declan asked. "I think I know where you're going with this, but I'd like to be sure before I sound like a crazy person."

"And, well, some of the stuff you wrote down struck me as a little—how can I put this without sounding completely insane myself?—it struck me as a little *familiar* to my own current situation. I guess what I really want to know is your personal take on this town. I know that's a bit ambiguous and a strange thing to ask, but—"

"It's not strange," Declan said. This seemed to be the answer he had been waiting for. "If it were Boston or Portland or some other place you were talking about, then maybe I might not understand. But Gilchrist... no, that isn't a strange thing to ask."

"No?"

"No," Declan said. "That's one peculiar town."

"Can I ask why you think that?"

"I spent months there, that's why. You only have to go there to know it." He paused, then added: "And you calling me from that house is only confirming it more."

"There is something off about it, isn't there? I just can't explain what it is," Peter said.

"But you can feel it, can't you? You can feel it in your heart."

"I swear it's like I've been here before. The first time I drove through town, it was like the biggest case of déjà vu I'd ever had, and I know I've never been here before. I'm sure of it."

"If there's one thing I've learned in my sixty-six years on this earth, it's that being sure of something doesn't mean diddly. It just means you're convinced. And people can be convinced of damn near anything under the right circumstances. For a time, people were sure that the world was flat, and we see how that turned out."

"Expectations shape our perception," Peter said dimly.

"Like I said, kid, you're intelligent. That's exactly right. It's simple—we spend our lives thinking we know what to expect, because there are rules, there is order that follows a set of logic we accept to be immovable. So when something queer comes along that doesn't quite align with what we anticipate, we dismiss it or rationalize it somehow and move on. You hear a bump in the night, and you say, 'Oh, it's probably the cat or the dog or a house noise,' but you only assume that because it's the only option we've been equipped to digest. Because monsters and ghouls don't exist, except for in our imaginations, right?"

"That's the consequence of growing up, I guess," Peter said. "The clay hardens."

"That's it, kid. That's exactly it. We forget how to bend our expectations. After too long, if you try, then you'll end up breaking something. And I'll tell you, Gilchrist is a place that can do that if you're not careful."

Peter heard the water shut off in the bathroom. "What did you mean when you said that me calling you from here confirmed it?"

After a somber pause, Declan resumed. "This is where things get a little weirder. And who knows, maybe there is a rational explanation for it, or I'm drawing conclusions I have no business drawing. But if there is, I haven't found it yet. And if you hang up on me, well, I wouldn't blame you. Before you do, though, think about what we just discussed about stubborn expectations."

"Okay, well you've certainly got my attention."

Declan breathed heavily into the phone. It was a hard sigh. "You know, a couple years back, I read about what happened to your son in the papers. It was a damn shame. That's the kind of thing that hurts to hear about, even when you're not the one it's happening to." It sounded like he had lit a cigarette on the other end of the line. "Thing is, I knew who you were back then, too. But not because of any book you'd written or because you were in the paper."

"What do you mean?"

"I was going through a bit of a rough time when I decided to rent that place. My wife and I were about two arguments away from divorce. I was drinking too much. I couldn't write. My life was a mess. So we agreed to try what I guess they call a trial separation. She took the house in Cape Elizabeth, and I spent six months at Shady Cove, hoping to find some sort of inspiration for a book I owed my publisher but couldn't write. It was after about the second week that the inspiration came. It just didn't arrive how I expected it to."

"The town," Peter said softly. "You were going to write about Gilchrist."

"Well, yes. But that wasn't how it started. For me, it was dreams. Real vivid ones. They started the first night I stayed there. I figured they were brought on by stress, but I'd been stressed before plenty, and I'd never experienced anything like this."

A tickle of unease ran across Peter's chest as a vision of that horrible church popped into his head, but he shut it out.

"What sort of dreams?"

"They started small," Declan said. "Little glimpses of a man and a woman. Nothing special about them. But they got more and more detailed, and it didn't take long for me to understand that the dreams were all set in Shady Cove. I figured the couple were unconscious representations of me at first. Freud stuff, you know? There was something odd, though—I could see their faces, but I didn't recognize them. And that doesn't usually happen. Not to me, it doesn't. When people are in my dreams, I either know them, or they're a Frankenstein mishmash of people I already know. But the couple I kept seeing were complete strangers to me. Nothing familiar about them. There was this sad bitterness surrounding them, too. Sometimes I'd even wake up crying, if you can believe it. I had a feeling it was my mind's way of telling me not to fuck up my marriage."

"I can believe it," Peter said. "Stuff tends to find its way out one way or another. Especially the emotions we try to bury. Simply doesn't work."

"Uh-huh. I thought so, too. But you may think differently when I finish what I'm telling you."

"Sorry. Go on."

Declan continued: "So, like any writer would do, I started to write about these people to understand them more. And in the back of mind, I had a hunch that maybe I would find a book idea if I did. Turns out I was right. I didn't know where I was going, or who they were, but the more I dreamed, the more I wrote. And the more I wrote, the more I started to know the couple and why they were at Shady Cove. That's how the story of *Jackson Hill* was born. At one moment I had none of it. The next, I had almost all of it being laid out in front of me. I just swapped Gilchrist for the fictional town of Jackson Hill, which was my own little tip of the hat to Shirley Jackson."

"I read that in your notes," Peter said.

"I'm sure you did." Declan took a pensive pause, then went on: "You know, I've always thought one of the stranger things about writing fiction is how characters take on a life of their own simply by writing about them. But this wasn't that. It was more like I was receiving a weak television signal, and I was transcribing the glimpses of pictures I saw as best I could and filling in the blanks. Not all the time. A lot of the story I knew I was in control of, I was calling the shots. But a lot of it… a lot of it was something else I'd never felt before. I didn't really think twice about it at the time. I didn't care where the inspiration was coming from, because I needed a book for my publisher. Besides, like you said, my clay had long since hardened, and I sure as hell wasn't thinking anything supernatural was actually at work. Not at first, anyway. Whatever the case, I wrote the thing during the six months I was there. It was published the following year in the fall of sixty-three. That would be almost three years ago now."

"I don't think that seems all that strange to me. Story ideas just sort of appear when you least expect them to."

Declan laughed again. The sound made Peter's skin break out in chills because the laugh sounded more like a warning to get prepared.

"I didn't think it was all that odd at first, either," Declan said. "Anyway, six months or so went by, and the book moved to the back of my mind as I worked on something new. Then one morning I was having my coffee and eating some toast, and I came face-to-face with the man from Shady Cove. The man I had dreamt about during my time there. I recognized his face immediately. I recognized *your* face, kid. Second page of *The New York Times*. It was an article about what had happened to your son. There was a picture of you. I nearly choked on my breakfast. What happened to you—*how* it happened to you— was practically identical to what I'd written in my book. And now you're in Gilchrist with your wife, staying in the exact same lake house where I kept seeing you. It's unbelievable. You know, I have never seen a picture of your wife, but I would bet my life that she's a redhead with blue eyes."

A dense stretch of silence sat between them on the telephone line. Outside, the sky opened up, and the rain became a torrential downpour. Peter could feel cool mist spraying in through the window screen behind him and settling on his neck.

"You still there?" Declan asked.

"I'm still here," Peter said.

"I'm right, aren't I? Is your wife a redhead?"

"She is," Peter said, and suddenly felt as if his mind and his body were separating and he was looking down on himself from ten feet above.

"Blue eyes, too?"

"Yes."

"Incredible. Absolutely goddamn incredible," Declan said, astonished. "Can I ask you something else? It's personal, but I think we should see how deep this odd-shit rabbit hole goes."

"Let me ask you something first," Peter said.

"Shoot, kid."

"This isn't some sort of joke, is it? I mean, I don't know you. How do I know this isn't some sick gag?"

"Be honest with yourself—do you really think that's what this is? Because I get the feeling you don't. I get the feeling your time there has already started to soften that clay a little and you're beginning to see that not everything is as it seems in this world. Especially not in that town."

Could not have said it better myself, Peter thought. But for some reason, he didn't want to confirm it aloud. "I don't know," he said. "But if it's a joke…"

"It's all in the book. Read it, and you'll know. Simple as that. Jacob and Sandra Thornhill have a child who dies by falling from a window in their home. Jacob's an author, just like you. Grief stricken and unable to cope with it, they move to a lake house to try and start fresh in a town where bizarre things abound. That's the mile-high view, but it sounds familiar, just like you said earlier, doesn't it?"

Peter had a feeling like he was holding the tether of reality and his grip was getting weaker, his palms sweatier, and now he was in imminent danger of losing his hold. Slipping. Slipping. Slip. And when he did, he was terrified to think of the dark void he would be cast into. Coming face-to-face with some ungodly horror. "So what do you want to ask me?"

"Your wife, she tried to kill herself, didn't she?" Declan asked cautiously. "Something to do with pills?"

Peter scoffed and shook his head. "Jesus Christ. How…?"

"I'll take that as a yes," Declan said.

"I don't understand. How could you know that? And it wasn't like that. It was an accident."

"The same way that I'm pretty sure you've been trying to have another child but just can't seem to make it happen, and that's really why you decided to get away and rent that place. Or that you've both quit drinking since being there. Or that you know if you two can't reconcile your marriage there, then it's probably never going to work. These things true, too? I'm going to go out on a limb and guess that they probably are. If I'm wrong, forgive me. I'm not trying to be rude."

"All of it," Peter said, starting to feel the pit of his stomach turn sour. "Jesus Christ, all of it's true. I don't get it."

"I don't, either, kid. But I can guarantee you it has something to do with that town. There's—I don't know—a thinness to that place."

"It could all just be a coincidence," Peter said, feeling a sudden flash of defiance. It was his practical mind's final death knell.

"Sure. Like I said before, people can be convinced of just about anything. It's all a matter of what you're willing to believe and how big a leap of faith you allow yourself to take."

"How can you be sure you never saw a picture of me and my wife? I've had articles written about me since my first novel. And these articles would've had my picture. Probably Sylvia's at some point, too. How do you know you didn't see one and forget about it? Maybe your subconscious dragged it up for whatever reason when you were staying here. Couldn't it be that's why you dreamed about us? All the similarities could just be bad coincidence. We're not the first parents to lose a child, and I doubt we'll be the last."

"Suppose you're right—then how would I know everything else that you've just confirmed is true? It's all stuff I wrote when I was there, when I was patching together these dreams and turning them into a book. It's like I was absorbing all this just from being in the house, from being in that town, even though none of it had happened yet. I don't know how that's possible, but you can't deny the facts." Declan hesitated. Then his voice took on an eerily sincere tone, and Peter could tell the man was telling the truth. "Look, I don't blame you for thinking this is nuts. It *is* nuts. Hell, I know it sounds like the ravings of a madman. But why would I make any of this up? I have nothing to gain from it."

"I don't know. Maybe you're just crazy," Peter said. But nothing in his tone suggested he actually suspected this.

"See for yourself. You said you just bought the book. Go ahead and read it. Everything I've just said to you is on record in *Jackson Hill*. That's why I wanted to know if you'd read it earlier. It's also why I thought you were trying to contact me in the first place. Ever since I read that article about your son and saw your picture in the paper, I thought I would get a call from you. I assumed either you or someone close to you had read the book, seen the odd similarities, and thought maybe I'd been trying to exploit what happened to you by writing a story about it. But a simple check of the timeline proves that's impossible. It'd already been published for six months when that happened to your family."

"God, what the hell is going on?" Peter pinched the bridge of his nose and closed his eyes.

"There's something else you should know, too. I don't know what it means, but…"

"But what?"

"The dreams eventually stopped when I was there," Declan said. "It was like you both just vanished. First her, then you."

"What happened?" Peter asked in a strangled voice.

"I don't know. But the last one I had was of you sitting at the kitchen table of Shady Cove. You were alone… and you were crying."

Peter scrubbed a hand over his face. "I feel stupid even having to ask, but do you have any idea what it means?"

"I don't know, kid. Like I said, this wasn't exactly handed to me on a silver platter all spelled out. I was piecing it together as it happened, discovering as I wrote."

"What happens to her in your book?" Peter asked. A wave of embarrassment wrenched through him when he heard the absurdity of what his question implied. The whole thing seemed silly on the surface, yet underneath it all, he could feel the dark weight of something very heavy and very real.

"It doesn't matter," Declan responded hopefully.

"Why not?"

"Because I knew I was making that part up. It didn't feel divined, I guess you could say. Not the same way the other stuff did. I only understood that you knew she was gone. Same way you can tell when your luck's about to turn bad in a card game.

It's just a gut feeling. That's as much as I got. Some things were clearer than others. You have to understand, much of this came at me piecemeal, and I did the stitching together as best I could, the way you do with any story."

"What happens?" Peter repeated bluntly. "I'm going to read it, so you might as well tell me."

He heard the splashing of water coming from the bathroom, the sound of gentle sloshing in a half-full tub. And all at once, he knew what Declan was about to say. For a horrible moment he was certain he could feel the water filling his lungs.

I don't want to hear it, he thought. *It's not true. None of this is true. It can't be.*

"She… Sandra Thornhill drowns herself in the lake," Declan said, the regret thick in his voice for having to taste the words. "But like I told you, kid, that was just story. That was me at the wheel, filling in a blank. As far as I knew at the time, she got taken away by aliens. She's okay now, isn't she?"

Aliens. Funny choice of word, Peter thought, as an image of that creature from his dream surfaced in his mind. He could see the gray thing with the shimmering face crouched over the window of his house, a witness watching as his son beat his little pink palms against the screen that would eventually pop out of its frame and send him crashing to the ground. He remembered how in his dream he had dove for Noah and come up short. Peter's hand went to his knee, then to his elbow, then to his forearm. The places were still sore. He had forgotten all about those mysterious scrapes.

"She's fine."

"Well, so that's good. Maybe not everything is true, then," Declan said. "Or at least not set in stone. I don't know."

"Yeah, or maybe whatever is going to happen just hasn't happened yet." With a heavy dose of cynicism, he added, "Are we seriously having this conversation right now? I mean, come on, this is literally right out of a horror novel. And if I'm talking to you about this, wouldn't you have put that in the book, too? When you were having your dreams, or visions or whatever, wouldn't you have seen that we talked at this moment and known all about it back then? Is that in *Jackson Hill?* Does what's his name—Jacob—stumble upon the book notes of a writer who stayed in the same place as him, and does he decide reach out to the guy?"

"No," Declan said flatly.

"Well, why not?"

"How should I know? Maybe it's the same reason you don't see your own nose even though you're staring at it all day. If there are rules to this, I sure as hell don't know them. God, kid, stop thinking I'm trying to sell you something. I'm not. I'm just telling you what I know. You can decide for yourself what to do with the information."

"I'm sorry. I'm just having a hard time wrapping my head around this."

"I know. You're certainly not alone on that one."

A moment of dead air grew on the line, and for a second it seemed there was nothing left to say. Peter licked his lips, staring across the kitchen and into the dimly lit bedroom. In the back of his mind, he was thinking about how nice it would be to hang up the phone and pour himself a tall glass of bourbon, then sit out back in one of those low Adirondack chairs and let everything melt away.

"Last week I would've thought you were insane," Peter said. "But today I'm inclined to keep an open mind."

"There isn't any real protocol for something like this," Declan said. "I'd say just be careful. Probably nothing will happen.

Maybe we changed something simply by having this conversation. It could be now that you know what might be coming, it won't happen."

"I hope you're right."

"Me too, kid. You want some advice?"

"What?"

"If I were you, I'd get out of that town and never look back. You and your wife pack up tonight and leave. Play it safe. That place might seem like a cure for what ails you, but I think it feels that way for a reason... and not a good one."

There was a rustling on the phone line, and Peter heard Declan, in a muffled voice, tell someone he would be done in a moment. Back to Peter he said, "I had this friend when I was a boy, Eddie Cavanaugh. He was one of those kids that always seemed to be sick. Whenever we'd stop by his house to see if he wanted to come play, his mother would tell us it was too dangerous for her Eddie to come outside. No, Eddie had to stay in so she could take care of her little boy and make him all better. Well, as it turns out, the crazy old bat was poisoning him a little each day. Making him sick just so she could make him feel better. He lost a kidney, and she ended up in a rubber room with a view. I guess she needed the attention. She fed off it, in a way. A sort of one-sided, symbiotic relationship."

"Like a parasite."

"Exactly," Declan said. "You know, I think maybe we've talked enough madness for one night. Don't you? Besides, it's getting late."

"Hold on. Let me just ask you this: why here? What's so damn special about this town?"

"I wish I knew," Declan said. "All I have is speculation. The honest truth is I don't have a clue. If you want my best guess, though, it's in the book. The research I did on Gilchrist to build the mythos of *Jackson Hill* led to some interesting things. Let's leave it at that and say goodnight for now. I'll give you my phone number, and if you want to hash this out some more in daylight, give me a call."

Peter wrote the number down on a scrap of paper and tucked it in his pocket. "This has been, without a doubt, the strangest conversation I've ever had, but I do appreciate you calling me back, Declan. Trying to see it from your shoes, that couldn't've been easy to say to me. I'm not sure I would've had the guts to."

"You bet, kid. Take care of yourself. Don't be too stubborn just because this doesn't seem practical. If something doesn't feel right, it probably isn't. Especially there."

"Good night," Peter said, and hung up the phone.

5

Peter stood in the doorway of the bathroom, watching Sylvia as she lay in the tub, a folded washcloth over her eyes. Her arms were draped over the sides, creating small puddles on the floor below her fingertips. That was good, Peter thought, because if she could see his face, she would've understood how completely shaken he was by the conversation he'd just had.

"Who was it?" she asked, her head remaining perfectly still. "Not a wrong number, I take it. You were on the phone quite a while."

"A colleague of mine," Peter said, stuffing his hands in his pockets and leaning against the doorjamb. "Someone I'd asked Tom to put me in touch with. He was supposed to get me the guy's number, not give him this one."

"Anyone I know?" Sylvia asked, her hand carefully reaching up and scratching beside her nose.

"I don't think so. A friend of a friend, really. I just had some questions I wanted to ask him. Research for the book, nothing that couldn't've waited until morning."

"I see," she said. "Would you do me a favor and get me my towel? I left it on the bed."

"Sure." Peter got it for her and put it on the back of the toilet tank.

He stood beside her, his mind racing with what Declan had just told him. None of it seemed possible. The whole thing felt caught in his throat, and he had the strange idea that if he just mustered one huge, whooping laugh, it would all come flying out. He should tell her, he thought. Then he would be rid of the absurdness of it all. He should tell her what was just told to him, and together they could decide what to make of it.

Yet he couldn't bring himself to do it. Every time he opened his mouth to speak, he couldn't find the words. It all felt too complicated, and too big, and in that stubborn part of him where the clay was hard, the idea was too ridiculous to be of any serious consequence.

"What's the matter?" Sylvia asked, tilting her head in his direction. The towel over her eyes stayed in place. "I can tell when something's on your mind."

"Nothing. Just wrestling with the end of the book. You know how I get during this stage of a project. Nothing's ever good enough." Peter hesitated, then asked, "Hey, Syl, how do you feel? Are you...?"

She smiled. "I'm okay, Peter. I feel... calm. I think coming here was a good idea. We needed this."

"Okay," he said. "Just checking."

"Don't worry," she said. "And you'll figure out your book. You always do."

"I know."

He stayed beside her a moment longer, a thin sadness settling over him. He couldn't shake that sensation of looking down from outside his body: a duality of being himself while at the same time watching a character who had just been thrust into a situation he could hardly comprehend, let alone navigate.

6

The sign on the construction fence read KEEP OUT in serious black letters. Jim Krantz looked down at the set of keys he had taken off Leo. The large ring held at least two dozen, but one key stood out. He used it on the padlock, and it popped open. Then he undid the chain securing the gate, pushed it open, and went inside.

He was two howling green eyes floating in the pitch-black night. He was the crunch of automatic footsteps wandering across gravel, driving toward a singular thought, compelled to move forward. It was dark, but he could see. It was all so clear in his mind. The wind whipped the rain sideways in sheets, sounding like pebbles against metal as it smacked into construction equipment. He felt none of it.

Four months ago the plot of land had been an acre and a half of woods, but it had been razed by bulldozers and was currently in the process of being blasted. A hundred yards of rock ledge needed to be excavated in order to accommodate the twelve thousand square feet of strip mall that was supposed to be built there the following spring. The late Leo Saltzman had partnered with his brother's construction company after realizing the potential in the location. The site was on the western side of Gilchrist, settled between Mill Road and Route 2 on a stretch of land where the two roads ran parallel to one another for about a quarter mile. It was ideal: close enough to a major artery to attract the highway traffic, and close enough to local communities to bring in a regular, more consistent customer base and provide local jobs.

At the back of the construction site, rubber blasting mats were stacked beside a large blue storage container. Jim went to the storage container, gazed down at the keys in his hand again, found the right one, and removed another padlock. He undid the latch and opened the door. Inside, the container smelled sweet and stuffy, like sawdust and bananas. Along the back wall, Jim lifted a dusty canvas tarp. Beneath it were wooden crates with the words WARNING: DYNAMITE HIGH EXPLOSIVE stenciled on the lids in red paint. Beside him on the ground were large coils of wire, and beside that were the detonators.

Jim took what he needed, then left.

Chapter Eleven

JACKSON HILL

From *Jackson Hill*, by Declan Wade (Foundry Press: 1963), p. 42:

Since the wake the day before, Sandra hadn't stopped with it. "Have you seen the thing?" she would ask anyone who would listen. "It's so small, it's teeny-tiny. Where do they even find something like that?" She was talking about the coffin. And every time she said it, she chewed her knuckles, each time a little harder, until eventually, she bled.

So they buried their son on a Thursday, on a gray October morning with a cold fog rolling in off the Atlantic. And Sandra had laughed at the funeral. Everyone in the church had heard her when she excused herself to the bathroom. At first it sounded like sobbing, but soon came the unmistakable whoop and cackle of hysterical laughter. Then, echoing through the hollows of the church, came her voice: *It's so small, so smaaalllll.*

Laughter. And more laughter.

Some understood what she was saying and why she was saying it. The others had a unified look of horror on their faces. Dear God, what was happening? Why was she laughing? Why wouldn't she stop?

Jacob, on the other hand, thought it was just about the saddest sound he'd ever heard. Something inside his wife had broken, a short circuit brought on by a surge of grief no human body was equipped to handle.

She was in a state of shock. That was what Dr. Lassiter would tell Jacob when he came to their house to give her a shot later that evening, not that he needed a doctor to tell him what he already knew. Of course she was in shock. Her three-year-old boy had just fallen from the window of their twentieth-floor Manhattan apartment and landed on the sidewalk. And she'd seen it all happen while she was on the phone with her sister.

"Her mind is having a hard time accepting what's happened," Lassiter said. "It's trying to protect itself. Sometimes these things manifest themselves in bizarre ways."

"But laughing at—" Jacob lowered his voice, looking in the direction of their bedroom, where Sandra was fast asleep. "But laughing at our son's funeral? That's more than a little bizarre, don't you think? I can't get that sound out of my head. She sounded... she sounded insane."

"Sometimes, when there's such an intense emotion, the body doesn't know how to react. It just needs to get it out somehow. It's almost like a mental sneeze, a way to clear out whatever's in there," Lassiter said. "She'll be okay. It might just take a little while. In the meantime, I'll write her a prescription for something to keep her calm. It'll help, especially with sleep."

Jacob didn't like the idea. Something inside him sent up a red flag at the idea of pills being his wife's coping mechanism. Looking back, he often pinpointed that exact moment as the place where he should've chosen differently.

"Okay," he said. "Thank you."

And so began the medicated life of Sandra Thornhill. A pill in the morning to start the day, a pill with lunch to keep things rolling smoothly, and a pill or two every night before bed to make sure the sandman showed up on time and her sleep was dreamless. It would go on this way for...

From *Jackson Hill*, p. 73:

Jacob had just enough time to duck out of the way as the plate smashed against the wall behind him.

"*Get out!*" Sandra screamed. "I don't care! I don't want to hear it anymore!"

"Just calm down, would you?" he said. "We'll keep trying. The doctor didn't say it wouldn't happen. He only said it was taking a bit longer than usual. That doesn't mean we can't."

"I don't want to keep trying. I'm sick of it, and I'm sick of you. You keep telling me everything will be all right. You've been saying that for the last two years, and nothing has been fine. Nothing has ever been fine."

She wasn't wrong about that. Nothing had been going their way. He couldn't argue that. But Jacob wasn't about to agree with her, not out loud. Of course not. If he did that, the whole thing would be over.

"Honey, why don't you take one of your pills and calm down. Okay?" Jacob said. "Once you're feeling a little better, we can talk about this more rationally."

Sandra laughed, appalled. "I don't want another pill." She grabbed the bottle off the counter and shook it. "Do you know how many of these I've taken since he died? Hundreds. Pill after pill after pill to pretend our son isn't dead. To pretend there isn't a problem when it's been a year, and I can't get pregnant. Maybe that's a sign. You let one die, you don't get another."

"San—"

"No. Shut up. I'm tired of not feeling."

Jacob found himself trying to work out the math in his head, even as he stood there getting screamed at. James had died in October of sixty-one. Now it was July of sixty-three. God, had it really been almost two years? It all felt like a dreadful blur—two years, two sadness-filled years, gone by as a smear of gray paint across a canvas. He counted them back. It'd been twenty-one months. And if Sandra ate four pills a day—oftentimes more—that was at least one hundred and twenty per month. Times twenty-one months. That's… She'd been wrong. She hadn't eaten hundreds; she'd eaten thousands.

"No one is forcing you to take anything," Jacob said, laying on the saccharine, I'm-not-your-enemy tone. "If you don't like the pills, then don't take them. You said they helped."

Then the bottle of pills was hurtling through the air at him. And this time he didn't have time to get out of the way….

From *Jackson Hill*, p. 98:

Jacob tried to wake her, but she was unresponsive. On the table was a half-empty bottle of gin. He stepped back from the couch, the fear slowly swelling inside him. Her skin looked paper-white against the dark blue of her bathrobe. The sleep looked far too peaceful. Far too *eternal*, a savage part of his mind suggested, to be mere alcoholic intoxication. Something crushed under his foot. He looked down and spotted the empty prescription bottle. The horrible, swelling wave inside him crested and came crashing down on the shore of his mind.

"Dear God. Sandra." He shook her. "Sandra, wake up. Wake up!" He slapped her.

And, of course, she did not answer him.

He shook her again, then slapped her cheek. But her eyes would not open to offer their irises. She was still breathing, but barely. Her chest was rising in shallow fits and starts.

How hadn't he seen this coming? Worse: what if he had and for some reason had chosen to ignore it?

He started for the phone, banging his shin against the coffee table as he turned. The bottle of gin clattered to the floor and began to empty itself onto the carpet in thick glugs and slurps. This stalled his mind. He stood frozen in the middle of the living room. He heard the traffic of downtown Manhattan outside, twenty stories below. A thought occurred to him, although it was more like a series of thought fragments that he slowly pieced together. If he called for a doctor, help might not arrive for at least an hour. It was a Saturday, after all.

He tried it from a different angle.

That's right, it was a Saturday, and people don't work weekends. Not people in his building. So people were home. His neighbors. A doctor. He knew a doctor down the hall. He'd met him at a Christmas party last year, the one where he and Sandra had both gotten too drunk and made fools of themselves. Sandra had fallen asleep on the bed of coats, and he'd used the broom closet as a lavatory. Certainly not their finest moment, but it was a moment that had left an imprint, and now he was recalling it. He was recalling the doctor's name, too. Bill. No. Will. No. Willams. Harvey Williams. End of the hall. Apartment…

He was knocking frantically on the door of apartment 20E, and he heard the locks turning. Someone was home…

From *Jackson Hill*, p. 117:

The town had a magnetism to it. It always had, from what he remembered.

Jacob hadn't been to Jackson Hill in over two decades, but he recalled even back then, the town had a palpable energy to it. It was a nervous type of caffeine energy, like everyone was waiting for the ground to crack open or for the boogeyman to jump out around every corner. Turned out, little had changed. He and Sandra had moved to town only a few days ago to start a new chapter in their life, and already the feeling was returning. It was all flooding back. And it was flooding hard and strong. Including the dreams. *Especially* the dreams.

Welcome back.

Jacob had been prone to vivid dreams since childhood. When he was six years old, he and his family had come to Jackson Hill to stay at Little Nook for the Thornhill family reunion. At the time, the house belonged to a distant cousin, Hezekiah Thornhill, the father of the cousin Jacob had bought the house from. Hezekiah had grown up in Jackson Hill and built Little Nook on a piece of lake property he had, if one could believe the local stories, won in a game of poker. During that weeklong stay for the reunion, Jacob had come down with an intense bout of night terrors.

After almost thirty years, he could still see visions of those bizarre nightmares. There was much he didn't remember—he could feel it more than he could see it—but he had never forgotten the face, that creepy colorful face, like the clear, shimmering brilliance of a soap bubble's skin. In his dreams, the face always leaned over him, and he could see his own reflection in it. But his reflection was distorted to show an aged and sickly version of him. In the nightmares, the face descended upon him, and right as it was about to swallow him, he would wake up screaming and sopped in cold sweat. And there was always the strong scent of campfire in his nose when he sat up, panting in the cold, dark room, trying to claw his way back to waking life. The house always seemed to have a smoky smell to it, even when they weren't barbecuing. In fact, the whole town seemed to. But it was particularly strong after a nightmare. He could almost taste the bitterness of ash on his tongue.

It went on that way for the six days Jacob and his family stayed at Little Nook. And when they did leave, the night terrors stayed behind in Jackson Hill. But it had left behind something special in Jacob. A channel had been opened in his mind, and now he was freer to travel to and from his dream space with much more ease and recall clarity. Back when he had been having the nightmares, he always imagined it as a construction project happening in his brain. A bunch of men had moved in during the middle of the night and started tearing up the ground, laying pipe, and changing things without his permission. What they had built was the channel. But they'd forgotten to build a door, and something had traveled up that channel and found him. The thing with the awful face. It had a name... a very old name.

And the name was *Gishet*...

From *Jackson Hill*, p. 267:

"Do you believe in vampires?" Professor Noonan asked, his face showing no signs he was joking. Leaning back in his desk chair, he removed his glasses and tucked them into his shirt pocket.

Jacob cocked an eyebrow. "Of the Bela Lugosi variety? Dracula and all that?"

"I'm serious," Noonan said. The tall stacks of mythology books in his office and on his desk echoed that sentiment. "There are many different kinds, but none are the blood-sucking sophisticates depicted in movies or books."

"To be honest, Mr. Noonan, vampires always seemed a little silly to me," Jacob said. "Nothing really believable about them."

"The way they're portrayed in fiction is a bunch of horse manure, yes. What I'm talking about is quite real, I'm afraid. There is a long history of it throughout the world. One only needs to know where to look to see it," Noonan said, steepling his fingers. "When I use the term 'vampire,' I'm not referring to what you probably picture. I use it to suggest the relationship between parasite and host, the reliance of one entity upon another as a means of survival. Nothing about a real vampire is elegant. They don't wear capes or have perfect hair or live in castles. They certainly do not turn into flying vermin, and cannot be defeated by crosses or garlic or any of that holy water nonsense. Religion has nothing to do with what they are, for the same reason it has nothing to do with the laws of physics." Noonan took a brooding breath. "I doubt very much they can be defeated at all, actually. No more than gravity can be. Some things are just a constant in our universe, a fixture that's always been and likely always will be."

"So what exactly are they, then?"

"Nothing with a resemblance to anything we're capable of fully understanding. Ghosts behind the veil, I guess you could say. These 'vampires'"—Noonan hooked his fingers to make quotes—"they exist in a different dimension, one far different from our own, both spatially and temporally. We don't see them, not usually, but they're still a part of nature, nothing supernatural about them. It just so happens to be a part of nature we don't yet understand. Am I making any sense?"

Jacob nodded tentatively. "I think I get the big picture. But if you can't see them, then how do you know they even exist?"

He had a vague sense of what Professor Noonan was talking about, but a lot of it was lost on him. He was starting to wonder whether or not coming to meet him was a mistake. He wasn't sure what he'd been looking for, but he hadn't expected invisible vampires. It all felt a little too foolish.

"The scientific approach. We can observe their effect on nature, make deductions from what we see. Find patterns throughout history. Think of it this way." Noonan lit his pipe with a wooden match and took a few puffs. "Consider gravity again. We can feel and see its effect every day. If I pick up a pen and let it go, it drops due to Newton's law of universal gravitation. But we haven't a clue what the hell is at the heart of the attraction that exists between two bodies with mass. What causes this attracting force? So we don't know *what* gravity is, but we know that it exists. It influences us in very conspicuous ways." He paused, and cracked a smile behind a haze of sweet pipe smoke. "And I didn't say we can *never* see them. I said we *usually* can't. After all, that is why you're here, isn't it? You've been seeing them?"

"Well, to be honest, I don't know what I've been seeing."

Noonan was looking at him sharply. "Describe it to me."

Jacob glanced down. "I don't know. It's like I can see them, but I can't. Like seeing a faint reflection of yourself in a pond. If you don't focus your eyes right, you'll see right through and miss it." He rubbed the back of his neck and sighed tiredly. "I always see a face, especially when I have those dreams I was telling you about. It's a colorful face. It looks like a mask, but at the same time, it's always shifting. Sometimes I think it looks like a pot of boiling spaghetti."

Noonan nodded along, then grabbed an old leather-bound book from a stack in front of him and started flipping through the pages. "You ever heard of a gishet?"

"I know that word," Jacob said, perking up.

Noonan looked up from his book. "You do?"

"Yeah. I'm not sure how. I just kind of do. It's like someone has been whispering it to me in my sleep. What is it?"

Noonan flipped through a few more pages and stopped. "Ah. Here it is." He turned the book around and set it open in front of Jacob. "This"—he tapped the page with his wrinkled finger—"is a gishet. Otherwise known as the Great Manipulator."

The rough sketch on the yellowed book page was an old drawing, and he didn't think it looked much like the thing he'd been seeing. It resembled a Chinese dragon. Around it was Gaelic writing.

"What are they?"

"No one knows for sure," Noonan said. "But if you believe the oldest texts, gishets are ancient harvesters. They build these worlds, the world you and I live in and call reality, as a means to cultivate. We are their puppets, and they are the masters pulling the strings. Our world is their stage. Do you believe in God, Mr. Thornhill?"

"Something like that, yes."

"And the devil?"

"Can't have light without darkness." Jacob smiled uneasily.

"Right. Well, gishets would've created them both. God and the devil. Light and darkness. All of it. Everything you know that exists, both real and imaginary, does so because they made it."

"Why?" Jacob leaned back in his chair.

"Simple," Noonan said. "Why do farmers build chicken coops or plow fields?"

"Forgive me, but that's a little…"

"Sounds like bad fiction, doesn't it?"

Jacob nodded. "Yes. Exactly. Is this what you honestly believe?"

"Not exactly, no," Noonan said. "Gishets feed on our energy. They're psychic parasites, in that way. They manipulate, creating chaos and disharmony because that's what they thrive on… that's what they have a taste for. And they can feed on it from their side. My guess would be that Jackson Hill must be a place where the barrier between our dimension and their own is thin, and that's why you're able to see them. On their side, Jackson Hill is probably something like a waterhole in the desert where animals gather to drink. A source of easy nourishment."

From *Jackson Hill*, p. 323:

Sandra waded out into the lake, her gown rising and drifting around her. The night was clear. The sky was a black slate of twinkling diamonds. The crickets sang to her. On the hill behind her, Little Nook stood solemn and empty. From inside its walls, she heard the crying. She just wanted it to stop. Her own child was haunting her, and she'd had enough. Time to put the baby to sleep.

She'd screwed it up the first time around with the pills and hadn't taken enough, but the second time, she aimed to make it stick. The lake had more than enough water to do the trick.

Her feet moved along the muddy lakebed, through the twists of tree roots and over rocks. The water was at her chest. She could smell the stagnancy of it. And for a split second, clarity seemed to flash inside her.

What are you doing, Sandra? This isn't you. It's this place. Where is Jacob? Tell him. He'll believe you. You know that there is something he isn't telling you.

But the clarity was strangled off by that delirious haze that'd fallen over her since arriving in Jackson Hill, a correlation she had been unable to see. She was headed toward darkness again, ready to let it swaddle her in warmth and take away all the pain.

The midnight sounds became muffled as she submerged her head. Her eyes were open, but they saw only black. Then an intense show of colors appeared before her, swirling, drifting, deepening. It was a face, giant and awful. Beautiful.

She opened her mouth and drew in a long cold breath of water. It didn't hurt like she'd thought it might. Her body began to tingle with a pleasant...

Chapter Twelve

IN THE LAKE

1

"Did you sleep out here?"

The words came to him as if they'd traveled down a great hall to find him. His face rested on a hard surface with an earthy smell. His mind was swimming out of a fractured sleep.

"Peter? Are you okay?" A little clearer now.

His eyes fluttered open. He blinked. His mouth was dry and bitter. Sylvia stood at the end of the kitchen counter in her bathrobe. He had fallen asleep sitting on one of the breakfast bar stools, and the wood countertop had been his pillow.

She started to reach for the book sitting beside his head, the one with all the creased pages folded back. "You really dog-eared this thing to death. What is it?"

A crick fired through his neck as he sat up. "It's research." With one hand, he grabbed his neck and began to massage it; with the other, he picked up the copy of *Jackson Hill* before she could take a look at it. He dropped it in his lap. "God, I think I really did it this time."

"Something you don't want me to see?"

"Just a drugstore paperback I grabbed yesterday. I was trying to find some inspiration. You're welcome to read it after I'm done." Peter bent back in the stool, stretching his back and yawning. "Excuse me. It'll be a little marked up, by the time I'm finished."

Sylvia seemed to lose interest. "Why didn't you come to bed?" She went to the stove and put on a kettle for tea.

"I did. But I got up. You were fast asleep. What time is it?" He checked his watch. Eight fifteen on Tuesday morning.

"Was something wrong?" She grabbed a mug from the cabinet.

"No, just couldn't sleep." Peter stood, working his head around in slow circles. "I thought I'd do a little reading. Time got away from me, I guess."

"Your neck bad?"

"Nothing some major surgery can't fix." He crossed the living room and opened the curtains covering the sliding door. Warm morning sunlight washed over his face. Big Bath's waters looked deep and black. The trees lining its shore were the lushest shade of green he had ever seen.

"Want some coffee?" Sylvia said. "I can make some, if you'd like."

"I'll pass. I think I might actually go for a swim. Maybe that'll stretch out this kink."

"Okay."

Peter couldn't help but notice that she was having a hard time making eye contact with him. He had an idea why because he felt it, too. There was a big thing hanging out there between them right now. Well, there were two big things—inexplicable things—but Sylvia only knew about one: the boy with his strange gift.

The other thing was *Jackson Hill* and his conversation with its author. But for the time being, that was Peter's burden to bear. And if he was being completely honest, he didn't want either of those things. He wanted to forget about both and just pretend that they'd never disrupted his world, especially after what he'd read in that book. It'd made his skin crawl.

After an hour of staring up at the ceiling last night, an arm tucked behind his pillow, Peter had given up on sleep. He had gone out to the kitchen a little after midnight, poured himself a glass of milk, made himself a bologna sandwich, and started reading.

He had an idea that reading the book might actually allay some of the unease he felt about everything recently thrown at him. The plan had been to crack the spine, read for an hour or two, and discover that everything Declan had described to him had been exaggerated and not nearly as specific or disquieting as he had made it seem. He wanted to poke a few holes in all the nonsense, let some of the pressure out.

Only it didn't happen that way. If anything, it had been worse than he was expecting. Some of the things he had read seemed as if they had been pulled directly from his head. The worst of which were the creatures in *Jackson Hill*—the gishets. The way Declan described them was eerily similar to the thing he had seen crouched above the window in his dream. Some of it could've been coincidence, he supposed. Horror novels often had monsters in them. But the detail about the swirling face of color felt all too much like the proverbial hammer striking the nail squarely.

Peter went into the spare bedroom, where his makeshift writing space was, and put the copy of *Jackson Hill* in the desk drawer for later viewing. Or perhaps later burning; he hadn't decided yet. Then he put on his bathing suit, grabbed a towel, and headed down to the little dock.

2

It was only eight thirty, but the air was already thick with humidity, and the thermometer nailed to the tree beside the porch sat at eighty-five degrees. The previous night's thunderstorms had cooled things off, but only temporarily. That small reprieve had come at a cost, though. The property was covered in fallen branches. Some of which looked thick enough to have done some real damage to a person stupid enough to have been standing there when they came crashing down. Peter recalled the caretaker's warning and understood what she had been talking about.

Peter went to the end of the dock and hung his toes off. On the other side of the lake, perhaps three hundred yards away, a group of what sounded like young children were taking turns running and jumping off a dock of their own. Behind them, a man stood with his hands on his hips. Peter wondered if the man was annoyed by the relentless wails of glee, or if he was simply used to it, the way he imagined a father might become accustomed to such a thing.

Peter glanced over his shoulder. Shady Cove sat up on its hill. He couldn't help but draw comparisons to the way Declan had described it in his book. The picture he had painted of the property was spot on. But then Peter's mind wandered down to a dark place. The last scene he'd read had been where Sandra Thornhill had drowned herself. It'd turned his stomach to see that scene play out in his mind's eye.

He found himself worrying all over again about whether or not he needed to keep a closer eye on his wife. She seemed fine, though. She seemed happy. But in the book, Sandra had seemed fine to Jacob, right up until she finished the job she had started with pills.

Is that what we're doing now? Are we living by the book? Are we agreeing that this is all really happening and going to happen?

In an attempt to free himself from his accelerating thoughts, Peter dove off the dock. The water was even warmer than the day before. He stayed under, riding the momentum of his initial dive, and didn't break the surface until his lungs began to burn. When he came up, he was fifty feet from the dock. Everything looked smaller, more picturesque from this viewpoint. Shady Cove could've been the backdrop of a Norman Rockwell painting.

He treaded water, occasionally taking in big lungfuls of air and floating on his back. He watched birds track across the hazy sky. His neck began to loosen up. Behind him, he heard the kids cannonballing into the lake, but their laughter took on a distant tone, waxing and waning as water lapped his ears. The morning faded away from him. And for a wonderful moment he was without a care, just existing. No past, no future.

That's when he felt a tickle on his finger. It was an odd sensation, like someone gently stroking his knuckle. His first thought was a fish. He righted himself and brought his hand out of the water to find a thin, pale tan line across his finger. Panic ripped through him, and he looked down in time to see the glint of his wedding ring as it descended in little fluttering arcs to the bottom of Big Bath, the sunlight kissing it goodbye.

"No. Dammit," Peter said, sucking in a huge gulp of air.

He torqued himself upside down and dove after it, his legs kicking and pumping. His hands grabbed wildly out in front of him, but he found only unpleasant pockets of icy water. His eyes were open, burning as he glided downward, but everything was a muddy blur. He kept going deeper. The water became frigid all around him, hugging him like a heavy lead blanket. After fifteen feet or so, the sunlight couldn't penetrate, and he was clawing through cold darkness. The pressure was building on his body. He could feel it pressing on his head and lungs, wanting to cave him in. He better touch bottom soon, he thought, otherwise he would have to turn around and swim for the surface. But the idea of finding the bottom struck a line of dread through him. It would be rough and tangled with God knew what. It would be sharp and hard like squid beaks. It would…

How deep is it right here? I'm only fifty feet or so from shore. It can't be more than twenty feet deep this far out.

But why couldn't it be? It might be a hundred feet deep, for all he knew. It could have a steep drop-off. He hadn't thought it through. And how the hell was he going to find a tiny ring in the pitch black at the bottom of a lake, anyway?

He was about to turn back and swim for the surface when he saw it. At first he thought it was a hallucination. It had to be. He had stayed under too long and was running out of oxygen, that's all. The black in from of him started to bloom with shimmering color.

It reminded him of the sparks that swam behind his eyes when he rubbed them hard with his knuckles. And perhaps that was what it was, because that far down, there was no difference between his eyes being open or shut. Maybe it was the water pressure pushing on his eyeballs.

He began swimming frantically for the surface, sure that if he didn't reach it, he would black out very soon. His legs kicked until his thighs caught fire. His arms scooped the water in broad strokes. But rather than fading, the color grew brighter. It took shape, forming features—horrible features—the same way a cloud can once the mind decides it sees a figure in it.

The surface light wasn't coming. The water should've been that muddy color by now. He hadn't gone that deep. Twenty feet at the most. Suddenly he was hit by the horrifying realization that he didn't actually know if he was swimming up or heading deeper. In the dark, it was hard to tell. What if the lake *was* a hundred feet deep and he was swimming toward his certain death? He was disoriented. His thoughts were starting to turn gray and syrupy. And no matter what direction he moved in, that face continued developing in front of him, becoming something he knew he didn't want to see. It was the face of the thing from his dream.

His lungs burned. His heart pounded in his chest, threatening to burst. It took every bit of willpower not to open his mouth and breathe in water. That would put the aching to rest. But it would also do the same for him.

Just keep going. Just keep going. Keep going… going… going… go…

A high-pitched scream tore out of the dark—a baby crying. It was his baby. He could never forget that sound. It was Noah.

I'm losing it, Peter thought. *I'm slipping away and going somewhere else.*

He swam harder, searching madly, trying to find some sign of which way was up. But at every turn, that expressionless, shimmering face greeted him, and that was all he could see. It was huge, with deep black eyes. Its gaping mouth opened. Wide. Wider. Peter was swimming into it. Something was inside, moving toward him—*hurtling* toward him. A bloodied face. A child's face. Noah's face. His skull was cracked open, his skin gray and rotting.

Then, as if the world had been pulled out from underneath him, he was falling, plummeting down a rabbit hole to a darker place. He felt his body being stretched and pulled apart. He had the distinct feeling that he was traveling.

So this is what dying feels like. It's not a peaceful thing—it's terrifying, loud, and jarring.

Then there was nothing. No crying. No colorful face. No dead Noah. No water. He could hear, though. There was no other sound, except his own breathing. His lungs no longer cried for oxygen. And everything echoed intensely.

Unable to think of anything else, he yelled, "Hhhhh-h-h-h—ellll-el-el-el-o-o-o-o." It didn't even sound like speaking; it sounded like electricity coming from his mouth.

No longer underwater, he was suspended in blackness—a vast nothingness. He could feel its immensity. That bitter smell of smoke hit him, and the water came crashing back around him, as if he had been inside a bubble and it had collapsed.

He looked up and saw a dim red glow. He swam toward it. Little hard pieces of debris needled his skin as he moved through the water. It was like swimming through a cloud of disturbed sediment, if the sediment had been shards of glass.

Peter broke the surface. Something was wrong. It was dark out, but the sky was an ominous red, swollen with black clouds. The air was ice cold. He was in that dream place that looked like a bad copy of his own world—a copy that had been molding away in a damp industrial basement for centuries. On the shore the trees all looked dead and smoldering. All that should've been green was black. He found Shady Cove where it should have been, but it was dilapidated, covered in black moss and strange membranous flowers. Ash, or something like it, fell from the sky, coating the surface of the lake in a gray film.

Peter started swimming to shore. His body stiffened from the cold. His jaw bounced up and down, teeth chattering as he breaststroked his way through the grimy water. It splashed in his mouth and tasted like rust. He wasn't going to make it to the dock.

I'm going to freeze to death in here.

He just wanted out of the water. It was all he could think about. His mind focused on it. Then the focus tightened, and the idea became everything. There was a quick flash, like a strobe of lightning on a pitch-black night, and just like that, he was standing on the dock. He was still cold and shivering but no longer in the water. He turned around and looked out over the lake. It was a plate of obsidian glass, not a single ripple even though he had just been swimming in it.

How had he just done that? Somehow he had moved fifty feet in the blink of an eye. The better question was: how was he there at all?

"Where the hell am I?" he said, testing see if he actually had a voice in this place. He did, but it sounded slowed down and sharp with reverb.

Something crashed in the woods behind him. He turned and looked over his shoulder. Another crash broadcasted from atop the hill beside Shady Cove. The sound of splintering echoed across the lake, followed by a wet, breathy flutter. A giant, colorful face shimmered through the woods. It was attached to a tall gray body with long swinging arms. It was coming for him. He knew it. He wasn't supposed to be there. He was an intruder. He wanted to be anywhere else.

In the back of his mind, an old memory rose, punching through the bedrock of his brain like a beautiful, determined flower through a city sidewalk. It was a good memory, born from a place of love and warmth. He hadn't even meant to think about it; the thought had just come. He knew nothing else but to close his eyes and accept it. And when he did, he was traveling again, once more suspended in an echoing sea of nothingness. But instead of a feeling of falling or being dragged down, he was being pulled sideways at an impossible speed. And as he traveled through cold, huge darkness, more blue light strobed in front of him. But it wasn't just flashes of light. It was life. Snapshots of places and things and events. They appeared to vary in time period from ancient to current to well beyond anything he could even begin to comprehend. He saw the violence of the universe—the eternal cycle of its birth, its death, its rebirth. He saw space and time folding in on itself and then expanding infinitely. It was like moving through the beam of some giant cosmic film projector, catching glimpses of a feature he was not designed to see.

Then the sensation of traveling stopped, and he stood on the shores of Crane Beach in Ipswich. However, it was still that same cold realm with the dim red sky and the look of rot. Giant black waves, cast out by a violent sea, crashed over sticky, rough sand that felt as though it had been soaked in oil. The place looked dreadful, yet somehow it retained the sentimentality of the memory that had projected him there from the dock of Shady Cove, more than eighty miles away.

He and Sylvia had come to Crane Beach with Noah when he was six months old. That was when Peter had taken the picture in the frame that sat on the desk in his office in Concord. He remembered exactly where they had all been standing when he took it, too.

Peter jogged up the beach toward the lifeguard station, his feet aching in the sand, the cold, dead air stinging his skin. As he approached the spot, he saw what looked like a smudge floating on the air, as if somebody had wiped a big streak of skin grease across a clean pane of glass. But as he got closer, the smudge came into focus, and it was moving. He could see his memory playing out, but it was a silent replay. He continued closer, and when he was only a few feet away, something powerful hit him. It was like stepping into a pocket of raw emotion. The joy of that day surged through him as if he were reliving it again. It was like he was absorbing it as radiation.

The image was faint, but it was there. They were all ghosts in this place—thin holograms. If the reality Peter knew was the detailed color print, then this place stored the negative.

"Noah," he said, overwhelmed. His son was a foot away, in his wife's arms. She looked so happy. They all did. He reached out, but his hand passed right through them without effect.

Peter began to cry. But they were tears of pure joy. The contrast of this beautiful feeling in such an ugly place only served to brighten the emotion. He could manage but one word: "How?"

He didn't know, and he didn't care. But he was certain of one thing: he wasn't meant to see any of this. He was sneaking a peek behind the cosmic curtain.

An intruding voyeur, he watched from this basement dimension as a younger, happier Peter Martell took photographs of his wife and son over two years ago during a Saturday trip to the North Shore. It was like stepping back in time and getting to experience it all over again, only the second time was somehow sweeter. He had a clear sense that if he closed his eyes and thought hard enough, he could make the whole sequence start over again. If he wanted to, he could watch it a hundred times— experience it a hundred times.

A great impact shook the ground, nearly knocking him down. The air seemed to tighten as if it were a rubber membrane being stretched to its ripping point. He looked toward the water. A massive splash was settling, but it wasn't a wave. One of those creatures—a gishet—was lumbering out of the sea, headed in his direction, its face a blaring kaleidoscope of intense, metallic color. It emitted a tubular vibrating sound, like a growling siren echoing down a long steel pipe.

He closed his eyes. Moving from place to place was beginning to have the feeling of intuition. He thought of Shady Cove, focusing on it, and he was traveling again. When he opened his eyes, he was in the kitchen of the lake house. But the room looked as though it had been sitting vacant for a thousand years. Everything was covered in dust and mold. Black moss grew on every surface. The windows were broken, the countertops cracked and rotting. Outside seethed black and red. He and Sylvia walked by—perhaps through—him silently, carrying bags. It was the day they had arrived in Gilchrist. They were looking around Shady Cove, inspecting their new digs. He watched himself reading the list of phone numbers on the refrigerator. He remembered doing that.

Too easy. Let's try something else.

So he tried for better, and the next time he opened his eyes, he was standing in his front yard in Concord. Once more it was a cold, rotten copy of the real thing. The red sky loomed overhead. The grass was black and greasy. The big sycamore beside the house looked charred and sappy. And the house itself resembled something that had been dragged up from the bottom of a swamp and set out to dry in an angry, unforgiving sun.

Nevertheless, a memory played against the backdrop for him to see. It reminded him of the eight-millimeter home movies his father used to show at Thanksgiving when Peter was a boy.

But what he saw in the basement dimension wasn't being projected onto any screen; he was being shown places, points in time, the raw footage of his life that had somehow bled through and left an indelible imprint on this place.

I remember this, too, he thought, watching the scene in his front yard. And of course he did, because it was thinking about it that had brought him to it.

He was washing the car in the driveway while Sylvia sat on the bottom step of the porch, doing her toenails. Noah bounced up and down in his walker. Every once in a while, Peter would turn the hose on Sylvia when she wasn't looking and get her with a shot of mist, just enough to grab her attention. She would look up, unamused, and Peter would look coy like he didn't know what had happened.

Peter laughed as he watched, tears in his eyes. The emotion felt like a drug. But it was a clean drug, and he was happy to absorb it.

Then something happened. A bright blue light flashed, and the memory disintegrated. His lungs began to ache and feel heavy, until the sensation exploded, and he doubled over and coughed up a mouthful of water. When he looked up, a scene came flooding back, but it was much more faint than before. And it wasn't the same one he had just been watching, either. He wasn't sure what it was. He hadn't advertently thought of any other memory. The new one came to him unexpectedly.

The front door of their house burst open, and a teenage boy came storming down the steps. Peter didn't recognize him. The boy was tall and lanky, with brown shaggy hair. He wore jeans and a faded black T-shirt with the words LED ZEPPELIN written on it—whatever that meant—and his face was familiar, in a strange way. After a few seconds, Peter saw himself follow the boy out of the house, only this version of him was older. His hairline had receded a little. His stomach was rounder. Wrinkles had begun to form around the corners of his eyes. He and the boy stopped in the front yard and began to argue. He had no idea about what because everything was silent and he had no recollection of the memory. As far as he knew, it hadn't happened.

"Not yet," he whispered. And just like that, he knew what he was witnessing.

Sylvia came out and stood on the porch, wearing an apron, hands on her hips. She said something with a stern face. Then Peter put his hand on the boy's back and led him inside, the way a father would.

"C'mon now, you're okay," a voice boomed from the sky.

Peter looked up, around. He didn't know who had said that or where it had come from.

His lungs felt heavy and full again. Warm water poured out of his mouth and nose. He couldn't breathe. Then his mind began to fade to white as foul air was forced into him, making him feel as though he might burst like a balloon.

The voice again: "Get it out, fella."

What was happening?

You know what's happening, he thought. *This wasn't a permanent trip. Don't kid yourself—you can't stay. You shouldn't even be here.*

The basement dimension was fading. No. Not fading. He was leaving it. *He* was fading. But he didn't want to go yet. He wanted to see more. There was so much more to see…

3

Peter tasted tuna fish and hot breath. A mouth was over his mouth. Teeth against teeth. Someone pinched his nose shut.

Another blast of foul air was injected into him. Then something was coming up.

"C'mon now, you're okay," a familiar voice said. "Get it out, fella."

Somebody rolled him over onto his side and gave his back a hard whack, and that brought out the stuff that was coming up. He spat a huge lungful of warm lake water into the grass on which he found himself lying.

A screen door slammed somewhere.

"Oh my God! What happened?" He recognized Sylvia's voice. Soft footsteps were running toward him across grass.

Peter blinked, his mind coming back to him. The first thing he saw was a set of wet, veiny legs wearing wool socks and work boots. Thick black stubble covered the pasty skin.

"It's okay, Mrs. Martell. I got him in time. He'll be okay," Sue Grady said.

Peter tried to push himself up. "What—"

"Easy now, fella. You almost drowned." Sue laughed, and helped him sit up. When she put her hands on him, he saw a bright flash and felt a hot wave flush over his skin. He could've sworn he'd heard the faint sound of screams, too. It conjured up a memory of the flash he'd seen in the car on Sunday as they drove into town. "Ain't no one ever teach you to swim? I came here to mow the lawn. It's Tuesday. Looks like I showed up just in time to see you go under."

Sylvia came and knelt beside him. "Peter, are you okay? I'm so sorry. I didn't…"

"I'll be all right," he said, and looked around dizzily. "I lost my…" He held up his hand to show his finger, but his wedding ring was right where it should be. "I… I thought I lost my ring. That's what happened. I went after it, and I guess I went too deep and got turned around."

He was selling it as a stupid mistake, but he knew something more had just happened while he was underwater. He had gone somewhere. It had been like his dream, only clearer, more coherent. He also understood something else: he had been lured toward his own death. But by whom? By what?

My eyes are opening, he thought, remembering what Kevin had said to him. *And this town is responsible. There's something about it.*

Sue laughed again. "Too deep? It can't be more than ten feet where you were. It's okay. This happens to city folks all the time. Haven't been swimming in a while, then they come out here and forget they're not in as gooda shape as they thought they were. We lose at least one a year. You're just lucky you weren't it. Yessir, you are."

"Ten feet? Really?" Peter said.

"That's right. Deepest part is thirty feet or so, and that's all the way out in the middle, nowhere near where you were. You'll be okay. Course, now I'm gonna have to go home and change my clothes. Things could be worse, I suppose. You could be a floater."

Peter looked her up and down. She was soaking wet, the slow curves of her stout body accentuated by the suction of her clothes. "Thank you. I don't know what happened. I think you probably just saved my life."

"Thank God you showed up when you did," Sylvia added, rubbing Peter's back with one hand. "I was inside, reading a magazine and…" She glanced back toward the house, looking completely horrified with herself.

Peter put his hand on her knee and got that same flash he had seen when Sue touched him. He shook his head, clearing away the feeling. "It's okay, Syl. This wasn't anyone's fault but my own."

She smiled wanly.

"Glad to help. I did what any person would do." Sue got to her feet, using Peter's shoulder to push herself up. She scanned the yard while wiping her hand across her nose. "Told you those storms're bad. Few good clobberers came down last night. Wouldn't want to catch one of those on the head. I'll get this cleaned up when I come back."

"You don't have to do that. I think you've done enough for us today," Peter said.

A perplexed look settled over her face. "No, I'll be back. That's my job. Leo would've chewed my hide if I let this place look so rearranged. Besides, I can't mow with all this in the way."

Peter looked up. "I heard about what happened to him. I was sorry to hear that. You two were friends, weren't you?"

Wrinkling her nose, Sue put her hands on her hips and nodded. "Yeah. I always told him he was gonna hurt himself fiddle-fartin around with his tools. He spends all his time behind a desk. He had no business playin out in his garage the way he did. Those things're dangerous. My father lost three fingers on a table saw when I was a kid. Pens." She shook her head and scoffed. "Strange hobby. I hope I still have a job come next week. I don't think his wife ever liked me much."

"I'm sure it'll all work out," Peter said.

"That's nice of you to say. I appreciate that," Sue said.

Sylvia helped Peter to his feet, and they all headed back toward Shady Cove. Sue picked up a few small sticks as they went and tossed them into the woods at the top of the hill. Then she got in her truck and left. But not before telling them she would be back to tidy up the yard and make it look how Leo would've wanted it.

Peter went inside and lay down on the couch while Sylvia made him breakfast, a look of guilt and disquiet haunting her face. But slowly that faded. Negative feelings never seemed to last long in Gilchrist.

Despite the fact that he'd almost drowned, his entire body and mind buzzed with euphoria. It was as if a dose of his old, happy life had been injected right into the mainline of his consciousness. He thought about how it had felt like he was drinking in the energy of his memories as he had watched them play out in that cold, basement dimension where things were stored. And that thought led to another, darker one: if he had been able to drink in that energy while he was over there, what else could? And what effect might it have?

Maybe there was a reason Gilchrist had such a knack for melting away stress and sadness. Maybe something was feeding on it in the same way he had. All of a sudden, *Jackson Hill* didn't seem so much like drugstore fiction.

Chapter Thirteen

MISSING

1

On his way to the station, Corbin spotted Ricky Osterman's car parked in front of the Gilchrist General Store. Something inside him boiled over at the sight of it. He pulled up alongside the black Biscayne, parked, got out, and waited.

When Ricky and Hooch exited the General Store a few minutes later, each carrying a Coke in one hand and a MoonPie in the other, Corbin was leaning against the hood of Ricky's car, hands turned inward and resting above his knees. He straightened slowly when he saw the boys.

"Ricky Osterman, just the person I'm looking for."

"Uh-oh, I must be in trouble." Ricky laughed. "What I do now?"

"You and I need to have a little talk, Ricky."

"Gilchrist's finest wants to talk with me? I'm flattered," Ricky said, and gave a condescending salute with his Coke bottle. "Thanks for keepin an eye on my car for me, Chief. I know she's a beaut, but she ain't for sale, if that's what you wanna talk about." He laughed as he stepped off the sidewalk. Then he walked by Corbin and went to the driver-side door.

Hooch didn't laugh. Instead he sipped his soda and took a bite of his MoonPie, his eyes looking anywhere but into Corbin's. He might've palled around with Ricky, but he wasn't cut from the same soiled cloth. He knew when to keep his mouth shut, and when a joke wasn't a joke at all.

Corbin followed Ricky, until he stood face-to-face with him. "That's cute, Ricky."

"Well, I'm a cute guy, Chief. What can I say? But I don't date cops. Sorry." Ricky grinned. He tried to open the door to get in, but Corbin caught the top of the trim and slammed it shut. "Hey! What the fuck, man? What's your problem?"

"First of all, watch your mouth. You talk to me like that again, and you and your pal here can spend the rest of the day looking for your teeth on the ground," Corbin said calmly. "Now, I said you and I need to have a talk, and we're going to do just that. We can do it here, or I can bring you to the station and we can chat there. If you prefer that, I can call your dad and have him tow your car home. I'm sure he'd love that. Might give you two something to talk about over dinner."

Ricky rolled his eyes and tossed his unopened MoonPie onto the roof of his car. "What the hell, man? I didn't do nothin. What're you hassling me for? I'm just tryin to have some breakfast."

Corbin eyed the MoonPie, but didn't allow himself to make any wild connections. Just about every kid in town ate them. It didn't mean a thing. His own daughter had them from time to time.

"I hear you like driving recklessly and scaring people off the road. That's going to stop. Today. You hear me?" Corbin said, his tone hardening. "No more speeding around here like it's the goddamn Daytona Five Hundred. You're going to kill someone."

Ricky laughed.

"That funny to you?"

"Maybe a little."

"And why's that?" Corbin started to feel his temper rising.

Later he would think that maybe he had blown his top so easily because Ricky seemed like the one problem in his life he could control at that point in time. All around him, the world he thought he knew was slipping away from him by odd, slow degrees. Or maybe he just wanted to impose his will on something, prove to himself he wasn't completely powerless.

"Because what're you talkin about? I ain't never scared anybody." Ricky shook his head. "I drive this thing like an old lady. You're makin all this up."

"You think people don't complain to me about your speeding? I hear about it all the time. I was just stupid enough to think you'd smarten up on your own. That's on me." Corbin took a half step toward Ricky and dropped his hand down on the roof of the car. The metal was hot. "I know you ran the Mayers off the road out on Waldingfield the other day. That sort of thing isn't going to happen again."

"That's crazy," Ricky said dismissively. "Who told you that?"

"Don't you worry about who told me. I know, and that's all that matters," Corbin said. "You're going to start following the rules, you hear me? If I find out you even so much as forgot to signal a turn, you and Mr. Collins here will be double riding around town on a bike. I bet the girls would love that."

Ricky's eyes narrowed to two dark slits. "Was it that daughter of yours? What's her name... Gracie, isn't it? Or is it Grace?

I always forget." He smiled slyly at Corbin, took a sip of his Coke, then licked his lips slowly, ending with a little kissing gesture. "I bet it was her who told, wasn't it?"

"What'd you say, you little pissant?"

"What? Gracie never told you her and I was good friends? We went for a swim up at the lake just the other day. It was real hot out. Needed to cool off, if you know what I mean," Ricky said, and winked.

Corbin felt the adrenaline dump into his bloodstream—a double shot. It was too late to tamp the flames. His chest tightened. His heart rate increased. His vision blurred. He didn't know when it had happened, but the hand he'd had on the roof was now around Ricky's throat, pinning him up against the car.

"I don't care how badly you had it growing up, kid. You stay away from my daughter. You hear me? She's too goddamn good for you." Corbin could feel his face throbbing in sync with his heart.

"Whoa, whoa. Take it easy, man," Ricky said in a choked voice. He was still grinning. "I was only kidding. Can't you take a joke?"

Corbin looked around. The street was mostly empty. "You want to see a joke? I think you'll like this one." He reached down and grabbed the bottle of Coke from Ricky.

"Hey, I'm still drinking that," Ricky said. He reached for it, but Corbin shoved him back against the car.

He pushed the mouth of the bottle against Ricky's cheekbone hard, then slowly ran it downward until it caught on the lip of Ricky's pants. He turned the bottle upside down, tucked it snuggly into Ricky's waistline, and let the Coke drain into his jeans.

Ricky tried to take it out, but Corbin smacked his hand away. "Let it."

"You just made a big mistake." Ricky sneered. "I thought we were pals, Chief. But not anymore."

Corbin noticed his yellow teeth, and for a fleeting moment, he felt something like pity for the kid. But the moment was just that—fleeting.

"A mistake? No, Ricky, I just made a joke. What's the matter? You don't find it funny?" Over Ricky's shoulder, to Hooch standing on the other side of the car, he said, "Chris, your friend here's had himself an accident. Poor kid made sissy in his pants. Make sure you help him get cleaned up, okay? Can't have him walking around town like a big baby who wet himself. That'd be embarrassing." Corbin heard his own words; they didn't feel like they belonged to him. He felt like a bully and didn't much care for the taste it left in his mouth. He had intended to be civil, but the kid had taken it in the opposite direction.

Hooch only nodded dimly. He was terrified, frozen with his soda in one hand, his MoonPie in the other.

Something dark and putrid clawed its way up from the depths of Ricky Osterman and surfaced on his face like a mask. The grin never broke. If anything, it spread and grew mean. Corbin suddenly thought Ricky had the dirtiest-looking face of any person he had ever known. It might've been the fine spray of freckles over pale skin, but it seemed like more than that. There was something grimy—oily—about him. Not surface filth, but inner filth. Something about it was familiar.

"Don't you have more important things to worry about than me speeding?" Ricky said snidely. "I heard two of your best guys killed each other over a piece of pussy yesterday, and you just stood there and watched. That true, Chief? You couldn't even stop two of your own from killing each other? How'd you get to be chief, anyway? You sure you're qualified? It doesn't sound like it to me."

Corbin's free hand balled into a fist, and he had a vision of bringing it down squarely in the center of Ricky's face. Perhaps two or three times. But then his mind turned to his wife and daughter. The kid wasn't worth all the trouble that would follow if he gave in to his immediate urge. It would be a temporary fix, anyway. Ricky's old man had probably been slapping him around his whole life. The few extra blows Corbin wanted to dole out wouldn't be the thing that finally set the boy straight. It was pointless. Tomorrow Ricky Osterman would still be a no-good punk, but Corbin would have changed for the worse. And he understood all of this in the time it took for his hand to become a fist and then open again.

"Go on and get the hell out of here, Ricky. I've already wasted enough of my time on you." He let go of him. Ricky's neck was bright red, with white marks where Corbin's fingers had been. It probably wouldn't bruise. But if it did, that was okay.

Ricky snatched the MoonPie off the roof of his car. Then his eyes snapped to Hooch. "Get in. Let's get outta here," he said, opening his door and slinking into the car. The Coke bottle remained in his waistband.

Hooch stalled a moment, then obeyed, fumbling with the door handle.

"Come on, hurry up!"

"All right, okay, I'm comin'," Hooch said sheepishly. He got in and shut the door.

Ricky started the car. The engine rumbled.

"I'll be seein ya, Chief." Ricky feathered the gas pedal twice—two small growls.

"Go," Corbin said. "Now."

Ricky backed out of the parking space, then paused in the street as he brought a pack of Lucky Strikes up to his mouth and pulled a cigarette out with his teeth. He lit it with a Zippo and turned to Corbin, grinning one last time. He winked, then ran a hand through his greasy copper hair.

The two of them stared at each other. Ten minutes ago Corbin had thought Ricky was only a troublemaker with a bad attitude, someone who was, for the most part, harmless. But now he wasn't so sure anymore. He found himself wondering whether or not the kid was capable of killing. Was he capable of running a chain across the road and then sitting back to watch it all go down? And it wasn't seeing the Lucky Strikes or seeing the MoonPie or seeing those two things together in the same place. It had been Ricky's eyes—the way they swam in his grimy face like two unpredictable bullets. If he had discovered anything in the last few days, it was that people were capable of great, terrible things.

Ricky dropped the car into drive and crawled up the street to the intersection of Main and Derby. He turned right and was gone. Corbin stayed there and listened for a long time. When the sound of Ricky's car had completely faded away, he got in his cruiser and left. The Benzedrine inhaler would've been nice right about now, he thought. But he put the idea out of his head.

2

"Mommy, I had a bad one. A real baddy," Kevin said, trailing his blanket as he came into the kitchen.

Laura looked up from mixing the potato salad she was preparing for lunch. "A bad dream, sweetie?"

He nodded and knuckled his eye. "Yeah."

"Was it one of your come-true dreams?"

"I think so."

"Okay, come here." Kevin came to her, and she picked him up. "What was it about?"

"I don't know."

"Why don't you try."

"It was very loud and very bright."

"What else?"

"That's all, Mommy. I don't know what it was, but I felt really sad."

"Are you sure it wasn't just a regular bad dream?"

"I don't know." Kevin dropped his head to his mother's shoulder and started to cry.

She held him.

3

Grace Delancey pretended the white painted line was a gymnast's balance beam. Her arms were out straight at her sides as she walked heel to toe down Town Farm Road in her blue plaid skirt, tipping from side to side, losing and regaining her balance. It was a silly thing to do, but she liked being silly. Recently, she had begun to feel her childhood slipping away from her, and while she understood it was the natural progression of things, she didn't like it very much. The reasons were many, but one in particular stuck out: everything got so damn serious when a person became an adult. Mainly, people took themselves too seriously, and that just seemed stupid. Growing up wasn't the stupid part—that was unavoidable. No, the stupid thing was that people acted as if they got serious for no other reason than they thought they were supposed to.

These types of trivial games—pretending she was a gymnast or other childish things—were something she did only when she was alone. It was her own way of making sure she never took herself too seriously. Perhaps, in a way, she was holding on to the childhood foundation upon which all future versions of her would be based. If she fed it every once in a while, watered it a little from time to time, it wouldn't die completely and would always be a part of her.

A crow alighted on the road ahead of her and started to pick at the flattened carcass of a dead squirrel. Another swooped down beside it. They both cawed, and Grace thought it was the sound of hazy summer days in New England.

It was just before noon, and it was hot. Sweat stippled her forehead and upper lip. She should've worn something lighter. It was a long walk. What had she been thinking? She was on her way to the library to check out the last book on her summer reading list: *The Sun Also Rises*. She didn't mind doing the reading, but she wasn't thrilled about Hemingway. She thought his writing was a little boring, which was why she had saved that one for last.

She was passing the Gilchrist Cemetery when she heard a car coming and stepped onto the grassy shoulder. In a deep place inside, she sensed a dark thing coming for her. Whatever it was, the little bit that remained of her fleeting childhood cowered at its looming presence. She turned to look behind her, and when she did, her heart sank.

Not this… not right now.

The whine and chug of the engine lowered as Ricky slowed and pulled up beside her. Hooch sat in the passenger's seat, and for a split second, the look in his eyes made Grace's stomach do an end-over-end roll. Hooch looked afraid. Uncomfortable.

Something's very wrong here, an internal voice warned.

"Hey there, Gracie," Ricky said, leaning out the window. "Where're you headed?"

"Nowhere."

"Nowhere? I think I know that place." Ricky laughed. "Get in. I'll give you a lift."

"Leave me alone, Ricky." She picked up her pace, but didn't want to show him she was scared. Kids like him could smell fear, and it only seemed to make things worse. She didn't even know what she was afraid of, but that same deep part of her advised that she should be.

He prowled along beside her, the car barking at her each time he fed it a sip of fuel. "C'mon, where you headed?"

"None of your business," she said, eyes straight ahead.

He flattened his tone to one of false sincerity, but acid still flowed beneath the surface. "What, are you still mad about the other day? Oh, come on. Look, I'm sorry. I didn't mean to scare anybody. Honest. Sometimes I just act like an idiot."

"You got that right." Another internal warning quickly came on the heels of her comment: *What are you doing? Don't provoke him. He's not someone to play with.* She didn't know why she had said it. Maybe because she was the daughter of the town's police chief, and occasionally that made her feel a little untouchable. She knew that was a dangerous way to think, but she couldn't always help it.

"C'mon, Ricky. Let's just go. This ain't worth it," Hooch said timidly.

Ricky turned to him, and from the corner of her eye, Grace saw his face bend into a mean, twitchy scowl. "Shut the fuck up. Stop being such a fuckin pussy," he said with a low, clenched-teeth hiss.

Grace's throat started to tighten. Her chest needled with budding fear as her vision went white in her periphery. Panic was coming. The crows in the road took flight as Ricky's car approached them and passed over the roadkill.

Leaning back out the window, Ricky said, "Just hop in. I won't bite. It's hot as hell out here. You wanna pass out on the side of the road? What kind of a guy would I be if I let that happen?"

"I'll be fine." Then, hoping it might help her situation, she added: "I'm only going up to Rockhopper's. I'm meeting my dad for lunch."

"That so? All right, then. Suit yourself." Ricky started drumming the side of his car with his fingers. He looked her up and down in a way that made her skin crawl. "Don't say I never tried to do anything nice for you. Adios, Gracie."

"Don't worry, I won't," Grace said, aware that she sounded as though she were mocking him. She hadn't meant for it to sound that way. It was just something she did when she was nervous.

Ricky slunk back inside his car. "Fuckin bitch," he said under his breath, but loud enough to be heard.

Grace thought it was probably intentional, but she bit her tongue.

He gave the Biscayne a full shot of throttle. The engine wound up; so loud that she could feel it in her chest. The tires spun and smoked. Ricky flew up the road, leaving two black streaks of burnt rubber on the asphalt.

"Asshole!" she yelled after him when she thought he was out of range.

Relief washed over her as he sped away. But the relief was short-lived. He slammed on the brakes a hundred feet up the road and squealed to a stop. He sat there for a moment, the smell of exhaust and bitter scorched rubber hanging heavy in the air. The crows had returned to pick at their carrion feast. And the fear she had felt washing away returned with them and was just as black.

Why did you say that, Grace? He was gone, and you had to open your big, stupid mouth. You've done it now.

She checked her surroundings to see if anybody else was around. She was alone and still at least a half mile from the library and a quarter mile to Rockhopper's, where her father was not actually waiting to meet her for lunch. Town Farm Road was a beautiful drive, but it was beautiful because it ran through a desolate part of Gilchrist. Besides the cemetery, there was nothing but deep woods, with a canopy so thick the road often looked like a green tunnel.

Run into the cemetery, that voice said. *Who cares if you look stupid—you run. He is unpredictable and dangerous, and there is no one here to help you. You really think Christopher Collins, a kid who prefers the name Hooch, is going to stop anything Ricky starts? He is too scared of Ricky to help you. And guess what? He should be… and so should you.*

Grace was frozen. A heavy stone in her throat slowly settled into her stomach.

Ricky's car switched into reverse with a dreadful *clunk*. Then the transmission began to whine and moan as he backed up. Seventy-five feet. Fifty feet. Thirty. Twenty.

And she just stood there, unable to act, regretting that she hadn't just let him drive away without saying a word. What was he really going to do to her, though? She was the police chief's daughter. But she wasn't finding much comfort in that, no matter how much she tried to convince herself that offered her some sort of protection.

She watched the rear end of his car grow bigger and meaner, its lightless taillights looking like a cold pair of eyes—a murderer's eyes. She took another step back from the road and folded her arms.

Please, God, let someone come along. Let me see one car come around that corner.

If Ricky tried anything, if he got out of the car or tried to make her get in, Grace decided she would run. She was fast, and she doubted he would take chase, not on foot. He wouldn't just leave his car sitting in the middle of the road.

Or was she just being a scaredy-cat, as Beverly sometimes called her? A small part of her—a naïve, hopeful part—thought maybe she was. Maybe she was letting her imagination get the best of her. Ricky was a bit of bully, but he was probably all bark and no bite. Bullies often were.

Then again, she thought, *what the hell do I know at all...*

Ten feet from her, Ricky revved the engine, and the next thing she knew, the back of his car was pointed at her and coming fast. She tried to move out of the way, but a great force clipped her hip and knocked her to the ground. She scraped her elbow and her knee as she landed on her side in a patch of gravel. Before she could process what had happened, the brightest pain of her life exploded from her foot as Ricky ran it over. There was a loud crunch, followed by a pop, and white-silver stars burst across her vision. At some point she had started to scream, although it didn't feel like her voice screaming at all. This couldn't really be happening, not to her.

The car had stopped, but her leg was still underneath it, between the front and back tire. The heat from the undercarriage wafted up her skirt, then hit her face. It smelled of gasoline and exhaust. She was on her side but managed to steal a glance down.

Big mistake. Her left foot didn't look the way it had when she'd woken up that morning. She couldn't see the damage inside her shoe, but it felt wet and warm in there. Her ankle was already purple, and things looked shifted around in a peculiar way.

Grace sobbed. "Oooow. Whyyy?"

Hooch got out and ran around the back of the car. He stopped and laced his hands atop his head when he saw her lying there on the ground. "Oh man. Ricky, she's hurt bad." He looked at her, sincere regret on his face. "I'm sorry. Oh God, I'm so sorry. It was an accident. I didn't want him to hurt you."

He knelt down and put his hand on her shoulder, but she snapped at him. "Get away from me! Don't come near me!" Screaming made the pain flare.

He jumped up. "Okay, okay. Relax. I only wanted to help."

The door opened, and Ricky stepped out. He hitched his pants and hawked a wad of phlegm onto the ground.

Grace looked up at him. "Luh-leave m-me alone," she said, and sniffled. She started to push herself away from the car so she wasn't underneath it. Her whole body ached. "Wuh-what's the matter with you? You hit me."

"I hit you?" Ricky said. "Oh, is that what that was? I thought it was a pothole."

Hooch went over to Ricky and spoke in a low voice with his back to Grace. "Jesus, man. What'd you do? You said you were just gonna scare her."

Ricky grinned. "Well, she looks plenty scared to me, doesn't she?"

He started toward her, but Hooch stepped in his way and put a hand on Ricky's chest. Ricky glanced down at it, then back to Hooch. "Get your fuckin hand off me. You crazy? You want to spend the rest of your life wiping with a hook?"

Hooch dropped his hand. "Sorry, Ricky. It's just—"

"Just what?"

"I'll say it was an accident. No matter what she tells anybody, I'll say she's lyin.'"

Ricky looked coldly at Hooch. "You saying I did this on purpose?"

"No. I just meant… No."

Ricky broke the tension with a smile. "Don't worry, Hoochy baby, we're gonna help her. I'm not an animal." He reached up, patted Hooch's cheek, and went around him.

With a seasick look on his face, Hooch turned and watched him go.

I told you he couldn't stop him, Grace's internal friend said.

She lay on her back, looking up at a sea of complex, blue polygons in the canopy of trees. She was dizzy. The world was spinning. Two hot tears rolled down the sides of her face. She was only vaguely aware of Ricky coming toward her.

"You all right, Gracie?" he said. "Me and your old man had an interesting talk this morning. He tell you about that yet?"

She looked over just in time to see Ricky's boot lifting off the ground. Then the heel was coming down. It grew and it grew, crowding her vision until there was only black tread. The crows cawed. A flash of red blinded her as the kick landed.

Then there was nothing.

4

Grace woke up on her side on a hard, uneven surface. She heard moving water. Her head throbbed. As she came further out of unconsciousness, all the pain spots in her body began to register, but her foot was by far the worst. She opened her eyes as best she could. One was blurry; the other offered a slit of vision. It was swollen almost completely shut. She tried to move her arms, but they were bound behind her back.

Somewhere nearby, two people were talking, but she didn't focus on what they were saying. Her mind was still rattled, but it was coming back to her.

He must've hit me and knocked me out. How long have I been unconscious? I left the house after an early lunch, but now it feels like afternoon. And oh God, did Ricky do anything to me while I was out?

She didn't think Hooch was the kind to do that sort of thing. But Ricky... Had he...?

Without moving, she focused her mind on where in might hurt, tried to see if she could feel anything. To her relief, she felt nothing to suggest she had been raped. Then her mind played devil's advocate: *Not yet, you haven't. Who says this is over?*

The last thought made her sick to her stomach.

She tried not to move too conspicuously. She didn't want to alert anyone that she had woken up. She looked around with her one good eye, trying to figure out where she was. She lay beside a river, probably the Gilchrist River. If that was the case, she had a pretty good idea of her location. She craned her neck back slowly until she could see up the river. In the distance, a black line stretched across the water. Silver Bridge. Sometimes kids went there to jump off, but right now it looked empty. If she had seen someone, she might've screamed for help.

The sound of talking grew louder and clearer. She moved her head down again, looking past the tips of her feet. Hooch and Ricky were about fifty feet away.

"Why'd we bring her here? You said we was goin to the hospital. I don't want nothin to do with this."

"Calm the fuck down. I told you I'm gonna let her go," Ricky said. "I'm just giving her a good scare, that's all. Let's have a little fun first."

"You're crazy. A good scare? Jesus, man." Hooch laughed humorlessly. "You ran her over with your fucking car. Her foot is busted. You wanted to scare her? Well, I think she got the message. God, man, she's the police chief's daughter. Do you think she's just gonna go home and say she sprained her ankle? And look at her face. You didn't have to kick her like that."

"Don't worry, she ain't gonna say a word. We'll make sure of that," Ricky said.

"No way. Forget it, Ricky. This is too far. You went too far. You gotta let her go, otherwise…" Hooch hesitated. Grace heard the meek defiance in his voice and doubted very much that he was going to be able to help her out of this. Ricky was a wolf, and Chris Collins was a domesticated little pup. "Otherwise, I'm not gonna cover for you. I'm not going to jail for this."

A moment of silence passed. A moment of contemplation. Ricky was thinking. Grace started twisting her wrists back and forth to see if she could loosen the knot. It was too tight. Since her injured foot made it impossible to run, she really had only one option: she had to get her hands free and somehow hurt Ricky. There were plenty of rocks around her. Maybe if she could grab one, she could get him in the head with it. If she did that, then she would have an easier time appealing to Hooch to get help. All of it felt so impossible, though. Too risky. Perhaps letting the situation play out was the best move, a safe part of her suggested. Maybe it was like earlier: if she hadn't called him an asshole as he had driven off, he probably would've kept driving. So maybe if she didn't struggle, he would eventually let her go.

Devil's advocate again: *You don't really believe that, do you? This ends one way. Ricky made up his mind a long time ago.*

"Relax," Ricky said. "No one is going to jail."

"This is kidnapping, Ricky. That's real-deal prison stuff."

The sound of the river filled another moment of contemplation.

"All right, fine, you pussy," Ricky said, his tone shifting. "You want to let her go, we'll let her go. You really think they'll buy it if we say it was an accident?"

This sudden change in Ricky seemed to catch Hooch off guard.

"I... I don't know. Maybe. But if we take her to a hospital, I'll vouch for you. Say I saw it all. I'll say she was walkin in the road and you hit her on accident. It was her fault, and she wasn't payin attention."

"What if she says we're lying?" Ricky folded his arms as if he were really concerned about these problems.

"It'll be two against one," Hooch said. "They'll have no choice but to believe us."

Even in her delirious state, Grace thought it sounded like just about the dumbest conversation she had ever heard. The logic was silly. And that didn't sit well with her, because while she didn't like Ricky, she knew he wasn't stupid. Crazy, sure. But stupid? No way. And she knew well that his was the most dangerous kind of insincerity.

"Well... all right. That's a stretch, if you ask me," Ricky said. "But if you think it'll work and you promise to get my back..."

"I do. I promise. Swear it, man."

Ricky unfolded his arms. "So go on, then. Let's get her back in the car. But if I lose my license because of this, you better get used to driving."

"Really? No problem, man," Hooch said, sounding a touch surprised.

"Really. You're right. I wasn't thinkin," Ricky said. "I'm too pretty for jail, anyway."

Hooch laughed uneasily. "Okay. It won't be so bad. You'll see."

They started toward Grace, Ricky leading the way with a cocky gait. He bent down, scooped up a rock, and chucked it in the river as if it were just another day in the park. Just a couple of pals down by the river, skipping stones. He picked up another and tossed it again, dropping back a little until he and Hooch were side by side.

When they were about thirty feet out, Grace closed her eyes. She didn't want them to know she was awake. The footsteps came closer. Every few seconds, a rock splashed in the water. Then she heard a sharp crack, followed by a grunt and a thick rumple. Instinct got the best of her. She opened her eyes again—and started to scream.

Hooch lay facedown on the ground, not moving. Ricky stood over him with a bloody stone in his hand. He looked at her and smiled, his yellow teeth winking at her from behind his thin, liver-colored lips. "Hiya, Gracie. Glad you're awake. Now I want you to keep those eyes open so you know what'll happen to you if you don't listen. Okay?"

"Help! Somebody help me!" she yelled, falling away to a sobbing whimper. It was pointless. She was surrounded by woods and farmland. "Somebody... please... Why are you doing this to me?"

Ricky cocked his head to the side, an animal watching its meal struggle. "Because I'm here and you're there. I decide, not you."

She screamed until her face was purple and her vocal chords felt like they had torn.

When she was done, Ricky laughed at her. Then very simply, he said, "Knock it off, Gracie. No one can hear you, and you're giving me a headache. Keep it up, and this'll be you next. You watching? Keep those eyes open. No cheating."

A soft moan issued from Hooch, but he didn't move. Grace looked on in horror as Ricky dropped to one knee and repeatedly brought the rock down on his friend's skull until there was nothing left but a pile of mush.

By the time he was finished, Grace was in shock. She was too scared to cry or to call for help, not that it did any good. Whatever hope she had been holding on to was completely gone. All that remained was a subdued numbness.

Ricky tossed the rock into the water, then made his way over to her. His arms looked as though they had been dipped in blood.

He pulled a pistol from his waistband and squatted beside her. He pushed the barrel into her cheek, then ran it across her lips. "Now I want you to listen to me, Gracie. Your old man went too far today, and left me with no choice but to teach him a lesson. He needs to know that I'm the judge around here. I decide, not him."

She pulled her head away but said nothing.

He grabbed her hair and dug the gun harder into her face. She could smell gun oil and spent gunpowder. She remembered it from when her father had shown her how to shoot. They still went every once in a while, but not nearly as often as they used to. Sadness ripped through her when she thought about how she might never again.

"You and I are gonna take a little boat ride and have some fun. If you behave, maybe I let you go. If you don't—if you piss me off"—he dug the barrel into her swollen eye until she saw red—"then things aren't gonna go well for you, Gracie. Wait here."

Ricky stood and tucked the pistol behind his back. He went over to Hooch and dragged him by the feet to the edge of the river. He patted his friend down and took a few dollars and a pack of cigarettes out of his pockets. Then he rolled Hooch into the water, waded out a few feet, and let the current take the body downriver.

When he was finished, he splashed water on his face and arms, washing off the blood. Then he walked out of view, moving in the direction of the woods that separated the river and the road. Grace turned and watched over her shoulder as Ricky pulled a canoe out from behind a bush and headed back toward her with it in tow.

5

After his experience in Big Bath, Peter spent the morning on the couch in a dreamless sleep. When he finally opened his eyes, it was almost two thirty, and he felt as if he had the world's worst hangover. The euphoric feeling had worn off, and his mind had the sensation of having been pressed in a vise.

He sat up and glanced around Shady Cove. "Syl? Syl, where are you?"

For the second or two she didn't respond, panic tickled him and he looked toward the lake. But the fear was short-lived.

"I'm on the porch," she said. "It's nice out. Come join me."

He got up, stretched, and went to her. She lay in the love swing, slowly drifting back and forth. On the ground beside her was a half-full pitcher of lemonade and a plate with sandwich crusts on it. She was still in her nightgown, a white, nearly see-through linen number that Peter jokingly referred to as her "Bohemian bed dress." It was the kind of lazy day Shady Cove had likely been designed to provide. And it was providing just that, but also, it would seem, so much more.

"I've been asleep for a while, huh?" He dragged a tired hand down his face.

"Almost five hours."

"Make room." He picked up her legs, sat down on the swing, and let her feet drop in his lap. He could feel the short stubble of her leg hair against his inner arm.

She looked at him curiously from beneath the forearm she had draped over her eyes. "Everything all right?"

"I'm a little out of it, that's all. Tired, I guess."

"You gave me quite a scare earlier," she said.

"I know. I'm sorry."

"Can we make a deal?"

"What?"

"From now on, no swimming without one of us to be on lifeguard duty."

He nodded. "That's probably a good idea."

"You think we should find a doctor?" she asked. "I'm sure there's one in town. It might not be a bad idea to get your lungs checked out. You don't want to end up with pneumonia or something."

"I'll be okay."

"You sure? You don't need to pre—"

"Syl." He sighed and looked at her good-naturedly. "I'm fine. Really. I just choked on a little water." *But it was more than that,* he thought.

"Okay. I'm dropping it," she said. "Want some lemonade? I just made it."

"Sure." He poured himself a little in the cup she had been using, and took a sip. It was the perfect balance of sweet and tart. "It's good. I forgot what this tasted like without vodka."

He blinked and stretched his face a few times to push away the tiredness. He looked out over the yard, his mind a simmering pit of sap. All the debris from the thunderstorms had been cleared away, the grass mowed and raked.

"It's hard, isn't it? We were drinking a lot. I didn't realize it until these past few days. Everything used to be with a drink."

"Yeah. It's kinda nice, though," he said distantly. His thoughts were elsewhere, dealing with apprehension.

Sylvia smiled after a moment of brief silence. "I think I'm in the mood for a hamburger." An afternoon breeze swept through the porch, rattling the screens. "I thought maybe later we could go to that place you were telling me about on the way up. I know it's a bar, but I'm sure it'll be fine. I'm okay if you're okay. Then maybe we can come back here and watch the sun set on—"

"Something happened, Syl," Peter said abruptly.

"Huh? What do you mean?"

He looked at her. "I'm going to tell you, and I want you to promise me that when I'm done, you'll just say 'okay' and leave it alone, no matter what you think of me."

"I don't understand."

"I need you to know what I saw, Syl." He shook his head in disbelief, tears welling in his eyes. "It was... I don't know. Maybe the most unbelievable thing I've ever seen. But it sounds—no it *is*—absolutely crazy."

He knew she would believe him; Kevin Dooley had poked a hole in any preconceived skepticisms either of them had about what was and was not possible. For Peter, that poke had started a slow leak in his mind that had quickly built to a deluge. Everything he thought he knew was being undermined and washed away. In the process, new, strange things were being unearthed. The problem he envisioned was that once he said what he was about to say out loud, then it would hang out there as unpredictable knowledge... and that could be dangerous. Knowing, he feared, might be worse for her than being kept in the dark. But she had a right to know.

Confusion crept down her face. "What are you talking about?"

"Just promise me you'll say 'okay' and that we'll get past this."

He knew that asking this guarantee of her made no difference, but he had to say it for his own peace of mind.

"How can I promise you that if I don't know what you're going to say?"

"You can't. But I need you to, just the same. Please, Syl."

"All right. If that's what you need, then I promise," she said. "Now what is it? You're scaring me."

Peter finished off the lemonade in his glass, then set it down on the porch beside him. "When I was out there, when I almost drowned, I saw something. I went somewhere, Syl. I know that doesn't make any sense, but I swear it's true... and I saw him, Syl. I saw Noah."

Her face steeled over. He had her undivided attention.

And for the next ten minutes, Peter told his wife in great detail about what had happened to him when he had gone under in Big Bath. He told her everything... except he never mentioned *Jackson Hill* or anything related to it. He didn't know why, but something told him not to.

When Peter finished, Sylvia was sitting up straight, looking out over the water. She didn't say anything, only stared ahead, her finger picking the side of her thumb.

"Syl, it was real. I swear it was. And you know I wouldn't say that if I didn't believe it. I'm not the type. I'm an evidence guy, and this was too close to a dream. But... I swear it was real somehow. Aren't you going to say something?"

She looked over at him, the faintest smile on her face. "Okay."

Peter snorted a small laugh. "Really?"

"What? You said that's all you wanted me to say."

"I know. But I didn't mean it quite so literally."

"I think we both know that there is something going on around here that neither of us really understands." She looked at him earnestly. "But I couldn't tell you if it's good or if it's bad."

Then he told a lie. "I don't know, either. I think it just is."

He was afraid if he said what he truly thought, it would lead to them leaving, and he wasn't quite ready to go yet. There was something special about Gilchrist, even if it was dangerous. Peter thought that maybe whatever qualities the town had, they were somehow causing his eyes to finally open.

"Do you think I might've imagined all of it? Be honest. I know it sounds more like a hallucination than anything else."

"You're telling me you slipped down some rabbit hole and saw our dead son. Should I believe he exists out there in some other reality? Probably not, no. But do I?" She reached over and took his hand. "I think I need to, Peter. Not for you... for me."

"I love you, Syl. You know that, don't you?"

She slid over and rested her head on his shoulder. They sat in silence for a long time, watching the afternoon sink lower on Big Bath and listening to the loons.

6

Grace spent twenty minutes on her back in the bottom of the canoe, watching the sky snake through the treetops as Ricky navigated down the river. It was silent, save for the slap of the canoe hull cutting water. Occasionally, steel-colored clouds drifted across the afternoon sun and dulled the day. Crepuscular rays, what her mother called Fingers of God, broke through and then faded. She saw it all, but she felt nothing besides a vague detachment from the world.

At some point they reached their destination. In the dense section of swampy woods where the river went narrow, the air felt crypt cool and smelled sharp. Ricky got out and dragged the canoe from the water with her still in it. Then they were moving again. He was pulling her in the canoe through the woods, the bottom scraping against the dirt.

Another five minutes passed. Then he stopped. The jarring drop of the canoe hitting the ground sent a gasp of pain through her whole body.

"We're here, Gracie. Home sweet home." He kicked the side of the canoe. "Get up, c'mon."

She sat up, which was hard to do with her hands still tied behind her back. It was thick woods as far as she could see in every direction. To her left was a little shack. Though old and falling apart, it looked as if perhaps someone had done a few minor repairs to it. She didn't know what the place was, but she could feel it seeping dread.

"I said c'mon. You're already pissin me off."

She looked at him, a feeling of stubborn disobedience rising up in her. "You broke my foot. How am I supposed to get out? I can't walk."

"Goddammit. Listen when I tell you to do something." He grabbed her by the top of her hair. The canoe tipped and spilled her onto the ground. He started dragging her into the shack.

"Let go of me!" she screamed. With her upside-down view, she could see the pistol sticking out from the small of his back. If her hands were free, maybe she could...

But your hands aren't free, Grace.

"Shut up. Knock it off," he said through clenched teeth as he tugged her inside. The smell of death and rancid meat hit her. She could hear his boots scraping against a grit-covered floor. Then he was dragging her across it, abrading her legs.

He pushed her into something hard and knobby in the center of the room. He let go of her, leaving her to sit upright against it. The rusty pipe came up through the floor about three feet high, then did a ninety-degree turn and ran out a little hole in the back wall.

He went over to a corner and stood with his back to her. "You like my place? It ain't much, but it's all mine. I don't usually have guests, so you'll have to ignore the mess." From his pocket, he took the cigarettes he had lifted off Hooch and put them on a little shelf in front of him. A necklace with a pendant hung from a nail below it. There were a few things on the shelf, but Grace couldn't tell what they were.

She looked around, her eyes adjusting to the dim interior. It was worse than she could have ever imagined. At first she didn't know what she was seeing. Then she did.

Ricky had nailed dozens of dead, eviscerated animals to the walls. Their bodies were pinned open like the dissected frogs from her seventh-grade biology class, and their entrails hung out like withered balloons. Some were dried and leathery looking, as if they had been there for quite some time.

He's been at this for a while.

"Ricky, why are you doing this? I didn't do anything to you."

He squatted and rummaged through a burlap sack on the ground below the little shelf. He pulled out a long length of rope and turned around, his face cold and calm.

"Your old man needs to learn he can't act any way he likes," he said, coming toward her. "And now that I think about it, I didn't really like the way you yelled at me the other day. I was only playin around with those folks, and you had to make me look stupid downtown in front of everyone. I wasn't actually gonna hit them. You had no right. That big mouth of yours is no good. It must run in the family."

"I didn't mean it. You scared me, is all. I'm sorry, Ricky. Really. Please just let me go. I swear I won't tell anyone about this."

"I know you won't. I believe you. Really, I do. Now, time for some fun." He grinned at her as he came closer. Then he was standing over her, his legs straddling hers. He dropped the rope beside her and started to unbuckle his belt. Icy, jagged fear tore Grace's stomach. This was it—what she had feared the most.

She recoiled against the pipe behind her, tucking her legs up despite the pain. "Please, no. Kill me, just kill me."

Ricky started to laugh. "Oh, you should see your face, Gracie. It's precious." He backed away from her and buckled his belt. "Is that what you think this is? I ain't that kind of man." He cocked his head to the side. "At least, I don't think so."

Crimson rage flashed in her head. "What's the matter with you! Get the fuck away from me, you sicko!" With her good leg, she kicked at him as hard as she could. She managed to connect a few inches below the knee, but it came at a cost to her as a great gouge of pain reported in her foot and ripped through her body.

Ricky's hand went to his leg, and he hopped back so she couldn't get in another shot. "Well, well, Gracie, aren't we full of surprises," he said, grimacing. "Didn't think you had it in you. You forgot about this, though." He reached behind his back and flashed the pistol at her.

Before she knew it, he lunged at her and caught her in the temple with the heel of the pistol grip.

7

When she regained consciousness, her situation was worse. She was kneeling, her knees raw from the grit of the floor. All she could taste was sour metal. Her mouth was full of it, and she couldn't move her jaw. Her teeth scraped against something hard and rough. Then she understood the situation.

He had secured her to the lateral section of pipe as if it were a pillory device (she had learned about these on their school trip to the witch museum in Salem), but her mouth was stuck open around it. The pipe was like a giant horse bit, and her head was bound tightly from the neck so she had no chance of removing it.

She tried to speak but could only make muffled sounds. She waited for Ricky to appear, to tell her what was next. *Just get it over with already*, she thought desperately.

Five minutes passed. Ten. Then after what felt like an hour, but could easily have been twenty minutes, she knew he had left. She could see through the shack's open doorway. Outside, wind soughed through the trees. Trunks creaked as they swayed. And she heard the crows again. So many of them.

Had they come to feed on her?

No. Not yet.

8

Ricky was back in downtown Gilchrist by six o'clock that evening. He was feeling pretty damn good, too, as he walked up the sidewalk. The grin on his face was at least a mile wide. He'd fed the dark thing, and it was paying him back. That was the deal they had struck long ago. But if he was being completely honest, he couldn't remember when exactly. In fact, so far as he could tell, the arrangement had always been in place, not that it mattered one way or the other. As his old man always used to say when he didn't understand something: *Don't waste no whys on it, Ricky. Just is.*

He figured someone would realize Grace was missing before long. She had only been gone since noon, but the idea that something might be wrong would probably set in right about now, when she didn't show up for dinner. Of course, there were other scenarios of how it could play out, but this one struck the truest chord inside him. The Delanceys seemed like the kind of family that respected dinner times.

He cupped his hands around his cigarette, raking his thumb down the flint wheel of his Zippo as he rounded the corner by Dale's Tavern. The moment the spark flashed, he was blind-sided. The lighter fell to the ground. He had walked smack into a person, their shoulders connecting solidly.

"Watch it, asshole," Ricky said automatically, and looked up. He didn't recognize the man or the woman with him.

"I uh... Sorry," the man said, picking up the Zippo and handing it to Ricky.

"Yeah, you are." Ricky snatched the lighter from the man. "Don't you look where you're going? What's the matter with you?"

The man stared at him, his eyes wide and black. "I didn't see you there."

Ricky looked up and down at the redhead on the man's arm. "Just watch it, okay? Jesus." He walked past the couple and continued up the sidewalk.

"You all right?" he heard the woman say as he walked out of range.

Any other time, Ricky might've gotten into it with the guy, especially since he seemed like he could be a tourist, and Ricky hated tourists. But he didn't have time for that. He had irons in the fire. Hot ones.

9

Peter stood in front of Dale's and watched the freckle-faced kid with the green eyes strut up the street, working to get his cigarette lit. His body was still ringing. Not from the impact, but from something else. The moment he'd run into that kid, a tiny explosion had fired off in the core of his mind and scattered fragments of something he didn't quite understand. Something about the boy sent a chill up Peter's spine. It had been like touching a live electrical wire and getting zapped.

"You all right?" Sylvia asked him.

He snapped out of it and looked at her. "Yeah. I'm fine. This is it," he said, painting on a smile and gesturing to the entrance of the bar. Laughter and muddied country music filtered out from inside. Something with twang. It sounded like a good time.

"You sure about this?" she said.

"Why not?" he said. "Who likes cold beer, anyway?"

Inside, the smell of stale cigarette smoke and pool chalk still ruled the atmosphere of Dale's Tavern. In a strange way, that was part of its charm. George Bateman was working the taps and pouring beers for a midweek evening crowd. He greeted Peter with a kind, familiar smile and said hello. Sylvia and Peter found two spots at the bar and ordered Dale's Delights. When George offered them two cold ones on the house, Peter declined for the both of them. Instead, they ordered two Cokes, and George asked no questions about it, because that was the kind of guy he was. Later, when the crowd was thinning out, Peter dropped a dime in the jukebox and selected The Righteous Brothers' recording of "Unchained Melody." He and Sylvia danced slowly in the smoky bar, stomachs full, and both happy in each other's arms. Two couples got up and joined them. As the song came to a close, George applauded.

When they returned to Shady Cove, they took a blanket down to the dock. And under the stars, while the loons spoke to the moon, they made love.

10

Grace had left for the library at around noon. She had told her mom she would be back in a couple of hours, but that was over seven hours ago.

Meryl Delancey had started getting nervous at around five o'clock. By six o'clock, she had started pacing through the house and glancing out the front widows every few seconds, expecting to see her daughter walking up the driveway. When that hadn't produced results, she had taken an unnecessary shower to pass the slow-playing time, hoping to find her daughter home when she got out. But the shower was rushed, and when she stepped out onto the cold tiled floor, she could feel the mean emptiness of the house mocking her. By seven, she had called all of Grace's friends to see if they had heard from her. All said they hadn't. Then nervousness quickly became panic. This wasn't like her daughter. Something was wrong.

She had one call left to make, and it was the one she dreaded the most. Once she called her husband, it became real. She would have to say out loud the thing she feared the most. And that would crystalize it. But the phone was already ringing in her ear. At some point she had picked it up and dialed the police station.

11

It had taken him a half hour to calm Meryl down. He said all the things he was supposed to say—that everything would be okay, that she shouldn't worry because Grace was probably just out with a friend, that she's got a good head on her shoulders.

Somewhere along the way, he had realized he didn't actually believe any of what he was saying. Then fear hit him, and his mind started to race. Maybe she wasn't okay. What did he know? He *hoped* she was. That was all. He had managed to hide his own panic from his wife—he thought so, anyway, although a part of him suspected Meryl knew he was peddling his hope as something more substantial—but alone in his car, he couldn't pretend anymore.

Meryl had kept saying one thing over and over again: *She wouldn't do something like this, Corbin. She wouldn't just tell me she was coming back and not show up.* And he couldn't deny that his wife was right about that. He wished she wasn't—dear God, he almost wished Grace *was* a bit of a rebel so that the possibility of her just being an inconsiderate teenager could be true. But no, Meryl had it right. Grace wasn't like that.

He had seen five deaths in his sleepy little town since Saturday. Now this? Gertie's words from her hospital bed were starting to grow heavier and take on a more defined meaning. He could admit that Gilchrist did have its odd moments, and maybe he had grown accustomed to it by being so close to it for so long, but so much darkness in such a short span was too much, even for Gilchrist. Something was changing. He just didn't know what the hell it was. But a deep feeling told him it was too big to just point a finger at and say, *There, that's it! That's the thing responsible!*

He had been driving around town, looking for Grace for the last two hours. Meryl had wanted to come, but he had convinced her to stay home in case their daughter showed up. So far, the only thing that had set off a buzzer in his head were the fresh skid marks on Town Farm Road. He hadn't recalled seeing them earlier in the week, and they were on the route his daughter would've taken to get to the library from their house. There was, however, a flattened piece of roadkill near the marks, so it could just as easily have been someone trying to avoid a squirrel. There were two sets, though.

One was a set of brake marks, and the other was a set of burnout marks. The latter had brought a specific person to mind immediately. But who was he kidding? He realized he had been thinking it the whole time. Perhaps the only reason he hadn't allowed himself to fully consider it sooner was because that meant admitting fault.

If I hadn't lost my temper earlier, then maybe…

It was dark by the time Corbin turned down the Ostermans' driveway. Nate's tow truck was parked in front of the house. He didn't see Ricky's car. He got out and went to the front door. Moths beat around the porch light. The place was dimly lit. Inside, Nate was laughing deep, sloppy laughs. Corbin had heard that laugh dozens of times down at Dale's. Tonight it sounded more lurid.

Corbin knocked on the door, hand resting on his pistol. The laughs cut off.

"Get that, Barb," Nate said. "I'm watching this. Why I even gotta ask?"

A soft woman's voice said something in a complaisant tone. Barbara Osterman hadn't been right since her fall down the stairs. Corbin knew Nate had likely been the cause of that fall, but there had been no way to prove it.

"How the hell should I know?" Nate said. "Maybe you should go find out."

The thin scrape of slippers shuffling across linoleum issued from inside the Ostermans' house. The door opened with a rattle. Barbara Osterman stood there in her dirty bathrobe, that hollow expression on her face. It was a sad thing to see. She'd once been a beautiful woman, but all that remained was a husk with ratty dark hair and unblinking, curious eyes.

"Hello, Corbin," she said in her slow, steady voice. There was an innocent, childlike quality to it. "Can I get you some water? It's hot out tonight."

"Hi, Barbara. No, but thanks for offering." He folded his arms. "Look, I'm sorry to call on you so late, but I need to talk to Nate."

"Nate? Of course. He's here. Want me to tell him you're here?"

"Could you, please?"

"Yes, I will. Thank you. I'll go get him." She started to turn away, then stopped. "I got my hair cut today." She ran her hands through it, fanning it out. "Do you like it?"

"It's lovely."

She smiled at him. "Really? You like it?"

Corbin clenched his jaw, understanding it wasn't her fault. "Yes."

"I'll go get Nate." She gave him a clumsy, flirtatious look.

"Appreciate it, Barbara."

She disappeared into house. With the door left open, Corbin could hear both sides of their conversation:

"Chief Delancey said he likes my haircut. I knew he would."

"It's Corbin? What the hell does he want?"

"I don't know. But he isn't thirsty. I offered him water."

"Go sit down. You're makin me nervous."

"Okay," she said.

The television volume lowered. Then heavy footsteps were coming to the front of the house. Nate appeared in the doorway in a T-shirt and underwear. He sipped his beer.

"Corb? Usually I get a call if you got tow work. What's up?"

Corbin stepped back from the screen door. "I need to talk to you. Why don't you step out here and shut the door."

"What's this about?"

"I just want to ask you a couple questions, that's all."

Nate came out onto the porch and shut the main door behind him. He swiped at the moths on the screen, then blew the wing dust off his palm. "Little fuckers are everywhere. What's going on?"

"You know where Ricky is, Nate? I don't see his car here."

"Aw, Christ." Nate hawked a wad of spit off his porch. "What he do?"

"I didn't say he did anything. I just want to talk to him."

"About what?" Nate narrowed his eyes, crossed his arms.

"That's not important," Corbin said. "Have you seen him or not?"

"Not since this morning. Must be real serious if you drive all the way out here without calling first. Way I remember it, if the police want to talk to you, you done something wrong."

"Did he tell you where he was going?"

"Going? How the hell should I know? He's a horny teenager. Probably out chasing wool. That's what I'd be doing." Nate laughed, and smacked a mosquito on his shoulder. A little streak of blood appeared on his thick shoulder.

"So you have no idea, then?"

"Shit, I don't know." He scratched the back of his head. "He and Chris were here earlier, workin on his car. That's the last I saw him. The two of em been headin up to the drag track in New Hampshire a lot. Could be there. I don't keep tabs on him, if that's what you think."

"Was it just the two of them you saw?"

"That's right. What the hell's this about, Corb? Ricky might be a dipshit, but he's still my boy. If he's got himself in some sorta trouble, I oughta know about it."

"He ain't in trouble, Nate. Like I said, I just need to talk to him."

"Well, if you can't tell me what the problem is, then maybe when I see him, I ain't actually seen him, if you know what I mean." Nate cocked an eyebrow and tilted his head.

Corbin looked coldly at him. "Don't fuck with me, Nate. Not right now." He turned and went down the steps, heading for his car. "You call me first when you see him. I want to know. You hear me?"

"Damn it, Corb, it ain't right comin to another man's house and talkin to him like that. Ain't no cause for it." He walked halfway down his front steps, railing in one hand and his beer in the other.

"Since when did you start caring about what's right?" Corbin got into his car. From the window, he said, "And careful on those steps, Nate. Don't want to have yourself an accident. That'd be a damn shame."

He started the car and backed onto the balding patch of grass that was the Ostermans' front yard. He headed out to continue looking for his daughter.

12

Nate stood on the steps and watched as Corbin's cruiser dipped and yawed through the potholes in his driveway. When he reached the end, he turned right and drove out of sight. What the fuck had that all been about? Whatever trouble Ricky had gotten himself into, this was the end of it. He was going to have to show that little prick who was boss.

He shook his Pabst to see how much was left. About a quarter. He tipped it back and finished it off. He crumpled the can in his hand and tossed it at the trash can beside his front steps. He missed.

"Shit." He stepped down onto the gravel landing with his bare feet, hobbling carefully over the sharp rocks. He bent down, grabbed the can, and dropped it in the trash. He turned to head inside but stopped when he saw someone coming out from behind the shed and moving toward him. "Hey, this is private property." He squinted to see better, but it did little to help.

"It's me, Pop."

"Ricky? What the hell're you doing back there? And what do the police want with you?"

"It's nothin. He's just got a hard-on for me," Ricky said. "Hey, check this out."

A shadow moved quickly toward him out of the dark. As Ricky's scowling face broke the boundary of the dim yellow porch light, Nate had time enough to see his son's arms raised overhead. Then the rusty head of the splitting maul cut an arc through the air.

Nate's eyes crossed as he looked up. "What the fu—"

13

The town of Gilchrist was fast asleep when Jim Krantz broke the pane of glass on the door. His elbow started to bleed. He looked down at it curiously, as if he didn't understand what it was. Something inside him temporarily lost its icy hold on him. For a moment his mind broke free, and a dose of clarity returned to him. He looked around, confused.

When he was younger, he and his friends used to do something they called "thumbing." They would crouch down, hyperventilate, stand up really quickly, then stick their thumb in their mouth and blow as hard as they could until they passed out. When done correctly, it would lead to intense visions and a not-so-unpleasant feeling of dissociative euphoria where the rules of time seemed to change. During these episodes, what felt like minutes usually only ended up being seconds. Standing there, Jim felt shades of that familiar misconception of time.

The last thing he remembered was the girl in his truck out by Big Bath. Sandy. There had been a car accident, too. How much time had passed since then? An hour? A day? Oh God, more? And what was he doing here? His body ached terribly, as if he had been worked too hard without rest. Strange day-dreamy recollections of long journeys through the woods flashed in his mind's eye, followed by a rush of free-floating anxiety. He had done something terrible… He was *doing* something terrible. But what?

"Where did you go, Pickle?" his mother's voice whispered to him from down a long corridor in his head. And whatever sinister thing had its hold on him returned. The clarity evaporated, and the compulsion to drive forward toward some unknown goal resumed its parasitic influence.

Jim's face glazed over cold again, and he let himself into the school. The white painted brick inside was festooned with children's arts and crafts. Taped up in the main hall, a banner of strung-together construction paper cutouts read MRS. PENNY'S PRESCHOOL. Below that: HAVE A NICE SUMMER! The cement-brick walls kept the place cool.

He drifted down the hallway, a phantasm carrying its stolen wooden crate. His boots clicked against the tiled floor as he moved slowly through the dark. He stopped when he found the innermost room—a small windowless space with a low wooden stage, drab carpeting, and chairs lining the perimeter. It was the heart of the preschool, where the children put on plays and the parents could come and watch. Afterward, there were always coffee and pastries spread out on banquet tables. For the kids, punch.

"Here?" he asked the empty room.

"Yes. In the ceiling, Pickle. That'll work nicely."

He put the crate on the floor, then grabbed one of the chairs. He dragged it back to the center and stepped up on it. He pushed in one of the drop ceiling tiles and slid it to the side, exposing pipes and other guts above. The main artery was a steel I-beam that ran the length of the room. Its lower flange would make a perfect shelf for the dynamite.

With his bare hands, Jim pried the nailed-down lid off the crate and set to work wiring the explosives. Somewhere behind a locked door in the basement of his mind, another voice, his own voice, raged against him: *Stop it! What's the matter with you? Don't do this? Don't listen to it!* But there was little he could do to stop it.

Outside, a car drove through a vacant downtown Gilchrist past midnight. It was a new day.

Chapter Fourteen

SEARCH PARTY

1

Peter had specifically bought an extra bottle of mint Rolaids before they had left, and he could've sworn he'd packed them, but they were nowhere to be found. He remembered putting them in the medicine cabinet on Sunday when they arrived, and yet this morning they weren't there.

The evening of sodas and greasy food at Dale's had been fun, and it had certainly been nice to feel a part of a small community where no one knew of their tragedy and didn't treat them as though they were somehow broken, but this morning they were paying the price for their dietary indiscretions. Both had awoken just before eight o'clock with searing cases of heartburn. Peter had volunteered to run downtown to get antacids after he couldn't find the ones he thought should be there, and Sylvia had offered to have a healthy, albeit bland, breakfast of oatmeal, fruit, and tea waiting when he returned.

So that was how for the second time in three days, Peter found himself walking into Quints Pharmacy. It didn't occur to him, not until it was too late, that going there at that exact moment wasn't just another random decision. And perhaps neither was coming to Gilchrist. In fact, later, Peter would think that these hadn't been decisions at all.

The door gave its little jingle when he pushed it open.

The pharmacist looked up from his newspaper. "Morning. Here for more books already, or you still reading the first one?"

Peter winced inside. A sinking knot of dread that was more than indigestion landed in his stomach. He didn't want to think about *Jackson Hill* or any of that weird stuff right now. It dredged up too much anxiety. There was something else, too— something had happened to him last night when he'd bumped into that kid on the street. He had seen something, felt something, but he wasn't sure what it was. It was lingering on his mind like a hair on his tongue, and when he tried to get it off, it eluded him.

"It's an interesting read," Peter said, which was perhaps the biggest understatement of his life. "I'm going to be coming back for another one when I'm done with it. That's a promise. You have Rolaids or something similar?"

The pharmacist smiled. "Course we do. Back wall, bottom shelf."

"Thanks." Peter went to the back and found the antacids after a moment of searching.

"Too much fun last night?" the pharmacist said across the store.

"Too much Dale's Delights is more like it." Peter's hand automatically moved to his gut as he approached the counter and put down the Rolaids. "You ever had one?"

The pharmacist laughed. "Oh sure. More than one. It's good stuff, but not so kind if you weren't born with an iron stomach." He pointed to the Rolaids. "This all? Just the relief?"

"That should do it for now."

The pharmacist pushed his glasses up and started punching keys on the register.

Looking around absently as he waited, Peter spotted a curious thing on the counter. It looked like a missing-person flyer. The clean, uncreased paper suggested it was freshly minted. From his angle, the girl's fuzzy, blown-up picture was upside down, but he could tell she was young. Just from the posture, he knew it was a yearbook photograph.

"What's that?" Peter asked, his finger tapping the corner of the flyer.

"The police chief's daughter went missing. He came in this morning, asked me to put this up. I was about to hang it out front." The pharmacist shook his head and sighed. "I've known Grace since she was in diapers. I just hope the poor kid's okay."

"When did it happen?"

"Yesterday, I think."

Peter slid the piece of paper toward himself and turned it around to get a right-side-up view. When he saw the girl, something inside him reacted. A fissure in his mind cracked open, and a flood of information bubbled up out of it, spilling all over his brain and threatening to short-circuit the whole operation. It was like his usual little knack for finding things, only this feeling was far more intense. There were shades of the strange, intense flashes he had been experiencing since arriving in Gilchrist.

"You recognize her?"

"Huh?" Peter glanced up.

"Maybe I read your face wrong. You looked like something grabbed you when you looked at her. Never mind."

And something *had* grabbed him, only he had absolutely no idea what to do about it. When he had bumped into the freckle-faced kid the night before, he had received a disorganized package of information that made no sense. But the moment he saw the picture of the girl on that flyer, all the jumbled pieces had shuffled together to create something more coherent. He had absolutely no business knowing what he did, but that didn't stop it from being true. Whoever that redheaded kid was, he was somehow responsible for the girl's disappearance. And she was still alive. That part he could feel like a warm glow.

"Sad, is all. I wish I could help," Peter said, a pang of shame sounding off inside him. It wasn't that he didn't want to say anything—he did want to—but he had no earthly idea how to offer up the information he thought he might have. He needed to think about it before just coming right out with it. Finding a missing person wasn't the same as helping a guy find his glasses.

The pharmacist stopped ringing up Peter's purchase and looked at him. His face suggested someone in the midst of a moral dilemma. "Well... you can if you'd really like to."

"How's that?"

The pharmacist's face wrinkled, and he threw his head back and fired a massive sneeze into a handkerchief he had managed to pull out just in time.

"Bless you."

"Thank you. Excuse me. Ragweed season." He folded the hanky and stuffed it back in his pocket. "Anyway, I wasn't going to mention it, seeing as you're from out of town and on vacation—didn't seem my place to put you on the spot—but if you really want to help, they're putting together a search party this afternoon to do a sweep of the woods. There's lots of ground to cover around here, and I know any help would be appreciated, local or otherwise. No pressure, but since you mentioned you'd like to help, that's why I said it."

Peter nodded, smiling. He understood. In a small town like Gilchrist, certain people got put to task when crises arose, and the pharmacist had apparently been told to wrangle as many troops as he could muster. "Would two extra able bodies help?"

The pharmacist looked pleasantly surprised. "Sure wouldn't hurt. I know that much."

"Then my wife and I would be happy to lend a hand. Name the time and the place, and we'll be there."

"Our Savior Lutheran Church at one o'clock." He pointed over Peter's shoulder. "It's right across the street, in case you were wondering. I'm going to close up early and go myself. Communities have to help each other out in times like these."

"We'll be there." Peter glanced at the flyer again, then back at the pharmacist. "How much for the Rolaids?"

He waved a hand. "No charge."

"Really? That's not necessary."

"Neither is you and your wife spending a day of your vacation out in the woods, looking for someone you've never met."

"Just seems like the right thing to do, I guess," Peter said, and shrugged. "And if you pay me for that, I'll feel cheap."

The pharmacist closed the cash register and pushed the antacids across the counter with the tips of his fingers. "I could say the same thing. Name's Teddy Halloran, by the way. Folks call me Tad, though."

"Peter Martell." He reached across the counter to shake. When their hands met, Peter was hit by the same violent flash he had seen when both Sue Grady and his wife had touched him, and he heard the same distant sound of a hundred screams all crying out at once. But this time, for whatever reason, he was hit with the name Lincoln. There was another name, too, but he couldn't see it. He could taste it, though, and it tasted like blood. He didn't know what it was, or why it was, only that it left a trace of sadness in its wake. He had stalled for a beat but finally said, "Good to meet you, Tad."

"Likewise. So I guess I'll be seeing you later, then."

"Guess so. Should I bring anything?"

"Bug repellant, water, and a good pair of walking shoes. Or boots, if you got em," Tad said. "And I think Meryl is making lunches for everyone, so I wouldn't worry about food. There'll be something to nosh on."

"Noted. Take care."

"Yep, you too."

Peter left Quints Pharmacy and stood on the sidewalk. He shook two of the antacids into his palm and chewed them. It was a gray, muggy morning, and the sky was spitting. Cars drove slowly through a town that seemed tired and oppressed. Everybody who walked past him looked as though they knew something they didn't want to know. His gaze shifted straight ahead to the steep granite steps that led up to a beautiful brick church. Our Savior Lutheran stood prominently atop a hill, set back fifty feet from the street. Seeing it reminded him of the decrepit church he'd dreamt about back in Concord, not in appearance—because the two looked nothing alike—but rather in the sense of foreboding it drummed up inside him.

He stared at it for a very long time, trying to feel God's presence. He didn't think that he could. Perhaps he had never been able to.

2

They arrived at Our Savior Lutheran Church at twelve forty-five and sat out front in the car, watching people trickle in. Sue Grady and George Bateman were among the earliest arrivers. There were plenty more Sylvia didn't recognize, but a few faces were familiar from their trip to Dale's. Sylvia spotted one of the couples who had joined them on the dance floor (not so much a dance floor as it was a sticky section of dining room that'd had the tables pushed aside).

Peter had his arms draped over the steering wheel, his chin resting on his wrist. Sylvia hadn't seen him so nervous since their wedding. She thought: *I think this place is starting to get to him.* Then farther down, a softer voice: *I think it's getting to me, too.*

(*it's changing me it's changing him*)

When Peter had returned to Shady Cove from his trip to the pharmacy earlier, he had told her about the missing girl. At first he hadn't said why he wanted to help so badly, just that he thought it was the right thing to do. But she had known there was more, and when she asked, Peter had told her. And she wasn't the least bit surprised when he mentioned that greasy kid from outside the bar last night because she had felt something about him, too. Something she hadn't been able to put her finger on. Whatever it was, she hadn't liked it.

Peter finally broke the silence in the car. "I think that must be him."

"Who?" Sylvia asked, trying to follow her husband's gaze. "The policeman?"

"Yeah. He looks like a police chief, doesn't he?"

A man in police uniform had come out of the front door of the church and stood looking around for a moment before turning and heading back inside. He was tall and broad shouldered, with a middle-age gut. His clothes were wrinkled, and his face sported a day or two of stubble. Something was fraught about him; Sylvia recognized the look of a person dealing with the unimaginable, the thing that was never supposed to happen to them, only to other people.

"We should go in. It's almost one." She secured her hair in a ponytail with an elastic she had taken from a collection she kept stored on the passenger-side door handle.

Peter looked at her. "How am I supposed to do this?"

"Let's just go in, and you can feel out the situation. You're good at that."

"What if I'm wrong, Syl? I probably just have a brain tumor or something. That would make a hell of a lot more sense than me suddenly gaining some sort of second sight."

"I don't think it's all of a sudden," Sylvia said. "I think you've always had a little bit of a gift. Think of it as powerful intuition. And maybe this town has a way of making it a little stronger. Who knows?"

"I sure as hell don't," Peter said.

She shook her head and smirked.

"What?" Peter said.

"I was just thinking about what someone would think if they heard us talking right now. We sound sort of—I don't know—silly, don't you think? I keep thinking Rod Serling is going to start narrating from the clouds at any moment."

Peter laughed. "Yeah, I've had more or less the same thought a few times since we showed up here. We're a long way from a week ago, huh?"

"Wasn't that the point of coming out here?"

"Yeah, I guess you're right."

"Ready to go?"

"As I'll ever be, I guess."

They got out of the Dodge and headed into the church.

3

At least fifty people were gathered inside Our Savior Lutheran. Most were milling around, drinking coffee out of paper cups and eating pastries off paper plates, talking amongst themselves. They were clustered in little groups in front of the raised pulpit stage. Five or six policemen were huddled around a foldout table, going over a map. Sylvia spotted the policeman she had seen out front. He was at the center of it all and clearly in charge.

Across the back wall, bagged lunches covered another table in neat rows. The woman behind that table was making sandwiches in a hurry, and a man in a wheelchair was wrapping them in parchment and dropping them into brown lunch sacks. The woman shared the same look as the fraught policeman—tired and pushed beyond anything she had ever thought she would have to endure.

The sense of community in the room was almost palpable. A beautiful thing to behold.

Peter leaned over and whispered, "What's our first move?"

"I don't know. Maybe we should find out what the plan is. Looks like they're still getting organized."

As Sylvia scanned the room, she inadvertently made eye contact with a blond woman in one of the small groups of people. The woman, carrying a clipboard, excused herself and approached them.

"I don't think I recognize you," the woman said. "I'm Beth Bateman. Are you here to help with the search? Please say you are." She smiled guiltily and pressed the clipboard to her chest, her fingers tapping the back of it.

"We are," Peter said, putting his hands in his pockets.

"Thank goodness."

"Tad Halloran told me this was the place. Said you could use some extra help. We're renting up at the lake, but that didn't seem like a reason not to lend a hand."

"Tad, what a saint. I expect he'll be here soon," Beth said. "What're your names? It's good to have a list of who's out there so we don't lose one of our own. Roll call when we head out, roll call when we return."

"Peter and Sylvia Martell," Peter said.

Beth wrote down their names. "All right, Peter and Sylvia. Just sit tight, and they'll go over everything soon. They're just trying to figure out where's the best place to start first. Time's always ticking with these kinds of things." She turned and went back to the group she had been talking with.

"You hear that? They need the best place to start," Sylvia whispered to Peter. "You said by running water... you heard running water."

"I know. I need to think. Let's grab a seat," Peter said, and shuffled into one of the pews. He and Sylvia sat, and he started chewing his nails.

"Martells, what're you doing here?" Sue Grady poked her ruddy face between them from the pew behind.

"Hi, Sue," Sylvia said. "Didn't see you there."

"I saw you," she said, and snorted a small laugh. "Didn't think it was you at first. Then I said I knew it was you. You here for the search?"

"Yes."

Sue nodded. "I knew you were good people. When I first met you, I said to myself, 'Sue, these are nice folks.' And darn it if I wasn't right. Not great swimmers... but nice folks."

"Have you done this before?" Sylvia asked.

"Oh sure. A few times. Lotsa places to get turned around out in them woods. Happens at least once a year." Sue's face stalled. "Course, with a teenage girl... well, the situation could be different. Don't have a good feeling about this one."

Sylvia hadn't known what to think of Sue when she had first met her three days ago. At first, she had thought Sue's personality was slightly abrasive, bordering on unintelligent. But she was starting to think she might've gotten it wrong. Sue simply said what she felt or thought, without any beating around the bush. And in that way, Sylvia respected her. When Noah died, she could've used a strength like that. Maybe if she had been able to say the hardest things to say, then she wouldn't have ended up nearly killing herself with a handful of pills. Maybe she wouldn't have needed the pills at all, ever.

Sylvia smiled politely. "I hope it turns out for the best. Which are her parents?"

That question seemed to grab Peter's attention. He looked up.

"The one making lunches, that's Meryl, Grace's mother. The big guy up there standing over the map, that's Chief Delancey. He's Grace's father."

Just as Sue was saying that, a man and a woman stormed down the aisle and went right up to Chief Delancey. The man looked angry. The woman like she had been trying to calm the man down on their trip over.

"And where the hell is the search party for *my* boy?" the man said.

All other conversations in the church stopped. A man wearing a clerical collar, who must've been Our Savior's pastor, went toward the commotion. But Delancey held up a hand while maintaining eye contact with the angry man.

"Let's go. Outside. Now," Delancey said. "If you want to talk to me, then we'll talk. I wanted to ask you a few questions anyway." He grabbed the man's arm and started leading him toward the door.

"That's Mr. and Mrs. Collins. They got a boy, Chris. He's a little older than Grace. He must be missing, too. First I heard of it. What the heck's going on around here? Pardon my French," Sue whispered, her eyes following the action.

Sylvia looked at Peter. He shrugged.

They caught a piece of the police chief's conversation as he walked the man up the aisle:

"We're doing a search. If Chris is out there, we'll find him. What're you thinking coming in here like this and making a scene?"

"Well, why the hell didn't you put up no flyers about Chris? I only see ones for your daughter."

"I didn't even know he was missing, Chuck. This is the first you've said anything about it to me."

This variety of common sense seemed to stump Mr. Collins.

"I'm sorry, Corb, but he didn't come home last night. Then I heard about this, and I guess I lost my head."

Delancey pushed open the big double doors at the end of the aisle, and he and Mr. Collins disappeared outside. Mrs. Collins watched them from the front of the church until the doors closed. Then she grabbed a cup of coffee and took a seat without speaking to anyone.

Sylvia looked at Peter, who was chewing the inside of his cheek. "Do you…?"

"No," Peter said. "Nothing about that. Wait here. I'm…" He stood up and scooted past her. "I'll be right back. Pay attention for the both of us."

Sylvia understood. Peter had made up his mind. Whatever he had decided to do, he was doing it. She watched him walk up the aisle, hands stuffed in his pockets. The room brightened and darkened again as he pushed open the doors and went outside.

After a moment, George Bateman came over, drinking a coffee, and sat down next to Sylvia. "Well, if it isn't the lady with the appetite and the dancing shoes. You have fun last night, I hope?"

Sylvia looked up and smiled. "Hi. George, right?"

"That's it. Sylvia?"

"Yes. I had a great time. It was just what I needed."

"You mind?" He pointed to the seat beside her.

"Not at all."

George sat down and glanced behind Sylvia. "Hey, Sue."

"How goes it, George? I was just telling Mrs. Martell here that I don't have a good feeling about this. Teenage girl goes missing, it's never a good thing. Lotsa *preverts* out there." She shook her head.

"Jeez, Sue. Always the optimist."

She threw her hands up. "I'm just sayin, is all."

"Yeah, well, don't let Corbin hear you 'just sayin' anything," George said.

"Yeah, yeah. I'm here, aren't I?" Sue leaned back and folded her arms.

"Where's Peter?" George asked. "I saw him here just a second ago."

"He had to get something from the car. He'll be right back."

"Ah. I see," George said and took a sip of his coffee. "You met my wife, I heard."

"I did?"

"Yep. Beth. She said she just signed you and Peter in."

"Of course, yes. I didn't know that was your wife."

"The one and only. She still can't believe someone as small as you took down two Delights and a side of fries and still had enough left in you to dance."

"And how, I wonder, did she hear about that?" Sylvia said, smiling. She felt her skin blush. She was neither proud nor ashamed, just unaccustomed to being the subject of such a conversation.

The room brightened and darkened again. Sylvia checked to see if it was Peter returning, but it was a man in a pharmacist's coat. He was unbuttoning it as he came up the aisle. "Sorry I'm late," he said to no one in particular.

She shifted her eyes back to George.

"That was a true accomplishment. I had to tell someone. She didn't believe me, though. To be honest, I think she was a little jealous." George winked at her, a friendly gesture. Nothing more. "I told her it was you after she signed you in. I think she believes it even less now."

Sylvia laughed, then promptly covered her mouth, realizing it wasn't the place for such behavior.

"Two? I could do two. No sweat," Sue said softly.

George and Sylvia both glanced back at her. She was fixated on picking something out of the tread of her boot using a small twig. Her lips were tight save for the tip of her tongue sticking out from the corner. Sylvia wondered where the little stick had come from. Had Sue been carrying a twig in her pocket? Oddly enough, she wouldn't be surprised if that were the case.

They turned back around. George rolled his eyes and shook his head slightly. He looked around the room, scratching the side of his face. "I just hope we can get this show on the road soon. Looked like it could start raining hard any moment now. We're burning daylight."

A loud bang issued from behind the pulpit stage as a heavy door swung open and found the wall. All heads swiveled in the same direction. Looks of confused disgust slowly emerged on people's faces. A few of the younger men, police especially, looked more amused than concerned. All the same, the room went cold quiet.

A naked man stood in the doorway at the back of the stage. He was holding something with wires attached to it in his hands. Despite the distance, Sylvia could see how green the man's eyes were. They could've been two glowing emeralds. He seemed torn—terrified yet determined. He trembled, the green metal device in his hands rattling thinly. The wires looped to the ground and disappeared through the doorway behind him, down what looked like a staircase.

Sylvia glanced over her shoulder to see if Peter was back yet. He wasn't. She didn't quite understand what she was seeing. Her eyes, coupled with the lack of concern on the policemen's faces, told her it was probably just a local drunk who wasn't a stranger to law enforcement. Sure, this was just something he did from time to time—get drunk and show up at church naked. But something deeper let out a distress call. She should go. She should get out of there.

"What's this happy horseshit?" George said.

"Oh boy," Sue said, leaning forward again. "He must be drunk as a skunk in a funk. Corbin's gonna lose it when he sees this."

One of the police officers took a step toward the man, hands on his hips, nowhere near his gun. He didn't seem worried, more so annoyed. "Jim, what the hell are you doing? Are you kidding me?"

"I'm doing their will. Please forgive me." The man pressed his hand down on top of the device.

Nothing happened. George and Sylvia looked at each other. He opened his mouth to say something. But the words never came. A hot, powerful rush lifted Sylvia skyward, pulling her in every direction at once. No pain, just force. Her final thought was that she had somehow been caught in a violent, crashing wave. Soon she would crash on a shore and sand would be swept into her bathing suit.

Then loud whiteness clapped her ears and swallowed her up.

4

"You're going the wrong way," Tad Halloran said as Peter headed down the front steps of the church. "We didn't scare you off, did we? I promise nobody in there will bite."

"Hi, Tad. No, I'm coming back. I just need to grab something before we head out."

"More Rolaids?"

Peter laughed politely. "That too."

"I'll see you in there," Tad said. "And don't forget bug repellant if you have it. That's always the first thing we run out of."

"Good to know. Just give me a minute."

Tad continued up the steps, and Peter continued down, their paths never to cross again.

When Peter reached the bottom, he sat against the stone wall, waiting for Chief Delancey to finish talking with Mr. Collins, who seemed to have cooled down. They were standing on the sidewalk across the street in front of a little coffee shop called The Daybreak Café. After a minute or two, Mr. Collins apologized and headed back toward the church, his head hung low.

"I'll make a call, Chief," he said when he reached the other side of the street. "See if I can't get a few of my guys to come help. How's that sound? I'll ask any of em if they seen Ricky, too. I got eyes everywhere. We'll figure this out."

Delancey only nodded. He stood there and watched him walk away. When Mr. Collins made it to the steps of the church, Delancey scrubbed a tired hand over his face, then hitched up his pants, his gaze shifting up the sidewalk.

He didn't look like an approachable man, not at the moment, but Peter crossed the street anyway. He was still unsure of how to go about this. Probably, he would just start talking and see where his mouth led him. What did he really have to lose? Well, maybe besides coming off as completely crazy and somehow implicating himself in a crime by possessing information he had no business possessing. He was, after all, a stranger in town. That thought wasn't entirely lost on him. But he had a wife who could provide an alibi, if it actually came to that. Maybe all it would take would be for him to give a vague description of the freckle-faced kid and say he thought he saw the kid with the girl, and that would point them in the right direction. Or maybe it wouldn't help at all. Only one way to find out...

"Chief Delancey?" Peter said, walking around the back of a parked car.

Delancey looked at him, his hand still clamped over his mouth. He dropped it. "Yeah. Do I know you?"

"You wouldn't, no," Peter said. "My wife and I are renting up at the lake. My name's Peter Martell."

"The writer?"

"Doesn't feel that way since I've been here, but yes. You a fan?" Peter asked, with an air of doubtful humor. He didn't realize the offensive implication until he had already said it, and it made him cringe a little inside.

"No. Small town," Delancey said, his voice controlled.

"That'll teach me."

"Uh-huh." Delancey narrowed his eyes, watching Peter closely. "You're helping with the search? I saw you in the church."

"I was told you could use the help," Peter said, shifting his gaze between the church and Chief Delancey. "You can thank Tad for that."

Delancey nodded, then folded his arms. "I appreciate it. It's my daughter what went missing. You heard that?"

"Yes. That's actually why I wanted to…" Peter trailed off as he noticed Delancey's attention shift to something behind him.

"Sorry, just a second," Delancey said, looking surprised. "Benny?"

Peter turned around. Coming up the sidewalk twenty feet out was a familiar-looking man. It took Peter a second to place him, but the name and the face came together. Last he had seen him, he had been falling-down drunk and coming out of Dale's on a Friday afternoon. It was the guy who had licked his face. Benny looked different, though. This afternoon he had on a clean chambray shirt, sleeves rolled up to the elbows. His pants looked worn but washed. And his hair was combed neatly to one side. In one hand was a cup of coffee, in the other was a cigarette.

"Say, Corb," Benny said.

"That you, Benny? You look…"

"Yeah, yeah. I know," Benny said, bowing his head a little. "Let's not make it a bigger deal than it is."

"How long?" Delancey asked.

"Three days or so. Not much, but it's a start."

"Dry is dry. Take it any way you can."

"Yeah." Benny took a pull off his cigarette, then flicked it into the street. "Anyway, I heard there was a search being put together for your girl. That true?"

"Uh-huh. We're heading out in twenty," Delancey said, almost reluctantly.

"How long she been gone?"

"Since yesterday." Delancey swallowed hard, then cleared his throat. "Between noon and nighttime so far as we can tell."

Peter was struck by the balance in Chief Delancey's voice. It was half scared father, half levelheaded law enforcement. He knew the territory all too well and suspected one side would win out over the other sooner rather than later.

"I'd like to help, if you don't mind," Benny said.

"Can you keep up?"

"I'll manage. If I can't, I won't be your problem."

"Head on inside, then," Delancey said, glancing at the church. "I'll be up in a minute to go over things. If anyone asks after me, tell em the same."

"Sure thing, Corb." Benny turned to leave, then got snagged on a thought and stopped. "Grace is a smart girl. I bet she's okay."

"Thanks, Benny. I'm sure you're right," Delancey said. But there was a doubt in his eyes that anyone could see. On top of that, he looked exhausted, completely sapped.

Benny turned to Peter and tipped his head, the two exchanging a polite, wordless glance. Peter didn't imagine he had any recollection of their meeting last week. He knew drunk, and when he'd first encountered the man, Benny had been just about as bad as a person could get without being on his back, out cold. It was a state where memories weren't made. Instead, they were shuffled through the mind in a hurry and flushed out the back before they could leave behind any trace.

Benny crossed the street and headed to the church, sipping his coffee carefully with a jittery hand. Chief Delancey and Peter watched him for a moment. When he reached the walkway that led up to the front steps of Our Savior, he hesitated and started to veer left and go down a narrower stretch of walk that skirted around the steps and looked like it led to a lower entrance in the basement of the church.

"That fool," Delancey said kindly. "He's going to the preschool in the basement." He cupped his hands around his mouth. "Upstairs, Benny," he shouted. Then to Peter, he added: "We used the preschool auditorium awhile back when his daughter… well. He must be confused."

"What?" Benny shouted back.

"Not Mrs. Penny's. We're upstairs," Delancey yelled to him.

Benny raised his cup to say thank you, then corrected course and doubled back toward the front steps. But it was all happening in slow motion. Something had shaken loose in Peter's mind. A big, mean thought was blooming. The name "Mrs. Penny" was a key sliding snuggly into a well-greased lock. And now the key was turning.

"What were you saying?" Delancey asked. "We should probably get back inside. Can you walk and chew gum?"

"It's your daughter," Peter said, dazed. It didn't even feel like it was him talking. "I saw…" He trailed off, his mind starting to race with undefinable terror.

"What about her?" Delancey asked, his tone sharpening. "Do you know something?"

Peter stared at the church, his mind unfolding. He saw them everywhere; there but not there. They were on the other side, in the other place… waiting to drink in the chaos, the dread, and all the horrible. The building, the whole area, was covered with gishets. They swarmed like tall, hungry insects with shimmering faces, squatting on the front steps, on the roof, in packs on the street. The strong scent of wet smoke hung on the air.

Peter looked up. The sky flickered red, as if some giant faulty lightbulb behind the sky had just been tapped. Then it returned to normal. The moment held the urgency of collision. This place, this time, was a cosmic intersection designed to bring about one thing: suffering.

Delancey dropped his hand on Peter's shoulder. "Hey, pal, tell me what the hell you're talking about."

Peter looked at him, his face a sheet of sad revelation. "Something's wrong. We have to get them out." He turned to run toward the church.

Delancey caught him by the collar. "What were you about to say? You know about what happened to my daughter? Spill it if you know something."

Peter looked at him, then back at the church. Benny had just mounted the first step but had stopped and bent down to tie his boot. There was a silent flash, followed by a hot blast of stinging air.

At some point Peter had been reoriented. He lay on his back, looking up as debris rained down and the wind carried thick black tendrils of smoke across the sky. His ears were ringing. He flopped his head to the side and saw a blurry Chief Delancey on his back, hands resting peacefully atop his chest. A six-inch red streak had appeared over his ear, and it was joining the sidewalk and pooling. He wasn't moving.

Peter tried to sit up, but the world started swimming. He fell back against the ground with a hard thud, his head landing in what felt like shattered glass. And right before he lost consciousness, the ringing in his ears turned to screams. One fading gray thought saw him off into darkness:

Was Sylvia among the screaming, or was she among the silent?

5

Ricky was just returning to his project since leaving her the day before. He had been a busy boy. Originally he had intended to go back to town, gather supplies, and return in time to have a little fun with Grace that first night. He had never really been able to take his time before, and he liked the idea of savoring this one, especially considering who she was. But one thing had led to another, and he had ended up burying a splitting maul in his father's forehead. That had needed cleaning up, but it was okay. Letting her spend the night out there alone was a fitting punishment, and his dark thing had liked the idea of seasoning her with a little fear.

After he had left the pump shed on Tuesday, he had gone to the General Store and picked up enough canned food, MoonPies, booze, and cigarettes to last him at least a week. The plan was simple, and Ricky liked simple. There was a certain elegance to simple, not that he really knew what that word meant. But he felt it. He would spend a few days out at the pump shed, which he liked to think of as his hideaway, with

Grace. And when he was done, after she had helped give him a proper sendoff from this version of Ricky Osterman, he would leave Gilchrist once and for all and become the thing he was always meant to be—his ultimate form. Maybe he would travel for a while, and when he found a nice place, a place where no one knew who or what he was, he would settle in and start over. Then rinse and repeat as necessary. That was the plan, and it was already in motion... perhaps it had been for a long time.

When he had finished picking up food and cigarettes for his big sendoff, he had driven to his house and parked his car out on the little access road that led to the town reservoir. He walked the short distance through the woods and stole the entire box of .45 ammunition from the glove box of his father's tow truck. His old man hadn't noticed the gun missing from under the seat for the week or so it had been in Ricky's possession, so Ricky doubted he would notice the bullets were gone.

It doesn't fucking matter, Ricky, he had told himself. *You're never going to see that fat asshole again.*

But he had been wrong.

As Ricky was leaving, Chief Delancey had shown up asking questions. He had figured that would be the first place the chief would check when his daughter didn't come home, especially after the confrontation they'd had earlier that day. But he had heard his old man refer to him, his own flesh and blood, as a dipshit. It was one thing if his father wanted to be a bastard to his face, but Ricky wasn't going to tolerate that piece of shit talking down on him behind his back, smearing his name when he wasn't even there to set the record right. So when Chief Delancey left, the judge decided, and the deal came down... so, too, had the ax. These things happen, his dark thing reassured him. These things happen.

After he had dragged his father's body behind the woodshed and covered it with a tarp, he had gone inside. His mom had been sitting in the living room, combing her hair in the reflection of a cloudy window. *Peyton Place* was playing on the television. Watching that show was the last thing Nate and Barbara Osterman did together. Of course, in public, Nate said the only television he watched was reruns of *The Honeymooners* or *Gunsmoke*.

"Hi, Ricky," his mother said. "Your father doesn't like my haircut. Do you?"

"Yeah, Ma," he said, and kissed the top of her head. "I gotta take care of something. You'll be all right now, huh?"

"Of course, sweetie." She stopped combing and looked at him over her shoulder. "Want me to make you some eggs? I know how you like breakfast for dinner."

He had when he was much younger, before her accident.

"No, Ma. Not hungry. Some other time?"

"Okay." She returned to combing her hair, a dull look in her dark, glassy eyes.

Ricky left, feeling an odd sensation he couldn't place. Then he drove to his father's shop, hid his Biscayne out back among the rows of junked cars, covered it in an old canvas, and fell asleep in the backseat almost immediately. At some point in the middle of the night, he awoke to the sound of a car driving slowly through the front parking lot, tires crunching across gravel. When he peered through a tiny flap in the canvas, he saw taillights pulling away. And he could've sworn they belonged to Chief Delancey's cruiser. The guy had been so close, but he hadn't fully committed to his instincts. The excitement of it had overcome Ricky to the point where he had been forced to pull his pants down and jerk off into an empty beer bottle.

After that, he had fallen back to sleep and dreamed colorful dreams.

But that all felt like a lifetime ago as he breasted the hill and came up on his hideaway now. It was thirty yards or so in the distance. He stopped, pulled the pistol from his waistband, and leaned up against a tree, setting down his duffel bag of supplies. He surveyed the scene, making sure there weren't any surprises waiting for him. He got the sense that Grace was clever, but after what his car had done to her foot, she was more or less immobile, even if she had somehow gotten free of his knots. And he doubted that very much.

Still, he stayed there for a few minutes, listening to the sounds of the woods. Two crows were perched on the sagging, mossy roof of the pump shed. His father hadn't taught him much, but one thing he had said to him that had always stuck was: *If you're going to do something, you might as well do it right.* He tried to adhere to that adage as much as he could, not because he had respected his old man, but because it made sense. He didn't want to screw this whole thing up for one little measly oversight. So he would be cautious.

When he was convinced nothing was lying in wait for him, he picked up the duffel and headed down the hill, pistol still at the ready. Bit by bit, he cut off the angle to the pump-shed doorway, until he broke into the sightline. Two terrified eyes glared out at him from the darkness of his hideaway. All knots appeared to have held fast. Relief mixed with excitement, creating a satisfying warmth in his chest.

"Gracie, how the hell are you?" Ricky said as he moved toward her. "Did you miss—" A loud explosion cracked in the distance and echoed through the woods. He ducked, stuttering forward a step. Fleets of roosting birds burst from the treetops, their panicked wings beating the sky. "Hot shit! What the hell was that?" He looked up and around, trying to determine which direction the sound had come from.

It seemed to have issued from the direction of Gilchrist. It was a powerful sound, and it excited him. He didn't know what it was or what had caused it, but he liked it much in the same way a shark liked any trace of blood it smelled. "Must still be blasting. Damn, Gracie, I think I nearly just pissed my pants," he said, and laughed.

He entered the shed, dropped the duffel beside her, and squatted down to meet her eyes. Grace breathed slowly, steadily, her gaze following him but not reacting to him. He didn't think she looked scared. *Hollow* was the best he could think of. Had her night out there alone broken her already? He hoped not. He had wanted to watch her break, to be there to catch the moment.

"You get any visitors last night? Sometimes coyotes come for my souvenirs." He gestured vaguely to the animal carcasses on the walls. "They sure woulda liked a fresh, tasty thing like you."

She didn't respond with anything other than a quick blink.

"All right, well, I brought some food. If you're nice, I'll let you have some. If I take this off"—he ran his finger over the winds of rope securing her mouth to the pipe—"are you gonna be a nice girl? I don't want to hear any yelling. No one can hear you, and it'll just give me a headache. Then I'll have to give you one."

No response. Not even a blink.

"I'll take that as a yes."

He stood, went around behind her, undid the knot at the back of her head, and unraveled the rope. He wound it into a loose coil around his arm, then dropped it on the ground in front of her. It landed with a ropey splat. She backed her mouth off the pipe, slowly moving her jaw up and down to work out the stiffness. Her teeth had left scratch marks in the rust. No longer attached at the head, she carefully adjusted her legs so that she wasn't kneeling anymore and instead was sitting with her legs out in front of her.

"Water. I need water, Ricky," Grace said hoarsely. "Unless you plan on having me die of thirst. In which case, you might as well just shoot me."

Ricky looked at her closely. "I ain't gonna shoot you. No, ma'am. What kind of a sendoff would that be?" He picked up the duffel and set it on an overturned crate. He opened it, pulled out a metal canteen, and unscrewed the cap. "Open up."

Grace tilted her head back, opened her mouth, and stuck out her tongue. It was white and filmy, with a brown tint running down the middle from the rusty pipe. He dumped small sips into her mouth and let her swallow in between.

After five or six, he said, "That's enough. I don't feel like filling it up again. You want a beer? Some whiskey? Maybe that'll loosen you up a little. We're gonna spend a little time out here, and I don't need an uptight bitch bringing me down."

"Which one is better for pain?" she asked.

Ricky smiled. He'd half expected her to flat-out refuse it. "Whiskey. Want a tug?"

"Okay," she said, wiggling her nose.

"What the hell are you doing?"

"My nose itches, Ricky." She glanced at one of her bound hands. "And I can't exactly scratch it."

"Rub it on the pipe."

"I'll pass, thanks." She kept wrinkling her nose.

"Knock that off. Here." Ricky dragged his knuckles roughly across her upper lip and nose. She winced, but it seemed to stop the twitchy nose thing that he didn't like.

"Thank you," Grace said.

Ricky turned and pulled a bottle of Old Grand-Dad bourbon from the bag. "Open."

"What's it taste like?" Grace asked, and worked her jaw from side to side again.

Ricky uncapped the bottle, took a long sip, and wiped his mouth with the back of his hand. "Like dog piss. Last chance. Open."

To his surprise, she opened her mouth. He splashed some on her tongue.

She pulled her head away and grimaced, but she held it all in and eventually swallowed. "It burns."

"Yeah, it burns," Ricky said, grinning. "That means it's good. More?"

Grace nodded. "Yes."

He tilted the bottle, and a thick stream jetted into her mouth. Her cheeks puffed out like a greedy chipmunk, but she didn't spit it out. She steeled herself and swallowed it all.

"Hot shit, Gracie. I didn't think you had it in you." He capped the bottle and put it back in the duffel. He bent and peered out the one window.

"Ricky?" Grace said.

He wheeled around on his boot heel. "What?"

"Are you going kill me?" she asked.

He let out a small laugh, then dropped back down on his haunches. Their eyes were level again. "Oh, Gracie. Gracie, Gracie, Gracie. Yeah... probably." He winked at her and then flicked her forehead. "And maybe, you know, maybe I lied about that other thing. Maybe we can do that, too. We got all the time in the world, beautiful."

She rested her head against the pipe and started to cry, but she didn't make a sound. They were silent tears.

Ricky pulled a little battery-powered radio from his bag, turned it on, and started to dance. "Hot shit, Gracie," he said. "I love this song."

It was "Paint It Black" by The Rolling Stones.

6

Peter awoke in a hospital bed with a gnawing headache behind his eyes. Sterile colors and antiseptic smells surrounded him. Unreality and reality duked it out in his first waking moments, oscillating between crippling sadness and a false relief that it had all been some terrible nightmare. In the end, reality landed with gruesome finality, and the full weight of tragedy settled over him to stay. If he could've turned away from it, he would have.

This is what he knew: there had been some sort of an explosion at the church, and Sylvia had been inside when it had happened. These two intersecting thoughts were part of a bigger truth he didn't want to face but knew he had to. So that was what he intended to do.

He looked down. His shoes were still on his feet. They hadn't put him in a gown. That was a good sign, he thought. His pants were covered in specks of black and a few tracks of blood. He looked at his arms. No IVs. He wasn't connected to any machines, either, so far as he could tell. He pushed himself up, confirmed it, squeezed his temples, and checked his wrist. He still had on his watch. It was twenty past two. They had been in the church at around one o'clock, which was just over an hour ago. But the hour seemed huge from his current viewpoint—a Grand Canyon gap in his life.

Peter glanced around the room. The windows were streaked with thin silver slugs of rain. The bed beside him was empty. Fuzzy memories flickered in his head: people standing over him on the sidewalk; being lifted off the ground, jostled; then a speedy ride in the back of a car.

He swung his legs off the bed. When the head rush had subsided, he stood. The floor was tilted. His balance was shaky at best, but he could manage well enough. After a moment, everything seemed to level out. He went into the hallway and spotted a nurses' station with a group of nurses behind the desk. He made his way up the corridor, his hand pressed across his forehead. He had never felt such a headache in his life. Each step he took brought up the urge to vomit.

When he was about ten feet away from the nurses, one stood and rushed around the counter to him. She was tall and thin, with a pretty face. "Sir, you shouldn't be up and walking."

"Where am I?" Peter asked, steadying himself against the wall. The nurse tried to take his arm, but he shook her off. "I'm fine."

"Gilchrist County Hospital," she said, watching him carefully. "They brought you in an hour ago."

"County hospital? Am I still in Gilchrist?" Peter angled his head down and winced. It felt like a shard of glass was trying to make its way through the arterial tunnels of his brain.

"No. You're in Hammond. Gilchrist is a few miles away, the next town over." The nurse lowered her head, trying to find Peter's eyes. "That's where you were. Do you remember anything?"

Peter lifted his gaze. "A little. What happened?"

"You really should be lying down. You've likely suffered a concussion, Mr. Martell."

Frustration was starting to boil up in Peter. "What happened?" he repeated, almost snapped.

"They don't know. There was an explosion. That's all anyone's told us so far."

"Where have they taken everyone?" Peter looked around. The place didn't appear particularly busy given the circumstances. "It doesn't seem like it's here."

"You were one of the lucky ones. Most are being brought to Worcester General or Boston. They're better equipped to handle something like this. You should be happy you woke up here. That means you're going to be fine."

"How did I get here?"

"You were driven. Not sure by who. They just said they found you unconscious on the sidewalk. They went back to keep helping." She tried to take his arm again and lead him back down the hall. "Let me take you back to your room. Doctor Graves will be in when he's finished stitching up another patient. He's the attending at the moment. You're going to be okay, Mr. Martell. That's a good thing."

"I need to find my wife," Peter said. Voicing those words brought up a thicker wave of nausea mixed with anxiety.

"Your wife?"

"Yes. Her name is Sylvia Martell. She was in the church."

The nurse looked as if a cold hand had gripped her from behind. "Mr. Martell... I..." She didn't know what to say.

Her sudden look correlated with what he feared he already knew. "I have to go," he said.

"But Mr. Martell, you—"

"I said I need to leave. Look, I appreciate whatever you've done to help me, but either call me a cab, or I'll start walking. And I'd really rather not." Peter winced again as another shard of pain squirmed through his brain. "And could I get something for my head? It's killing me."

As it turned out, the nurse wouldn't call him cab, but she understood enough to know he wasn't going back to his room, either. So she gave him the number for a local cab company in Hammond and let him use the phone. Ten minutes later, a taxi arrived out front.

Before Peter left, the nurse approached him in the front lobby. "I shouldn't do this without the doctor's consent," she said, "but these should help with your head. I hope your wife's okay." She handed him a paper cup. Inside were three Darvocet.

"Thank you," Peter said, and swallowed them dry.

He went outside and got in the cab.

7

The Massachusetts State Police were on the scene when Peter returned to downtown Gilchrist. Troopers were everywhere. Their vehicles lined the street. And in all the commotion, he didn't see a single uniform from the Gilchrist police force. A horrible thought hit him all at once: what if they were all dead? The church had been full of Gilchrist's finest, who had been there helping plan the search for the chief's daughter. In such a small town, that might've been half the force, probably more. And if none of them had made it out alive, then…

Peter shook his head to push the thought away because of the inevitable conclusions it forced him to draw about Sylvia.

She's gone. I can feel it. But I need to see it. I need to see…

The Darvocet hadn't begun to work yet, and the motion of his head fired off a flare of pain behind his eyes. He grimaced and pressed down on his temples. That offered a brief respite from the gnawing pain.

The cab stopped at the intersection up the street from where people were gathered behind orange A-frame barriers. All Peter could see were people's backs, everyone looking in one horrible direction. Many appeared to be crying and consoling each other.

"This is as far as I can go, pal. Looks like the road's blocked off up ahead." The cabbie leaned forward over the steering wheel, squinting. "What the hell happened here?"

Peter dropped five dollars over the seat and got out without saying a word. He looked across the roof of the cab before shutting the door. Fire trucks from three different towns were parked in the street and around the block. Whatever familiar, cozy feeling the town had once held was gone. It felt like a foreign and dangerous place now. It was a threat and always had been, but he had been unable to see it.

He didn't remember starting, but he was running up the sidewalk, the rain smacking his hot face. Each footfall sent a vibration up his legs that ended as an excruciating sliver of pain in his head.

Why am I running? I already know what I'm going to find. Please, dear God, let me be wrong. Let this all be a mistake. Maybe it was the building beside the church. Maybe...

The closer he got, the harder the truth hit. The sidewalk shimmered dully with shards of broken glass. All the storefront windows along Main Street had been shattered. The road was covered in debris. Pieces were scattered as far back as the intersection where he had gotten out of the cab. And the scattering grew denser the farther up the road he went. Mostly it was splintered wood and pieces of crumbled brick. And the worst part was that he recognized the brick. It was the same shade as the church, if he remembered correctly. And he did. It seemed impossible how much there was. The road, the sidewalk, and the cars were littered with it.

Each piece that he marched past as he made his way closer to the crowds of people brought back a recollection of how powerful the blast had felt. It had been like getting hit in the chest with a sledgehammer. One moment he had been talking to Chief Delancey, and the next he had been looking up at the sky, slipping into unconsciousness. All of these pieces, his own mental debris, were coming together, and as each interlocking thought joined the bigger picture, his hope broke apart. It hadn't been some small accident. And it wasn't something a person could just walk away from.

Peter stopped when he reached the edge of the crowd and could see what they saw. Suddenly he felt as if an invisible rubber mallet were playing against the base of his spine. Hardly anything remained of the church. What still stood looked like a two-dimensional slice of the back wall. The entire front had been reduced to a heap of rubble crawling with police and firemen, presumably looking for people buried beneath. The steeple had fallen forward and was in pieces across the front lawn. On a small patch of grass to the left, a dozen or so white sheets covered small mounds. At first Peter wondered why they were making little piles of bricks and covering them with sheets, but the absurdity of that thought gave way to the realization that those sheets hid bodies. And then came a worse realization: one of those piles of bricks was probably his wife.

The back of his throat ached, but he swallowed the urge to cry. This wasn't the time for it. Instead of trying to make his way through the crowd, he skirted it until he found a young-looking state trooper standing at a gap between a brick wall and the crowd. On the other side of the trooper was the beginning of the church's granite front steps. Peter glanced at the name tag below his badge: B. CONWAY.

Conway put up a hand as Peter approached him. "Can't go through this way."

"I need to get some information," Peter said.

"Yeah, you and everyone else," Conway said, not making eye contact. "Get back in the crowd. You can't come through here."

"I'm not trying to go through."

"Good, then step back."

"What's the matter with you? My wife—"

"The matter is"—Conway gave him his eyes—"we can't do our job when people keep trying come up here. It's dangerous. And nobody seems to know what the hell caused the explosion to begin with. So I'll say it again… step back."

"Listen, you son of a bitch, my wife was in there. I'm not trying to get by you. I'm trying to find out where she is. If you can't help me, then tell me who can, and I'll talk to them."

"What'd you call me?" Conway's face had turned a hard shade of red, and his jaw seemed to have somehow grown squarer.

"I'm just trying to figure out where the fuck I start," Peter said. "Jesus H. Christ! You don't have to act like such a stupid asshole." He could feel people starting to look at him.

Let them, he thought.

"That's it." Conway unfolded his arms, stepping forward.

Peter backpedaled as Conway came toward him. But Conway reached out, grabbed the front of Peter's shirt, and pushed him up against the brick wall. "Come on. Get your hands off me."

"You need to learn some manners, pal. You're lucky I don't

throw you in the back of my cruiser and let you cool off. I told you to get back. What didn't you understand about that?"

Peter showed the palms of his hands. "You're right. I'm sorry. Please, I just want to know if my wife is one of the survivors they took to Worcester or Boston. That's all I'm after."

A spiteful look washed over Conway's face, and the corner of his mouth gave a little upward curl. "Survivors? There ain't nothing but body parts in there."

Something inside Peter popped. He shoved Conway as hard as he could, his back pressed against the wall for leverage. Then he stepped forward and punched the man square in the jaw. Conway's head snapped back, but he stayed on his feet. His hand went to his face. He worked his jaw back and forth a few times, then spat blood on the ground.

Peter stood there, frozen. What the hell had he just done? He had never hit someone before—*way to pop your cherry on a cop*, an internal voice said—and the impact hurt his hand more than he had thought it would. "Hey, look, I shouldn't've done—"

"You stupid moron." Conway started toward him again, fists clenched.

"What the hell is going on over here?" someone yelled.

Both Peter and Conway looked in the same direction. An older trooper with a stocky build was heading over to them. He didn't look amused. This was exactly the type of goddamned thing this guy didn't have time to deal with.

Conway's demeanor tempered—beta in the presence of alpha. "This guy struck me, Sarge."

"That true?" the older trooper asked Peter.

"I did," Peter said.

The older trooper looked at Conway. "Well, what the hell you do to piss him off?"

"Nothing. He was trying to get through. You told me to keep everyone—"

"I wasn't trying to get through. How many times do I have to say that?" Peter said. Then to the older trooper: "My wife was in the church when it... Look, I'm just trying to find out where she might be. Jesus, I don't even know if she's alive."

But he did know. And the answer was: she wasn't. He was just going through the motions, waiting to be told what he already knew. A strange memory hit him, one he had all but forgotten. He was ten, hiding in the closet in his parents' bedroom. They were discussing Christmas, and his father was telling his mother that it was time to stop the Santa Claus charade. The boy was getting too old, and it was time they started taking some of the credit for the toys. Goddammit, they paid for them, not some fat make-believe asshole! Since the first grade Peter had suspected Santa Clause wasn't real, but he had held on to the idea as long as he could, until he had heard it from his own parents' lips. Life had just seemed better that way.

The older trooper sighed. "Okay. Trooper Conway, why don't you leave us alone. Keep doing what I told you to do, just try not to do it in such a way that makes people want to knock your block off."

"Sarge—"

"Go. Now. I won't tell you twice."

"Yes, sir." Conway gave Peter a cold look and then walked away, holding his jaw, his tongue working the inside of his cheek.

"I'm Sergeant Babineaux. Let's step over here a moment." They moved from the street to the sidewalk, away from the crowd. A good many were still watching them, curious about the fight that had nearly broken out. "We'll just pretend this never happened, okay? Given the circumstances I'm going to assume Trooper Conway had it coming. He usually does. Unfortunately, his attitude is bigger than his brain. You all right?"

"I'm fine," Peter said.

"You said your wife was in the church?"

"Yes." Peter pinched the bridge of his nose and shook his head, once again holding back an urge to break down and start sobbing. "What the hell happened?"

"Well, that's what we're trying to find out. All we know at the moment is that there are a lot of casualties."

"I was taken to the hospital," Peter said. "I was outside when it happened. But the staff at Gilchrist County said that people were being taken to Worcester and Boston. Is that true?"

"A few people were, yes." Babineaux ran a hand across his mouth. "But they weren't inside the church when it went off. My guess was that they were outside, like you... probably a little worse off. This whole thing is a mess at the moment. It's going to take some time to sort it out."

"What about them?" Peter pointed to the bodies covered by sheets. "What if one of those...? Shouldn't I try to identify her?"

"What's your name?"

"Peter... Martell."

Babineaux put his hand on Peter's shoulder. "Peter, if one of those is your wife, you don't want to see under that sheet. Whatever did this, it was a heck of a blast."

Peter nodded. His eyes were starting to blur. It was hard to tell if it was rain or tears. He supposed it didn't matter.

"If you want my advice," Babineaux said, "go home and get some rest. If your wife's alive in there, we'll find her, and there will be a record of where she's taken. But standing out here in the rain and waiting for us to pull a body from the rubble isn't going to do you any good. That's as hard to say as I'm sure it is to hear." Babineaux crossed his arms. "Now, can you listen to that? Or am I going to regret overlooking the fact that you assaulted a member of law enforcement?"

"I lost my head. I'm sorry," Peter said. "I just…" He didn't know how to finish the sentence.

"I know," Babineaux said, and patted Peter on the arm. "Just hang in there."

Then he went around Peter and disappeared back into the commotion. Peter stood on the sidewalk a moment. At some point he looked down. Among the broken glass was a maroon pool of blood. He was standing directly where he had been when the explosion had knocked him off his feet. The pool of blood, he suspected, belonged to Chief Delancey. One of his last fuzzy thoughts before he had blacked out had been of a head wound. A long slice in the shape of a frown.

Peter headed up the street, hands in his pockets, head down. His clothes were wet, feet damp, and even though it wasn't cold, he shivered. It was a windless afternoon, made mean, tall, and deep by death. He didn't know where he was heading. Then he did. He hadn't even meant to go that way. He was walking in the direction of his car, which was still parked on the street where he'd left it earlier that afternoon. His brain was completing a forgotten circuit.

They had parked at least a hundred feet from Our Savior Lutheran on the opposite side of the street. The Dodge was clear of the crowds of people. A long spider crack ran the length of the windshield, and pieces of brick were scattered across his hood and roof.

Peter didn't care. He opened the door and got in. The keys were still in his pocket. So much was where it should be, yet so much was lost, out of place. He started the car and turned on the windshield wipers. They scraped debris across his windshield in a strained sweep, leaving muddy, clay-colored streaks on the glass.

He looked across the seat, listening to the squeal of the wipers. The rain drummed on the roof. Sylvia's hair elastics were where they always were—on the door handle. Peter brought his hands to his face and started to cry.

8

Returning to Shady Cove without Sylvia might have been the hardest thing Peter had ever had to do. Cradling his dead son's lifeless body in his arms had been bad, but losing Sylvia was worse. When Noah died, at least he hadn't been alone to face it. He felt a vague sort of guilt for even thinking it, but he and Sylvia had both borne that grief, its weight distributed evenly between them. They had suffered together, and there had been something less tragic about that awful bond they shared.

This time, though, it would be only him looking into the sinking void, and he wasn't so sure he wanted to face that alone. What was the point? To prove his mettle? To whom? To what? He was tired of staying strong. He had seen enough of this world, especially in Gilchrist, to know there was no God. Not the kind that people believed in and leaned on for strength. Not the kind that traded in faith. What existed out there wasn't a benevolent, just, or compassionate creator. It was a cruel, greedy manipulator that cared for nothing except its own thirst.

And he didn't want to feed it. He didn't want to feel what he was feeling because he knew that those emotions were precisely what it wanted. The series of subtle—and not so subtle—manipulations had all been designed to bring him to Gilchrist and march him toward tragedy. This town had probably been suffering the consequences of its own nature forever, and for whatever reason, his life had been caught in its undertow and dragged down. Just another meal. He supposed this sort of thing happened every day, all over the world. Whatever people called it—bad luck, tragedy, evil—it was all the same. Never random, never without reason.

But he was done with it. Done with all of it. If there was one thing he had learned to do over the last few years, it was how to avoid feelings. He and Sylvia had practically become professionals in that arena. And if anything was going to drink up his misery, it would be him.

He sat down at the table and set the bottle of vodka in front of him. He had purchased it on his dazed drive back to Shady Cove. He hadn't been planning to drink—the thought hadn't even touched his mind as his world began to fall apart before his eyes—but then he had spotted the liquor store and realized that maybe he had been planning his next drink his whole life.

He looked around the kitchen of Shady Cove, blinking slowly. Nothing had definition anymore. It was all muted and fuzzy. Except one thing. The bottle of Rolaids was still on the counter. He sniffed, his smile faint. The last thing they had shared was a bad case of heartburn. But at least it had been brought on by a good night of honest-to-goodness fun—a night of dancing, laughing, and making love. They had created a good memory, and he wondered if he would get to maybe see that again one day. Was there a negative of it stored somewhere in that basement dimension, waiting to be watched? He hoped so.

He closed his eyes, uncapped the bottle, and downed a third of it in one long drink. The Darvocet had kicked in, and he was already riding that dull wave of loopy warmth. But the immediate effect of the alcohol was a welcome addition. He hadn't taken a drink in almost a week, but it all came flooding back, like seeing an old friend whose company he had forgotten he enjoyed so thoroughly. He took another long swig and sat in the silence of Shady Cove, listening to the duck clock tick and tock, letting the sharp corners of his pain be rounded down as the liquor went to work on him.

After a few minutes—it could've been an hour; he couldn't be sure—an idea came to him, irrational yet totally perfect. He stood, wobbled, steadied himself on the back of a chair, then made his way into the bathroom. He opened the drawer and reached all the way back. It took him a second, but eventually he found the bottle of Equanil he had hidden behind the first-aid kit. He swallowed five, after chewing them first, and washed it all down with more vodka. The bottle was already half gone. He didn't know if his intention was to kill himself, or if he just wanted to feel closer to Sylvia in some strange way. Maybe if he could align with her past state of mind, try to put himself in her shoes, he could grasp one final glimpse of her, somehow preserve her inside him. It was hard to say for sure. His mind was on sideways, sliding down the embankment into the void. His thoughts were clumsy, tumbling wooden blocks.

He looked down at the knuckles of his right hand. They were black and blue from socking that arrogant cop. He opened and closed his hand. He liked the way it felt: sore and tight, like it was made of rubber. In fact, he had liked the way all of it had felt—the quick building anger that had erupted in an indelible act of violence. He wasn't a violent man, had never even punched someone before, but the pained look of surprise on the trooper's face had been satisfying. It said: *I didn't see who you truly were, but now I do.*

Peter took another drink and set the bottle on the back of the toilet. He glanced up and looked at himself in the mirror. The side of his face was covered in thin scratches he had no recollection of receiving. "Look at me now," he said, and grinned. "Where d'we go from here, my friend? Where d'we go?" His speech was starting to slow and slur.

He punched the mirror. It spiderwebbed, and a few jagged pieces fell into the sink. He laughed madly. Outside himself, looking down, he saw a stranger, but the smile on his face fled as the cabinet door swung open slowly. He saw the bottle of antacids, the bottle he had been unable to find that morning. The Rolaids were sitting on the cabinet shelf, exactly where they should've been. Still, he was certain they hadn't been there this morning. He had checked twice.

He stared at them for a long time. And in another quick act of uncharacteristic aggression, he grabbed the sides of the medicine cabinet, tore it off the wall, and threw it into the tub. Tears ran hot down his cheeks, but he wasn't crying.

A thin pain issued from his palm. He looked down, eyes bleary. A long cut stretched from the base of his thumb to the base of his pinky. He looked at it, seeing it but not really understanding it. He must've cut it on the medicine cabinet. He wiped it on his pants, then wrapped a hand towel around it.

Silvery stars and clouds floated across his vision. His head was spinning. The booze was working. The drugs were working.

He stumbled into the bedroom and found his wife's suitcase. It was still full of clothes she hadn't unpacked. He picked it up and dumped it out on the bed, pushing it all to the side where she had slept. Then he lay down beside it. It smelled of her perfume. But it was more than that. It smelled of her life. He buried his face in it, held it tightly, and wept, until dizzying blackness fell over him and carried him off.

Chapter Fifteen

OUT IN THE WOODS

1

It was ten past eleven on Wednesday night when Corbin knocked on the door of Shady Cove.

"Mr. Martell? Peter… are you in there? It's Chief Delancey." He softened his tone. "It's Corbin."

No response. He knocked again, harder.

"Maybe he isn't home," Benny said, leaning from the passenger's seat of Corbin's pickup truck.

Corbin's cruiser had been parked in the church's back parking lot and was demolished by large pieces of flying debris. His head had suffered similar injuries, but he had been far luckier. Thirty-six stitches and a bottle of pain medication had fixed him up well enough to be out at Big Bath, looking for a man who may or may not know something about his missing daughter. Just a couple hours ago, firemen had pulled Meryl's body from the wreckage and Corbin had identified her. It hadn't been pretty. His wife was dead, and he would have to face that soon enough. But his little girl might still be out there somewhere, and the time to grieve would have to come later. If there was a chance of finding Grace, he had to take it. The nurse at Gilchrist County Hospital, where Corbin had been treated, had told him Peter Martell was brought in around the same time he was and left on his own in a cab. Two ships passing in the night. But at least Corbin knew the guy was still alive.

"His car's here," Corbin said over his shoulder. He tried the door and it opened. "Stay here."

"You sure?"

"I'm sure."

Corbin went inside. The lights were all off. Somewhere in the dark, a clock ticked off seconds.

"Hello. Anybody home?"

Deep silence.

He made his way up a hallway and stopped at the first doorway on his left. His eyes weren't adjusted, and it was too dark to see anything but rough shadows. He reached his hand through the doorway, felt around on the wall, and found a light switch. He flicked it up. The bathroom light came on overhead. There were shards of mirror glass in the sink. The medicine cabinet was in the tub. Dime-sized spots of blood dotted the floor. A brownish handprint was smeared on the wall beside the towel rack. A half-empty bottle of vodka sat on the back of the toilet tank.

"Jesus. What the hell happened here?" he said under his breath. He had a feeling he knew, though; the scene echoed in his own heart.

He left the light on and continued up the short hall, his faint shadow stretched out ahead of him. The next doorway opened to a bedroom. In the dim light, he could see someone curled up in the fetal position on a bed, back facing the room. The bed was covered in clothes.

"Peter?" Corbin said. No answer. The room smelled sharply of alcohol mixed with an undertone of perfume. He went to the person, whom he presumed to be Peter Martell, and gave the man's shoulder a gentle shake. "Mr. Martell." He shook again, this time harder.

Peter shot up like a spring, looking around frantically. He drew in a long, confused breath. "What... What is it?"

Corbin took a startled step back. His hand reached instinctively for his gun and then dropped away. "Mr. Martell, it's Chief Delancey. It's okay. Didn't mean to scare you."

Peter looked at him, blinking rapidly, coherence returning slowly to his eyes. He wiped a hand down his face, breathing ragged breaths through his fingers. "What're you doing here?"

"I've been trying to track you down for the last few hours."

"Jesus, my head." Peter reached up and squeezed his temples.

Corbin looked around for a moment and found the light switch. He pointed to it. "You mind?"

"Go ahead." Peter looked at the bloody towel wrapped around his hand, then turned and planted his feet on the floor. The light washed the room yellow. He squinted, angled his head down, and rested his elbows forward on his knees. "What time is it?"

"Just past eleven."

"Still Wednesday?"

"Uh-huh." Corbin took a seat in the chair beside the door. "You all right? You don't look so good."

Peter glanced up, his eyes bloodshot slits. "I could say the same."

Corbin's fingers went to the long line of shaved hair and blood-crusted stitches that ran from his left temple to behind his ear. "How're you?"

"Concussion," Peter said.

"Could've been a lot worse."

"It was a lot worse," Peter said. "For both of us, I think. Your wife was in that church, wasn't she?"

Corbin folded his arms and looked sideways for a moment. "She was."

"So was mine. I'm sorry."

"So am I," Corbin said, fighting the urge to think about it. *Not yet*, he told himself. *If I fall apart now, I don't stand a chance of finding Grace.* "But I didn't come here to talk about that."

"I know you didn't," Peter said.

Corbin leaned forward, forearms on his knees, mirroring Peter's body language. "Do you remember what we were discussing before the explosion?"

Peter nodded. "Your daughter. Grace, right?"

"That's right. Listen, I'm going to need... No, I'm going to insist you finish what you started. Grace is all I got left. If you saw something, you tell me. The state police are busy figuring out what the hell happened at Our Savior, and pretty much all my guys short of dispatch are gone. So it looks like I'm on my own for the time being. You're the only lead I have. And I don't even know what that lead is. Let's start there."

Peter stared at the floor for a beat, massaging his temples with his one good hand.

"Mr. Martell—"

Peter's eyes snapped up. "Stop calling me that. Peter... just call me Peter. I'm not holding out... I'm thinking. What I know—or think I know—isn't going to be what you're expecting."

"Okay," Corbin said, leaning back and putting up his hands. "But this isn't something I can wait on. So why don't you just go ahead and try me, okay? We'll start there."

Peter shook his head and scoffed at whatever he was working out internally. "I'll tell you what I know. You can take it or leave it. I'll even tell you how I know it. You won't like that part. But it'll be the truth."

A door opened and shut in the front of the house. A few seconds later, Benny appeared in the doorway. "Everything all right in here?"

"I told you to stay put," Corbin said over his shoulder.

"I know, but…" Benny looked at Peter and nodded politely. "I'll go back in the truck. Name's Ben Feller, by the way. Not sure we've met," he said to Peter.

"We haven't… not really. But it's fine. Stay," Peter said. "Look, guys, I appreciate you letting yourselves in and waking me up out of a rather pleasant blackout, but do you think we can take this into the kitchen. I need a cup of coffee or something. My head's splitting in two." He eyed Benny suspiciously. "You don't have a scratch on you. How'd you manage that?"

"Not sure. Probably the angle of the steps saved me. Blast went straight o'er me. Bent down to tie a loose lace, and next thing I know, brick's raining down. Curled myself into a ball and prayed."

"You oughta play the lottery more," Peter said tiredly, but with an air of dry humor.

Corbin reached into his pocket and tossed a prescription bottle on the bed beside Peter. "Help yourself. That should fix your head."

Peter picked up the bottle, read it, and tossed it back. "Thanks, but coffee's probably a better idea at the moment."

They all went into the kitchen.

2

Peter was on his second cup of coffee by the time he finished telling Corbin and Benny about his run-in with the freckle-faced kid outside Dale's Tavern. Corbin had poured himself a cup at the outset, but he hadn't taken a single sip. Benny sat at the breakfast counter, looking at his hands the whole time.

"So that's it," Peter said, setting his mug down and rubbing the side of it with his finger. He liked the warmth of it. "Chief, your face looks exactly how I thought it might. You think I wasted your time, don't you? That I'm just about the craziest person you've ever met? I don't blame you. Before coming to this town, I would've thought the same thing."

"I think I don't know what to think," Corbin said. "But I've lived in Gilchrist long enough to know strange things happen, probably at a higher frequency than most places. And this week certainly hasn't made me think otherwise."

"Fair enough," Peter said. "You know, at one point I was just going to lie and make up a story that sounded more believable, say I witnessed something that could point you in the right direction with your daughter. But after what happened today, I'm having a hard time seeing the point in caring what people think anymore. I think I knew that was coming, too, but I couldn't do anything to stop it. I know I'm not crazy. You don't have to believe me about Grace, but at least I'll know I tried."

"Thing is"—Corbin scratched the back of his head, his face embroiled with rightful skepticism—"the kid you're describing is exactly who I thought might have something to do with this. His name's Ricky Osterman. He and I had a bit of a disagreement yesterday. And I'm not going to ignore a coincidence like you landing on him, especially when that's the best we got. It's just…"

"I believe you," Benny blurted from his seat at the counter. "And I ain't even know you, neither. But I believe you. I think maybe I got a little of what you got, too. Only it's not the same. I just... well, I see things around here sometimes that I don't think other folks see... or maybe they do. Things that'd make you turn tail and run, that's for sure."

Corbin looked at Benny. "You do?"

Benny nodded. "I know with my history that don't mean a whole lot, but I ain't lyin about it."

"Can't say as I was expecting this conversation to end up here," Corbin said.

"We should listen to him, Corb," Benny said, gesturing to Peter. "What choice do you have? If he says he thinks Grace is near running water, that probably narrows it down to the Gilchrist. And if it is Ricky, then I'd wager he stuck to an area he knows, which means probably in town. We ignore that, then we have hundreds of acres to cover. That's a dead end. At least this gives us something to go on. We could head out there tonight and start at the northern part of town and make our way down. Me on one side of the river, you on the other. It's prolly five or six miles. We could do that before sunup. You got any better ideas, let me know."

Peter watched them. His head was still a tumbling mess. His thoughts didn't seem entirely his own at the moment. But he did feel strangely unburdened. A weight had been lifted. And that was good.

"Do you know where?" Corbin asked Peter.

"Like *exactly* where?" Peter said. "No. It's not like that." He paused, thinking of Sylvia's remark in the car. "It's more like intuition. And it doesn't always make sense."

"You said a slaughterhouse. Well, there ain't no slaughterhouses around here," Corbin said.

"I don't know if it's a slaughterhouse. I never said that. I said she was surrounded by dead animals. Could be a taxidermist for all I know."

Corbin looked at Benny, then back at Peter. "All right, look. You and I have a lot to hate about the world right about now, but do you want to help do something useful? Three guys can cover more ground than two can. You feel like going for a hike? If you wanted to lend a hand, now's your chance."

Peter looked up. Part of him wanted to just be left alone, but a bigger part, a part that felt engrained with his wife's will, thought he should keep pushing forward. Besides, he had originally gone to the church to help. Perhaps he had felt so compelled to do so because of what had happened to Noah. It was a chance to save one. Or maybe that's the very thing that had been used against him. Maybe...

He cut off that mode of thinking; it felt an awful lot like the what-ifs that had haunted him after Noah. He would help for one reason, and it was a good reason: this was his opportunity to finish the last thing he and Sylvia had started together. It didn't seem like much, but it was enough to hold on to. And at the moment, he needed that.

He conjured a thought, forcing himself to hear it in her voice: *See it through, Peter.*

"All right," he said. "Where do we start?"

3

They arrived at an empty gravel parking lot just before one o'clock in the morning. Corbin parked near a building at the back. The headlights illuminated a sign out front that read

FOOTE BROTHERS CANOE RENTAL. There were a few picnic tables, a rack with oars and life vests hanging from it, and a Coke machine with a trash can beside it.

Peter sat between Corbin and Benny, an old army bag in his lap. They had stopped at the police station on the way and picked up flashlights, walkie-talkies, and a few canteens of water.

Corbin shut off the engine and got out. Benny did the same, and Peter slid out after him. He could hear and smell the softly burbling river, but he couldn't see it yet. The rain had picked up again—a steady, cool drizzle. They were all wearing rain slickers and muck boots, also courtesy of the Gilchrist Police Department. There wasn't much talking until they went around to the back of the truck and Corbin dropped the tailgate. Peter set the bag down. Corbin pulled it over to him and unzipped it.

"All right," Corbin said. "Each man takes a flashlight and a radio. Water, if you need it, too."

Peter reached in and grabbed one of the canteens. "I need it."

The hangover had set its hooks in, and it was worse than his usual brand. The Equanil still had a weak hold on him, too, and occasionally he felt as if his head were floating away from his body.

"I know you do," Corbin said. "You smell like a distillery. No offense."

"None taken," Peter said, and gulped down a mouthful of cold water.

Benny didn't say anything on the subject. He grabbed a flashlight and tested it a couple times to see if it turned on and off. Then he picked up a walkie-talkie and tucked it inside his jacket. Peter and Corbin did the same.

"Benny, you take the right bank of the river," Corbin said, printing his flashlight beam on a wooden footbridge that crossed the Gilchrist. Water glistened like dull brass sparks as it passed underneath. "Peter and I will take the left, spread out a little to cover more ground. I figure it's best to cover both sides at once. Keep the radios on, but only use them if you need to. We'll check in every half hour or so. I have no idea what we might find, so it's best to keep the element of surprise on our side. Speaking of which…"

Corbin leaned into the bed of his truck and dragged a rolled-up tarp to him. He unwrapped it and flashed his light down.

"Shit, is this a search party or a hunting party?" Benny said, lighting a cigarette. "You think we actually need those?"

A shotgun and two revolvers sat on the tarp.

"I don't know. Hopefully not. But wouldn't you rather have one and not need it than the other way around?" Corbin said.

"I suppose you're right," Benny said.

Corbin picked up the shotgun and pumped it. "Listen, let me make something clear right now—and if this doesn't sit well with either of you, then I'll do this myself and won't think lesser of you for it—but I'm not going out there as law enforcement." He removed the badge from the chest of his uniform and dropped it on the tarp. "If my daughter is in these woods, I intend to bring her back. And if it turns out Ricky has his hand in this, I'll tell you one thing… that kid's a wolf. Trust me, you don't want to be the sheep that crosses his path."

Benny reached down and grabbed one of the revolvers, winking one eye shut and pointing it into flat darkness as his cheek glowed orange from his cigarette. His hand trembled. "Is it loaded?"

"Wouldn't do a lot of good if it wasn't," Corbin said. He put his fingers on the barrel of Benny's gun and gently pushed it down. "You sure you know how to shoot that thing?"

Benny tucked it into his waistband. "Does a bird fly?"

"Depends on the bird," Corbin said.

"I can shoot," Benny said. "Don't you worry about me."

"How 'bout you, Peter?" Corbin said. "You feel safer with a little steel to grip?"

"I'm okay. I'll take my chances."

"You know something we don't know?" Corbin said.

And even though he said it with a tone of nervous incredulity, Peter could tell there was sincerity there. He could tell Corbin was scared, his poker face held together by weak thread. One light tug was all it would take.

"I know that I've never shot a gun before in my life," Peter said. "And I'd hate to have it somehow end up in the wrong hands, pointed at one of you two on my account."

"All right, then." Corbin bundled his badge and the remaining pistol in the tarp, then walked around and put it in the cab of his truck and locked the door. "We oughta get a move on."

4

They stuck together until the footbridge. Then Benny kept straight and went across to the other side, his flashlight sweeping left to right ahead of him in slow arcs through the rain.

Corbin veered left, moving south along the bank of the river. "This way," he said across his shoulder. "It's narrow here for a few hundred yards, but it opens up. We'll spread out then to cover a wider swath."

"Okay," Peter said, fighting back a wave of nausea. His stomach continued to turn over on itself.

He followed closely, watching Corbin's big frame maneuver over the moss-covered remains of fallen trees and wild jags of wet roots. The week had been downright sweltering for most of its days, but tonight had the raw feel of autumn in New England. It was as if a cold, iron hand had closed around the town and was slowly tightening its grip. Everything was being brought together.

It's just another manipulation, Peter thought.

And if it was, he had no idea of its purpose or where it led. Perhaps, he mused, that was the trick of it, how everything can seem completely under control, until it no longer is and it's too late. In hindsight, it all seemed so foolish, so easily avoidable. You say: *Man, I should've seen it coming… I should've known.* Yet you didn't.

The what-ifs. They were the far-reaching teeth of tragedy that could bite at any time, from any distance. The little things, the seemingly innocuous choices of life, that could've been done or made differently. For as long as Peter had been familiar with the concept, he had thought of it as nothing more than a way for him to torture himself about the randomness of life, but now he wondered if it was just a way to retrace the path that had been deliberately drawn for him. And if that was the case, it brought him to a bigger question: where had that path begun and where would it end?

Where it always ends, where they *want it to end… in suffering and tragedy.*

He and Corbin walked in silence for a few minutes. Then Corbin stopped and pulled his radio from his pocket. He pressed the button, and it squelched. "You there, Benny?"

Peter heard Corbin's voice come through his own walkie in his pocket. He looked right and could see the flicker of Benny's flashlight across the river. It stopped moving forward for a moment.

Benny's voice crackled on both their walkies: "Yeah. I read you loud and clear."

"Just testing," Corbin said, wiping rainwater out of his eye.

"Gotcha," Benny said.

Corbin tucked the radio back in his jacket and kept trudging ahead. Peter moved along, feeling like a wind-up toy that had been spun up, set down, and was now headed toward some inevitable destination.

"What was your wife's name?" Corbin asked, slowing his pace until he and Peter were walking beside each other.

Peter looked sideways at him. "Was?"

"Shit. Hey, look, I'm sor—"

"It's okay. It was Sylvia," Peter said. "No one who was inside that church is walking away from it. I'm not naïve enough to think otherwise."

"No, you're right. They pulled my wife's body out a few hours ago. I had to identify her. Never thought I'd ever have to do that, I'll tell you that much." Corbin hesitated, then said, "You'll have to do it, too, for yours. It won't be easy, but you'll do it just the same, and then it'll be done. I'm sorry that you have to."

"You trying to cheer me up?" Peter said. "Because I hate to be the one to tell you, but you're not doing a very good job of it."

"Don't mean to sound cold. I'm just trying to speak to you honest," Corbin said. "It's good to know what's coming, don't you think? Although I suppose you know a damn sight more about that than I do."

"I'm not some sort of psychic, if that's what you're suggesting," Peter said. "Maybe what I told you back at the house makes it sound that way, but I'm not. I just pay attention more than most, I think."

"I didn't mean to suggest anything or sound ungrateful. I truly do appreciate you offering what... well, I guess offering what you saw." Corbin looked at him and nodded a vague apology. "But if not psychic, what would you call it, then?"

"I don't know."

"Well, what's it like?"

Peter sighed, thinking it over, but also wanting very much not to discuss the subject at all. It felt too fantastical. "I've always had a knack for finding things people lose. Ever since I was a kid, really. Even if it was a random woman at the market who lost her car keys, somehow, if I just focused a little, I could find them sitting in a crate of lemons back in the store. Or if my dad lost his watch, I could tell him it was on the shelf above his workbench in the garage without even having to go out there... and I'd know I would be right. But I never thought it was anything special... a parlor trick at best." He paused a beat before adding: "Then I came to Gilchrist, and things got weirder."

"So what... you focus on what you want to find, and then you get a vision or something?" Corbin said earnestly.

"It's more like being in a large crowd of people and everyone is talking. But your eyes are closed, and you can't open them to see. If you don't pay attention to anything in particular, all the voices around you just blend together to white noise. But if you focus, you can grab on to a conversation, hone in, and hear it clearly. And if you listen really closely, you can start to feel your way to the source of the voices. That's sort of what it's like for me. I focus on a conversation and follow the voices until I find what's talking."

"Is that what happened when you bumped into Ricky?" Corbin asked, dodging a rock on the riverbank.

"No. What happened with Ricky was new," Peter said. "That was like being in that crowd of voices... but for the first time, I could see. My eyes weren't closed anymore, I guess."

Peter thought of what Kevin had said at dinner on Monday about opening his other eyes, and smirked. The little dude knew all about it.

"I haven't figured out what the hell I'm going to tell Grace about her mother," Corbin said, then hesitated. "You got any kids?"

Peter heard the hope in Corbin's voice, speaking about his daughter in a way that kept her alive in his mind. That was good, but also dangerous.

"I had a son, but he died."

Corbin turned sharply to him. "Aw, jeez. I'm—"

"Please don't try and cheer me up again," Peter said, shielding his eyes from Corbin's flashlight. "I don't think I could take another one of your pep talks. No offense."

Corbin laughed good-naturedly. "None taken. Where are you from, Peter? You a loc—"

"Do you mind if we knock off the small talk?" Peter said in a tired tone. Not rude but honest. "It's nothing personal. I just don't feel up to it right now."

"I understand."

And Peter believed that the Gilchrist chief of police did, in fact, understand. He found the man's brute integrity comforting in a way.

They walked in silence for another five minutes. The sound of their collective footfalls snapping damp twigs and crushing wet leaves became their conversation. And when the woods opened up, Peter shifted a hundred feet or so to the left, but stayed close enough to keep Corbin's flashlight in view.

5

Ricky had fallen asleep in the corner after he was through having his fun for the night. He was snoring, leaning upright against the wall, the pistol sticking out of his waistband. He had promised her a second round of celebrating in the morning, followed by a grand finale he said she would never forget. The kerosene lantern sitting on the overturned crate Ricky had been using as a table flickered dirty yellow light around the shed. Grace had gotten used to the smell of the dead animals, but seeing them pinned to the wall reminded her it was still all around her. And with the tape he had put across her mouth, she could only breathe through her nose.

That bastard.

Grace watched Ricky closely, timing every movement with his snores to cover any trace of sound she might make. The doorway in front of her was a rectangle of black.

The ropes were tight, but with little lateral jerks, she managed to slide her hand down the horizontal pipe to where it made a ninety-degree turn and ran down into the floor. The elbow fitting had a sharp, rusted edge. She maneuvered the rope tied around her wrist so that a side of it was pressed against the sharp pipe fitting. Then she started to saw it back and forth in small movements. Slow and steady.

Her eyes stayed on Ricky. She watched his chest slowly rise and fall. She found the rhythm and made sure to stay in time.

Inhale: saw.

Exhale: be still.

Inhale: saw, saw, saw.

Exhale: be still, be still, be so still.

She looked at his disgusting mouth and could taste the cigarettes. The thought of it made her feel sick to her stomach, but she couldn't worry about that. If she didn't at least try, then she would be dead by this time tomorrow.

Inhale: saw.

Exhale: be still.

He had said he was going to kill her, and she believed him. Her foot throbbed and burned with fiery pain. And she hurt in new places. For the most part, she was numb, and that was okay. She thought it was probably for the best right now. But she wondered if she somehow made it out of that shed alive, would that feeling, or lack thereof, ever fade?

Grace continued to work at the rope, minding the rhythm, and watching the fine cotton filaments begin to fray. Little by little. Bit by bit.

Inhale: saw.

Exhale…

6

Peter's walkie spoke to him from inside his jacket.

Corbin's voice: "We've gone about three or four miles. I think we're coming up on the back side of John Marini's cornfields. Have a moment, fellas."

"All right. Ain't seen nothin over here yet. But we still got a ways to go," Benny said.

Peter pulled the radio from his jacket, fumbled with it for a second, then depressed the button. "Nothing over here."

"Okay," Corbin said. "Smoke em if you got em."

Peter tucked his walkie away.

That was the fourth radio check-in, which put them at about the two-hour mark. And each time, Corbin's voice seemed to lose a little more enthusiasm. Peter looked in his direction and saw Corbin's light still about a hundred feet out.

Peter trained his flashlight on his watch. It was five past three. They were in the heart of darkness. *It doesn't get any more night than this*, he thought.

Luckily the rain had fallen away to a fine mist. Or perhaps this deep in the woods, the canopy was sparing them from the big stuff. He shined his flashlight around and spotted a tree stump at the top of a small hill ahead of him. It looked like a good place to sit and rest for a few minutes while they took a break. He needed it, too. The boots he had on loan from the Gilchrist Police Department were about a size too big, and his heels were blistering badly.

He went to the stump. When he reached the top of the hill, something below in the distance caught his eye. It was faint at first, but he turned off the flashlight, and within twenty seconds he could see a small structure about thirty yards away. It looked like a little shed, with a single dimly lit window. His heart fluttered.

"Holy shit," he said under his breath, fumbling for his radio. He got it out and spoke softly, dropping away from the top of the hill to shield his voice. "I got something, Corbin. Come to me. Stay quiet. We're close by."

"I can't see you," Corbin responded, a radio whisper.

Peter turned his flashlight back on and waved it down low.

"What is it?" Benny said.

"Hold on. Stay quiet," Peter said.

He looked in Corbin's direction. A flashlight beam began to move toward him. After a minute, he heard the sound of his footfalls. Then Corbin was standing in front of him, the shotgun still resting back on his shoulder. His face was a wet stone.

"Something talking to you, Peter?" he said, breathing heavily.

"It's nothing like that. Follow me," Peter said in a low voice. "And shut off your light. Maybe kill the radios, too, just in case."

They went back up the hill, flashlights off, radios silent. Peter showed him.

"Holy shit," Corbin said, and crouched.

Peter did the same, resting his arm on the tree stump for balance. "Yeah. My sentiments exactly. What is it?"

"I think it's one of Marini's old pump sheds. He stopped pulling from the river ten years ago after he dug his retention pond." Corbin turned to Peter, astounded. Renewed hope slowly emerged across his face. "Son of a bitch, I don't believe it. You were right."

"Looks like someone's home," Peter said.

"Sure does."

"Think it's them?"

"Only one way to find out." Corbin rose off his haunches. "Stay here."

7

Corbin brought the shotgun off his shoulder as he crept down the hill to the pump shed. He kept one hand on the forestock, and the other ready on the cold curve of the trigger. His back had broken out in a nervous, prickling sweat, his skin in welts of gooseflesh. He was mindful of every footstep, making sure to be as quiet as possible. The soughs of wind provided some cover from the rigid silence of night. The closer he got, the stronger the awful smell became.

He made his way to the small window in the side of the shed. When he reached it, he peered inside. His body tensed, another dose of adrenaline surging through him. His daughter sat in the middle of the room. She had tape across her mouth, and her arms were tied to a pipe out in front of her like one of those medieval torture devices. She was working her wrist against something.

Attagirl, he thought. Then he noticed her swollen, black-and-blue foot nearly bursting out of her shoe and clenched his teeth so hard he was sure they would all shatter.

His first reaction was to go to her, to save her, but he fought the instinct. It might've been the hardest thing he had ever had to do, short of pulling that sheet back and identifying Meryl. But he couldn't be hasty. The final moments were always when tragedy struck. People seemed to abandon all common sense in the face of intense emotion, and that was often the last mistake they ever made.

He surveyed the room through the window. A small lantern. A duffel bag full of canned food. A few bottles of booze. Some empty beer cans. There was what looked like a folded wool horse blanket in the corner. He found the source of the rotten smell. The walls were all covered in dissected animal carcasses.

Surrounded by dead animals…

But he didn't see Ricky anywhere. That was either a good thing, or a—

It felt like someone punched him in the shoulder blade. His hand squeezed involuntarily on the shotgun's trigger, and it fired off a round into the dirt, then dropped to the ground. His back began to burn and ache, sharp pain traveling up his neck and into the crown of his head. His right arm lost all its strength. It coursed with painful pins and needles, like little jolts of electricity. Something was wrong.

"I go to take a shit, and looky what I found. Come to join my big send-off, Chief," a familiar voice said from behind him.

Ricky pressed a cold piece of steel behind Corbin's left ear, digging it hard into bone. He didn't need to turn around to know that it was a pistol.

8

Grace had pretended to be asleep when Ricky woke up and went outside. She didn't know where he was headed, but once the sound of his footsteps faded, she went to work double-time on the rope. It was risky, she knew, because he would be able to see her well before she could see him returning. But this was her last chance.

(*now or never*)

If she could at least get an arm free and keep it hidden, then maybe she could grab the gun from his waistband when he wasn't expecting it. If he leaned down to try to kiss her again, she would let him. And when he was off his guard, she would bite down on his lip, tear it off if she could, and at the same time, grab the gun. Then she would aim at the center of mass just like her dad had taught her and squeeze—not pull—the trigger, until all the bullets were gone and Ricky Osterman was dead. Her biggest concern was shooting using only one hand—she had never done that before—but as she saw it, that was her best and only option, a risk she needed to take. Plaguing her like a cancer in the back of her mind was the knowledge that plans never went the way they were intended. She would cross that bridge when she came to it, though.

She had just gotten through the rope on her right hand when she heard the gunshot and the commotion outside. Before she could decide what to do, her father appeared in the doorway. One hand was on top of his head, his elbow winged out, but the other arm hung limply by his side. His face looked pained.

Ricky stood behind him, gouging him forward with his pistol. "I caught us some din-din." He laughed, and jabbed Corbin in the back again. "Move. Come on. Family reunion time."

Grace's eyes peeled wide, and she screamed muffled sounds through her taped mouth. But her mind said this: *Dad! No! Don't hurt him, you psycho!* Then deeper down, her subconscious answered: *You are supposed to save me, Dad. You are my protector. Do something!*

Nothing made sense anymore. But through it all, she forced herself not to move her freed hand. It was the only thing she had left.

"It's okay, Grace," her father said in a calm voice. "Don't be scared, baby."

Ricky laughed again. "Yeah, sure, everything looks *okay*, doesn't it?" He pulled Corbin's service weapon from his hip holster and tucked it behind his back.

"What do you want, Ricky?" Corbin said.

"I want you to go kneel next to Gracie. We're all gonna have a little fun now."

"It's Grace, not Gracie. Or are you too stupid to get her name right?" Corbin said.

"Shut up! I know what it is, asshole." Ricky brought his arm up and cracked her father on the back of his head.

Corbin dropped to his knees and fell forward; only one arm came out to brace his fall. Then Grace saw why his other arm hung useless the way it did. The handle of a hunting knife protruded from her father's shoulder blade. For a moment it looked fake because she couldn't see any blood on his green raincoat, only tiny beads of rain. But she looked farther down and saw little rivulets of red on the side of his pants.

He looked at her as he crawled toward her. Something about his actions seemed deliberate. His eyes looked hard at her hand, the one that was free. Then he looked at her. "It'll be okay, Grace. I swear it'll be okay. Don't be scared. I'm hurt, but I'll be fine. You hear me?"

She looked at him, terrified.

"Do you hear me?" her father repeated.

She nodded.

"How sweet. Yeah, everyone's gonna be fine. Kneel," Ricky said, training the pistol on Corbin. "How many more of you are there? Don't tell me none, because I ain't stupid."

"None," Corbin said. He turned around and knelt in front of Grace, looking up at Ricky. "Wait. I'm wrong. It's a dozen. Or maybe two dozen. I can't remember."

Her hand was maybe ten inches from the knife handle. It was shiny black with a silver butt. She looked at it, and her heart began to thump in her chest. *Stay calm*, she told herself. *You wanted one chance, and this is it.*

Ricky wound up and kicked her father in the ribs. He stepped back and pressed his forehead against the side of the gun. "I know he is. I know," he said, talking to no one. He tapped the pistol against his head. Then he looked toward the doorway, one eye staying on Corbin. "Try and come in here, and I'll shoot em both!" he yelled to the night outside. "You hear me?"

"Who are you talking to? There's no one out there," Corbin said.

"Don't fucking test me." Ricky pointed the gun at Corbin's face. "You know, I was going to kill you both. But I think I'll just kill you.

And right in front of your daughter, okay? Let her live and think about it. See how she copes with witnessing her old man getting his brains blown out. All her fault, too." He looked at Grace. "It's all your fault. Do you understand that? He came out here for *you*, and now he's going to be dead. Blood's on your hands, bitch."

"Grace," Corbin said. "I love you. You hear me? Don't listen to him."

She nodded.

Her father looked at the empty doorway, his face sprouting anger. "Hey! I told you guys to stay back. I'm handling this."

She didn't quite understand. Then she thought she did.

Ricky flinched, looking sideways at the door for a fraction of a second to see who Corbin was talking to. But that sliver of time was all there was to act. Grace reached forward, grabbed the handle of the knife, and pulled it from her father's back.

He winced, then lunged forward.

"What the fuck!" Ricky steeled his arm, re-fixing his aim. But Corbin had already reached up and grabbed his wrist, dragging him down to close the distance.

Grace pulled herself up on her good foot, cocked her arm back and drove the knife down as hard as she could into Ricky's forearm. A seam of white-and-pink flesh exploded open as the tip of the blade slashed deeply across his arm, exposing two bulging cross-sections of tendon, vein, and muscle. She almost cut into her father's thigh on the follow-through.

Ricky screamed, his face contorting. It didn't sound human. He cried one word: "Mother!"

Corbin jumped up, his hand still clamped around Ricky's wrist. He brought his head back and smashed it into Ricky's face. Gouts of blood spouted from Ricky's mashed nose and fell to the floor.

The gun went off—four shots in rapid succession. But they all fired into the floor or the ceiling as Corbin controlled Ricky's arm.

Debris rained down, landing on the back of Grace's neck, some in her eyes.

Corbin drove his head into Ricky's face again, then twice. It sounded like meat being tenderized… if the meat groaned and grunted when getting hit.

"Drop it, you little shit," Corbin said, and pushed the top of his head into Ricky's chest to move him around the room. Blood was spilling everywhere from Ricky's arm and nose.

He tried to backpedal and throw punches with his left hand, but they landed clumsily against Corbin's neck and seemed to have little effect. Her father had at least eighty pounds on Ricky.

Grace watched, frozen, as it all unfolded like a movie. Then she snapped out of it and realized she was still holding the knife. She started to cut at the rope on her other wrist. And just as she freed herself from the pipe, her father and Ricky slammed into the doorjamb, tumbled outside, and were swallowed by the darkness.

She tore the tape away from her mouth and began to drag herself toward the door. She could only hear a scuffle outside— then another gunshot and a quick flash of yellow.

"Daddy!"

She couldn't see anything. Then, from out of nowhere, a white light streaked across the darkness. There was a loud *crack!*

Then stillness.

9

Peter stood over Ricky, the flashlight in his hand. The bulb had flickered but hadn't gone out when he connected with back of the kid's head. He shined it down. Ricky wasn't unconscious, but he was slowly moving around on all fours, moaning like a hurt animal. The sizable gash in his arm oozed blood. Peter picked up the pistol on the ground beside Ricky and pointed it at the kid, his hand unsteady. He had never held a gun before, let alone pointed one at a person who needed one pointed at him.

"Who hit me?" Ricky mumbled.

Corbin picked himself up off the ground and fell on top of Ricky, driving his knee into the center of his back.

Ricky didn't put up a fight, only wheezed at the weight holding him down. "Get off me," he said, a pained groan.

"Helluva swing you got, Peter. You all right?" Corbin grabbed his pistol, which was still stuck in Ricky's waistband, and holstered it. Then, one hand at a time, he pulled Ricky's arms behind his back and pinned them under his knee. He looked up at Peter. "You want me to take that, or are you good?" he asked, gesturing to the pistol.

"I'm fine," Peter said, looking around in a semi state of shock. The whole thing felt surreal. It had happened so fast. Then he caught scent of something foul. "What's that smell?"

"You don't want to know," Corbin said.

Ricky started to yell incoherently. "I am the judge! I decide! Get the fuck off me! I decide! Not you!" His screams started to sound like a pig's squeals. "Get off me! Get off me! I decide… I decide!"

Corbin tried to reach behind and lift his coat. He groaned and let his arm hang at his side. "Do me a favor and grab my handcuffs off my belt and put them on this nitwit. The bastard stabbed me. My arm isn't working so good right now."

Peter got the handcuffs and secured them on Ricky's wrists. Then Corbin turned him over and sat him up. Ricky crossed his legs Indian style, let his chin drop against his chest, and fell silent. The front of his white T-shirt was covered in blood.

"Daddy? Say something… please," a girl's voice called from inside the shed.

"Hold tight. I'm here, baby. I'm here." Corbin started toward his daughter. "Watch him," he said on the way by. "If he moves, hit him with your flashlight again. Or shoot him. I don't care which."

Peter's gaze followed Corbin, and he looked into the shed. He saw a young girl in a dirty blouse and a plaid skirt leaning on her hip, dragging herself toward the door. She was squinting, looking out. One of her legs looked badly injured. Then from the corner of his eye, Peter saw a flicker of light and heard snapping groundcover. He turned. In the near distance, Benny emerged from the woods and came into the clearing. He was soaking wet.

"I swam across the river when I heard a gunshot. Then I heard a lot more. Everyone okay?" he said, approaching. He had his gun drawn like a slick cowboy, but Peter thought he looked a little like Elmer Fudd.

"Looks like it," Peter said.

"What the hell happened?" Benny shined his flashlight on Ricky. "Holy Moses. How's the other guy look?"

"Okay, I think," Peter said.

Ricky lifted his head, eyes shut. "Get that thing out of my fucking face," he said hoarsely.

Benny sniffed but moved the beam off the kid's face. He and Peter both looked toward the pump shed at the same time. The silhouette of Corbin came walking toward them, his daughter's arm around his neck as she hobbled forward on one leg.

"Corb," Benny said, rushing over. "Grace, you all right?"

Grace didn't say anything. Peter thought she was probably in shock.

"She's okay," Corbin said, eyes straight ahead. He continued away from the pump shed, all of his focus devoted to Grace. "We need to get to a hospital. Her foot's broke bad. Probably her leg, too."

Benny stayed outside the shed's doorway and watched them pass by for a moment. His attention seemed to slowly shift to what was inside. "Christ. Peter was right. Look at this place." He flashed his light on Peter, then to Ricky, then back inside the pump shed. "This is sick." After a short moment of what looked like contemplation, Benny brought a handkerchief to his face and disappeared inside, his flashlight sweeping around wildly.

From where he was standing, Peter understood well enough what was causing the smell. The shed was full of dead animals. He glanced down at Ricky and took a half-step back. Then he looked at Corbin's daughter. He could only imagine what it must've been like to be stuck in there for as long as she had been. Then he saw the look on her face. And he saw the look on her father's face, too. Something was already festering there. What else had gone on in that shed? Peter wasn't so sure he wanted to think about it.

They stopped near Peter. For a moment he thought Corbin was going to do something dramatic like say: This is Peter Martell, the man who helped find you. But that didn't happen, and he was glad it didn't. Instead, they all stood in silence, a bloody, and probably dying, Ricky Osterman sitting between them.

He snapped his head up, showing a bloodied and swollen face. "Ahhh, Gracie, why'd you do this to me? We had so much fun together, didn't we?" He smiled. His front teeth were all missing, and he wiggled his tongue between the gap.

"Shut your mouth, or I swear to God I'll leave you out here to die and let the birds pick your bones," Corbin said.

Ricky started laughing. But it was the weak, tired laugh of a delirious mind. "You can't do that... You could, but you won't. Chief ain't like me. Chief ain't got my friend." He dropped his head again and went quiet.

"How are we getting out of here?" Peter finally asked. It seemed to be the biggest question of the moment. The way Corbin was looking around, he appeared to be pondering the same thing.

"There's a canoe somewhere. That's how he brought me here," Grace said. "But I don't know where it is."

Head down, Ricky muttered, "No. That's my vessel. Don't touch." More laughs. Then he continued with a little chant: "Chief ain't like me, Chief ain't got my friend. Chief ain't like me, Chief ain't got my friend..."

They ignored him as he repeated it over and over again, weaker and weaker each time.

"Hold on," Peter said. "I'll look around." It took him about thirty seconds to find the canoe sitting behind the pump shed. He dragged it over. There was one oar inside, and a few empty beer cans. Schlitz.

Corbin looked at it, then looked at his daughter. "Can you do a boat ride, Grace? It's a mile or two to the Sawyer Falls fish ladder. Could be there in forty-five minutes or so. I can radio ahead to their department, tell em we're coming. It'll be a whole lot quicker than any other option we got."

"Uh-oh, he found it," Ricky said in the background, breaking his chant.

They continued to ignore him, until Benny said in a tone of complete shock, "It was him."

Peter turned to see Benny standing outside the pump shed, looking down at something in his hand.

"What's wrong, Benny?" Corbin said.

"He killed her, Corb." Benny held up what he was looking at, shining his flashlight on it. "It's Maddie's necklace. I bought it for her on her birthday. It was missing when they found her. I..." He turned to Ricky. "It was you... You killed my girl. I always knew it wasn't no accident."

"All these years, and here I was, right in front of you. Ta-da." Ricky turned his bowed head to Benny and smiled. "Benny like me now. Benny got my friend in his heart."

Benny pocketed the necklace. Then raised his pistol as he moved in front of Ricky and pointed it at him. "It was you. Dear God, it was you." He wiped a hand down his face. "Why?"

"Because she was there... and I'm here. I decide," Ricky whispered.

A low sound rose up, like tubas playing underground at a barely audible frequency. The smoke smell permeated the air. Everything went tight.

Peter glanced back over his shoulder. Corbin stared at Benny, a look of awe dawning on his face. Grace's forehead was pressed against her father's shoulder, eyes closed.

When Peter turned back around, fear grabbed him. A gishet stood behind Benny, but Benny didn't seem to notice its presence. It was there but not there. The shimmering face loomed over him like an electric cloud. Peter knew if he looked hard enough, he would see the ominous red sky on the other side, in that basement dimension where all was stored. Where all was waiting.

"Do you see that?" Corbin said. "Please tell me you do."

"I do."

"I've seen it before," Corbin said.

"So have I."

"What the hell is it?"

Peter wanted to answer: *I think that's our maker.* But instead, he said, "I don't know." It seemed like the only thing to say. And it was closer to the truth.

"Benny..." Corbin said with an unsteady tone in his voice. "I can't just—"

"Go on," Benny said. Something in him had switched, a softness hardened. "Go on now, you hear me? Take care of your daughter. I'll take care of this monster."

Peter thought maybe there would be some sort of argument on the matter. There wasn't. But neither he nor Corbin could tear their eyes away from what they were seeing. The creature just stood there, a witness, a puppeteer. And Peter knew why: it was drinking it all in. It was harvesting what it had sowed.

Ricky sat up straight, staring at the gun Benny held on him. Beneath the blood on his face, his skin was pale. If Benny didn't kill him, the severed artery in his arm would soon enough.

He started to scream again: "I decide! I decide! I decide! I decide..." Louder each time. Angrier, more defiant each time.

"We're going, Peter," Corbin said. "Now."

"Okay," Peter said, dazed. Finally, he broke away.

He helped Corbin get Grace into the canoe. Then together they dragged it through the woods, leaving the pump shed behind. But what had happened in there, Peter knew, would not disappear for Corbin and Grace quite so easily.

No one spoke as they went. Ricky's two repeating words—*I decide*—played the whole way, a haunting soundtrack that faded more with every step they took. Everyone was waiting for the silence. Peter kept his eyes straight ahead, knowing that if he looked into the dark pockets of the woods, he would see one of those horrible faces. It wanted him. It wanted them all. It had planted sadness and anger in them and wanted to reap it. That was its doorway into the heart. Hate made a person vulnerable.

I decide... I decide... I decide... I decide, Peter thought, one hand on the canoe, the other holding the flashlight and lighting the way, his eyes knowing only the next ten feet. Then the next. Then the next. Until they finally reached the river. The moon had broken through the clouds, and the water caught little silver peaks. It didn't look so black anymore.

"Get in," Peter said. "I'll push us off."

Corbin stepped into the canoe and sat down up front so that Grace could lie back against him, her swollen foot resting on the gunwale. "I have you," he said. "Just close your eyes and be still. We'll be away from here soon."

She wrapped her arms around her father's leg and started to cry quietly.

Peter launched them most of the way, then got in. He gave a final push with the oar, and they were heading down the Gilchrist River in the direction of Sawyer Falls. He paddled gently, kept them centered in the river, away from any shores. And after a few minutes, the punctuation mark they had all been waiting for finally came. Six gunshots rang out, even and calm in their spacing. Decisive. Deliberate. They echoed through the woods, and in their wake, complete silence came, save for a flock of crows that took to the sky and flew away forever.

Day would break soon, and so much lay ahead.

"Is Mom mad at me?" Grace asked. "I hope she's not too worried."

"No, baby. No. She's not mad."

Peter watched Corbin's broad back bend down as he kissed the top of his daughter's head. His shoulders were wide. Strong. They would bear what they had to.

Peter continued to paddle, each dip and pull of the oar taking them away. Just away.

Chapter Sixteen

TIME TO GO

1

Peter returned to Shady Cove after the night in the woods. It seemed the only place to go. Corbin and Grace had been taken to the hospital, and Peter had been offered the same by the Sawyer Falls police, but he had declined and instead asked for a ride. He was tired, and he didn't want to think anymore. He just wanted to wrap himself in deep folds of sleep and forget about his problems for a while. He knew they would be there waiting for him when he woke up. But for the moment, it was enough already. Enough.

When he walked into Shady Cove, he pulled off the muddy muck boots, stripped down to his underwear, then went into the bedroom and fell asleep immediately.

He slept for twenty-four hours.

2

He awoke on Friday morning. And when he did, he wasn't sure what to do. So he did nothing. In a way, Shady Cove felt like a sort of purgatory where his problems and responsibilities couldn't quite reach him if he didn't want them to. He knew he needed to call Sylvia's family, to tell them what had happened to their daughter—although he had no official confirmation of her death yet—and begin to unravel the knot. But he didn't know how to start. The damned thing seemed too huge, somehow elusive, and he didn't know at which angle he should come at it. So he chose a passive approach. Or, rather, the passive approach chose him. The solutions to his problems would find him when they should.

And they did.

One by one, they did.

3

Peter's first answer found him the next day. He was sitting down at the dock, his feet in the water, when Corbin showed up. There was no awkward hug or anything like that, because they hardly knew each other. And Corbin wasn't that sort of guy. To be honest, Peter wasn't, either. Not at that moment, anyway. But there was a bond between them, ugly as it might've been, so Corbin sat on the little bench on the dock, and the two of them talked for a little while.

Corbin told him his daughter was doing okay, despite a shattered foot and a broken leg. But when he said it, he squinted a few times and looked everywhere except into Peter's eyes. The subject changed quickly, and Corbin thanked Peter once again for what he'd done; even if, he said, he didn't understand it. Peter said he didn't understand it himself—not entirely—but that he was glad Grace was home safe.

"How'd she take the news about her mother?" he asked, trying to be delicate.

Corbin folded his arms, unfolded them, then scratched his temple with a finger. "She took it," he said. "She's a strong girl. Just like Meryl. She'll be okay."

Peter was staring down at his feet in the water. "You want some advice about losing someone?" he asked, lifting his gaze.

Corbin looked at him curiously. "What's that?"

"It'll always hurt, but you'll learn to live a life with it. It doesn't sound like good advice now, but you'll understand eventually."

"I'll try and remember that," Corbin said, studying Peter closely.

Peter returned his gaze to the water. "You hear from your friend yet?"

"Benny? No. Not a word," Corbin said. "But something tells me I won't."

Peter looked at the rippling reflection of his face between his legs. "Are we going to talk about it?"

"Talk about what?" Corbin said. "I didn't see it, if you didn't."

Peter realized they could've been talking about any number of things, given the ambiguity of that statement. But he knew they were on the same page; he had seen the haunted look on Corbin's face.

"Something's dangerous here," Peter said. "You know that, don't you?"

Corbin leaned forward, elbows on his knees, and sighed. "I know it. Jesus, I know it." He paused. "I think I always have."

"It's not going away," Peter said.

"No, I don't think it is. And I have no idea what to do about it."

"It doesn't strike me as the sort of thing you can do anything about."

"That's what scares me the most," Corbin said.

When the conversation eventually began to sag, and both of them had been staring out across Big Bath long enough without a word spoken, Corbin finally said, "You know why I came here today?"

Peter looked at him sideways. "No. Should I?"

"I don't know."

"I told you I'm not a psychic," Peter said. "But now I'm starting to suspect it wasn't just a friendly drop-in."

"Right now, I think I wish you were psychic, Peter," he said, and his tone carried no humor in it. "God, it would make this a whole lot easier."

Peter's heart dropped, and he closed his eyes. He had been waiting for this. He just hadn't known how it would actually arrive.

4

Peter identified Sylvia's body on Saturday, August 27, 1966. Corbin had been right that night in the woods: it wasn't easy, but Peter did it, and then it was done. They only needed him to view her from the neck up. Her face was surprisingly unblemished in spite of the way she had died. Actually, he thought she looked almost peaceful. But he could see the shape of her wasn't what it should be under the rest of the white sheet. Things were missing, her topography misshapen. He didn't want to imagine what it might look like, but he knew there would be many sleepless nights ahead where he wouldn't be able to turn away from the temptation to torture himself.

After he left the morgue, he stopped at the little ice cream shop near Big Bath called The Junction and ordered a chocolate milkshake and a hot dog. It felt like something of a last meal. He ate it out front at a picnic table and listened to how quiet the world seemed... how empty. Occasionally he heard a loon call out, but that was all. The giant wave of despair that had been building on the horizon had finally crashed and rolled through, churning things up for a horrifying moment, and now the water had begun to draw back and glass over calm again. But everything had been disturbed, and when things finally settled back to near where they had once been, they would be different. And there would be another wave, Peter knew. And another after that.

For the entire half hour that he sat there in the beating sun, considering this and drinking his milkshake, he didn't see a single other person besides the pimply kid slinging milkshakes and pork products. It seemed a touch odd that on a hot summer day no one would be hanging around an oasis like an ice cream stand. But Peter thought he understood why. The town was still trying to comprehend what had happened at Our Savior Lutheran Church. The religious, as they were wont to do, focused most intently on the why and found ways to craft comfort there. Almost everyone in Gilchrist, in one way or another, had been affected. Some had lost family members, and some had lost friends. Many had lost both. But everyone had lost at least an acquaintance. In a town as small as Gilchrist, death casts a wide net.

Most were still referring to it as "the accident" and were speculating that it was probably the fault of a defective boiler, and thank God there weren't children in the preschool when it happened. That was a true miracle, by God! But others, those who couldn't understand why a heating boiler would be on in the summer at all, were starting to talk about suspicious things. The smell of bananas was one such topic, which, according to the man who ran the hardware store and who used to mine coal in Pennsylvania, was what dynamite smelled like.

Corbin had filled him in on these little pieces of gossip. But Peter didn't care about any of it. His wife was dead regardless of what had caused the explosion. And no matter what the police finally uncovered as the true reason, he knew what had really caused it. The same thing that would cause it again, in Gilchrist and probably elsewhere.

He finished his milkshake, sat a little longer, then left. When he returned to Shady Cove, he sat at the kitchen table, looking through to the bedroom where his wife's clothes were still piled on the bed, from when he had fallen asleep with them… with her.

He remained there until the sun set. And then he sat a little longer.

5

After identifying Sylvia's body, Peter stayed three more days at Shady Cove before deciding it was time to go. There was nothing left for him there. His last days were spent sitting down at the little dock, feet hanging over the side, staring out at the water and trying to figure out how best to tell Sylvia's family that she was dead. At the very least, he needed to do that. It was the right thing to do.

He thought about calling Sylvia's mother, but he and Ruth had never gotten along, and he knew the news would not be rationally received coming from him. Sylvia's mother was the type to interpret such an act as some sort of malicious attack, as if Peter had called her for no reason other than to destroy her life. He hated to admit it, but there was a faint bittersweetness that came with knowing that Sylvia's death would sever his familial obligation to his in-laws once and for all. A final gift from his wife, Peter thought, finding a morbid beauty in the notion, silly as it was.

In the end, he decided the best option was to call Sylvia's sister. And so on Wednesday morning, exactly one week after his wife had died, he reached outside of his purgatory place and made the call that would finalize her death. He told Evelyn what had happened as best he could. There had been an accident—a *freak* accident—and Sylvia had been one of the unlucky victims. He had come to hate the term "unlucky," especially after his time in Gilchrist.

Evelyn had been justifiably upset, and once she had calmed down, she apologized for any blame she seemed to have cast on him. She was just upset, okay? Upset. In shock. But Peter said he understood and not to worry. After a moment of silence, Evelyn offered to shoulder the responsibility of telling her mother. Then she said she would be up there that evening to help figure out where to begin with setting the arrangements. Peter gave her the address and the phone number, and then it was over.

After Peter hung up the phone, he found a scrap of paper on the kitchen counter. He sat down and stared at the blank page, the wooden pen Leo had given him poised above the paper. He had been staring at the scrap of paper for at least a half hour when a knock came at the screen door.

"Are you leaving now?" a small voice asked him. It took him a moment to recognize it was Kevin's voice... and another moment to realize he had heard it in his head.

Another voice spoke for real: "Hello? Peter? It's Laura... Dooley? You liked my meatloaf, remember?"

"Just a second." Peter went to the door to find Laura standing outside with Kevin right beside her.

The boy was still wearing the oversized Red Sox cap. Kevin tilted his head back and waved with a big goofy smile.

"Hey guys," Peter said, and opened the door. "Come in, come in."

"I told you he didn't go yet, Mommy," Kevin said.

"I'm still here," Peter said.

Laura and her son stepped inside Shady Cove. "Well, we don't want to keep you. I just wanted to see how you were doing. Give you my condolences in person. That's the right thing to do."

"You heard about what happened, I guess," Peter said, and stuffed his hands in his pockets.

"I'm so sorry," Laura said.

"It's okay," Peter said, then corrected himself. "I mean thank you. I don't know why I always say that."

"I did the same thing when his father passed. It's normal, I think. 'It's okay' really just means '*I'm* okay.' You're not saying it's okay that they died. That'd just be weird," Laura said, and laughed.

"I never thought about it like that," Peter said. "I'm okay, then. How's that?"

But he knew he wasn't.

"Better," Laura said.

"Better," Kevin parroted.

"You guys want something cold to drink?" Peter started toward the kitchen. "I don't have anything made, but—"

"You have tea?" Laura went past him and opened a cabinet next to the refrigerator.

"I do," Peter said. "It should be there."

"Ice?"

"Yes again."

"I'll make us some iced tea, then. Sound good?" Laura pulled down the box of Lipton and a bag of sugar.

"I won't refuse a glass if you make it," Peter said.

"I like when she makes icy tea," Kevin said.

"Okay, sport. Icy tea it is."

After Laura made the iced tea, they all went and sat out on the deck for an hour or two and just enjoyed the blue-skied afternoon, slowly finishing off the pitcher, each glass a little more watered down than the last. Kevin had brought two toy bulldozers and spent most of the time pretending to level a section of the garden. He said he was building a headquarters for his troops. Nobody spoke a whole lot, and Peter liked that. Mostly he wanted to be left alone, but he enjoyed sharing his solitude for a little while. It was okay.

But when the iced tea was gone, their visit was over, and Peter thought he was ready to leave, too. He picked up the empty pitcher, and Laura grabbed the glasses. Then they went back inside.

"Come on, buddy. Let's say goodbye," Laura said to Kevin, who was still building his headquarters.

Kevin reluctantly picked up his dozers and followed her inside. He was quieter than usual. He seemed sad about something, and Peter thought he knew what.

"Are we going?" he asked, looking down at his feet.

"We're going, sweetie. I think we've bothered Peter long enough." She looked at Peter and smiled.

"Nonsense," he said, flicking the brim of Kevin's hat. "It's been a pleasure." Kevin didn't look up, so Peter dropped to a knee. "Take care of your mom, sport. And remember, take care of that hat, too. It's one of my favorites, and I might have to come back for it someday… if I can."

Kevin jumped forward and wrapped his arms around him. "I'll stay in touch. Maybe I'll even come visit you," he whispered—or maybe Peter had heard it in his head; he couldn't be sure. He pulled away and looked at Peter. "Are you sure you have to leave now?"

Peter nodded. "I think so."

"You miss them, don't you?"

"Yeah, sport. Yeah, I do."

"Okay," Kevin said, and hugged him again. "Be careful."

"I will. I promise."

Peter stood and thanked Laura for coming and keeping him company for a couple hours. He said it was a fine way to spend his last day there. She gave him a hug. Then they left, and he was alone once more.

He took a seat at the table and looked at the blank scrap of paper again. He hadn't written anything yet, but he knew what he needed to do. He picked up the pen, found the right four words, and wrote them down.

After leaving the note on the counter and securing it under a glass saltshaker, Peter wandered down to the dock for the last time. It really was a beautiful place. But it reminded him of a poisonous flower—pretty at a distance, dangerous to anyone who got too close. And deadly to those who touched it... or let it touch them.

He stood on the edge of the dock, toes hanging off, and closed his eyes. The wind breathed slowly across the water. The sweet smell of fresh-cut grass drifted by. The people of Gilchrist were already getting on with their lives, putting tragedy behind them. They were doing it how they did it best— by ignoring. It was their gift and their curse. That was life, though. One long, sharp, double-edged sword. If you weren't careful, it would cut. And sometimes, what the hell, it cuts you anyway.

Angling his face up to the sun, Peter conjured thoughts of his son and of his wife. He had so many good memories of them, enough to last a lifetime. And memories, he knew, were such wonderful, powerful things. They lived on, existing long after the shutter of life opens and closes and the cosmic camera grabs its picture. They were just waiting to be seen.

Chapter Seventeen

EPILOGUE / A NEW START

On the Friday before Labor Day, Corbin turned down Lakeman's Lane for the last time. Grace sat beside him in the passenger's seat. Her leg was wrapped in a hard cast, and the bruises on her face had all but faded. She had been staring sideways out the window since leaving the house... since leaving the pump shed, if he wanted to be honest with himself. He hoped she would be okay, but he had no idea. The external stuff would heal, and that, he knew how to handle. But the internal stuff? He really could've used Meryl's help in that area. He missed her a lot, and he knew Grace did, too. He would be there for her, though. That was all he knew how to do—be there.

He kept his eyes on the tarped-over boxes he had piled in the bed of his truck as he navigated the landscape of potholes in the road. He had packed everything they would need to start a life someplace new. Someplace away from Gilchrist. He had made up his mind a week ago after thinking about Barbara Osterman. He had been thinking about her a lot, actually, after what happened with Ricky. But one night the connection just clicked in his head. For as long as Barbara and Nate Osterman had been an item, there had been abuse. Corbin had been called out to their house at least a dozen times, and each time, he tried to offer her help. She never wanted it, though. Corbin was subtle at first, but toward the end, around the same time she had her accident on the stairs, he had directly told her he would help her if she wanted to leave Nate. But she'd refused. She said Nate loved her, and that he had just lost his temper and that he really wasn't all that bad once you got to know him—all the normal stuff abused people convince themselves of to defend their abusers. And Corbin understood it. He didn't like it, but he understood it. Once a person gets used to something, even if it's a bad thing, they can learn to love it, get comfortable with it.

And that, Corbin came to realize at his wife's funeral, was Gilchrist. He had lived in this town for so long he hadn't noticed how bad, or bizarre, things had gotten. It had become a one-sided relationship. The town took and it took, but it never gave a thing back except heartache and suffering. So it was time to move on. In his eyes, Gilchrist had soured and become too dangerous. And something told him if he didn't leave, then there would be no hope for his daughter. Somehow this place would use it against her. The same way it had caught Ricky young and used him.

Corbin pulled into Shady Cove's driveway and parked next to Peter's car. The layer of pine needles on the windshield made him uneasy.

"He must still be here," he said. "Want me to leave it running so you can listen to the radio?"

"Okay," Grace said, staring out at Big Bath.

Corbin went to touch her shoulder, but decided against it. "I just want to say goodbye. I hardly know the guy, but it feels like

the right thing to do. He lost his wife in the church. And he…
Well, I'll just be a minute."

He got out of the truck and left it running. He made his way
down the beaten path to the door. It was open, except for the
screen slammer that stayed shut under the tension of a spring.
He knocked. "Peter? You home? It's Corbin."

No answer.

He opened the screen door and went in. "Peter?"

Still no answer. He kept expecting him to pop his head out
from a doorway at any moment, but that never happened.

He continued up the hall and looked in each bedroom. The
pile of clothes was still on the bed. A suitcase in the corner.
Water cups on the nightstands. It looked how it had the last
time he had been there. But no Peter.

He turned around and went into the kitchen, where he spied
a piece of paper sitting on the counter. He lifted the saltshaker
and slid the note toward him.

I've decided to go. That's all it said. Four words. It seemed like
an obvious statement, but something about it felt deeper.
Corbin went to the sink and looked out through the window at
the dock. He thought maybe he would see Peter sitting down
there. It was empty. But he did see something sitting on the
railing. A little black square.

He went outside through the sliding door and down the
little side path that led to the dock. Corbin opened the wallet
sitting on the railing. Peter's license was the first thing that
greeted him. Peter Martell, Concord, Massachusetts…

A loon called out somewhere across Big Bath.

Corbin took a seat on the little bench on the dock and
dropped the wallet beside him. He looked out over the water.
The sky was growing dark over the trees to the west, and a cold

wind was starting to batter the leaves around him and turn them silvery. Thunderstorms were rolling in. And from the sound of the deep rumbles in the distance, it was going to be a real doozy—an end-of-season whopper.

Corbin glanced up at Shady Cove. Its windows scowled back at him like disapproving eyes. He had never seen a place seem so empty. He shifted his gaze to his truck. Grace was fixing her hair in the side-view mirror, tucking strands behind her ears.

A big fat raindrop came down and smacked him right in the forehead, running down into his eye. He knuckled it out. Then another landed on his knee, and the dock began to turn spotted.

"Take care, pal. I owe you one," he said, and headed back up to his truck.

When he got in, Grace looked at him. "You find him?"

"No, he wasn't here," he said. "Put the window up. It's starting to rain."

Grace did. Then she slid over and rested her head on her father's shoulder. "Can we go now?"

"Yeah, baby," Corbin said. "We're going."

He put the truck in reverse and backed out of Shady Cove's driveway. When he reached the end of Lakeman's Lane, he went right. He drove until he reached the highway. And from there he headed north, away from Gilchrist.

ABOUT THE AUTHOR

Christian Galacar grew up in Ipswich, Massachusetts, a small suburb north of Boston. He attended the University of Massachusetts Amherst, where he received a BBA degree in Finance. Although interested in writing fiction from a young age, it wasn't until 2012 that he decided to pursue it as a career. *Gilchrist* is his second novel.

To receive updates on future book releases and other announcements, subscribe by email here: www.christiangalacar.com. He promises not to fill your inbox with unnecessary newsletters.

Follow on Twitter @Christian_Lang and on Facebook.
Or reach out through email at cgalacar@gmail.com.

OTHER WORKS

ONE LAST THING

So you've made it this far. Congratulations! You're awesome and I already think you deserve a lifetime without ever having to visit the DMV again. Unless, of course, you like that sort of thing, in which case I cannot help you. All I ask is that you take a moment to write an honest review. The power of your opinion is greater than you may know and helps bring my work to the attention of others. Thank you for any consideration you give this, dear reader, and I hope you continue to read what I write.

www.christiangalacar.com

37568444R00302

Made in the USA
Middletown, DE
28 February 2019